Wyldling Trials

Book Two of the Wyldling Dream Series

A.R. Grimes

A Cycle of Tehara novel

Printed in the United States of America: First Printing, 2023

ISBN: 978-1-958718-02-5 (ebook)
ISBN: 978-1-958718-03-2 (paperback)

http://cycloftehara.com

Editors: Huckleberry Rahr and Weslee Imrisek
Cover art: GetCovers.com

Map designed using Inkarnate software (Inkarnate.com):
Northern Marches

For all the damsels

Who ever dreamed of saving

A knight in distress

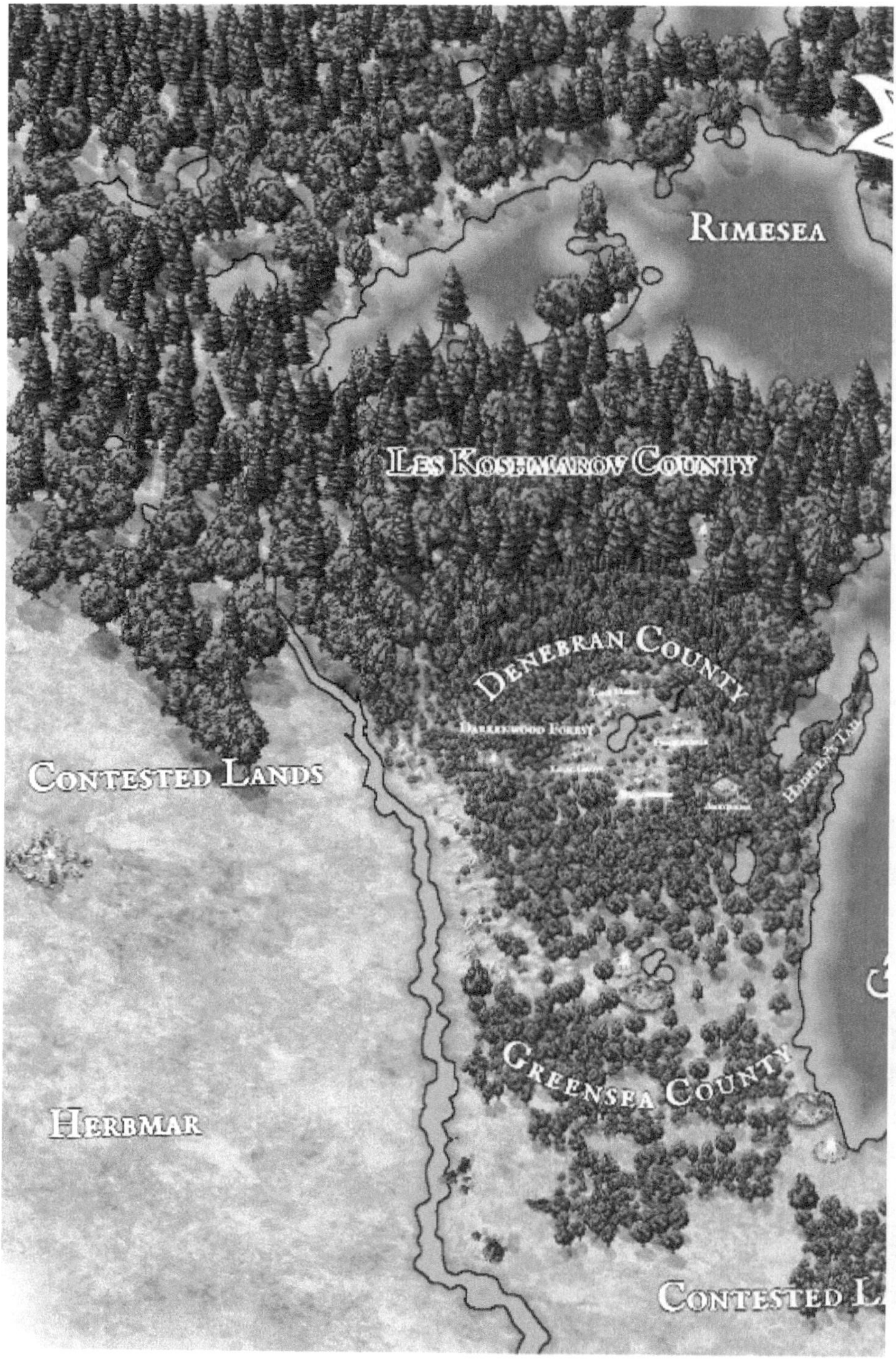

RIMESEA
LES KOSHMAROV COUNTY
DENEBRAN COUNTY
DARKENWOOD FOREST
CONTESTED LANDS
HERBMAR
GREENSEA COUNTY
CONTESTED LANDS

NORTHERN MARCHES
FELLSEA
SANCTUARY ISLES
FELLWOOD COUNTY
JAGGERSEA
GREENSEA
MIRRORSEA
NORTH
LANDS

The Deep End

"What are you waiting for? We have to save Enoch!"

Annabelle's voice echoed in the resulting silence that fell in the glade. Eight pairs of eyes stared at her from shocked faces—six human-looking, two not. Cheeks heating, she hugged herself and ducked her head to hide from their scrutiny. Moisture from the wet soil soaked into her jeans, and the earth beneath her rocked like a boat on rolling waves. She frowned. Why was it doing that? Did the ground normally move around on Tehara, or was she dizzy?

Back on Earth, Annabelle Leigh Wells wasn't a girl known for taking risks—certainly not risks on the level of jumping into a wormhole that led to another planet. Neither was she comfortable speaking up in strange company and making demands of grown men. And now, having done both those things, she wondered if she'd plunged into the deep end of the pool with an anchor strapped to her legs.

Actually ... She licked her lips. *Water would be nice. I'm as parched as the Sahara.*

Throat-clearing sounds drew her attention to the wounded soldier lying beside her on the damp ground. Dark-skinned with light-brown hair, his name was Simon Halloway, Enoch's best friend and the leader of his guardsmen. "Don't you ... worry yourself over it, Miss Wells," he said, somewhat breathless, as he reached out to touch her wrist. "Finding Enoch ... is a concern for me ... and my men." He winced as if something pained him. Annabelle took his hand, but he gave hers a squeeze, let go, smiled, and then continued, "Once the Commander's apprised ... of the situation, he'll hunt down that renegade and his accomplice ... sure as the suns rise in the west."

Five soldiers chorused: "That's right, Sarge."

"The young knight will be found," a heavily accented tenor voice spoke from her right, biting off words as if they'd offended him. "The ones who took him will suffer severe punishment."

Annabelle peeked through her lashes at the white-furred man with a short, canid muzzle who knelt at Simon's feet. He was called His Excellency, Lord Raeden von Bleistaff, and he'd given her a huge tunic smelling of cardamom and pepper to cover her torso after she'd destroyed her shirt to make bandages. At first, she'd thought him a werewolf, but she'd learned this wasn't the case.

With those black splotches on his tail, upper arms, and ear-tips ... Aside from the copper-red hair on his head, his coloring reminded her of the Dalmatian her family had owned during her childhood.

"Pardon," the dog-featured man said, rising to his feet. "He must search for spoor left by that murderous rogue." His eyes glittered, and his voice roughened into a growl as he stalked toward the gray-stoned wall behind Annabelle. "Fear not, Freylin; your servant will make Ravenos pay for his crimes."

My servant? What's he talking about? And who is this Ravenos person? Her head reeled with confusion. She hadn't arrived on Tehara until after Enoch's abduction.

The soldiers argued about what to do, talking over each other. Noise buzzed in her brain like a mouthful of fizzy candy. Whimpering, Annabelle hunched her shoulders and clapped her hands over her ears.

"Everybody simmer down!" bellowed a nearby voice.

With a squeak, Annabelle sat bolt upright, and then grimaced at a wave of dizziness. Every soldier's mouth snapped closed. Sir Thomas was the eighth man in the group. Although it was debatable whether she should refer to a talking toad the size of a large tomcat as a man. Enoch called him Toad. Annabelle loved amphibians. Part of her itched to gather up said toad in her arms to cuddle, but the coldness in his expression warned her against touching him.

Toad hopped from his perch on Simon's chest to a rock that raised him another foot off the ground. "Anyone know where Commander Storm is?"

As he lowered his gaze from the sky, one of the other soldiers said, "He's investigating bandit activity in the South District. Isn't that why he left, Sarge?"

Simon grimaced. "That's right, Bart. Although ... I'm thinking that's all ... subterfuge ... crafted by Ravenos's true employer ... draw him away. Make it easier to nab E."

"Jeremiah's ever-loving Bullfrog," Toad groaned. "Of course it was a trick."

Brow furrowed, Annabelle looked askance at him. How could a toad from an alien planet know about a character from a classic rock song? Perhaps she'd misheard him.

"Sir Thomas," prompted a man with close-cropped curly hair. "What about Enoch?"

Yes, Annabelle thought. *Please, let's discuss rescuing Enoch now.* Finding the friend who'd become like a brother to her consumed her thoughts.

"We'll find the kid," Toad announced, glaring at each trooper. "That goes without saying. But the first order of business is getting help for Halloway, here." And then, he issued a series of orders, sending three soldiers off to fetch a tracker, inform the garrison captain and dispatch a messenger to call back Commander Storm, and arrange a search for Enoch.

The toad addressed the two remaining soldiers. "I want you to build a litter-sling ... whatnot, to transport Halloway to the garrison infirmary." After giving him the fist-to-chest salute, they jogged off to do his bidding.

"It's called a travois," Annabelle whispered. None responded, but she thought she saw Simon quirk a smile. A warm glow thawed the edges of the chill inside her. Thank God! The young sergeant would survive his injuries. She could carry that news to Enoch once they found him.

Rubbing her temples, she considered Simon as she recalled the blue glow outlining everything in view while the warm, liquid energy rushed from within her to bring the man back from death's door. Both femurs snapped, ribs broken, and internal bleeding. He'd been unconscious and dying ... and then, suddenly, he wasn't.

What happened? She wondered for the hundredth time. *For sure, God answered my prayer to heal him. Well, the worst of it; his legs still seem to be broken. But why did I see blue light, feel that warmth swelling from within, and then pass out?*

It's as if the healing power all came from ... me.

Annabelle glanced sidelong at Toad to find his attention fixed on her. She shuddered as pale blue eyes pierced her like icicles. "And now," he said, squinting, "the big question. What should we do with you, kiddo?"

Why wouldn't the ground stay still? Head swimming, Annabelle struggled to form words, but nothing came out. *You don't need to* do *anything with me. Tell me how I can help find Enoch.* She worked a drop of saliva around a mouth as dry as ashes. *And I'd like a drink of water.*

Toad's eyes seemed far too knowing as he pinned her with his gaze. She drew in a breath, certain he would remark upon Simon's miraculous recovery—and pose questions she couldn't answer—but he didn't speak. He merely stared at her.

Annabelle was about to ask him if she'd grown a third eye when Raeden returned. He hunkered beside her and Simon, not touching, but close enough for her to feel his body heat. Why was it so cold? It was supposed to be summer here. She masked a shiver by pulling the borrowed tunic tighter around herself.

"There is a dark feeling to this place that makes the skin creep and crawl," the dog-like man said, his ears laid back. "The little maiden must be brought to safety, Sir Thomas."

"Right," the toad muttered, hopping off Simon's chest. "Safety. That means the garrison. Or ... maybe we can stick her somewhere in Lilac Manor. Crap; let me go call one of those guys back." He filled his vocal sac as he bounded through a gap in the bushes, then sent out a booming, bullfrog call: "Marsh! Ainsley!"

Annabelle frowned, her indignation rising in a salty wave. *"Stick her somewhere?"* Like a porcelain doll or a fragile knickknack on a dusty shelf? No way, José! She wasn't either of those things. And she didn't want to be safe—not if "safe" meant they'd shut her away like some hapless princess locked in a tower. Her fingers curled to form fists.

I want to be useful and find Enoch! Otherwise, what's the point of me being here on Tehara? Everything blurred, and Annabelle blinked to clear her vision.

"Lord Raeden?" Simon asked. His voice sounded stronger than before. "Any sign of where they might've taken him? Can we track them?"

Yes! Please, Lord Raeden, tell me you found a trail that leads to Enoch and you're ready to go after him. And take me with you. She tried to speak, but her voice still wouldn't work.

Raeden growled. "*Nich*, Sergeant Halloway. This one scented all around the clearing and along the wall and brush. Aside from the stench of burning on the path, there is nothing. No scent of Enoch or any other. No spoor. And such should not be possible." He flexed his fingers. "This one is uncertain—the Lord Commander could tell for certain—but he believes the rogue and the other you saw with him spirited away our young knight ... with witchcraft."

Annabelle's eyes widened. "What do you mean? They used ... magic?"

"*Shach.*" Raeden nodded, upper lip lifting to expose fangs. "It is like Enoch—how does one say it? —has been banished without a drawing."

What the heck? His last words made no sense. A frisson shook Annabelle. If Enoch's captors erased all the evidence, how could they locate him? Why would someone take Enoch? What did they want from him?

"Perdition," Simon replied in a hollow tone. "That's ... real bad." His lips trembled and his eyes shimmered. Fists clenched at his sides, he turned his head so she couldn't see his face.

Is he crying? Annabelle's throat tightened. *Oh, no ... don't you dare start the waterworks! Quick; think of something else.*

There must be something I can do .... She nibbled her lip. *Well, if they can't track him, then I'm going to try. Please, God, help me find him.*

Annabelle closed her eyes and imagined herself in the void place, streamers of shining blue radiating from her body—the extensions of her awareness that she called thought-tendrils and Enoch called kythim. *This time, I might reach him.* She must bypass the aching, hollow *absence* that had once been the warm, vibrant presence of Enoch. She stretched out, straining with her kythim.

Maybe if I reach a little farther ...

Vertigo struck her and spun her about.

"Miss Wells?"

A calloused hand gripped her wrist, and the earth settled. Her eyelids lifted to reveal a world saturated by a blue haze.

Simon stared at her, wide-eyed. "Merciful Yshua, her eyes are glowing!" He jerked his hand away.

Raeden snapped something in another language that reminded her of German cussing. She groaned, swaying, as the ground rolled beneath her like a boat on troubled waters. Male voices shouted, ringing in her ears like the cries of gulls. She turned to see Raeden reaching for her. Before she could understand everyone's concern, the world went fuzzy and sideways.

As darkness descended in a black wing, she screamed with all her might in a voice muzzled by silence.

Enoch, where are you?

Spirited Away

Soot Panther

Five Hours Earlier...

Knights were blistering crazy, and baron-knights were the craziest of them all. No wonder the Dreadlord wanted them all blotted from the continent.

William glared at the bound and unconscious youth slung across his companion's shoulder like a sack of potatoes. Sir Enoch Northward, Acting Baron-Knight of the Northern Marches, had put up quite a fight when they captured him. Even with the collar of the wyldling snare clasped around Northward's neck to suppress his powers, being battle-trained by the best warriors in the realm made him difficult to subdue.

Biting back a moan, William adjusted the trousers he wore under his burkheld and rearranged the brown robes to prevent himself from tripping on the hem. His stones were still tender after Northward's lucky—or unlucky—blow to the groin.

May the suns burn and blister the confounded knight to charcoal.

His companion, Zakaar Ravenos, halted. Brown-furred ears lifted as he sniffed the air. Besides his tall and muscular build, the harkhurz possessed the acute senses and grace of the canine lykharim he resembled. These attributes made him an excellent warrior and assassin—when he wasn't suffering fits of the Blood Rage madness.

"Now what?" William grumbled. "We can't stop for everything you smell. Master Tenebris'll flay us if we don't—"

Zakaar pivoted on his heel, moving like a dancer despite the knight draped over his shoulder, and put a finger up to his short muzzle. Amber eyes gleamed as he murmured a single word in his native tongue: "Panturos."

Soot panther! William swallowed a curse. *That's right; the Veil went down. Wild beasts can get through now.* He backed against a tree trunk and scanned the surrounding trees, taking care to look up. The dark gray predators often ambushed prey from above, dropping from tree limbs to rake their hapless victims with sharp claws.

The harkhurz squatted, grimacing. The raw stub of his amputated tail still bothered him. William still couldn't fathom how Zakaar had got his tail half-burned off while slaughtering the three soldiers who'd come to Northward's rescue.

Zakaar removed the unconscious captive from his shoulders, setting him at William's feet. Grinning, he unsheathed his short swords. "Time to hunt." He slipped into the surrounding shadows as easily as a man donned a dressing gown.

Ugh. Not again. William had long since given up trying to comprehend Zakaar's capacity for bloodshed and murder—as well as Master Tenebris's desire to encourage it.

William searched the canopy for soot panthers. *I suppose the harkhurz's murder spree didn't turn out all bad. After all, Northward came into the Darkenwood looking for the dead maidens—and fell right into our clutches.* Perhaps Master Tenebris was wilier than William gave him credit for.

A low, coughing growl interrupted his musings. It came from somewhere in the copse ahead where Zakaar had gone. William's right hand went to the bone knife in its sheath made from several layers of human skin. He pressed back against the rough bark of the tree. The knife's primary purpose was ceremonial, but nothing prevented him from using it as a weapon if Zakaar failed to subdue his prey.

However, William had full confidence in him where killing was concerned. He'd once seen Zakaar walk away unscathed after eviscerating a terror bird that overtopped him by a span. William's lips twitched. *We feasted well that night. But that was before the Eastern Marches. Before the harkhurz began his descent into madness.*

Soft, rhythmic grunting emerged from the night. Another hunting call. He froze. *That was three trees away from me.* He recalled that soot panthers hunted in pairs or small family groups. This thought did little to settle his nerves. He dared not move, not even to take out his whiskey flask for a therapeutic sip.

Naturally, clouds chose that moment to blot out the starlight. *Suns burn it. I can't see.* The sound of his own hot blood rushed in his ears, deafening him to anything else. William spoke the words of a guttural cantrip through clenched teeth. A dim, blue-green werelight sprang to life on his left to hover over the body of his comatose prisoner. Depleted of energy, his arkhabala—the spellform tattoos Arkhadhans etched into their skin—prickled in sullen warning under his robes.

The sudden light surprised a soot panther creeping up on him. The huge cat crouched with one broad paw lifted in mid-step. And then its lips peeled back from ivory fangs. William stared at its teeth. *The fangs would be perfect as tokens for an Arkhadahn's Web.*

The soot panther bunched up, preparing to spring, when a whirling silver blade struck its flank. Blood sprayed black in the blue-green light. The great cat screeched and fled into the undergrowth, shedding the weapon—one of the assassin's short swords.

Birthed from the shadows, Zakaar fell upon the beast with his other weapon, hacking at its neck as if he was splitting a log for firewood. The soot panther shrieked like a woman in agony.

William cringed. His vision swam, and his awareness seemed to split in two. A woman's voice cried out in pain, sobbing, *"No. You can't take him. Stop. It hurts. Don't do this. Yvres, please, stop ..."*

He clapped his hands over his ears, but in his head, he could still hear the woman screaming in unison with the beast, even as its cries dwindled into piteous mewls. Burning suns! What in nether perditions was happening? He gritted his teeth. *Whose voice was I hearing?*

Yellow eyes shining in ecstasy, the assassin chopped until the spine was severed. The cat went silent. So did the woman. William turned aside and covered his face to block out the image of blood spurting from the headless neck. An urge to weep threatened to overtake him.

Zakaar chuckled. "There is no more to fear. You can uncover the eyes now. The blood has stopped flowing."

William took a few deep breaths to steady himself, lowered his hands, then gagged. The harkhurz was licking the black gore from his swords with a blissful expression. Shuddering, he averted his gaze to the limp figure lying at his feet. The prisoner's silvery jacket had swirling patterns stitched in black thread. Like the thorny, vine-like arkhabala tattooed across William's own shoulders. The flickering blue-green light made Northward's face look sickly and wan, but his brow furrowed, and his lips moved as if he was trying to puzzle his way out of his predicament in his dreams.

William snorted. *Good luck with that, Northward.*

A grisly popping noise made him look up. His glance met the glazed eyes of the dead soot panther, opaque in the werelight's faint glow. He shuddered again. One by one, Zakaar extracted the dead soot panther's fangs. William flinched as he wrenched out each tooth.

Outer darkness! The fangs were *huge.* William had never seen them close up before. He could use them to boost the range of his spellforms. But why was Zakaar taking them? "What are you doing?" he demanded. "We don't have time for this!"

Zakaar kept his eyes fixed on his task. "There is always time for this. I hunt. I kill. I claim my—how does one say it? Ah, yes, my trophies."

William swallowed the sourness creeping up the back of his throat. Zakaar wouldn't let him take the fangs, then. *Void freeze it.* "Well, hurry up. We need to clear away your butchery in case someone comes this way looking for Sir Fancy Jacket here." He nudged the supine form with the toe of his boot. *At least I won't have to wrestle with this idiot again. My soporific formula should keep him asleep for the next twelve hours.*

The assassin insisted on cutting out the beast's heart as well, and then—to William's disgust—taking a bite out of it. Afterward, he dragged the carcass up into a tree to hide it amid branches and thick foliage. While Zakaar disappeared into the copse and dealt with his first kill, William scuffed dirt over the bloody gore on the ground and covered everything with leaf mold.

He prodded Northward's buttocks with the toe of a boot. "Not that you can respond, or anything. But it's blazing inconvenient, having to clean up the mess after Zakaar's kills. I wrapped up and buried every one of your little friends—you're welcome, by the by—and then what does he do? He digs them up and moves them to where anyone can find them!" He threw his hands up in the air. "As if I hadn't already spent entire blistering *days* piling stones over not one, but *three* corpses in the dungeon pit."

Scowling, he nudged the bound youth again with his toe, a little harder this time. "I told him he was better off leaving them where I put them first—where it was nice and cool. Otherwise, they putrefy. I can't imagine *that* tastes very good. Blech! Why not gobble them up right away? It would've made for less work for me in the long run. Stupid harkhurz."

Zakaar slunk out of the shadows. "I can hear all you say, my friend. The 'stupid harkhurz' has cleaned all his mess. You need not do any work piling up stones." With a grunt, the assassin hoisted the human cargo upon his shoulders, and they continued on their way.

Tenebris had better be happy. William clenched his jaw. He'd done all his master had asked of him. Everything the Dreadlord employed them to accomplish here in the Northern Marches had come to fruition. Just as it had in the Eastern Marches. They'd assassinated two baron-knights and captured a wyldling. And yet, William knew his master would point out some tiny flaw in this task's execution.

He always discovers fault in whatever I do.

They met with no other wild beasts, although canine howls of lykharim sounded from the north, and not too far distant. Unless someone put up another wardspell, ferocious animals would overrun the Darkenwood within the week. He wondered who was even capable of such a massive enchantment. Perhaps the Dreadlord could accomplish it. Or that namby-pamby Lord Evanrudhe and his self-righteous Dwelfnic Council hiding in Y'Dendordenelle. No one else had the raw power.

William licked his lips at the thought of that much power in his own hands. *By Villem's scepter, what I wouldn't give to tap into the Aethyr and the Arkhabadh simultaneously and feel all that energy coursing through my veins ...* He'd experienced it, once.

The wind rustled in the damp foliage of the trees. Large droplets splattered on William's head. Cursing aloud, he wiped the moisture off his face, rattling off a vile insult in nehmwight dialect when Zakaar laughed.

William sneered. "Remember who makes your elixir. Unless you *want* to go mad?"

His companion subsided into silence. However, William's small triumph did little to uplift his mood. Even the prospect of a reward for delivering their captive to the Dreadlord's fortress failed to raise his spirits, because that remained a vague promise for the future, and William knew from long experience it was far more likely that disappointment—and pain—loomed ahead of him. Certainly, Master Tenebris would ensure that he received pain.

"Pain is the crucible in which I'll melt away your dross, William. And then, I shall forge the miniscule ore that remains into a tolerable Arkhadahn."

He sighed. Master Tenebris claimed that, because of his mixed blood, they must burn away the kadorei dross before William could rise from apprentice to acolyte status, let alone full Arkhadahn. Hence, the unremitting object lessons.

He glanced aside at the youth slung like a trussed-up lamb across the assassin's broad shoulders and snorted contemptuously. "I wonder how much pain this pampered little kadorei can tolerate."

Zakaar grinned, revealing his sharp canines. "You want me to find out?"

William rubbed his forehead. "Like I told you before, as soon as we get to Fastness and the Dreadlord sees him alive and well, *then* you can beat him up—so long as it doesn't show. And after the Dreadlord's done with him, you can do whatever you want, short of killing him. Otherwise, no elixir to keep the voices away."

The harkhurz grumbled. "I will hold you to this. The warlock owes me a debt of honor." He placed a hand against his side, where the young knight had slashed him with his sword.

A debt of honor? Burning nonsense!

However, William kept his opinion to himself.

One More Indignity

Serpent watch was well underway when William and Zakaar arrived at the ruined castle. The clouds cleared a second time to unveil a panoply of stars. William extinguished his werelight. The night drew to a close. He felt it in his bones—the tingling approach of firstdawn that those of nehmwight lineage could sense.

An unwonted flurry of activity occurred in the western quarter of the courtyard. His master was making use of the servants that the Dreadlord had lent them; six armored nehmwight warriors were loading crates of equipment and traveling trunks into a wagon under his direction. If they resented being treated as common laborers, then their handsome faces revealed nothing of their emotions. Doubtless, they measured their own positions as inferior to that of Tenebris, and no warrior below the rank of Warlord would dare defy a Master Arkhadahn—and even Warlords stepped carefully around a sorcerer with thirteen circles.

William's lips twitched on the verge of a smile. *Unless, of course, one is a fool or has grown weary of life.* Tenebris loathed the Warlords with a hatred hotter than the three suns combined. Especially Warlord Vespyrahl, the most powerful and brutal of them. If given the chance, Tenebris would cheerfully kill the man. Tenebris had never explained why, and William was afraid to ask.

As if reluctant to carry him into the courtyard, William's feet grew heavy. Zakaar slowed down to match his pace and glanced at him sidelong. With one eye on the nehmwights, searching among them for his master, William yanked his cowl up to cover his head. He was rewarded by an icy trickle of rainwater down his neck. A curse flew from his lips.

"Must you make enough racket to wake the dead?"

William's heart frosted over and plummeted into his stomach at the sound of his master's voice, like steel caressing silk. He clamped down tight on the whimper threatening to escape his throat, composed his features, and turned around.

Master Yvres Tenebris, Arkhadahn of the Thirteenth Order, stood behind him like a tall, black pillar of unremitting disapproval. With his hands tucked inside opposite sleeves of his black robe, he seemed at rest, but William knew better. A composed expression adorned the thin, ash-gray face, and black eyebrows arched in question. Even the arkhabala seemed quiescent, like thorny vines twisting up the column of his neck to unfurl along his jawline. But William knew better, because the carnelian eyes locked on his own blazed like twin gateways into perdition itself.

All his thoughts burned to ash and blew away as he spluttered, "How?"

Tenebris favored William with a predatory smile. "Apparently, you didn't notice the tracer I wove into your aknalud."

William's eyes widened. Tenebris wove a tracer spell into his underwear? How long ago had he done this?

His master's eyes glittered. "Very good; you're paying attention. I cleansed our traces from the entire area and began packing as soon as you departed, for I knew that regardless of your success, my distraction would only hold the Commander's interest for several hours. We must hurry, now, if we are to make it to Fastness before the new moon. Bring our guest." Tenebris turned on his heel and strode away, his black cloak trailing behind him like wings.

A snide voice in William's head whispered: *"Always have to have the last word, don't you, Tenebris?"* William seized hold of that scrap of insubordination and then tucked it away like a boy hiding treasures in a locked box.

Instead of acting on his master's demand, Zakaar watched William and waited on *him*. A warm glow filled him at the assassin's shifting allegiance. "Oi, pick him up. Let's see what kind of conveyance Ten—I mean, *Master* Tenebris, prepared for Sir Fancy Jacket, here. I hope it's a used chicken crate with dung all over the inside."

Especially after the dirty skink-face kneed me in the stones.

Northward's transport—a black lacquered palanquin with heavy red curtains—delighted William. It would get hot and stuffy inside the thing. The kadorei would be miserable. *Even more miserable*, he amended, as the prisoner's head lolled against the assassin's shoulder. *Because I'm not taking off that collar.*

He scowled at the fine jacket, trousers, belt-pouch, and boots the youth wore. His footwear looked newly made. Not that William desired such clothes for himself; they reminded him what a pampered existence the fool led. An idea took shape. He grinned. "How about we strip Sir Fancy Jacket, Zakaar?"

The harkhurz's eyes gleamed. "To humiliate the warlock? Yes."

William extracted the triangular key from his sakkhelt—the many-pocketed sash under his robe he used to carry spell components—and touched it to the wyldling snare binding Northward's ankles. Following the Dreadlord's instructions, he reached for the violet spark inside himself and envisioned the metallic bonds loosening. The snare uncoiled and then wound around the key. Zakaar bared his teeth and backed away, shivering.

"There's nothing to be afraid of, you rabbit-hearted ninny," he said, pulling a sack from inside his burkheld. "Now, get over here and help me."

The boots came off first, then the belt, the buckskin trousers, the brocaded jacket, and the light tunic. William rubbed the cloth between his fingers before stuffing it with the rest inside the sack. He suppressed a sigh; his own underclothes were dull and rough in comparison. He looped the belt through his sakkhelt. Investigating the attached pouch's contents could wait until later.

He knelt and activated the snare. It wrapped around the unconscious Northward like vine tendrils. The youth looked pathetic and runty, lying on the ground dressed in nothing but his small-clothes. Hardly dangerous at all. William resisted the urge to punch him.

"Annabelle..."

Half-risen, William froze with a forearm braced on his knee. He could have sworn the captive's lips hadn't moved. He'd spoken, though.

"Dulciber?" Zakaar asked. "Is something wrong?"

He didn't hear that? William's brow furrowed. First women screaming in his head, and now Northward's voice. He must be wearier than he thought. "It's nothing." *Probably.* He swept aside the palanquin curtains. Zakaar deposited the captive—none too gently—onto the cushions inside.

William shoved the sack at the harkhurz. "Put this in my trunk. His sword, too," he added, looking pointedly at the blade dangling from Zakaar's belt. "There should be room."

Zakaar snarled, gripping the hilt. "I have earned the warlock's weapon by right—"

"No, you didn't," William shot back. "*I* did. When I subdued him with the wyldling snare. He was helpless against anything you did to him after that."

Amber eyes blazed like Lachesis's rays. William met him glare for glare, hands fisted at his sides. His sluggish arkhabala stirred and pain rippled through him.

I have nothing left if he attacks, but I mustn't back down.

The harkhurz growled and lowered his gaze, detaching the sword from his belt and tossing it on the sack. He straightened in a military posture and thumped his chest with his fist. "It shall be done." After gathering up the kadorei's effects, he carried them toward the pack-wagon.

William released the breath he'd been holding. Blazing suns! For a moment, he'd thought Zakaar might cast aside their alliance and attack. He shook out his cramped fingers as he observed the youth the Dreadlord wanted so badly.

What did the Dreadlord plan to do with a wyldling? He would ask him once they reached his stronghold. *He's answered my questions before. Perhaps he'll even allow me to help carry out his plans.*

Four of the Golorum—elite warriors—came over, and one acknowledged William with a nod. Their faces revealed nothing of their thoughts as each man took a corner and heaved up the litter until the poles protruding from the fore and aft rested on their shoulders. From beneath his cowl, William watched them jog toward the western gate. He rubbed his chin, frowning. Annabelle. What did it mean?

"William!" Tenebris snarled from right behind him. "Suns burn you, stop woolgathering. It's past time we left."

Despite himself, he flinched. How did Tenebris sneak up on him like that? "Yes, Master. I ..." His voice trailed off. *Merciful*

Valeshka, my treasures! He forced himself to meet his master's gaze. "I'll be along in a moment. I just remembered a place you probably missed in the cleansing—one of the towers."

Tenebris scowled. "Bumbling fool," he muttered. Louder, he added, "Go on, then; take care of it. Quickly." With a departing glare, he spun on his heel and strode after the cart rattling over the uneven pavement.

William stood alone in the center of the courtyard, staring into the west. The Annabelle mystery would have to wait. He tilted back his head and closed his eyes. He listened to the humming in his bones that heralded firstdawn. Klotho, the smallest of the three suns, would rise in about three hours. Unlike his mentor and the six warriors, William did not fear the rising of the suns.

Unlike them, he was a freak.

William snorted. *Not that it's all bad. Even though my mother abandoned me, being half kadorei offers its compensations. Apparently, being able to walk abroad in the sunslight without going blind is one of them.*

He drank whiskey from his flask, then turned around and went across the detritus-strewn courtyard of the crumbling fortress. His boots crunched over the brittle skeletons of past autumns' fallen leaves and small animals alike. Above, in the east-facing tower of the castle's weathered corpse, he reclaimed the leather satchel containing the scrolls the Dreadlord had given him. It also held the items he'd taken from the knight with the golden kythim. Tenebris didn't know about any of them, and William preferred to keep it that way.

Once back down in the courtyard, he glanced up at the sky. Starlight still pierced his soul like needles despite their incalculable distance. Lonely distance. *Do stars have mothers?* He scowled. Where in perdition had *that* thought come from?

He took another swig of whiskey, tucked the flask away, and inhaled deeply, concentrating on the air entering and leaving his lungs. The fragrances of night-blooming orchids and midnight everlasting mingled in his nostrils, triggering a memory of a dream he'd had ...

Enough! Firstdawn is coming. Dreams can wait. It's time to leave.

William regarded the massive ruin that had been his home for a season. "Good riddance," he muttered. And then, he walked through the archway without a backwards glance.

In the Doctor's House

Adrift

Annabelle had her suspicions from the beginning—the dark blue armor she wore and the raft made of ice were dead giveaways—but she knew for certain she was dreaming when the silver dragon appeared.

As she admired an enormous moon and rainbow-hued stars in a velvet night sky, the creature flashed overhead, its serpentine length undulating like an eel through waterless currents. Either it reflected the moonbeams or it glowed with its own argent light, for it appeared bright as the moon. She followed its progress, its long, shining shape rapidly diminishing with distance until it was yet another winking star amongst thousands.

Okay, she thought. *Even though it's silver and not my* blue *dragon, any dragon is pretty awesome. Too bad it's gone.* She stared at the part of the sky where it had disappeared.

Wait, what was that?

Clambering up on her knees, she squinted into the night sky. The silver pin prick was growing larger again. An expectant breath caught in her throat. The creature was returning!

Outstretched wings cast moon-shadows as it passed and a human figure clung to the spines behind the reptilian head. The passenger wore full-body armor chased with silver, like the dragon's scales. Armor much like hers. Joy filled her. *It's the silver knight. The brother of my heart. Enoch.*

The dragon danced in the sky, chasing the wind. Every movement was carefree yet silent. Neither the silver dragon nor the silver knight appeared to be aware of her. As she watched, the pearlescent moonlight darkened to orange. Black threads like parasitic worms crawled across the forbidding disk and reached for the silver dancers.

When she opened her mouth to warn them of the danger, no sound emerged. Soot-gray tendrils cocooned the silver knight, wrenched him from his seat, and tore him away to disappear into the orange moon. Bereft of its rider, the dragon convulsed. It threw back its head in a soundless shriek—and then vanished.

The moon winked out and the sky went black. Wind howled in a wordless lament, whipping her hair around her face. She wept, the image of the silver figures dancing with the wind and the stars scalded into her memory.

Her fingers curled into fists. "With God's help, I promise I'll find you. I *will*."

A man's voice spoke. "Welcome to Tehara, sapphire lady."

With a gasp, she ripped her gaze from the void. A tall figure stood on the edge of her ice raft, cloaked in shadows and outlined with violet light. She identified this man from her previous dreams, although she couldn't see his face. He held an instrument resembling a mandolin.

"Grieve not, Ahdmerel," he said. "Face the Moonlight Trial. Earn Daar-Lûsin's allegiance, and you shall bring Skelsdaran home."

"Moonlight trial? Dahar-what?"

The bard plucked out a mournful tune, and a glowing dagger appeared between them. Shattered bits of the rainbow shimmered along the blade like the large opal set in Grandma Rosemary's ring. Her breath hitched. *So beautiful. Is that what he's talking about?* When she reached for it, the dagger flashed white, then vanished.

Annabelle blinked to clear her vision. Her lips parted. Before she spoke, the bard changed the melody he played. Notes like clear water spilled from its strings. They pierced her soul with needles made of ice, painful despite how quickly they melted.

The ice raft groaned, cracked, and burst asunder. She plunged into a world of water where her armor seemed light as pumice. Cradled in blue, she breathed without trouble in a crystalline blue liquid that thrummed with murmuring voices.

"Fear not, Ahdmerel."

Was that part of her name? It seemed to fit her—almost—like garments she needed to grow into. Just as 'Skelsdaran' suited the silver knight, Enoch.

She closed her eyes. But someone took him away. Enoch was gone.

Her eyelids flew open. She reached out. "No! Enoch, come back!"

Back ... back ... back ...

The sapphire world contracted and then exploded, shattering like ice, the shockwave sending her spinning.

I have to save Enoch!

Silver starlight pierced the blue-black depths. She swam toward the surface with an effortlessness she wasn't accustomed to in the waking world.

Enoch?

Annabelle's eyes snapped open. She whipped her head around, trying to locate the young man, but her vision remained shrouded in darkness. Everything was hushed, and a warm softness surrounded her.

Where am I?

Heart palpitating, she attempted to raise her arms and lunge to her feet, but something held her down. *Did those loathsome dark ropes snare me as well?* The horrible image of dark gray tendrils exploding from an orange moon and wrapping around her body flashed across her mind. Panic seized her. She thrashed about to free herself.

"Enoch, help me!"

Footsteps thudded, followed by the click of a latch and the faint creak of hinges needing oil. A slice of yellow light spilled in through the opening door and across a pale counterpane. Annabelle went still, blinking. She was lying in a bed, cocooned in blankets instead of entangled in the coils of the monstrous worms that had taken Enoch away.

A woman bundled in a large shawl stood in the doorway, regarding her with hooded, dark eyes set in an oval face hanging over the hurricane lamp she held. There was something pleasant and comforting—even familiar—about her features.

Annabelle squinted myopically at her hostess. With the lamp in hand, the woman shut the door and rushed to a chair on the right side of the bed.

"Steady now, Miss Wells," the woman said in a soothing voice. She set the lamp on a table beside the bed, next to a pitcher and a glass. "You're safe here in the doctor's house. There's no reason to be afraid. Take a deep breath."

At the sound of her voice, Annabelle's tension loosened. *Oh, yeah. She's the doctor's assistant; what's her name, again?* Her memory was spotty, but she recalled strong arms bearing her aloft, the scent of cardamom, and someone—*Lord Raeden, the dog guy?*—carrying her into a house where a middle-aged woman directed him to lay her upon a bed. Before the fog of oblivion descended, another man in the house—whom her bearer had called Dr. Fourtier—addressed the woman by name.

I remember, now.

"Verbena," Annabelle said, rubbing her eyes. "I'm sorry I woke you; it was just a bad dream. What time is it?" She placed a hand over her chest. Her heart still beat like a hammer. She remembered ...

Eyes wide, she gasped, "Simon! The soldier. Is he all right?"

With a slight smile, Verbena reached over and patted her hand. "Sergeant Halloway is on the mend. My father is tending to him. He's lucid, free of infection, and doing well for a man with fractured femurs. Before long, he'll be up and about, charming any young lady within a three-mile radius." Sighing, she shook her head. "It's as if he's had several weeks of convalescence over eighteen hours. Father and I are both mystified by it."

Annabelle slumped back against the pillows. So, she hadn't imagined it. Something had happened with Simon. He'd been at death's door. She'd prayed, and then ... the blue power came. But had that been God answering her prayer to save Enoch's friend—

Enoch!

She struggled to sit up. "Oh, gosh. Enoch's missing. I have to go find him."

"You will do nothing of the sort, young lady," Verbena Fourtier said, her voice low. "Klotho has not yet risen; it's scarcely Frog Watch." As she spoke, a clock chimed five times, the sound muffled by the closed door. A smile twitched at her lips and she added wryly, "*Now* it's Frog Watch."

Klotho—as in Klotho, Lachesis, and Atropos? What do the Grecian Fates have to do with anything? Oh, that's right. Those are the three suns. And Frog Watch is five A.M. Wait ... wasn't it early morning when I arrived on Tehara?

Annabelle gawked. "Holy cow. How long have I slept?"

Moving the lantern closer, Verbena peered into her eyes. "Since Lord Raeden brought you here yesterday morning, around Atropos-rise. You'd fallen into an exhausted stupor." She leaned closer. "Good; your color's improved. Allow me to check your pulse." Humming an odd melody, the woman held Annabelle's wrist. "A little too fast. Breathe, dear. Deep, calming breaths." She continued humming.

Annabelle obeyed, focusing on her nurse's face. The woman's pleasant features and voice soothed her. *What is that lovely tune? It sounds a little like Gaudete, or some other medieval-era music.* She breathed. In and out. Gradually, her heart rate slowed.

Verbena smiled. "Better." Letting go of her wrist, she poured liquid from the pitcher into the glass and handed it to Annabelle. "You need water."

"Thanks." She drank eagerly, emptying the glass. As the water flowed down her throat, she felt her body waking up. Demanding more.

Verbena refilled her glass. Once. Twice. Three times. Her eyebrows rose. "My, you're thirsty. How are you feeling?"

With a sheepish smile, Annabelle placed the empty glass on the table beside the empty pitcher. "Like I have to pee," she said, as she began extricating herself from the blanket cocoon. Slowly, she pushed herself up. Good. No dizziness. She shoved the covers away and swung her legs over the side of the bed. Her bare toes brushed against a soft rug.

Verbena held her arm, leading her to a curtained alcove where a chamber pot awaited her, then back to her bed. "You still seem a trifle unsteady. I can brew some soporific tea to help you get back to sleep."

"I've slept enough. Enoch needs me. I've got to find him."

"I share your concern, Miss Wells," she replied, "but you aren't familiar with the area. The troopers are all out scouring the forest. Leave the search to them."

"But Verbena ... there must be something I can do to help." Eyes burning, she plopped down on the bed. She stared at her hands. "If I hadn't told Enoch I'd come through the wormhole ... It's all my fault he's gone."

Verbena knelt and took her hands. "Annabelle, look at me." Vision fogged by tears, Annabelle met the woman's gaze. "Enoch disobeyed the Commander's order to stay out of the Darkenwood. You are not to blame for whatever happened to him because of that disobedience. Do you understand?" Annabelle nodded. "Good." Verbena gave her hands a squeeze and then let go. "I have faith that, in the end, this shall all work out as the good Lord Yshua wills it. Whatever comes of all this, remember: Enoch's soul is in Lord Yshua's hands."

A tightness formed around Verbena's hazel eyes and her voice trembled when she spoke of Enoch. Memories of this woman, which Enoch shared with her earlier, swirled beneath the surface. A memory unfolded like a rosebud.

Weeping, the small boy curled up on the cot gazed at the woman kneeling beside him.

"Want mama," he sobbed. "Mama, mama."

"Poor Enoch," she murmured, stroking his hair. "I can't replace your mother—not even a little—but I will care for you as if you were my son. I'm here, child. I'm here." She began humming a sweet melody.

After a while, the boy's crying subsided. He watched the woman with glassy eyes. "Little ... mama," he said, his voice creaky. "Little ... mama."

Annabelle blinked, her eyes meeting Verbena's. Older now, with fine wrinkles and streaks of gray in her dark hair, but the same woman who had consoled a lonely orphan in the memory.

"You were like his mom," she mused aloud. "His little mother."

Verbena jerked as if someone slapped her, placing a hand over her heart. "How—" She cleared her throat and tried again. "How did you know he called me that?"

Annabelle averted her gaze. "I'm not sure. It's weird. I can recognize people Enoch knows after a while—it's like something clicks in my brain—but I don't *know* anyone, myself. Our minds were connected until he ... was gone." She fretted at her lower lip. "Whether it's my fault or not, I still want to help."

Verbena shook her head, her face shadowed. "Unless you know something the rest of us don't, there isn't anything you can do right now, except rest and regain your strength." She rubbed Annabelle's back, her voice brightening. "Since sleeping is out of the question, I'll brew you a nice cup of tea and fix some breakfast. That should do you a world of good."

"Okay," Annabelle replied, her mind already working on the problem. She knew something the others didn't. She could help find Enoch by using her special connection to him. Although she'd failed the last time. Perhaps the fatigue of traveling through the wormhole had temporarily sapped her ability to contact him. *Maybe I'll reach him if I try again.*

Resolved, Annabelle shut her eyes and imagined herself in the void place. *Enoch,* she called, reaching out with her glowing blue kythim. *Enoch, where are—*

A great weariness fell over her like a heavy quilt. Head spinning, she slumped, the world tilting to the right until her pillows smacked her cheek.

"Miss Wells!" Verbena was at her side, taking her pulse, straightening out her body to lie flat on the mattress, then tucking her in as a mother did for her child.

The room danced around her. Annabelle's eyelids grew leaden as Verbena stroked her hair and hummed the haunting tune. "No," she murmured. "I can't fall asleep. Enoch needs me."

"Rest, Miss Wells," Verbena whispered. "We'll speak later. As for what's being done about Enoch—" the woman cleared her throat before continuing— "that's all in Commander Storm's hands, now."

Verbena

A feminine voice spoke her name, and warmth touched her brow. The pleasant scent of herbs tickled her nose. Annabelle blinked in the morning light as the room around her and her hostess came into imperfect focus. Verbena had discarded the shawl. She wore a plain blouse tucked into a long, dark skirt and her braid wrapped around her head. A cloth bundle draped over her left arm.

Verbena smiled warmly. "Good morrow, Miss Wells."

"Morning," she mumbled, rubbing the sleep from her eyes.

Verbena placed the bundle at the foot of the bed. "I brought clothing for you, if you feel up to dressing."

Annabelle sat up under the woman's watchful eye, steeling herself for dizziness that never came. She grinned. "Yeah, I feel much better." When she set her feet on the rug beside the bed and stood, she wobbled a little, but her companion steadied her.

After helping her to the commode, showing her where to wash, and how to clean her teeth with something resembling a paint brush and powder that tasted like baking soda, Verbena assisted Annabelle in donning unfamiliar clothing: a singlet-type undergarment that also secured her breasts, an ecru cotton shirt under a sleeveless dress with a fitted leather bodice and divided skirts, and thin, fawn-colored trousers tucked into mid-calf leather boots.

She paced around the room, twirling to watch the divided skirts fly out around her like bird wings. Everything fit and allowed free range of motion, even the boots. How had Verbena had time to acquire boots for her small, wide feet? But where were her own clothes? At least she'd found her glasses sitting on the bedside table.

With a glance at her benefactress, she managed a tremulous smile. "Thank you for the clothes. They're a good fit." She smoothed her hands over her belly, pleased at how the undergarments slimmed her down without binding. She wished there was a mirror so she could see if she looked skinnier. Her empty stomach grumbled its protest.

Verbena beamed. "You are quite welcome, dear. Now, how about some breakfast?"

Annabelle paused with a slice of buttered toast halfway to her mouth and gaped at Verbena. "I slept for *how long?*"

"Another twenty-four hours since you last woke." Verbena sipped tea. Her expression seemed pitying. "You needed the rest and there was nothing you could do in the meantime."

Annabelle ran through some calculations and her eyes went wide. "But that means today's my birthday." At Verbena's perplexed look, she added, "I'm sixteen today."

"Sixteen Turnings? You're of an age with Enoch, then."

Turnings must equal years, Annabelle mused.

With a wan smile, Verbena nodded at the toast in her hand. "You'll want to finish that, dear. Replenish your energy."

"Has anyone found out anything about Enoch?" Gaze fixed on Verbena, she took a large bite of toast, and warm, buttery goodness filled her mouth. It felt denser than the bread she ate at home. "Mmmm."

The woman set down her teacup on its saucer and turned it slowly. She frowned at it as if it had offended her. "All I know is that the troopers searched the area where you ... arrived ... quite thoroughly. Last night, Commander Storm informed me he found nothing—no inkling what became of Enoch." She raised the cup to her lips. "There was talk of sorcery."

Annabelle swallowed the last of the toast and washed it down with tea heavy on cream and honey to cut the bitterness. "Whoever took him, and whatever happened, it must've been before I arrived." She bit her lip. The last thing she remembered from the clearing was the soldiers asking her questions she couldn't answer, the toad-creature giving orders, the dog-man shouting something—and then everything went blank.

She spoke her musings aloud, and Verbena responded. "Lord Raeden carried you all the way to the infirmary after you collapsed, and then to my house after my father examined you." A wan smile curved her lips. "I've been looking after you since. Here," she said, shoving a plate of sausages closer to Annabelle. "Eat up."

Annabelle stabbed a sausage with her fork. Before she shoved it into her mouth, she asked. "Just what is this Lord Raeden guy, anyway? We don't have dog-people on Earth—at least, not that I've seen." Her eyes widened at a sudden thought. "Cripes, I hope I haven't offended him by saying something stupid."

Verbena chuckled. "I don't believe you offended him in the least; he seemed more concerned about your state of health than about anything you might have said. Lord Raeden is one of the Wensallen-kaen people, or a 'kaenhir' for short. Not that I've met any apart from him. If memory serves, he arrived with Commander Storm and Enoch. When I met him, Enoch was just a wee toddler asleep in his arms." She became teary-eyed and her lips trembled. She passed a hand over her face and cleared her throat. "Forgive me." Meeting her gaze, she smiled brightly. "Now, tell me about yourself, Annabelle. Are you apprenticed in a trade yet?"

Annabelle swallowed. "Trade?" She was taken aback at the thought of herself as a plumber or an electrician. *Uh, uh. That's an accident waiting to happen.* "No, I'm still in high school. But I'm thinking of going to college and studying biology." Verbena's furrowed brow prompted her to explain. Afterward, the woman's confusion seemed to lift.

"Ah! I see. You wish to become a scholar." She smiled. "As a doctor's assistant, I find I never stop learning about ways to treat ailments or the mysteries of the human body." Her expression grew appraising. "You said you enjoy learning about living things. Do you have any interest in herbal remedies and healing? I could always use a helper with a clever mind and a compassionate heart."

"That sounds neat!" Annabelle grinned, and then her sunny thoughts clouded over. Verbena spoke as if she'd be staying here. She blurted, "What about finding Enoch? He's like a brother to me. I want to help. I think I'm here, on Tehara, for that reason."

Verbena shook her head. "You can be very helpful right here in Lilac Grove without risking life and limb out in the wilds. Leave finding Enoch to Commander Storm, Miss Wells. It's far too dangerous for a young lady–especially one without battle-training—to travel anywhere on Tehara." She shivered. "There will be trials you can't even imagine."

"What do you mean?" Annabelle frowned. "Wait ... who *is* this Commander Storm?" Had Enoch told her anything about him? The name filled her with foreboding. Memories not her own swirled like colored patches in a whirlpool but refused to coalesce into images that made sense.

Verbena picked up her teacup and peered into its depths. "Commander Storm is Enoch's mentor and guardian, now that Sir Rick has ... passed." Blinking rapidly, she swallowed some tea. "He's in charge of all the military forces under the Dwelfnic Council. Hundreds of thousands of warriors. When he gives an order, everyone hops to it." Dryly, she added, "He's also skilled in every weapon in creation and knows every route, path, and trail on the continent. If anyone can find Enoch, it's him."

Annabelle raised her eyebrows. *Wow! Sort of like a Five-Star General, weapons master, and ranger all in one.* She cleared her throat. "This guy sounds pretty, um, capable. He'd be able to protect me, right? Why can't I go with him?"

Verbena winced. "Miss Wells, Commander Storm is not known for his tolerance of females. Especially those embarking upon journeys without proper training. He'll see you as a hindrance and his gruff ways would make you miserable. Trust me; I know him." She patted Annabelle's hand and smiled as if to soften a blow. "It's far better if you stay here, with me, and learn medicine and the ways of healing until we can send you home again."

Is that what I should do? Uncertainty chased her thoughts into a tangle. *Verbena's probably right. But I can't just stay here, even if it's safer. I'd always wonder about Enoch. Unless I go, I'll never know if he's okay.*

Annabelle dropped her eyes and stared at her empty plate. When had all the food disappeared? She glanced up to see Verbena watching her with a troubled expression. She'd mentioned healing. *Should I ask whether it's normal for people to heal using magic on Tehara?*

Annabelle took a deep breath to steady herself and was just opening her mouth to speak when a noise like rolling thunder shook the house.

Exodus

Annabelle perched on the edge of a wingback chair's seat in the front room while her hostess answered the front door, tucked around a corner and out of her view.

"Commander," Verbena exclaimed. "I expected you to be gone on your way already."

A deep, resonant voice sent fear shivering into her bones. "I would have, but for one small matter I must attend to before departing. Has the womanchild finally awakened?"

"She has," Verbena replied, sounding reluctant. "Please, come in."

Ducking his head beneath the transom, a giant clad in a supple leather duster entered the room. Two baldrics crossed over his waist with two curved swords in scabbards hanging at either hip. The hilt of a third sword reared above his left shoulder. In one hand, he held a satchel. With the other, he unstrapped a helmet and removed it from his head, tucking it under one arm. Eyes like chips of dirty ice speared Annabelle.

"Good morrow," he said, his tone of voice implying it was anything but.

Annabelle felt her stomach drop when he looked at her. She stared into the reptilian visage of the largest—Man? Creature? — being she'd ever seen. Andre the Giant has nothing on this guy. *He's huge, like a freaking dinosaur!*

Verbena shot him a nonplussed glance as she hurried to her side. "Miss Wells, this is Commander Storm. He will ensure Enoch returns to us."

Trembling, Annabelle leaped to her feet as the stranger approached, giving him a little wave. The floorboards groaned beneath his huge black boots. "H-hello, Commander." Inwardly, she grimaced. *I sound like a scared little girl.*

"Greetings, womanchild." The huge warrior arched an eyebrow as he hooked the satchel on his belt. "I trust you are prepared to leave? Mind, I'll not stand for any lollygagging—even in a female."

"Womanchild?" And what the heck did her sex have to do with anything?

"Um ... yes?" *With confidence, Annabelle!* She straightened her spine. "Yes, I'm ready to leave." Fiddling with her skirt, she asked, "So. Where are we going?" Her breath quickened. "To save Enoch?"

He stopped midway into the room and regarded her through narrowed eyes, like a craftsman examining his tools to determine their fitness for the task ahead. His fingers drummed a regular staccato against the rim of the helmet. "Aye. I plan to rescue the lad. Alone. However, duty demands that I deliver you to a place of safety first."

Annabelle gaped at him as her heart plummeted. "But I want to ... I thought that ...." She swallowed past a sudden blockage in her throat. *I'm not a package to be dropped off somewhere!*

Verbena placed a hand on her back. "What do you mean, 'deliver her to a place of safety?'" She scoffed. "She's perfectly safe right here in Lilac Grove!"

"No, she is not, Miss Fourtier," the Commander said icily. "And neither shall anyone else be, should she remain here."

With his chin lifted, he turned back to face them. "I shall bring her to Y'Dendordenelle. Aside from her own realm—where she ought to have stayed—it is the safest place for her. Had the Void-Bridge remained open, I would insist that she return, but that avenue is closed."

The wormhole was gone? Her heart skipped a beat. "You mean I can't go home?"

"Aye." He squinted. "Hopefully, the Dwelfnic Council can open a way to your realm."

"But—but I don't want to go home until Enoch is safe," Annabelle cried. *Oh, God, what am I doing—shouting at this scary guy?* Shaking, she forged ahead. "And I don't want to be dumped at ee-den-dor-whatever-it-is. I want to save Enoch."

Commander Storm approached until he stood a pace away. He looked down at her, his gray-eyed gaze icy with disdain. "What you want or don't want is immaterial." Something stirred the hem of his duster—a tail the same brown color as his scaly skin.

He has a tail! Annabelle leaned back into Verbena's steadying hand between her shoulder blades. Had David felt this way when he faced Goliath? She blurted out, "Oh, my gosh. Are you some kind of dinosaur-man hybrid?"

"I am an evainghir, not a ... dinosaur-man hybrid." His thin lips contorted around the words. "Whatever that is." His grimace bared teeth too pointed to belong in a human mouth. Donning his helmet, he stepped closer, floorboards singing out in protest. "Come, womanchild, it's time to leave." He held out the largest hand she'd ever seen. Annabelle looked at it and swallowed her protest.

He could crush me with no effort.

The doctor's assistant tsked. "Commander Storm, you are giving Miss Wells no choice in the matter. And I still believe she's better off here, with me. She—"

"I want to go," Annabelle interrupted, her heart hammering.

Verbena's hand dropped away from her back. "Are you certain, my dear?" Anxiously, she peered into Annabelle's face.

Annabelle met her gaze and nodded. Traveling with the evainghir, there was a chance—however minuscule—that she could convince him to take her along on his journey instead of leaving her in the safe place with the odd name he'd mentioned. If she stayed here, then she might never know what became of Enoch.

"Commander," Verbena protested, "you could at least wait until Lachesis has risen. A few hours won't make a difference. If you mean to take Miss Wells ..." She sighed. "Lord Raeden will be most displeased that you didn't wait for him."

He frowned and shook his head. "Waves and waystones wait for no man. Or womanchild. We must leave now. If he wishes to join us, then His Excellency will catch up. I expect delays as it is." His steely eyes rested on Annabelle.

Oh, so I'll cause delays, will I? Umbrage rose within her, hot and bitter. She swallowed it.

The Commander's thin lips twitched into something like a sneer. "I am accustomed to traveling with warriors and those prepared to face hardship—not the soft and weak. Only the battle-trained and the strongest survive in the wilderness. Expect no coddling from me, womanchild. You have five minutes to bid your farewells." He nodded at Verbena, turned in a swirl of coattails—and real tail—and left the way he had come.

Annabelle stared after him. *Only the battle-trained ...* Her knees shook and nearly gave way under her. Verbena steered her back to the chair, and she sat, the woman rubbing her shoulder and murmuring reassurances. She clenched her hands into fists in her lap. Her vision swam. "Verbena," she sobbed, "I have to go with him—I feel God has called me to this. And yet ... I'm weak, like he said, and ... What if I end up being useless? I don't know anything about being a warrior or fighting with swords, like Enoch." She snorted. "Phys. Ed. is the one class I've never got an 'A' in." She inhaled through her nose. "How am I going to do this?"

Verbena knelt before her and took her hands. "Miss Wells ... Annabelle. If this is your choice, then know this. The Almighty has a plan for you, and he equips all those who love him for the trials they will face in life. Trust in him."

Her eyes crinkled at the corners in a smile. "Warrior or not, I suspect you have as yet untapped reservoirs of strength inside you." She gave her hands a squeeze. "And despite what he said about survival, Commander Storm will protect you and prepare you for what lies ahead. His honor demands it." Wryly, she added, "He'll most likely train you to use a sword."

Annabelle sniffled. "Thank you, Verbena. For everything," she replied in a watery voice, and ventured a smile. *But no swords for me. They're meant for killing people, and I could never bring myself to do that.*

The Commander's rumbling basso drifted through an open window. "Have you finished your dad-rotted sniveling?"

Verbena rose, muttering. "Honorable or not, someone ought to give him lessons in basic civility." Louder, she said, "We'd better get you moving along. Come; I packed a few things for you."

My backpack! The sudden shock of recall jolted Annabelle out of her grief. Wiping away tears, she leaped from her chair.

"Verbena, did you … did someone find my bag? I brought some clothes, toiletries, and other essentials along with me."

Verbena frowned. "You'll have to ask the Commander. If the troopers found anything, he'd know about it."

Outside, birds chirped and whistled in the trees in the pale, early morning light. Paving stones rang dully beneath Annabelle's boots as she stepped from the back door. The fresh perfume of lilacs mingled with herbal scents, making her nose twitch. Her hands tightened on the straps of the pack Verbena had provided as she hesitated between two lilac bushes flanking the door. A large garden sprawled from the end of the paved area to the forest beyond; red daffodils, blue tulips, and yellow hyacinths lined the path, leading to a wrought-iron table and four matching chairs beneath a flowering crabapple tree. She envisioned herself drinking tea with Verbena and Enoch and her heart gave a little wrench. *It looks so homey.*

A rumbling, throat-clearing noise pulled her back into the present. She pushed her glasses higher on her nose and peered around the lilac bush to her left. The Commander waited beside a stone bench against a low, wrought-iron fence. As she stepped past the bush, he hefted a huge pack-frame and slipped it on his back like it weighed nothing. Annabelle's eyes widened. The bulky pack was larger than her! How much did it weigh? *He's so … massive. A bodybuilder on steroids would look puny standing next to that guy.* She swallowed.

"Time's a-wasting, womanchild," he said. "I believe this belongs to you." He waved at a familiar item sitting on the bench.

Annabelle brightened. "My backpack! You *did* find it." Grinning, she went to claim her property. A few strange lacerations discolored the tough, green fabric, but the relief welling up inside her overwhelmed any bitterness.

He did not return her grin. His expression darkened. "Of course, I searched your ... satchel for dangerous contraband. Fortunately for you, I did not find any."

She clutched the backpack and her voice rose an octave. "You went through my stuff?"

Gray eyes narrowed. "It should please you I returned it at all." He snorted. "His Excellency insisted you be given the benefit of the doubt—despite your dubious origins."

"His Excellency. Do you mean Lord Raeden?"

Commander Storm scowled. "Aye." He jerked his head toward the woods. "Enough bantering. Come along. We're wasting daylight."

Whatever we were doing, it wasn't bantering.

Annabelle frowned and slipped her arms through the backpack straps, carrying it in front. *I feel like a turtle.* Her cheer dampened, she followed the evainghir, jogging to keep up. His cloak-draped tail swayed from side to side, mesmerizing her. They passed through a small gate and then on along a narrow dirt path winding among trees and bushes. Fern fronds brushed against her legs and dewdrops scattered. An earthy, damp scent rose that reminded her of the woods around her grandparents' house. She swallowed thickly.

The dim forest lightened. Before long, she was puffing under the weight of the burdens she carried. Where were they going, and how far away was it? Visions of Frodo Baggins trudging a harrowing path toward Mordor flashed through her mind.

Hopefully, I won't have to drop a magic ring into a volcano to save Enoch.

"Um, Commander?" she ventured, timidly. "Are we walking all the way?" She'd never be able to keep up with his long-shanked strides.

He glanced over his shoulder. Something like amusement glinted in his eyes. "No. That would be utter folly, untrained for hardship and weak as you are. I prepared a mount for you."

A mount? But she didn't know how to ride a horse! Annabelle fretted at her lips. Sighing, she bent her head and focused on the end of his tail again. His words stung. But for Enoch's sake, she would endure any hardship.

I don't want to be a burden, but I must be part of this—of getting Enoch back. I just wish I knew whether he was okay. What must he be going through? Are his abductors torturing him? She shuddered. Maybe it was a good thing their bond wasn't working ...

No. Her fingers tightened on the backpack straps. *What an awful, selfish way to think.* It didn't matter how horrible his experience was, she'd rather have the connection back and share in his pain than always wonder what was happening to him. At least then she'd know he was alive. *Please God,* she prayed. *Let us find him soon!*

The birds twittering overhead seemed to mock her.

Abruptly, the Commander stopped and Annabelle stumbled into him. "Be more cognizant of your surroundings, womanchild," he said. "I know little of your realm and the threats you may face in your daily life, but Tehara holds many perils. The Veil that once protected these lands has gone down. There are beasts lurking in the wilderness that will rend your flesh from bones and devour you whilst you still live."

She cast a glance over her shoulder. "What kind of beasts? Like, lions and tigers and bears?" *Oh, my! All I need now is a yellow brick road, and we're all set.* She sucked her lips between her teeth to trap the nervous giggle bubbling in her throat.

He turned to face her, blocking her view of the path ahead. "If those are deemed huge, ferocious predators in your world and capable of eviscerating a man as casually as one swats a fly, then, aye. Exactly like that. Also, bandits and mercenaries roam the countryside despite my efforts to eradicate them. These are battle-hardened men who will show you no mercy, should you stumble across them."

Is it really that bad, or is he just trying to scare me? She gaped at him.

The Commander squinted. "If you value your skin, then remain vigilant, womanchild. Wandering minds lead to maimed bodies." He stepped aside, waving her on.

Annabelle scowled. Under her breath, she muttered, "And being a nasty jerk leads to getting smacked in the—"

She stared past him, eyes wide.

From where it stood under a tall tree, a horse-sized beast with liquid brown eyes blinked at her—a white-tailed deer, a buck with antlers still in velvet. He bore a bridle, a saddle with a bag fastened to the front, and panniers on either side of his haunches. Seeing the giant deer jostled something loose from Enoch's shared memory.

Enoch tends to the beast in a dimly lit stable, removing the leather gear it wore and offering a handful of limp greens. Enoch, laughing, as the deer nuzzled his cheek ...

Unbidden, a name floated to the forefront of her awareness. "Tinker," she said. The buck trotted forward to nuzzle her cheek—just as he'd done to Enoch in the memory. She giggled as he touched her forehead with his moist, quivering nose. She scratched him under the chin. He half shut his eyelids and grunted with pleasure. "Your name is Tinker, isn't it boy?"

"It matters not what its dad-rotted name is," the Commander said. He opened his mouth to say more, then narrowed his eyes. "How do you know the beast's name? Did the boy tell you?"

"N-No. Not exactly." Grip tight on the backpack's straps, she licked her dry lips. "I ... had a flash of memory. Enoch's memory about Tinker."

"Explain how you acquired these memories," the reptilian warrior demanded. "Are you in direct communication with the lad? Do you know where he was taken?" His fingers brushed the hilts of his twin swords as he loomed over her. "Such information would be ... useful."

Annabelle flinched. Her breath grew choppy. "No," she replied in a small voice. "Not anymore. I don't know where Enoch is, or who took him." He kept gazing at her with those cold, gray eyes like steel augers, and her tongue was wagging before she could stop it, spewing out words faster and faster. "I used to share dreams with him. We connected through our k-kythim, I think it was called—mine is blue and his is silver—and I could feel his presence, but now it's broken. Our connection. And I can't feel him or find him, no matter how hard I try ..."

Choked by rising tears, her voice tapered off. The Commander stared, silent. His visage looked even grimmer. Annabelle swallowed with difficulty, then took a shuddering breath.

Oh, dear. Should I have told him all that? He already thinks I'm completely useless! How would she convince him to bring her along now? She must get back their connection. Somehow. Then, perhaps she could help the Commander find Enoch.

"That is an unfortunate development," Commander Storm rumbled. "Give me your satchels, womanchild." He took her bags and secured them in the panniers. Before she could protest, he added, "Get up into that saddle, now. Or I'll put you there."

Annabelle cast a net through her mind, pulling up everything she'd ever read or seen on television about riding a horse: not much. Steeling herself, she grabbed hold of the cantle with her right hand and the pommel with her left. Her thigh pressed against her stomach as she shoved the toe of her right boot in the stirrup. She hopped on her left leg while hauling herself up. *Not enough upper body strength.* Tinker sidled away, dragging her.

"I can't do it," she sobbed. Her arms trembled with fatigue. "I've never ridden before. I don't know how."

Oh, please God, help me. Please don't let him leave me—

Commander Storm seized her by the belt and the back of her leather vest. Annabelle squeaked in surprise as he plopped her down in the saddle. She arranged the divided skirts until both sides hung down around her legs instead of bunching in the front.

Gruffly, the Commander gave directions on how she should sit erect with her shoulders back, the way her feet should go into the stirrups—with toes pointed toward the sky—and then gave her the reins. "When the beast moves," he snapped, "Move in rhythm with it." He took up the lead for the animal and continued along the path.

Commander Storm led the deer along at a distance-eating trot. Annabelle bounced, teeth rattling until she adapted to Tinker's gait. Reluctantly, she admitted that the Commander's advice was sound. Once she had grown less fearful of falling, she loosened her grasp on the reins to examine the saddlebag in front of the pommel.

When the loose flap moved, she flinched, swallowing a scream. *Oh, my gosh! There's something inside.* Visions of fang-filled mouths set in slathering jaws, and curved talons reaching out to tear her flesh, flashed through her mind.

The leather cover flipped back, and a huge toad with pale blue eyes leered at her. "Having fun yet, kiddo?"

Into the Wilds

Rules of Engagement

Annabelle gasped, her heart leaping into her throat. "Oh!" She blinked at the creature in her saddlebag. Tentatively, she asked, "Sir Thomas, right?"

The toad snorted. "In theory." His throat sac pulsed. "Not that I can remember anything about being Sir Thomas. Just call me 'Toad,' for now. Fits me better."

Yeah, it sure does. She huffed a brief laugh as she wriggled in the saddle. *It feels weird to sit with my legs so far apart.* Loosening her white-knuckled grip on the saddle horn, she said, "Okay, 'Toad' it is. Are you coming along to save Enoch, too?" She bit back a groan and the urge to smack herself on the forehead. *Duh, Annabelle. Of course he is.*

He glared at her. "No, I hang out in random saddlebags for the fun of it. What do you think, kiddo?"

Face warming, Annabelle squawked with indignation. "I was just asking; there's no need to be a sarcastic jerk about it."

Commander Storm glanced back over his shoulder. "Ah. Sir Thomas," he said. "Quit needling the womanchild and impress upon her the need to keep her voice down. Best she adapts the habit of traveling quietly before we pass through the waystone and into the true wilderness."

Hey, I'm right here! Annabelle scowled.

"Yes, sir," Toad replied. He fixed his pale blue eyes on her. "You heard him, kiddo."

"Then why didn't he tell me so directly?"

Toad smirked and shook his head. "He's my superior officer, and he's chosen to funnel orders through me. It is what it is."

What if I don't feel like playing that game? With a sigh, she leaned forward. "Commander Storm, what's a waystone?" she asked, albeit more quietly. The word rang a bell, but she couldn't quite place it. Enoch's shared memories were fragmented. "And can you say anything about where you're taking me? You mentioned some kind of council ... Please. We left in such a hurry. I want to know what's going on." She squinted at her companion and added sweetly, "I'm sure Toad would like to know, too."

"Hey!" Toad shifted around in the bag, squatting lower. "Leave me out of this."

"She will cause trouble if I don't," the evainghir muttered, as if completing a conversation begun inside his head. He dropped back to walk alongside her mount. His steely gray gaze was level with her own. She stared, fascinated, at his reptilian visage. Small, brown scales a shade darker than his skin surrounded his human-looking eyes and mouth and lined his square jaw and jutting cheekbones. His nose was a mere suggestion defined by slits, like a lizard or snake. And yet, hair poked out from under his helmet.

Is the Commander a mammal or a reptile? I still *think he's a dinosaur-man hybrid.*

After measuring her a moment, he returned his attention to the path ahead. "Very well. There are certain things I shall tell you now. But before I do, know this: if you wish to survive the journey, you will obey my every order. When I tell you to be silent, you will be silent. If I tell you to run, then you will run." He looked at her with narrowed eyes, his upper lip curling to reveal a fang. "Do you understand, womanchild?"

Heat rose to her neck and a chill coursed down her spine. *He's ... scary. Hopefully scarier than any of those wild beasts he said we'll meet.* She clutched the reins tight to mirror the rigid set of her shoulders. "Yes," she whispered, unable to break his gaze. "I understand."

Commander Storm nodded, then faced forward again. "Good." He picked up the pace and continued, "As I have already told you, we travel to Y'Dendordenelle. Or 'Treehome' as it translates into the Trading Language. The folk who reside there—in particular, the Dwelfnic Council—will have information concerning the best means of rescuing the lad."

Hope stirred inside Annabelle, but the Commander's next words pinned it down and wrapped it up tight as a fish in a net. "In addition, the First Councilor possesses the ability to return you to your own realm. And if he cannot do so immediately, then you shall abide in his care safely enough, whilst I carry out my mission."

She gave a little squeak of protest. Without bothering to look at her, the reptilian warrior continued. "To answer your other question ..." Curious despite her exasperation, Annabelle listened with bated breath as he explained. "Waystones are a means of crossing great distances in moments. They exist as stone circles with monoliths in the center, all linked in a vast network spanning the entire planet. A necessity, given the many perils of the landscape. The trick is knowing which waystone opens at a particular destination and exactly when that path becomes accessible. The Council documented much of the information in seven copies of an almanac. Without it, very few have the knowledge to use waystones to their advantage—"

"Let me guess," Toad muttered, his voice muffled within the saddlebag. "You're one of those special few."

"—or possess tokens keyed to specific locations," he spoke over Toad's interruption. "And yes, lad, I am one of those few. Baron-knights also receive an almanac and access tokens upon their ascension; I believe Ursanovir kept his under a floorboard in his office." He eyed the saddlebag. "You would have learned of it before he passed, had you not so rashly run off chasing shadows in the Darkenwood."

Toad grumbled something under his breath about finding lost children.

"Waystones are portals," Annabelle mused aloud. "Like a magic instant transit system." She frowned. "Do they run on a schedule—and how does that work? Is it like busses or trains that come every fifteen minutes or half an hour?"

Toad rolled his eyes. "Pretty sure he doesn't know what those are, kiddo."

Oh, and you do? Annabelle snorted.

"The 'schedule,' as you call it," the Commander replied in a level tone, "is based on calculations involving complex astral and planetary alignments."

Cool! Annabelle grinned. "Commander, please, can I see it—the almanac, I mean?"

The evainghir gave her a puzzled look. "I don't have an almanac. I don't need one." He hesitated. "I am ... attuned to the waystones. In a manner of speaking."

"Attuned, how? Like a musical instrument?" She considered her clarinet, practicing the duet with her best friend, Kensi. She thought of her parents and siblings. Of home. A pang went through her. Would she ever see them again? Well, if this 'Council' insisted on sending her home, then she might see them pretty soon. Dread and anticipation filled her in equal parts.

The Commander shook his head. "It has naught to do with music. 'Attuned' means that I know where the waystones are and when to pass through them."

"Wow, that's neat." She was silent for a moment, thinking. "So, what happens if we get to this waystone too late?"

He stared at her, his regard as sharp as the swords he carried. "It is of the utmost importance that we reach the waystones on our journey at the proper time. If we do not, we miss our window of opportunity to attain our goal. However, unacceptable as it is, that is merely the best outcome."

Annabelle licked her lips. "W-what's the worst that can happen?"

Commander Storm's jaw tightened. "If you made the attempt at the wrong time, without a vashenta—that is, a gem keyed to the desired destination—you could end up stranded somewhere you didn't intend to go. Somewhere lethal." He squinted. "I possess the vashenta. That is all you need to know. As you value your life, you will obey my orders. With that in mind ..."

From the assortment of deadly utensils attached to his wide belt, he selected a short sword in a brown leather scabbard. "I brought along a weapon for your use." He held it out until she took it, adding, "You will keep it on you at all times, always close at hand. Go on, draw your blade. You must grow accustomed to its weight."

Toad chuckled. "Just try not to cut yourself with it, kiddo."

Hesitantly, Annabelle gripped the weapon's hilt and—after a few tries—pulled it from its sheath. She held it aloft. As long as her arm and heavier than her clarinet, its blade glinted in a shaft of the first sun's pale light. She switched the sword from one hand to the other before sheathing it. Not knowing what to do, she cradled it against her bosom. *This is one dangerous baby I'm holding.*

Her mind retreated to a memory that was not her own.

Twelve-summers-old Enoch quivered with excitement as he admired the way the blade glinted in the sunslight. It was his first real, edged weapon. Sir Rick had given it to him as a Name-Day gift. Simon and Sharky had both praised its balance and keenness; Enoch was relieved to have their approval.

That morning, Commander Storm had arrived from his tour of the Western Marches, come especially to assess Enoch's readiness for the next level of the sword-dance.

A shadow fell over him and his shiny blade went dark. "Time you had your own blade, lad," the Commander said. "Now, show me the first sequence of Summoning the Wind."

Blinking, she emerged from Enoch's memory. Was "summoning the wind" some kind of special fighting move? Sword-fighting scenes from her favorite books and movies ran through her head. None of them helped. "I've never used one of these before. I don't know how."

How many times am I going to say that while on this journey?

Commander Storm's mouth twitched. "It's quite simple, womanchild. The pointy end goes into the enemy. In a bind, use it as a bludgeon." Matter-of-factly, he added, "If it comes to pass that you must use it, I will be dead and our mission a failure."

Oh, please, dear God, no. Perish the thought. Her heart hammered so loud she feared her companion could hear it. "Are ... are you planning to teach me how to fight?"

*Like he taught Enoch? And me—*fighting? *With a* sword? Her senses revolted.

Unpleasant emotion flickered across his scaly visage. "I do not train females in the art of war," he rumbled. "Sir Thomas and I will train you in self-defense. Nothing more." Gravel crunched under his boots as he took the lead.

"But I ..." Annabelle's voice drifted off as she stared after him. "What am I supposed to do with this thing?"

Toad chuckled. "You can start with putting on the belt, kiddo. Are you right-handed?" She nodded. "Thought so. The scabbard should hang at your left hip."

After strapping on the belt and adjusting the sword, her gaze settled on Toad. "I've been wondering. I can't fight. I want to help find Enoch, but ..." She fretted at her lower lip. Without her connection to Enoch, what use could she be? "If I learn how to fight, do you think I can convince the Commander to bring me along?"

"Search me." The oversized amphibian managed a credible shrug. "Commander Storm moves in mysterious ways." He snorted. "But if I were you, I wouldn't count on your fighting ability being the deciding factor. It takes years to master the sword-dance. And we don't have that kind of time."

Riding Mishap

Commander Storm's long-legged lope set the pace at a steady canter for another hour—although it felt like an eternity. Annabelle clung to her mount and prayed that she wouldn't fall off. Her knees ached from the pressure it took to keep her upright. What sort of perils did Tehara hold? Was Enoch okay?

Thanks to the Commander's talk of wild beasts, she kept envisioning horrible monsters descending from the trees to tear her to pieces, as well as worrying about Enoch and all the things that could go wrong. By the time the Commander slowed, pulling them off the trail and into the surrounding forest, her nerves sang with anxiety and she had worked herself into a low-grade panic.

Annabelle clutched the reins while scanning all around. "Is something wrong, Commander?" she asked, her voice growing strident. "Why'd we leave the path?"

Tinker halted beside the huge warrior. His stony gaze was level with hers, seeming to pierce right through her like the twin swords at his hips. It made her want to squirm. "Nothing to worry about," he replied, his voice rumbling like distant thunder. "There's a stretch up ahead I must assure is clear before we proceed. Hunters and trappers use this part of the wood. I wish to avoid undue notice. Sir Thomas, do you follow?"

Toad poked his head out of the saddlebag. "Yes, sir. Loud and clear."

"Good. Begin instructing the womanchild whilst I reconnoiter."

"Er ..." Toad blinked, glancing at her sidelong before responding. "Yes, sir."

Pausing, the Commander narrowed his eyes. "Stay here and obey Sir Thomas." He slipped between the trees, fading from view amid shifting shadows and shafts of green-gold light.

"Great," Toad grumbled once he was gone. "I'm stuck babysitting a moody teenager. I didn't sign up for this when I became a knight."

Annabelle's jaw dropped. *I'm not moody!* She lifted her chin. "If you're supposed to be a knight, then why aren't you acting more chivalrous?"

Toad laughed. "Hate to break it to you, kiddo, but real knights weren't very chivalrous. All that nonsense comes from fairytales. Aren't you a little old to believe in that stuff?"

She glared at him. *He wouldn't know chivalry if it fell from the sky like an anvil and squashed him.* She snorted as giddy laughter bubbled up her throat at the cartoonish image.

"Anyway," he said, cutting her off, "the Commander told me to train you, so that's what I'm gonna do. The good news is, for your first lesson, you won't even need to dismount. Let's get started. Draw your sword."

Annabelle pursed her lips. Carefully, with her trembling right arm, she unsheathed the blade. "Now what?"

"Okay, the part you're holding is called the grip, or handle, of the hilt. The round bit is called the pommel. The flat bit protecting your hand from the blade is called the crossguard. Now lift your sword."

Frowning, she held the grip with her knuckles and the edge facing forward. "Like this?"

He nodded. "See what you're doing? That's called the hammer grip; great for striking downward with the edge. You'll need to learn how to adjust your grip. Be versatile. You're right-handed, so we'll start there. Practice switching grips so the guard is in line with your arm. It always needs to be in line with your arm for strength and stability. And keep it loose until contact." He described several ways to rotate the position of her fingers and thumb, and how to keep the blade at a forty-five-degree angle. "Roll your fingers toward your palm. Focus pressure on the pinky and ring finger; loosen your thumb, move it ... there. That's it. Good."

A glow of pride replaced her confusion. "I can see how a person would need strong wrists for this." She laughed.

"Yeah, don't worry. We'll work on strengthening your wrists, kiddo. But strength isn't everything in swordplay. Now, hold it out to one side, parallel to the ground, for as long as you can. When you get tired, switch arms. I want to see what I have to work with here."

Annabelle grimaced. *A nerdy bookworm with no upper body strength, that's what.*

Toad's disconcertingly cold blue gaze rested on her. She pursed her lips and concentrated on keeping her arm level.

"Don't forget to breathe, kiddo."

She released her pent-up breath. After two minutes, her arm quivered, its muscles screaming for respite. Annabelle's jaw clenched as she strained to hold the sword steady.

"If you're tired, then switch arms."

I hate being so weak. She held the sword out on the left side. The quivering heat of muscle fatigue set in even sooner, and the sword tip drifted downwards. She growled, struggling to lift her arm.

I have to do better than this, or these guys'll never take me seriously.

"Okay, that's enough," Toad said, sounding disgusted. "Stop, before you hurt yourself. I've got a baseline for your strength."

Under his breath, he muttered, "Criminy. Save me from mule-headed teenagers."

With a scowl, Annabelle awkwardly sheathed her weapon. "What strength? I've just proven how weak I am."

"That can change," he replied, "with time and hard work. No pain, no gain. If it doesn't kill you, then it'll make you stronger. Get used to the idea now."

Annabelle sighed. "Some birthday this is. I get a sword I can barely lift and a quest I'm ill-prepared for." She stared at the short sword in her lap. "This sucks! Why does everything here have to be so hard?"

"Oh, knock it off, kiddo," Toad snapped, his eyes flashing with inner fire. "You wanted to come along on this trip."

"But, Toad," she whined. "Nothing here is how I expected it to be. Enoch's in trouble, and I don't know how to save him. Everything I learned in school means nothing here. I feel so useless."

Toad glared over the brim of the saddlebag. "*You* feel useless?" He snorted. "Try being me, kiddo. I know how to use a sword and fight—everything involved in being a knight—but this stupid toad-body won't let me do any of it, so I couldn't prevent the kid's abduction. What's more, I'm supposed to be Sir Thomas, but I can't remember anything about *being* Sir Thomas, the person. Only what he could do. At least you can remember who you are and where you come from. You have a human body that *somewhat* works." He laughed humorlessly. "You think you have it bad? You have no clue. So, suck it up, buttercup."

Annabelle blinked away tears. "Oh, Toad. I ... I wasn't thinking. It must be terrible for you, being stuck in the body of a toad. I'm so sorry." She leaned over and kissed the irascible amphibian above his snout.

Toad went still. And then he shuddered, squalling out a vulgar epithet that made her jerk back with a scandalized gasp. Still cursing, Toad leaped out of the sack and onto Tinker's neck. Snorting and shaking his head at the unexpected weight, her startled mount bucked. Annabelle clamped her legs and gripped the saddle to keep from falling off.

"Calm down, you stupid deer-thing!" Toad snarled, clinging to Tinker's fur with his stubby digits as Tinker thrashed about and attempted to fling him off his neck.

Annabelle cried out, snatching for the reins. She shrank closer to the deer's body and clung to the saddle horn like a rodeo cowgirl. "Tinker, stop! Whoa, boy!" Fear lanced through her like an arrow as her mount increased his gyrations.

Oh, God, save me!

Suddenly, Lord Raeden was there, planting himself before Tinker and grasping the bridle with both hands. Nose to nose with the giant deer, the kaenhir snarled something in a dialect that sounded like German. Whatever he said had a calming effect upon the frightened stag, because Tinker ceased his wild dancing and head-tossing. He stood still, trembling, chest heaving and nostrils blowing.

Raeden barked out a command. Staring into the beast's eyes, he held out his right hand parallel to the earth and lowered it. With a confused grunt, the stag folded his legs and eased down on his belly, stretching his neck on the forest floor. Annabelle felt her feet touch the ground. Raeden hunkered in front of the deer, not breaking their locked gaze until the animal was calm.

His pale eyes bulging out even more than usual, Toad slid down, vocal sac pulsing rapidly as he emitted gulping sounds.

"Are you well, Freylin?" The kaenhir sidled around Tinker's head until he was right beside her. He leaned closer to peer into her face, ears pricked, his green eyes dark with concern. "Have you an injury?" He touched her hands; the warmth of his fingers and the fur brushing up against her knuckles seeped into her. She heaved a shuddering sigh.

"I'm okay," she said, examining him. He wore a leather vest over a light cotton tunic, buckskin trousers tucked into tall riding boots. Traveling clothes. Incongruously, he wore a monocle over his left eye and his coppery hair was tied back with black ribbons.

"How did you find us?"

"Your servant tracked you," he said, eyes sparkling with humor.

Annabelle furrowed her brow. *I have a servant? Who is he talking about?*

He tipped his head. "Can you stand, or do you require assistance?"

"Let me try," Annabelle said with an embarrassed smile. "You'll catch me if I fall?" He nodded and stood up, poised and alert. She pulled one leg across the back of her mount and rose on unsteady feet. Silently, he offered her his arm, and she took it, catching her breath. "Thank you," she whispered, closing her eyes and breathing in the faint scents of cardamom and pepper. "I'm so glad you came."

"As is your servant," Raeden replied.

"Who's my servant?" Annabelle looked around. "There's nobody else here. And I don't have a servant. People don't have them where I come from."

Raeden raised an eyebrow. He tapped his chest. "This one is your servant."

Toad muttered a curse from the side of the trail.

"This one what? Oh ..." She grinned. "You mean yourself, don't you? Do you always refer to yourself in the third person? That's hilarious. But why would you be my servant? I mean, aren't you a lord?"

Raeden's whiskers quivered. "Yes, Freylin, he is a lord, but he is also your servant. This is as it should be—until he has fulfilled his service. But this must not be spoken of again." Green eyes glinting as they rested on her, he held out his free arm with his hand palm up and then raised it. Tinker lurched up on his hind legs. The kaenhir barked out a command, and another giant deer trotted up the path toward them, saddled for riding and bearing a bulky pack. The buck was larger than Tinker and possessed a ten-point rack, still impressive despite being encased in velvet.

"They obey you so well," Annabelle remarked. "How do you know what to do?"

"Your servant helped to train this stag." He scratched Tinker's chin. "All the courier beasts are trained by the folken." He nodded at the other deer. "That one is your mount's sire. He is called Lorun. Your servant has trained him for battle. Now." The kaenhir turned to Annabelle, head tilted, his brow furrowed. "How is it you come to be in such danger?"

Sheepishly, Annabelle let go of his arm and grabbed the reins of her mount. She stroked Tinker's muzzle in mute apology. "It was all my fault, Raeden," she said in a rush. "I startled Toad, and he jumped, and then Tinker spooked ..."

"*Ach so?*" He peered at the oversized amphibian crouching under a patch of ferns. "Is this the truth, Sir Thomas?"

Toad muttered another curse. "Dumb girl thinks the world revolves around her." He shot a baleful glance at Annabelle. "I always take full responsibility for my own actions, kiddo. So don't try to cover for me. I spooked the deer-thing, and it nearly killed you. End of story." He swiveled to hop into the shadowy brush. "I don't need anybody's friggin' charity."

"Toad, wait!" She prepared to charge after him into the wood, despite the jelly-like quality of her leg muscles.

Raeden grabbed her arm before she took a single step. "Let him go, Freylin. That one needs—how does one say it? —solitude. He shall return when he is ready, *nich*?"

Annabelle turned to him. "Why do you call me that? Fraylin. Did you forget my name? It's Annabelle. Or you can call me 'Ann', if that's easier."

Raeden let go of her and stepped back, his spine rigid, but his green eyes held warmth. "Your servant forgets nothing. The folken remember all they see and hear." He tapped his head, mouth twitching in something resembling a smile. "If he has given offense, then he offers his apologies." Placing a hand over his heart, he bowed. "But he cannot address a little maiden in familiar ways. Such is not proper. Until he has known you a season, he will address you as Freylin." He nodded and clasped his hands behind his back, ears quivering.

That's fine, but what does 'Freylin' mean? Hmmm. I wonder if he'd let me touch his ears. Are they silky, like a real dog's?

Annabelle opened her mouth to ask—not sure which question would tumble out—when Raeden's ears lifted, and he turned to one side.

Branches parted and Commander Storm charged into view, gray eyes wide and bright, gripping the hilts of his swords, ready to draw. He crashed to a halt and glared at them.

"The courier beast spooked, Lord Commander," Raeden said, giving the fist-to-chest salute. "All is now in good order."

"By the Great Below," the evainghir said, his eyes shifting from one to the other. Annabelle cringed, expecting a fiery diatribe regarding her inability to control her mount, but the Commander's gaze settled on Raeden. "I was uncertain whether you would come, your Excellency. What of the duty to the realm that you swore to uphold as the Lord Seneschal?"

"'Seneschal' is no longer this one's title," Raeden responded, eyes narrowed. "He has resigned the position, for the baron-knight who requires his service is no longer in residence. This one has found a higher calling." He let go of Annabelle and then stepped between her and the huge warrior. His voice roughened into a growl. "With respect, Lord Commander, why do you not wait for your servant? You take the young knight's heart-sister into the tomb of perils, like a thief in the dark, despite the agreement. For both insults, he will face you in the trial by combat, though he loses his very life."

"Do not dress yourself in motley, Raeden," the Commander said. He folded his brawny arms, looming over them. "I would never accept a challenge from you. Regardless, the womanchild is my ward. She goes where I take her."

Annabelle stared at him. *His ward? Since when? And I have a name; why won't he use it?* When she tried to protest, only a squeak emerged.

She moved up beside Raeden, close enough to feel him trembling, his body rigid and taut as a strung bow—but whether from outrage or terror, she couldn't tell.

"How shall this conflux then be dissolved?" snapped the erstwhile seneschal, gesticulating with both hands.

"We have no *conflict*," Commander Storm replied, enunciating, "that requires *resolution*, your Excellency. I need not explain my actions to you. I have declared martial law. In the absence of a king, I need not answer to anyone save the Council."

Annabelle searched the Commander's visage as he spoke, but to her surprise could find no trace of derision or scorn. The two men stared at one another, both making odd gestures with their fingers.

"Is that sign language?" she blurted.

Abruptly, the two stopped their digital contortions and looked at her, as if surprised to find her still standing there.

"Many apologies, Freylin," Raeden responded, slamming his right fist against his chest and bowing to her. "It is a great rudeness to speak before you in a language unknown to you. Your servant's anger ran away with him." He glared at the Commander. "He is concerned for your safety."

Commander Storm's eyes narrowed. "No harm shall befall her in my care, your Excellency." His face went expressionless as he turned to Annabelle. "Now, womanchild, go ahead along the trail and take the deer with you. I must discuss something with his Excellency. Without interruption."

Great, now I have to wait to ask him anything.

With a sigh, Annabelle retreated to make the acquaintance of the new animal. Lorun enjoyed chin-scratches as much as Tinker did. She took Lorun's lead and brought him over to Tinker. Her throat constricted and her heart hammered at the thought of climbing into the saddle again. Instead, she looped the lead around the saddle horn and took hold of Tinker's reins.

Dragging her feet, she continued along the trail with her eyes fastened on the packed dirt lane stretching straight ahead. Golden green light dappled the path and the surrounding foliage. She looked around. Where was Toad? Would he ever come back? Was he gone, like Enoch? With her back against a tree, she concentrated, reaching out with her kythim into the void place. A sharp pain went through her, and she stopped before she blacked out again.

Enoch ... Please, God, let me get our connection back!

Sniffling, she wiped her nose on her sleeve. She wanted to call for Toad but feared that he would make fun of her for crying.

"Don't be such a baby," she imagined him saying. *"How do you expect to earn the Commander's respect if you're bawling all the time?"*

"Shut up, Toad," she muttered.

"What for? I didn't say anything." A familiar gravelly voice came from a patch of unfurled bracken fern a few paces ahead of her. Startled, she stopped. Toad hopped out from behind the ferns, a mouse-tail disappearing into his mouth. He swallowed. "Sheesh, kiddo. No need to be surly. I was just finding myself a snack."

"Sorry," she replied, unable to meet his pale eyes. Something about his gaze made her feel vulnerable and tender, like newly healed flesh beneath a scab.

"Don't be," the oversized amphibian replied. He glanced back to where the Commander stood with his arms crossed, watching them. "Like I said before, it was my fault. Come on, kiddo. Let's make like a tree and leave. A dinosaur must've farted, 'cause it sure stinks."

This time, Annabelle did nothing to suppress the laughter bubbling up in her throat.

To Start a Fire

Shadows were lengthening, and the daylight had waned into the crimson glow of evening when Commander Storm called a halt. Their little group hiked up a steep incline until the trees thinned, where they found a small clearing on the crown of the hill with a sandy pit ringed with stones in its center. Several weathered logs with splintered edges lay at regular intervals along the perimeter of the clearing.

Travelers must use this place regularly, Annabelle mused as she staggered, panting, her feet throbbing in the new boots. She bore no ill feelings toward her mount; however, she had refused to climb back into the saddle. Instead, she strode along the trail as quickly as she could with Tinker's reins in hand. She stuck close to Raeden and took his arm for support over the rougher portions of the trail.

At first, he suggested she overcome her fear by riding—he promised to remain near her—but she insisted she was not afraid, that she only walked because she needed to stretch her legs after sitting in the saddle for most of the day. He did not press her but adjusted his own pace to hers, the ten-pronged stag ambling in his wake.

The gloaming time unnerved Annabelle. On Earth, she'd never seen skies take on such a lurid crimson hue, as if the entire world were drenched in blood. Was it because Tehara circled three dissimilar stars?

I wish I had a book about Tehara ... its natural history, geography, people, and cultures.

There's so much she didn't know; the more she considered her ignorance, the more fear stirred in her breast like a hungry eel. The sheer magnitude of her circumstances made her senses reel. Questions whirled and roared in a tempest. Where, in all of this vast new world, had Enoch's abductors taken him? Would they be able to find him? Could she learn enough new skills to be useful on this mission? The last thought struck her as she swayed. She tightened her grip on Raeden's arm.

"Freylin, are you unwell?" Holding her arm, he led her over to a fallen log and supported her as she sat down.

"She had better not be," the evainghir said. "She has much yet to do this evening in setting up camp and preparing the meal. Your Excellency, you will scout the perimeter."

"You want me to do what?" Annabelle's heart plummeted like a rock into a deep, cold well. She glanced appealingly at her companions. "But ... I've never been camping before. I've no idea what to do."

That jerk you sit next to in band class, Neal MacReady, would know what needs to be done, a snide little voice taunted her. *Maybe you should have paid closer attention to his endless Boy Scout camping anecdotes while you were still on Earth, eh?*

Raeden peered into her face, his white fur stained a deepening rose color in the twilight. "Freylin, it is not expected for you to work alone and without guidance." He turned to address their expedition leader, placing himself between her and the evainghir. "Lord Commander," he said, standing with hands clasped behind his back, "this one must respectfully protest—how does one say it? —the assignment of duties. Freylin is exhausted and knows not the ways of traveling. This one proposes he stay here to instruct her about what she needs to know in the days ahead." His tone sounded calm and even, but his tail lifted, the fur along its spotted length bristling.

Commander Storm did not reply, and Toad poked his head out of the saddlebag. "Sir? His Excellentness has a point. You wouldn't expect a raw recruit to wield the sword in battle without training first. How is this any different?"

Warmth filled Annabelle, and a smile tugged at her lips despite her weariness. Thank God! Both Toad and Raeden were sticking up for her.

With a sideways glance at the toad, the huge warrior sighed. "So be it. Although I do not see the point. A few blankets and a fire should not be beyond her abilities to arrange."

Raeden's ears twitched. "This one has also brought a tent and a soldier's cot with a suitable bedroll for her comfort. He has heard from Miss Fourtier, who fretted that these items were not included."

"Criminy! Not touching that one." Toad slid to the ground, backside first, chuckling. "I don't have a death wish." He hopped away into the shadowy underbrush.

"Your Excellency," Commander Storm said, "you know my intentions are to travel light and swiftly. We are already behind schedule. So long as she desires to be included, the womanchild must do without such comforts on this journey and gain the skills necessary to take part. Her survival depends upon it."

My survival depends on being uncomfortable? Annabelle frowned. *How does he figure?*

Raeden made a sweeping gesture toward Annabelle, tapped himself on the chest, and then brought his hands close together, thumbs and forefingers darting together in odd motions that reminded her of sewing. What did those signs mean? She'd have to ask him to teach her.

The evainghir snorted. "That is certain to be the death of you, Raeden." The two men regarded one another in silence. Raeden stacked his right fist over his left. The huge warrior puffed out his cheeks with a plosive sound, running his hand back through his hair. He shook his head. "On your own head be it, then. I wash my hands of the matter." He dropped his pack-frame underneath an oak tree. "I shall check our back trail whilst you two set up camp." Without a backward glance, he strode from the clearing and vanished into the surrounding forest, every tree a stark silhouette against a blood-red sky.

After he left, Raeden swept his gaze around the glade, ears pricked up. Nodding with satisfaction, he then turned to her. "You are weary, Freylin," he said. "Do not move from that place. Your servant will set up the camp and tend to the beasts. Watch, and learn from what he does. Ah! But first ..." Eyes bright and whiskers quivering, the kaenhir went to his mount, removed something from a saddlebag, and strode over to Annabelle.

Puzzled, she eyed the leather-wrapped object he held as he approached. *Is that what I think it is?* Breath quickening, she straightened, her eyes darting from his face to the bundle.

"One did not wish to soil the stream, Freylin, in mentioning this earlier in the Lord Commander's presence, but your servant has brought something else for you. Something to help you learn. This belongs to Enoch," Raeden said, as he offered her the rectangular parcel. "One believed it may offer some ... comfort."

The object was heavier than Annabelle expected and she nearly dropped it. Hands shaking, she placed it in her lap and peeled aside the leather, which felt supple and almost greasy. She gasped at what she revealed. *It is!* She exulted, bouncing a little as a grin spread across her face. "A book!" she squealed, running her fingers over embossed designs and rune-like symbols.

"A book," Raeden echoed. "As your servant understands it, this book contains something of true history."

Finally, some information about Tehara. Thank you, God!

And then she frowned. "Wait. I can't read this." Carefully, she opened the cover to the first page, and saw the same runes in a large script. Underneath in smaller letters, however, were five words that—if she tilted her head and squinted past a weird swimming in her vision—she found she could decipher.

"Fortulles Evaingynon Seprima. Legendary ... Tales ... of the ... Sages," she read aloud. *Huh. I hope I pronounced that correctly.* She looked up to meet Raeden's green-eyed gaze. "And it's Enoch's book?" A thrill went through her. *This is so cool!*

He nodded. "He had great love for it, and the tales within. It may be of help to you in days to come, or it may not. Only the Threefold One knows."

Warmth bloomed inside her. "Oh, Raeden! It's already helpful, because it *is* a comfort—to have something of Enoch's. Thank you so much."

"It was your servant's duty and great pleasure." Gravely, he placed his fist against his chest and bowed.

Annabelle was tempted to touch the ears within her reach. Instead, she hugged the book. "I'm so glad you're here. You showing up made my day, you know."

He straightened, looking at her with his head tilted. "'Made your day,'" he repeated, brow furrowed. "How does one 'make a day,' Freylin? Surely, that is in the realm of the Threefold One, and not for your servant to do."

Laughing, Annabelle said, "It's a figure of speech meaning you made me happy—the happiest I've felt all day—because you're being so kind to me."

The kaenhir raised his ears and wagged his tail. Before he moved away, she set the book down, jumped up, and threw her arms around Raeden. His body went rigid in her embrace, his arms raised with elbows bent out from his sides.

Annabelle let go and backed away. "Oh, dear! What did I do? I'm so sorry!"

Green eyes wide, he began to shudder and make odd clicking noises in his throat.

"Perdition, take it all!" Commander Storm stalked into the glade with a bundle of sticks under one arm. "You little fool," he hissed, tossing the wood into the center of the clearing. "Wensallen-kaen are not used to physical displays of affection," he said, grimacing. "You have rendered the kaenhir incapable of intelligent speech. Pah!" He threw his hands in the air.

Annabelle heard a familiar voice laughing from under a patch of bracken ferns. "In other words," Toad said sarcastically, "you broke him, kiddo."

Had Toad been observing them all this time?

Annabelle turned away, blushing. "I'm sorry; I didn't know. I wish I knew more about this planet and its customs ..."

Hopefully Enoch's book will help fix that.

Muttering to himself about the dubious value of "womenchildren," Commander Storm began unloading the baggage and gear from his pack and the panniers on the deer.

Behind her, a warm presence weighted the air. "Freylin," Raeden said, his voice shaky, "Do not fret. No matter what others say, your servant finds no fault in you. Come, sit. There is much for you to learn."

Annabelle managed a smile. "Alrighty then," she replied and returned to her log. She eyed the book, her fingers itching to caress the embossed leather cover again, turn its pages, and peruse its contents. However, it was growing too dark to examine.

I guess it'll have to wait until Raeden gets the fire going and we have more light.

While the Commander tended to the animals, Raeden assembled a cot and then a small tent that he staked up around it. The strange reddish light and his swift, deft movements prevented her from seeing any details.

"Um, Raeden? Could you please show me again? It's hard following you."

The kaenhir paused. "Apologies, Freylin," he said, then explained what he'd done. Annabelle nodded along, her mind drifting elsewhere.

Raeden must be as worried about Enoch as I am if he quit his job at the Manor to come along with us. Whatever his reason for leaving, she was grateful for his presence. He'd been kind to her, even though he had no reason to be. Maybe it was because she reminded him of Enoch.

"Your Excellency," the Commander said, and she flinched. He had finished stripping the beasts of their burdens. "Whilst reconnoitering, I saw a small herd of dolkibar just south of here. I would fancy a bit of roast meat tonight."

"Of course, Lord Commander," Raeden replied. "This one shall set the fire and—"

"No, your Excellency. The womanchild can attend to the fire. Assuredly," he added, turning to her with raised eyebrows, "such a homely task could not be beyond her skills."

Annabelle's insides chilled as Raeden picked up a bow and quiver of arrows from behind his saddle. He nodded at her solemnly. Consternation grew inside her as he prowled from the clearing. Her advocate had left her alone to deal with the huge warrior.

"You'd best get to it, womanchild, before you lose the light." Commander Storm stepped closer, his expression dubious. "You know how to cook, do you not?" He held out a small box, a stone, and a metal bar.

"Of course, I know how to cook!" Annabelle retorted as she took them.

You know how to cook on a stovetop, you dope, not over a campfire in the woods.

She examined the three items, muttering to herself. "Um ... so this is flint and steel. I've never started a fire without matches or a lighter before." She laughed, her face warming. "This ought to be interesting."

First things first: she must get a fire started. Hastening to the stone-circled sand pit, she grabbed the smallest branches and snapped off the tiniest twigs for the tinder. The open clearing provided enough light for her to build a small twig tower in the center. She recalled that much from Neal's camping stories. The tower kept collapsing under her shaking hands.

Darn it!

Hairs prickling on the back of her neck informed her of the Commander's vigilance. His contempt hung like an oppressive weight upon her shoulders. But she couldn't afford to break down under his steely gaze.

This is a test, isn't it? Enoch must have had to go through something like this. She gritted her teeth. If he could learn to do it, then so could she.

Toad hopped over from his hiding spot and peered into the pit. Annabelle steeled herself for caustic criticism.

"For love of Jeremiah Bullfrog! That's never gonna work. Listen. You need a nest of fine material in the middle that'll catch a spark, like shredded birch bark."

How does he know about Jeremiah the bullfrog? It has to be a coincidence.

Eyes wide, she stared at him with her mouth hanging open, then began shredding the birch bark. He grumbled, "No, no, not that. Don't you know anything? The box has tinder in it. Yeah, that fluffy stuff. Take a pinch and put it in the middle ... good. Now, set the twigs exactly like I tell you ..."

Annabelle glanced over at the evainghir; fortunately, he wasn't looking. She bit her lower lip and concentrated on Toad's directions, sweat pooling under her arms and bedewing her forehead. She placed each twig and branch around the nest of tinder and tree bark just as he instructed her. The little tower of sticks didn't tumble apart. After placing the last stick, she sat up and heaved a sigh, regarding her work.

She grinned. "I did it!"

"Well?" Commander Storm said. "Do you plan to light the kindling, or are you waiting for lightning to strike from the heavens?"

Annabelle cringed. She was only halfway done with her task. Bent over the pit, she glanced pleadingly at Toad. Pale blue orbs met hers and gleamed in the gathering darkness. He remained silent. She was on her own now.

She felt Commander Storm's gaze boring into her back.

I'll show him I can be useful!

Lips pursed, Annabelle picked up the flint and steel. She scraped the metal against the stone. A feeble spark flickered against the tower of twigs but failed to ignite. Beside her, Toad gazed at the wood.

Come on. Ignite, darn it! She struck the steel against the flint. Sparks flickered in Toad's eyes, but the fuzz pile in the sandy pit remained unlit.

"Dear God," she prayed under her breath. "Give me strength. Please ... just help me light this stupid fire. In Jesus's name, Amen."

She glared at the flint and steel, then dragged the iron across the stone. The largest spark yet drifted down into the nest of kindling. She held her breath, waiting, and then wilted in desolation when nothing happened.

Why wasn't it igniting?

Toad's eyes narrowed, but he said nothing. He leaned closer to the stack of wood, as if to examine the tinder.

"Again," demanded the implacable evainghir.

"Wait," said Toad, his entire body tensing.

A flame rose from the kindling, tiny and golden and perfect. Annabelle's heart lifted. She closed her eyes and sighed.

Thank you, God!

Within moments, the campfire burned strongly. The flames reflected in Toad's pale blue eyes. "There it is," he rasped as he slumped down on the rock. He sounded exhausted. "You done good, kiddo. Oh, by the way ... happy birthday."

Captive

William returned from gathering last autumn's dead and dried tassel-grass for the cooking fire. He paused and leaned against a standing stone to watch the Golorum play Fate, the warriors' favorite gambling game. It was the squad-leader's turn to roll the bones.

Six tetrahedral spindles fell with a clatter on the flat stone's surface. Four of the upward facets showed stylized daggers and the other two showed crowns. "Yes!" the squad-leader grunted, pumping a fist into the air. "Assassin's Triumph." Five warriors groaned and put coins in a helmet for the pot.

One loser turned and frowned at William. Looking away from the warriors, he continued toward the fire-pit he'd dug earlier, wringing the dry grass like he would a pigeon's neck.

The warriors sent by the Dreadlord obeyed Tenebris out of fear and respect for his power, but they'd made it clear they would not extend this to include a lowly apprentice. His hands tightened around the withered grass stalks. Not yet, anyway. But someday ...

"William! I told you to gather tinder for the fire, not muck about making a mess."

William jumped at the whip-crack of his master's voice, fumbling with the bundle he'd gathered. "Yes, master," he replied breathlessly, and heaped the grass in the center of the hole. Zakaar hunkered beside it, skinning the five rabbits and three grouse he'd caught that afternoon while the nehmwights slept in the shelter. The harkhurz's eyes glittered in his direction, but he remained silent. He was gradually reverting to the sane man William remembered from before the Eastern Marches.

Now that I've made him an elixir that actually works.

William knelt and laid out dead branches he'd collected from bushes as they traveled. His skin crawled as he imagined his master's gaze scorching his back. The sensation only lasted a moment before the Arkhadahn returned to setting up wards around their resting place inside the stone circle. Although it was no longer active and wild beasts shunned them, Tenebris took no chances. Muttering to himself, William helped Zakaar light the fire and set up the assembled spits. He leaned back on his heels to admire their work.

Whispers tickled his ears, sounding like large, feathery wings flapping and wind soughing through the leaves of trees. William froze. *There aren't any trees out here in the Herbmar.* He stood and scanned the sky for an airborne source of the sounds.

"What is it?" Zakaar was on his feet, too. His eyes gleamed amber, reflecting the firelight.

William choked out words past his tight throat. "Did you hear that? It sounded like a blazing huge bird just flew by overhead."

The harkhurz tilted his head, ears twitching. "I heard nothing of that nature." He sniffed. "I scent nothing dangerous." He looked up at the sky and then at William. His regard softened. "I see nothing, my friend. Perhaps you hear things because you did not sleep well?"

Is this a prelude to more taunting ... or does he think of me as a friend?

"You know I didn't," William snapped, looking away. "But that's not the point." He stopped his hand before it reached the flask inside his burkheld; Tenebris might see and take it away. Instead, he curled his fingers into a fist and forced the hand down to his side.

As if from a distance, a familiar voice spoke, *"Where am I? Annabelle, are you there?"*

He frowned. *Villem's bloody flail and scepter ...* He'd measured out Northward's dose exactly. How was the wretch already awake?

William glanced at his companion. Strange; the harkhurz acted like he hadn't heard their captive's voice. Was he imagining things? Better to investigate and not leave anything to chance. William assumed a fierce expression. "Oi, Zakaar. Make yourself useful and scout the perimeter. I'm going to check on our guest." He didn't wait to see whether he complied before pivoting on his heel and stalking toward the palanquin.

"Lord Yshua ... please deliver me."

He thrust aside the curtains, mouth open to snarl an oath, but it died in his throat. Silver vapors rippling like pennants in an intangible breeze radiated from the captive, white brilliance at their core, dancing in strange shapes. Northward's eyes were open and staring right at him. William gasped. Quickly, he checked the wyldling snare. Yes; the dark gray, metallic cords binding Northward remained intact. His magic was leashed.

Then why is his kythim manifesting so strongly? And what do the color white and flame-like symbols mean?

Meeting the captive's gaze, a chill swept through William like winter's breath, his vision doubling and shifting. He clutched at the palanquin's frame to steady himself, glimpsing a dark figure with glowing orange eyes backlit by the starry sky—*is that me?* —

and then, the image shivered and the silver-limned captive reappeared before him.

"Orange eyes," Northward murmured.

William took a deep, shuddering breath. "Burning suns and freezing void! What in all the prickle-burr nether-gardens was that?"

Still staring at him with glazed eyes, Northward chanted in dreamy sing-song:

"Eyes flare orange fire! Know your grim plight.
Flee from the harrows of deepest dark night.
Ware nehmwight hordes! They scheme for death;
Draw swords and fight till your final breath.
Stalkers of night, all mongrel bred;
Without just cause, they'll strike off your head.
Arkhadahn's Web ensnares as he could
All good folk in black strands by rite of blood.
Far worse than these, legends all tell:
The Daywalker shall reign as king over Hell."

A grip like iron clamped on William's right shoulder. "What's going on here?" Tenebris narrowed his eyes at the captive, whose chin had sunk down to his chest after his recitation. "You fool, I told you to dose him with valerian and kavalha. Why is he already conscious?"

William flinched away from his master's fingers. "I did, Master." He scowled at the prisoner. "And what the blazes was *that*—poetry?"

Tenebris sneered, but the expression seemed forced. "Kadorei drivel from a muddled brain. Pay it no mind."

Eyeing his master sidelong, William shook stray bits of grass from his burkheld. *What don't you want me to know, Tenebris?*

Northward's eyes opened again and his brow furrowed in confusion. His voice was rough. "Who's there? Annabelle ... are you there?" More softly, he asked, "Why can't I feel you?"

William laughed aloud; the fellow looked and sounded so utterly stupid. Northward's eyes widened as he peered out of the palanquin, searching the darkness. "Hello?" he said, his tone stronger, but still uncertain. "Who's there? Why am I bound? Is ... is Annabelle with you?"

"No," William replied, chuckling. Annabelle was a sort of girl's name, wasn't it? She must be a person Northward cared for. Perhaps one of the children Zakaar had killed.

William cast a werelight so the prisoner could see his leer. "Annabelle's dead, you bat-faced buffoon. Zakaar ate her for breakfast. You know how he likes the taste of maiden-flesh."

Suddenly lucid, the prisoner fixed his furious eyes on William and cried "murderers!" He thrashed and strained against the wyldling snare like a bird in a net.

"Enough!" Tenebris snapped, tattoos writhing. He made a grabbing gesture and the shouting cut off. The prisoner's eyes bulged as he struggled to draw in air. The Arkhadahn leaned over the youth, grabbed his chin, and forced him to look at him. "You will cease your tantrum. Now."

William grimaced, rubbing a hand over his own throat. His master had used that spell on him just the other day. He tethered the werelight to a point a foot above his right shoulder and drew in closer to his master. It would be interesting to see somebody else receiving an object lesson from Tenebris for a change.

So long as there's no bleeding involved. He shuddered.

Northward stopped struggling and gulped in air. He kept trying to speak, but no noise escaped his throat. The fellow was lucky that Tenebris allowed him to draw breath. William smirked. The spell wouldn't last much longer, but the stupid kadorei didn't know that, now, did he?

"Very good," Tenebris said, a faint smile thinning his lips. "I am your host, the Arkhadahn Yvres Tenebris of the Thirteenth Order, Master of the Nine Rods of Dominion, Highest of the Grand Khabal. However, you may refer to me as Master Tenebris, or Varazslo."

As always, William felt a thrill at his master's use of his full title. *Someday, that'll be me. Just you wait, Tenebris. I'll defeat you in the Arkhadahn's Challenge. And then* I'll *be Varazslo.*

Tenebris's smile faded and his regard sharpened. For a moment, William feared his master sensed his traitorous thought, but Tenebris still faced Northward. "Listen to me, kadorei filth. I'll only tell you this once. If I find myself repeating things, there will be pain. There are four rules you shall follow going forward, and if I find you violating them, there will be pain. And I can make the pain last a very long time without leaving a single mark on your body. Now, the rules are very simple. Even an infant can understand them."

William shifted his weight from one foot to another. *I know what that expression portends.*

"Rule One," Tenebris said, his voice like silk caressing steel, "you are not, by any means or in any way, to attempt escape from me or my companions. Rule Two: you will not, by any means or in any way, attempt to alert others not of this party of your captive status and thereby solicit aid in escaping. Rule Three: when I speak to you or ask you a question, you will respond both truthfully and with all the polite civility drummed into you by your elders. Rule Four: you will eat and drink the sustenance I provide for you. I have put fail-safes into effect to prevent you from ending your life. However, I shall be most vexed if you attempt it. Most ... vexed." His jaw tightened and his eyes flared with orange light.

William grinned. *This is quite entertaining.*

"Now," Tenebris continued, mildly, rising to his full height. "In a moment, I shall release your voice. Your first words to me had better be polite acceptance of your circumstances and willing compliance, or there will be pain." He delivered this last in a jovial tone William learned to fear as a child. It usually heralded a beating. Goosebumps prickled his flesh and his grin faltered.

Tenebris made a gesture similar to a dismissive wave, and the spellform collapsed. It would've dissipated in another ten seconds, but the captive couldn't have known this.

William tucked his hands in opposite sleeves of his burkheld. *Better that our prisoner knows as little as possible concerning the limitations of our power.*

The moment he could speak, Northward sucked in a breath and yelled: "Go to perdition, nehmwight son of a goat!"

His face expressionless, Tenebris beckoned to the harkhurz. "You may deliver my rebuttal," he said. "But not too vehemently. The Dreadlord wouldn't appreciate receiving a damaged parcel."

Zakaar stepped forward, ears pricked up and eyes alight. He crouched and punched the bound and helpless youth in the solar plexus, driving the wind out of him. Northward curled in on himself, gasping as he struggled to breathe.

"I'll leave you to ruminate over that for a bit," Tenebris said with a grim smile, sliding the curtains closed. The heavy fabric muted the prisoner's spluttering. He turned to William. "I'll not have his noise bring terror birds down on us. Water him, and then give him some poppy-milk."

William raised his eyebrows. *What's Tenebris on about? Terror birds don't hunt at night. And he knows the Dreadlord won't like his prize addled by laudanum.* Aloud, he replied, "Yes, Master." He glanced at Zakaar. "Hold him down while I pour, will you?"

Eyes glowing, the harkhurz bared his teeth in a rictus. "With pleasure, my friend."

The Sword, the Syrax, and the Spring

A Bad Dream

"Let him go!"

Annabelle fought to reach Enoch as writhing, dark gray strands cocooned him and took him away. Her body grew cold and unresponsive as the same cords bound her. And then, she was falling ... She awoke and rolled off the narrow cot, thudding to the earth. Gasping for air, she clutched at her head.

Not that dream again.

"Freylin," a voice whispered from outside her little tent. "Are you well?"

She swallowed thickly. "I'm okay," she replied in a shaky voice. "A bad dream, that's all."

"Ah," Raeden said. "Your servant has also had unpleasant dreams these three sleeps since the young knight was taken. Of what did you dream? Perhaps to speak of the fear will help chase it away."

Annabelle rose to her knees. The tent ceiling brushed against her head. While she'd slept in her tent, Commander Storm and Raeden had made do with their bedrolls on the ground outside.

She smoothed her hands back through her hair and then down her wrinkled clothing, the same set she'd worn the day before. Her eyes felt grainy and blurry. "I dreamed about Enoch. These horrible dark gray ropes came out of an orange moon and tied him up. And then the ropes came after me. They felt like metal but moved like worms, or snakes." She shivered and rubbed her arms. "It was so cold."

"You dreamed of the lad's abduction?" Commander Storm rumbled from right outside, and she flinched.

"Um, kind of? More like a symbolic representation of it." Her voice grew small. "I had this dream before, with the dark gray ropes wrapping around Enoch and carrying him off." She focused on her breathing.

Calm down. It was only a dream. A regular dream, and not in the dreamscape. Wasn't it?

The evainghir grunted. "Hmm. Come out once you are clad. Raeden, break down the tent. Second-dawn is imminent."

Good thing I slept in my clothes. Annabelle scowled as she crept toward the entrance of her tent. "Yes, sir," she grumbled under her breath. "Right away, sir. A 'please' would be nice."

"Please," the Commander growled from right outside the tent. "And be quick about it."

Raeden tutted. "Lord Commander, you must learn how to speak with better politeness."

"That's rich, coming from him," Toad chimed in from under her cot. "He can barely string a sentence together without garbling it."

Was he under there the whole time? Heat rose in Annabelle's cheeks. "Toad," she hissed. "Don't be nasty. He can probably hear you."

"He can," Raeden said coldly. "He may not speak the demon trading tongue to perfection, but there is nothing wrong with his ears."

"For a dog's ears," Toad laughed.

"You're incorrigible," she said.

Toad sneered. "Is that even a real word?"

She lifted her chin. "Of course, it is. I collect words, so I should know. It means you're stuck in your bad habits."

"Whatever." Toad grunted, pushing the sword in its brown leather scabbard out from under the cot. "Speaking of habits, don't forget your sword, kiddo. Or do you want His Excellentness to fetch it for you?" He snickered.

Annabelle snatched up the weapon, pushed through the tent flaps, and clambered to her feet. "Just ignore him, Raeden."

In contrast to her shabby and rumpled appearance, Raeden looked impeccable in a black leather vest and buckskin trousers, red hair slicked-back and tidy. He tilted his head, ears pricked. "Your servant cannot ignore him. Worry not; he has decided not to take offense at those who talk about trash in the rubbish pile."

Annabelle burst out laughing and brushed away tears. "Oh, you're so funny. Thank you; I needed that."

Toad hopped outside, rolling his eyes. "Please," he groaned. "That's too much hilarity so early in the morning."

Raeden tilted his head the other way, his monocle glinting. He was about to speak when the Commander said, "Enough chatter. As soon as Raeden finishes, we're leaving. The day advances and we cannot tarry." The warrior strode off to the clearing's edge, where he packed up a leather bundle of weapons.

Annabelle frowned after him. *Something's up. I'd better ask the Commander about my dreams.* While strapping on her sword-belt, she started toward him.

Raeden touched her shoulder, halting her, and then handed her a steaming mug. "There is time enough for the tea," he said.

"Okay." Annabelle sipped the hot beverage cautiously. It tasted earthy, like mushrooms, with a hint of sage and something else she couldn't name. She made a face; the flavor wasn't what she'd expected. "Not that I'm complaining—it's not bad, just weird—but what is this?"

"It is a special tisane," Raeden responded, meeting her gaze. "Your servant blended it for your health. You must drink it every day. Without fail."

Her eyes widened. "Why? Do I have some kind of disease?"

Toad burst out in croaking laughter. Raeden pinned his ears and glared down his nose at him. "One does not see the humor in this, Sir Thomas. The tea is not to treat illness, Freylin," he explained, turning back to her, "but it will make you safe, while we travel." He shifted his weight, glanced away, and clicked his tongue. "The women of the folken use it, at certain times, when they must travel through the wilderness made dangerous by hunting beasts who track by scent." At her blank look, he leaned closer and whispered. "It is to prevent the moon-blood."

"Oh! That." Face warm, Annabelle buried it in the mug and focused on drinking the strange beverage. She hadn't even considered how her menstrual period might impact their journey. *Sometimes being a girl is downright inconvenient.* Toad had hopped away, but she could hear him still chortling at her expense. The jerk.

A strange thought crossed her mind. *I wonder if Toad's been having bad dreams, too. I'll ask him later. Before I do that, I need to talk to Commander Storm.*

Once finished, she thanked Raeden, gave him the mug, and stood, fussing with the hang of her sword. *Maybe—someday—I'll get used to wearing a murder-stick. Hmm. "Murder Stick" sounds like a good name for a sword. After all, murdering people is what swords are made for.*

With a sigh, she walked over to the Commander. He glanced up from repacking his collection of assorted deadly utensils as she approached.

"C-Commander? Can we talk about my dream? I think it means something." She smoothed her hands down her skirts.

Commander Storm's expression was unreadable, but the look in his eyes seemed bleak. "Indeed, womanchild," he replied. "Dreams often have meaning. Even more so for those who are connected in dreams. However, it can be perilous."

"First there's danger everywhere and now I can't even have dreams. Is there anything safe in this world?"

The evainghir raised his eyebrows. "No. Aside from Treehome, there is not. And anyone who tells you otherwise is either a liar or a fool."

"But what do you think it means—the gray metal ropes?"

He gave her a measuring look. "Nothing good."

She swallowed. "What do you mean, 'nothing good?'" When he didn't answer, she tried a different tack. "So, you said these dreams are dangerous?"

"Indeed. To lessen the danger, I will teach you to guard your mind," he said, "but I must prepare for your lessons. We shall speak more about this soon. In the meantime, continue familiarizing yourself with your weapon." He nodded at the sword hanging from her belt. "Sir Thomas and Raeden shall both instruct you today in skills necessary for your survival. If they deem your progress adequate, then you may have an hour to peruse that book His Excellency brought along for your amusement."

Oh, so now Commander Storm is resorting to bribery to get me to train?

Biting back a sarcastic comment, Annabelle fiddled with the sword's pommel. "Speaking of, isn't there a book I can read on sword-fighting? I'd feel much better if I could get the theory down before applying the knowledge."

He grunted a laugh. "Not in my possession, little one. I'm afraid you must forgo studying theory in favor of application."

Toad hopped over. "This isn't high school, kiddo," he put in. "You aren't graded on this stuff. Welcome to real life."

Being Useful

Commander Storm insisted they abandon the "extra amenities" Raeden had brought for Annabelle's use. He cached the tent and cot up in a tree. She didn't dare protest, lest he take away the book about Tehara's legends, too. Besides, she needed to prove to the Commander that she was tough enough to travel without luxuries. At least Toad wasn't heckling her about it.

When she balked at riding, the Commander narrowed his eyes and hissed, "Mount that beast, or I will tie you across its back like a gutted dolkibar."

"Reading may be easier in the saddle, Freylin," the kaenhir reassured her.

He's right, but ... no way I'm repeating that crazy, hopping dangle-dance from yesterday.

Despite her misgivings about riding, she asked Raeden to give her a boost into the saddle and mounted without incident.

"Thanks, Raeden." Annabelle picked up the reins in trembling hands and pressed her calves against Tinker's barrel. "Go on, boy," she whispered. The stag looked back at her, snorted, and then trotted after Commander Storm.

Raeden followed close behind. *He* had leaped effortlessly onto Lorun's back. Feeling irked, Annabelle watched with a mix of admiration and envy.

Commander Storm fell back to walk beside her. "You must keep me informed regarding your dreams," he said without looking at her. "If anyone speaks to you, be it the boy or someone else, you will inform me."

Annabelle winced; her muscles were sore from yesterday's riding. "Okay. I don't remember talking to anyone. Just the ropes taking Enoch away and then wrapping around me." She shuddered. "I've never felt so cold. Empty. It was like when ... I lost the connection to him."

He glanced at her. "We shall speak more of this when we reach our destination."

"But ..." Afraid to see the contempt settle its hard lines in his visage, she looked at her hands. Her heart hammered. *Ask, you coward.*

Taking a deep breath, she asked, "Would I be useful to you if I could locate Enoch?"

Commander Storm stared at her. Annabelle held her breath. Finally, he replied, "Womanchild. Your 'usefulness' on this journey—such as it ever was—is a moot point."

"What?" She sat up straight in the saddle. "I can be useful! Just tell me what I need to do."

He measured her with his gaze, then shook his head. "The risk is too great. To you, as well as to others. Once we reach Treehome, I will leave you behind in the care of those I trust to keep you safe and continue my mission. Alone, if I must."

Annabelle felt as if the ground had dropped out beneath her. "No ... there must be some way to get my connection back. Please, Commander Storm. I don't want to be 'safe,' I want to help you rescue Enoch. I'll go with you to the end! Please, train me in whatever you need to. I'll do whatever you say." Her throat thickened. "Just ... don't leave me behind."

Some elusive emotion flickered in the Commander's eyes and he glanced aside, a line forming in his brow. "Perhaps there is a way," he muttered, touching the hilts of his swords. "Do not get your hopes up—it is better by far if you stay with the dwelfnim. However, I pledge to delve into this matter further ... We shall see when we arrive in Y'Dendordenelle; it is out of our hands and beyond my control."

Arching his eyebrows, he added, "Now, it is time to focus on that which we can control. Your training." He cleared his throat. "Sir Thomas, Raeden—attend."

Before Annabelle could question him further, Toad popped up from the saddlebag, saying, "Yes, sir?" just as Raeden drew near with a "Lord Commander?"

The Commander assessed them both. "Take it in turns to train up the womanchild. See what you can make of her. I do not expect miracles—she is soft and weak because of excessive coddling—but push her toward a working knowledge of self-defense." His cold gaze settled on Annabelle and her throat constricted. "I'll leave you to it." He took the lead once more.

Toad gave a low whistle. "Criminy. No pressure, then."

Annabelle stared at her whitening knuckles as she squeezed Tinker's reins. Alternating waves of hot and cold anger swept over her in turns. "That jerk," she grumbled. "What's the point of training if he's only going to leave me behind in Treehome?"

"From what I heard," Toad answered, "there's a slight chance he won't. And a warrior must always be prepared for any eventuality."

"Sounds just like the Boy Scouts," Annabelle muttered. She took a few deep, shuddering breaths, and then glanced at Raeden pleadingly. "Are you guys up to working a miracle and teaching me how to defend myself with this thing?" She patted her sword.

"All things are possible with the Almighty, Freylin, and he is always with you. Your servant will gladly help you train." The kaenhir raised an eyebrow as he regarded the toad. "Unless Sir Thomas would like to seize the strings?"

"Oh, no," Toad replied as he fell back into the saddlebag, half-laughing. "Don't let me interfere. You volunteered, so this lesson is your dog-and-pony show, Excellentness."

Raeden lifted his chin and narrowed his eyes. "Sir Thomas, dogs and ponies have nothing to do with the sword training."

While Toad snickered, Annabelle clapped her hands over her mouth to stifle the giggles bubbling forth. "Well, maybe not the ponies," she said, "but we have deer." *And Raeden is kind of like a dog,* she mused.

Raeden cleared his throat. "Freylin, are you ready?"

"Um, yeah." Annabelle gave him a dubious look. "But we're on the move. Shouldn't I dismount?"

Raeden shook his head. "*Nich,* Freylin. Sword lessons can be done in the saddle, so long as you take care. You must learn his weight and how to hold him before the dance."

Him? Dance? Annabelle's eyebrows crawled up her forehead. Was he talking about the sword? *Oh, that's right.* Raeden's first tongue wasn't the Trading Language. She recalled her German class and how the nouns had genders. "Sword is a masculine noun in your language?" she asked, touching the hilt of Murder Stick.

"Naturally," Raeden replied. "The sword is a weapon used by men. Among the folken, men protect the women and children. Their clan."

"Really? Then why don't you have a sword?"

Raeden shuddered, his expression darkening as he pinned back his ears. He grasped the length of his queue as if he wanted to rip it out of his head. "One does not speak of it," he rasped. He shivered, and added in a mild tone, "You must not speak of it again, Freylin."

"I'm sorry!" Annabelle blurted, her heart hammering. Warmth mantled her cheeks. *Great job, Ann. Open mouth, insert foot.*

"Hey, now," Toad said, poised as if to leap. His eyes fixed on Raeden. "No need to get all wound up, Your Excellentness. It's a valid question. I wondered, myself."

The kaenhir released his queue and turned to them. With a hand placed over his heart, he bowed. "Your servant casts no blame and freely forgives." His regard softened. "You are a stranger here, Freylin. How could you know what is taboo?"

"She's not the only one," Toad grumbled.

"Thank you." Her throat felt thick. "I won't ask again." *At least, for now.*

His whiskers twitched. "Although he does not own one, and prefers to use his bow or staff, your servant has had some little training with the sword-dance. He will aid Sir Thomas as he can, and learn more from him alongside you."

Brow furrowed, Annabelle looked between them. "But, Raeden, if you aren't an expert, then why are you teaching me?"

Toad sighed. "Do I have to spell it out to you, kiddo? Eventually, you'll need a sparring partner." He averted his gaze, his tone growing bitter. "And for obvious reasons, it can't be me."

Raeden eyed him sidelong. "Sir Thomas, this one has been praying for your—how does one say it? Ah, yes—your restoration to the proper form." He cast a glance ahead at the Commander and then bent closer. "Perhaps a cure will be found in Treehome, and then Freylin will have a suitable sparring partner."

"A cure?" Annabelle glanced between them. "Does that mean Toad could become Sir Thomas again?"

Toad grunted noncommittally. "That's the hope." A sharp look made Annabelle swallow the other question rising to her lips. "Let's just get on with this."

"As you wish." Raeden nodded and turned to Annabelle. "Draw your weapon, Freylin. Carefully. Then, hold him up and point his tip at the sky."

"Yep," Toad said, brightening with mirth. "Exactly what I would've suggested, Your Excellentness. That's quality training, right there."

Raeden shot him a nonplussed glance, shook his head, and then raised an eyebrow at Annabelle. He mimed drawing a sword.

With a sigh, Annabelle reached across with her right hand to pull Murder Stick out of its scabbard with a slight ringing hiss. She held it aloft, rotating her wrist. The blade glinted in the sunslight, reminding her of Commander Storm's pitiless gaze. Unbidden, an image from a favorite cartoon came to mind.

She grinned, declaring, "For the honor of Grayskull!" With a soft snort, she lowered the sword, then blushed as Toad burst out laughing.

Raeden's ears perked up and his eyes opened wide. "What manner of oath is this?"

"Oh, sorry. Just goofing around."

Ahead of them, Commander Storm cast a glare over his shoulder.

Raeden winced. "Sir Thomas, Freylin, you must be quieter." Shutting his eyelids, he breathed in and out through his nostrils. "Now, follow your servant's directions. You will hold the sword in different positions. Each has a different number ..."

The kaenhir ran her through exercises in which she held Murder Stick at varying distances and angles from her body.

Periodically, she switched hands, learning the numbered positions, working until her muscles trembled and sweat ran down her back.

"You must do this every day, Freylin, to build up the arm and wrist strength. Both in the saddle, as now, and when you rise on the morrow. Your servant will show you more this evening, as Sir Thomas directs."

And then Toad took over, explaining how to maintain her weapon, hone the blade, and keep it clean. "After a battle," he said, "always wipe the blood off your sword. You don't want it to tarnish."

Annabelle's jaw dropped. "Like I'm going to be cutting or stabbing anyone, Toad!" She shuddered.

"Seriously," Toad said in a dry tone. "Did you think the sword was just for show? Of course, it's for cutting and stabbing anyone who attacks you."

"Do not frighten her, Sir Thomas," Raeden said. He tapped his breastbone. "While this one has breath in his body, he will take on the burden of killing for her."

She laughed nervously, her eyes widening. "Whoa now, wait a minute ... Why are you so certain we'll be killing anyone?"

"Oh, I don't know," Toad drawled, "maybe because of all the desperate men with weapons who could be lying in wait anywhere along our route. Travelers have died—"

"Attend!" the kaenhir interrupted in a sharp tone. More softly, he added, "Freylin, please show your servant the number two guard position."

Raeden taught her until they arrived at a part of the forest with giant trees and scarce undergrowth. Commander Storm dropped back to check on her progress and inform them he was scouting ahead.

"Be sure to stretch your arms and rotate your wrists, womanchild," he advised, then addressed Toad. "Sir Thomas, we shall rendezvous when Lachesis is at her zenith. His Excellency knows the place."

Annabelle watched him jog away, frowning, as she chafed her wrists. *I haven't a clue how he could tell where the suns are, what with the dense canopy overhead.* Perhaps the evainghir had a sixth sense, his body mysteriously attuned to the natural rhythm of Tehara and the celestial spheres. After all, he claimed he knew the waystone schedule like it was built into his bones.

With a wry smile, Annabelle pulled out the leather-bound tome and began paging through, skimming the translated text for any mention of the dark gray metallic ropes from her dream. She squinted as the words swam and wavered before her eyes. The text stabilized when she concentrated on reading. Before long, she was engrossed in a story about how each Sage established a magically protected colony in a place after his own heart and devoted it to his Aethyric Aspect.

She scrunched her nose to push her glasses up. Aspects. Aethyr. What were those? They seemed familiar. Flipping back a few pages, she discovered a brief discourse on the seven Aspects of Aethyr—air, water, flame, stone, mind, flesh, and void—embedded within the previous story.

So, it's like the four elements from antiquity, with three more thrown into the mix.

About to turn back to the colony story, she hesitated when an odd, familiar word caught her attention. She traced underneath the sentence as she read. *"Phoenixheart settled the matter of the rogue wyldling, Josiah Horn, by binding him with the wyldling snare. He sentenced him to a full generation in the*

Outcast's Tomb, although some argued that the snare's impediment of his wyld was punishment enough ..."

Wyldling.

Annabelle frowned. Hadn't Enoch mentioned that word in one of their dreams? He'd believed he might be one of these ... wyldlings. Her breathing quickened. *I need to read more about this!* She examined the words more closely.

A raucous cry shattered the idyllic calm of the summer afternoon. With a gasp, Annabelle jerked up her head as a pink comet crashed through the forest canopy. She clung to the saddle with one hand and held the book to her chest with the other, suppressing a scream. Tinker startled and would have bolted had Raeden not seized the stag's bridle and barked out a command while reining in his own mount.

Toad poked his head out of the saddlebag, shouting curses that made her ears warm.

They use that awful word here on Tehara, too?

With another piercing shriek, the noisy, pink projectile unfurled its wings and landed with surprising grace on the trail in front of Tinker. "Lawks-am-awesy!" he said. "You fellas are hard to find. Good thing I figured y'all would be headin' for Y'Dendordenelle to ask Lord Evanrudhe for help. Hey, now, who's this?" Sparkling hazel eyes set in an aquiline head with triangular ears—like a cat's—looked up to appraise her. "Heya, toots." He waggled the feathery ridges above his eyes.

Raeden snarled. "Peter ..."

Toad groaned. "Criminy. By all means—let's add to the traveling menagerie."

Annabelle gaped at the creature. *The front half is a bird of prey and the rear half is from a great cat—if either of those animals could ever be pink.* Despite his outlandish appearance, there was something familiar about him—something stirring along the edges of memory ...

She blurted out, "What the heck are you—a pink griffin?" Hazel eyes sparkling with humor met hers. Shakily, she added, "And for your information, my name's not 'toots,' it's Annabelle."

"Anna-wanna-rub-my-belly-O!" he replied in sing-song. "My name is Peter and I'm a handsome syrax-O." In a normal cadence, he added, "Hey, sweetie; I brung you a present!" Puffing up the crest of pink feathers between his triangular ears, he pulled something winged and bedraggled out of his harness. With a twist of his neck, he flung it up to her.

Raeden turned from the deer and plucked the feathery missile out of mid-air. He bared his fangs at Peter and growled. "Peter, do not be forward with the little maiden!"

"I'm not dealing with this joker." Muttering further complaints, Toad ducked back inside his saddlebag.

Peter pinned his ears and hissed at Raeden. "Damp-off, Dogface. You've got no right takin' Annie's present." He crouched and wriggled his tail like a cat poised to spring.

The eerie sense of familiarity settling over her strengthened. Her vision blurred.

In her mind's eye, she saw the pink creature hunkered in a similar attitude and a younger-looking Enoch, who stood several feet away with laughter in his face. He swung a feathery ball attached to a length of twine, faster and faster, while his winged companion followed it with his hazel eyes.

Raeden stood beside him, eyeing the pink creature with disdain. "He should do his messenger work for Sir Frederick.

You will spoil him with too much play, Enoch. And you should be training."

Enoch kept spinning the toy. "Aw, Red. Don't be like that. He's got an hour before he has to leave; surely there's time for a game? It'll be a moon before I see him again. Go get it, Peter!" he yelled as he let go, launching the feather-ball flying into the sky.

With a joyful screech, flapping wings stirring up dust, Peter sprang after it. Enoch whooped in encouragement ...

As abruptly as it came, the tableau dissipated. Enoch's laughter still rang in her ears. A sense of great loss swept over her. She inhaled sharply. *That was one of Enoch's memories.* Her shoulders slumped as she let out a pent-up breath. Once more, she watched Peter squaring off against Raeden. Other similar scenes from Enoch's memories teased the edges of her awareness but failed to surface. A smile twitched at her lips. Silly and obnoxious as he acted—and ferocious as he looked—Peter was a friend.

I need to defuse this.

Annabelle tucked the book into a pannier and directed Tinker closer. "What is it?"

The kaenhir held *it*—the tail-feathers of a deceased bird that resembled a mourning dove—between a thumb and forefinger, his right arm stretched out to one side as if to keep *it* as far away from Annabelle as possible. Peter gave up his aggressive posturing and puffed out his chest. Eyelids lowered in smug feline fashion, he cast sidelong glances at Raeden.

"Er, thank you, Peter," she said while struggling to keep a straight face. "I'll have you know, when a boy likes a girl, he gives her flowers—not dead things. But ... I suppose it's the thought that counts."

Raeden's eyes narrowed. "His thoughts better not be counting in the ways of courtship. Do not encourage him, Freylin."

"Um ... it was a joke." Her face warmed.

Raeden shook the dead bird and then glared at it. His visage twisted with disgust. "*Sturlz und dradst!* It crawls with the vermin." He threw it away into the bushes and then flapped his right hand to dislodge any unwanted guests.

"Hey!" Peter cried, glaring at the kaenhir and laying back his ears again. He seemed on the verge of tearing off into the bush after his "gift." Annabelle called out for him to wait.

"Well, now, Annie-O," he said, sitting down on his haunches and curling his tail over his front talons. He jerked his beak over his left shoulder. "What can I do ye for?"

Annabelle laughed. "Oh, my gosh! You're so funny. Um. I have a few questions about syrax anatomy and natural history. For one thing, are they all eagle-lion hybrids, or are there other blendings? And do they lay eggs like birds or give birth like mammals?"

Peter looked as pleased as a cat with a bowl full of cream. "I'm allus happy to discuss my natural history and suchlike with a purty lady." He waggled his eyebrows, and Raeden snarled something in his native tongue.

Before Peter answered her questions, the Commander stalked around the bend, his gray eyes flinty with disapproval. "I thought I heard the buzzard. This explains your tardiness. Peter— with me. Report on Sir Beauregard's response." He jerked his head and strode along ahead of them.

The syrax padded along the trail in his wake with tail lowered and ears drooping. "Talk at ya later, Annie-O."

Annabelle strained to listen, but she caught only fragments of their conversation. At one point, Commander Storm balled his hands into fists and raised his voice: "Time is a luxury we cannot afford." Peter flinched and Annabelle grimaced in sympathy. She exchanged a look with Toad, who frowned and said nothing. After that, the syrax flew off.

As they traveled under the eaves of the dim wood, the day grew warm, humid, and oppressive. Annabelle's tunic clung to her body and sweat slid down her back as she rode Tinker along the trail in the Commander's wake. She stared up into the green and gold dappled canopy. Despite her terror of heights, she envied Peter's freedom to fly above in the open air.

Concentrating on the book proved difficult, but she gleaned what information she could about wyldlings and Aethyr. Enough to confirm her suspicions that Enoch was a wyldling. She brought out her notebook to record her questions and insights until the constant sliding of her glasses and the occasional cloud of gnats became too distracting. With a groan, she tucked her study materials into the pannier and dragged out her depleted waterskin. She grimaced at the lukewarm, flat taste of the liquid.

Some fresh, cold water would be great right about now. What I wouldn't give for a lovely, spring-fed pond with frogs and ducks frolicking around it. She pictured it in her mind. A tension, like a rubberband stretching, built in her gut. Now what? She swallowed a groan, rubbing her abdomen. Was she coming down with something?

Although the feeling increased as they descended a hill, pulling her to the left, she didn't dare complain aloud.

I wish the Commander would let us take a break. I need to go ... somewhere.

The discomfort reached a crescendo. Her breath coming in gasps, Annabelle pressed her right thigh against Tinker's side and opened her left rein. He veered off the trail, plunging between the dark boles of tall trees and bounding over a low bush. Raeden shouted, but she ignored him.

Eyes wide, Toad emerged from the saddlebag. "Kiddo, are you out of your gourd? Get back on the trail!"

They emerged into daylight and fresh air. She leaned back, drew on the reins, and Tinker halted. The landscape had changed, as if a giant lumberjack had waded in with his ax and swiped down the ancient wood of behemoths. The sunslight was harsh and bright after the dimness of the old-growth forest. She squinted ahead at clumps of vividly colored wildflowers and drooping willow fronds across a sparkling expanse of water. Chorus frogs called and a fresh, fishy tang filled the air.

"Kiddo?"

Annabelle blinked, staring. "It's my pond."

An overwhelming compulsion to go to the water swept over her. Leaning forward, she pressed her knees into her mount's barrel. Tinker grunted and trotted toward the pond. Commander Storm barked an order. Abruptly, Lorun blocked their path and the younger stag drew to a halt, snorting and shaking his head.

Raeden dismounted. "Freylin!" His eyes flashed as he grabbed Tinker's bridle. "You must not stray from your servant." Annabelle bent double, grimacing as a cramp rippled through her insides. His visage softened. "Freylin, what is the matter? Do you wish your servant to help?"

Unable to speak, she nodded, then leaned toward him. She tried to swing her leg over the saddle horn. Raeden hesitated, then grabbed her around the waist and lifted her down. He released her almost immediately, but she clung to his arm and he steadied her, his posture stiff.

"Thanks," she grated out from between clenched jaws. She let go of him as the cramp subsided. She sighed in relief, but the pulling rubberband sensation still tingled at her core. Why wouldn't it let up? *Are these cramps, or what? Perhaps my body's adjusting to that "moon-blood" preventative I drank.*

"Criminy, kiddo. Are you okay? What was that all about?"

Commander Storm approached. "Explain yourself."

She shrank against Raeden, who flinched away, then touched her arm. "Freylin?"

"I need..." Swallowing, she gestured at the pond. "Water."

The Commander's gaze grew sharp and appraising while his expression remained unreadable. "Hmph. Might as well make use of the resources at hand." He tossed several empty waterskins at her feet. "Find the spring and fill these. And do not be dilatory about it; we'll not tarry here for long. Your Excellency, watch her whilst I reconnoiter."

Tinker and Lorun moved toward the pond. Annabelle and Raeden took the flaccid waterskins and followed the stags to the narrow, stony beach.

"Wow. It looks like the place I envisioned."

Raeden furrowed his brow, but said nothing.

"Well, I'm out," Toad said. "There's bound to be minnows in this pond." As Tinker bent to drink, the oversized amphibian leaped into the pond with a splash. He torpedoed away underwater, and fish shadows scattered like arrows.

Annabelle led the way along the shoreline, seeking a likely place to fill the waterskins. *We need clean water, fresh from the spring.* Possible pathogens and parasites lurking in the water, unseen, flashed through her mind. There was also the prospect of duck droppings—not to mention fish poop. Her throat tightened at the faint odor of algae and damp; it reminded her of playing near the pond on her grandparents' property in Rothschild.

The rubberband tugging at her middle faded as she headed for the eastern edge of the pond and a patch of crimson lilies, amid which reared up a mossy rock cleft down the middle.

Bees droned and buzzed in the hyacinth-like blooms as she drew near the rock. Were the bees on Tehara neon-green or purple? To her chagrin, only black and yellow bees hovered around the flowers. She turned toward the shore, skirting a clump of golden flowers and busy pollinators. The ground felt firm beneath squelching moss as she approached the cleft stone.

Placing her feet with care, she waded through the crimson lilies and their spade-shaped dark green foliage. A sharp, fresh scent with a hint of pepper wafted from the blooms. Metallic green and blue damselflies flew up from their hidden places, and she gasped. *Fairies!* But they were just insects and disappointingly similar to their counterparts on Earth.

Stop being such a dweeb, she told herself as she inched her way around the stone and toward the water. It had to be there. *Ah, there it is!* Water trickled into the pond from the cleft rock. As suddenly and mysteriously as it had come, the tension in her middle departed.

"Very good. You have found the spring without your servant's help."

Annabelle whirled, her heart hammering against her breastbone. She'd forgotten Raeden was with her; he was so darn stealthy. The kaenhir stood several yards away beside the clump of blue hyacinths farthest from the water. With ears pricked, his eyes gleamed as he scanned the water. His hand hovered by a large knife with a carved ivory hilt hanging from his belt.

"Raeden," she exclaimed with a huff. "You scared the living daylights out of me."

"*Echt?*" Without removing his gaze from the pond, he tipped his head. "Freylin, your servant is confused by your words. How can the light of day be alive to feel fear? And how does it come out of you?"

Annabelle laughed. "It's just an expression. I'm not sure how to explain it. Basically, you startled me." She came around the stone and crouched beside the spring.

"The trading language is of the devil," Raeden muttered. He stood silent vigil as she filled the waterskins, scanning the forest behind and around them but more often glaring at the pond as if it had offended him. The water bubbled forth at a steady pace and the skin filled quickly.

When next she glanced up, the kaenhir was still eyeing the pond. "What's wrong?" she asked, suddenly concerned for Toad. "Are there sharks in the water?"

Raeden's eyebrows rose. "Sharks? Absolutely not. Perhaps something worse than sharks dwells within the water."

She cast a surreptitious glance at the pond. What threat could lurk beneath the crystal-clear water? She put the cap on the waterskin and looked down. Two pale orbs peered back at her from the depths, rocketing to the surface. She gave a faint cry of surprise and almost slipped into the pond herself.

Raeden hauled her back from the edge. "Freylin, great peril may lurk in the water—"

Toad burst out of the pond. "Boo! Did I scare you, kiddo?" He crawled onto the rock and smirked at Raeden. "'Great peril?' Sheesh! Your Excellentness, are you wound up tight. There's nothing but fish and frogs. I'm the scariest thing in this pool." He dove back into the pond, croaking laughter.

Raeden glared after him and muttered in his native tongue. He hunkered beside her, eyes bright as he handed her another empty waterskin. "Do not worry, Freylin. Your servant will protect you from all the world's evils."

She couldn't help but smile as her heart warmed. "Thanks, Raeden. That's sweet of you." *No one's ever offered to do that for me. But I should be able to take care of myself. I'm sixteen years old, for goodness' sake.* With a sigh, Annabelle watched the water dribble into the new waterskin.

"Freylin?" Raeden's voice was gentle. "Are you well?"

At least her stomachache—or cramps; whatever it was—had gone away. She shoved the plug into the nozzle. "Sometimes I wonder if I should be here at all."

Raeden's ears went back. His whiskers flickered in a manner she'd learned emoted discomfort. "Freylin," he responded gently, yet vehemently, "You are here. If the Almighty Threefold One did not mean for you to be here, then you would not be here."

Annabelle's heart leapt. Eyes wide, she searched the earnest, canid features she'd come to rely on. "Are you saying you believe it's God's will that I'm here on this ... this quest?"

This is a quest. Just like in the novels I've read back home— and like the story about King Gideon's journey in Enoch's book.

Raeden nodded. "Your servant is certain of it. 'All things work together for the good of those who love the Almighty; for those who are called according to his purpose.'"

She stuck the plug into the waterskin and jumped to her feet. "That's what I thought, at first. But now I wonder. What do you think my purpose is? I don't know how to fight, or hunt, or forage, like you guys. Even Toad has special knowledge about fighting and stuff. I'm pretty sure that's why Commander Storm's planning to leave me behind at Treehome." She hugged the waterskin, a sudden longing to be held sweeping over her. Her booted feet scuffed at the moss. "I know it's wrong, but I feel so ... useless. Helpless. How do I stop feeling that way, Raeden?"

"This one does not know, Freylin," he replied, ears drooping as he rose to his full height. "He would take such feelings away from you if he could and rip them to shreds." He regarded her while tapping his chin. Then his ears lifted.

"Freylin," he drawled, as if testing out the words he spoke, as a man does when he walks upon thin ice. "Your servant knows how to kill the useless-feeling inside of you. One must first make your useful-feeling grow, and then the useless-feeling will wither."

Beckoning her with a head tilt, he went over to the deer and put away the full waterskins. Annabelle followed with a curious frown, her waterskin sloshing in her arms. She hung it from the saddle horn.

Raeden stood with hands clasped behind his back. "First, know that finding the spring on your own was a useful thing."

Annabelle pushed up her glasses and rubbed her nose. How had she found the spring, anyway? She'd never had that knowledge back home. There was no need for such a skill on Earth where water was accessible by turning on a faucet.

I wonder if there's something in the book that explains it … like, maybe water has magic properties on this planet.

She shrugged. "Yeah, I did. But I'm sure you could've done just as well, Raeden."

"This is truth. Locating water is a skill all travelers should have." He eyed her sidelong through his monocle. "But your servant believes you wish to have a special skill that none other has, *nich vihren?* He wonders about a thing. In your homeland, what are tasks you did well?"

Annabelle hunched her shoulders and toyed with Murder Stick's pommel. There were so many practical things she couldn't do; it was difficult switching gears to consider what she was *good* at. "Um, I can play a clarinet. And sing in the choir at church. Oh, and cook, I suppose—now that I've figured out how to light a fire." She chuckled. "Also, I guess I'm good at anything to do with school. Learning things from books. Retaining knowledge. Getting good grades. I'm supposedly *smart.*" She rolled her eyes and sighed. "All stuff that's useless here."

"The ability to learn is not useless, Freylin. To retain knowledge is an advantage, a gift from the Almighty." He leaned closer. "Your servant is glad to teach you new skills, as you wish. He knows you will learn them swiftly. Shall he teach you a new thing on this day?"

She made a face and met his gaze. "It's not more fighting, is it?"

Raeden's whiskers quivered. "*Nich.* It will please you." Eyes alight, he rummaged through Tinker's panniers. With a triumphant exclamation, he extracted a black leather valise about half the size of her backpack. He knelt and indicated she should do the same. Once she did, he presented the black bag to her with reverence, as if he offered his greatest treasure.

"It is heavy," he warned. "Allow your servant to handle it." He placed it on the ground between them. Inside, paper crinkled and bottles clinked.

"What is it?" Annabelle glanced at him, then unlatched and opened the case. Her eyebrows lifted as she surveyed its contents. *Is this an old-fashioned medical kit?*

"The Lord Commander has given you a sword," he responded wryly. "He and Sir Thomas will train you in its use, but your servant knows from Miss Fourtier that your heart lies along a different path."

Annabelle reached for a stoppered bottle made of amber glass, then hesitated. "You'll teach me healing?" She recalled kneeling in the glade beside a dying man, water soaking into her jeans. The flash of blue, the surge of warm energy, and Simon Halloway miraculously healed.

She frowned. *Did that healing power come from me? I'm still not sure what happened. Could I do it again? I hope I don't have to wait for a life-or-death situation to find out.*

"*Shach,*" Raeden replied, startling her. "Your servant will share his little knowledge of battle medicine with you." His green eyes darkened and his voice hardened, sending a chill down her spine. "And he fears you must learn battle medicine to prepare for what comes."

Silent Knight

Life or Death

William missed the days when his dreams weren't out to kill him.

His footfalls rang against stone as he fled down the corridor. He'd no idea where he was in the dreamscape, only that he needed to get away. This was no ordinary dream; things that happened here had repercussions in the waking world.

Breath rasped in his throat and his heart pounded like a prisoner seeking escape from his cell. Leg muscles burned with fatigue, and yet, he must keep running. This was a matter of life or death. If he stopped to rest, then he'd lose all the ground he'd gained. And possibly, his life. He wasn't sure if a person could actually die in the dreamscape, but he wasn't willing to test it out.

He was coming—the knight with the golden aura. The knight Tenebris had flayed, slicing into his torso with his bone blade, bleeding him to the point of death. The knight William had then, somehow, transformed into a toad ... and who now sought vengeance.

Valkor's Scythe, I'd rather be pursued by a pack of hungry lykharim!

Moonlight shone through windows, beams of silvery white flashing to interrupt the dark gray walls as he passed them. Where were the exits? Did this blazing fortress not have any?

William uttered another oath as he came to a junction. He chose the left-hand path. The new corridor appeared identical to the first: narrow windows set into walls made of soot-colored stone on either side, a ceiling hidden in the blackness above him, and a hard stone floor beneath his feet.

But that's highly improbable, after all the twists and turns I've made. Why would there be windows on both *sides—surely, there must be interior walls? Why are dreams so irrational?*

Robes flapping in his wake, William tore down the corridor as if Valkor—the Deathbringer, himself—was after him. "Don't be a fool," he muttered in between gasps. "He doesn't exist. It's all mythology. That rubbish is for gullible idiots and vapid children."

But the golden knight who hunted him was all too real. The cursed man had been waiting for him in the dreamscape, with eyes blazing blue fire and an abiding hatred. He spoke not a word, but his naked chest bore the bloody testimony of Tenebris's slashing knife. The mere sight of the man rendered William powerless, leaving him helpless before the fiery blade the knight wielded. William suppressed a whimper. His choices had been to flee or die.

The corridor came to a dead end. He pounded impotent fists against the blank wall until they ached. Tears gathered and stung his eyes.

"Burning, blistering suns above! Is there no way out of this ridiculous maze?" He spun and back-tracked the way he came. Hopefully, he'd gained enough ground, but if not ...

William strained for the power reservoir in his arkhabala. The tattoos remained quiescent, cold, and bereft of energy even though he'd gone to sleep with them fully charged. Why wouldn't it work? Even summoning a werelight proved impossible. Not that William needed a light. He was no longer a child who feared the darkness.

I am one with the darkness.

Breathing deeply to calm himself, William slowed as he neared the junction. He must go cautiously; the golden-limned hunter could lurk just around the corner. If only he could extend his senses ... but perhaps he could. He concentrated, reaching for the wellspring of Aethyr he'd discovered while setting up the surveillance spell using the stone circles. Merciful Valeshka ... the power was there!

I don't care what Tenebris says about the Aethyr. This is a matter of life and death. I'm using whatever power I can if it helps me survive.

William sent his awareness ahead, kythim spooling away from him like threads made of amethyst ... why in perdition were they purple, instead of gray streaked with orange as they'd been in the past? Ridiculous dreamscape. He'd worry about that later. Muttering a cantrip, he extended his kythim to fan out past the intersection. Impressions flooded his senses: the chill of the air, the dusty flavor of the stones, and a tomb-like silence. Nothing. His pursuer wasn't there.

An obliging wall propped him up for several heartbeats while he caught his breath and reeled in his kythim. Then he tore across the junction, eyes forward, arms pumping. A crackling tension filled the air. His hair stood on end and his skin pebbled with goosebumps. *Keep going.*

The hallway curved. As he rounded the bend, a moon-lit forest glade came into view, distant, yet attainable. Freedom drew closer with every step. It filled his vision. Just three paces away, now. He just had to reach it before that vengeful knight—

William crashed into an invisible barrier. It drove the wind from him in a wheezing gasp, and he staggered backward. No! Rage and fear mingled like a spicy brew in his gut. Jaw clenched, he tucked his chin and slammed a shoulder against the unseen wall. Pain jarred his body. Violet ripples spread from the point of impact, but the barrier stayed firm.

"Void freeze it!" Rolling his abused shoulder, he whirled to face his tenacious pursuer. He pulled out his dagger and curled his other hand into a fist at his side, willing it not to tremble. He pursed his lips firmly. Powerless or not, he wasn't going down without a fight.

William blinked in astonishment. Instead of his silent, cold-eyed, and bloody nemesis, a cloaked figure stood twenty paces away with hands clasped at his waist. Kythim shimmered in a violet corona. A shadowy cowl hid his face.

"You have led Helzarvenn a merry chase, nehmwight's get," spoke a man's resonant baritone, "and successfully eluded him. Bravo." Raising his gloved hands, he clapped three times, slow and measured. "But," he continued in a lazy tone, "as you are now, it shall avail you nothing, in the end."

Backed against the barrier, William narrowed his eyes. "Who are you? What do you want? And what do you mean, it 'avails me nothing?' I escaped the suns-burnt knight!"

"I am called by many names," the cloaked man said, sounding amused. His violet kythim shook with silent laughter. "The traveler of dreams. The questor of nightmares. The wandering bard who never leaves his prison. And as for your other question, nehmwight's get ..." Reaching over his left shoulder, he grasped the long handle of something strapped to his back. "I shall show you the perils of roaming the dreamscape without the proper tutelage."

William tensed and his breath caught. What was that, some kind of weapon? *Probably a sword. Well, he won't take me down so easily.* He tightened his grip on the knife's hilt as his palm grew clammy. The shark-hide binding prickled against his skin. Why did his dreams always place him in mortal peril?

From over his shoulder, the man pulled not a sword, but a stringed musical instrument made of dark wood inlaid with mother-of-pearl and amethysts.

"What's that, a lute?" William scoffed. "Here I thought you had a proper weapon."

"My delightful companion? She is a lytarra, an instrument from another Age. Her name," he said, setting his fingers to the strings, "is Lyrica Harmonious. And in the hands of a master bard she is—alas for young fools untrained in the ways of the dreamscape—a proper and most potent weapon."

Suns burn and blister me to ash. I need to learn to keep my mouth shut.

William shrank away, pressing against the barrier as if it might relent and allow him to pass through. He'd read about the type of magic a master bard wielded. Hastily, he sheathed his knife and plugged his ears as the man began to play. A pointless gesture; the music wormed its way through minuscule spaces and into his mind. Images of Zakaar tearing out the soot panther's fangs assaulted him. The memory had haunted him for days. And now, the music promised he would suffer the same fate as the hapless beast.

This traveler of dreams meant to take away his teeth.

Of their own accord, William's hands lowered and his feet shuffled across the rough stone floor. He shambled like a drunken kadorei but remained upright by the will of his captor. His lips quivered with the effort of keeping them together. That much was left within his control.

So the bard could have the pleasure of prying his jaws apart?

The music brought him to a halt a pace from the cloaked man. The instrument turned to mist and disappeared. William struggled to move; whatever enchantment the musician had cast still bound him. He swallowed the urge to curse aloud. His nostrils flared with every inhalation and exhalation. Strong fingers grasped his chin and tipped his head back.

"I'm curious," the man whispered, his face still hidden. "I wonder if defanging you here will limit you in the waking world. Shall we find out, nehmwight's get?" Pressure increased on his jaw. A pair of pliers approached his mouth.

No. Please, no. A useless plea. He'd long since abandoned hope that anyone was listening. Terror jolted through William's frozen body and his eyes widened. "Nnnnnn."

Laughing, the cloaked man released him and stepped back. "Your little fangs are pitiful things, nehmwight's get—hardly worth the effort. But I will take them from you. When I see fit." His voice lowered to a threatening rasp. "If Helzarvenn does not incinerate you, then I shall teach you the ways of the dreamscape. And the meaning of humility."

He snapped his fingers, and William sagged, tumbling boneless to the pitiless stone floor.

Head throbbing, William roused from fitful sleep. The details of his nightmare fell away like cobwebs, leaving behind a vague impression of pursuit and a narrow escape. With a soft groan, he rolled from his pallet and glanced around a room shuttered against the suns' rays. A lamp lit with conjured werelight hung from the ceiling cast its dim, blue-green glow throughout the shelter.

The captive's palanquin rested in one corner, its occupant silent. Zakaar was absent; probably out hunting. His master and their escorts still slept, save for the lone warrior guarding their slumber by the door. William's bed was nearest the exit. Of them all, Tenebris had insinuated, William was the most expendable.

He rubbed his temples. With his headache, it took him a moment to recall where they were. Tenebris possessed five day-shelters strategically placed across the Contested Lands between the Northern and Western Marches. This one lay four nights' travel from the ruins of Grivvensfel.

The man by the door glanced up from honing his dagger. He raised an eyebrow. "Still having trouble sleeping, Arkhasuhl?"

William gaped at him for a heartbeat. None of the men had addressed him before, and certainly not by his proper title as the Arkhadahn's apprentice. He ran a hand down his face. "Suns curse it, yes." He bit his tongue to keep from adding: *I should think that's rather obvious.* One of the Golorum was willing to speak to him; this could prove useful. Best not reveal too much of his weakness, though. Warriors appreciated strength. "But it's nothing debilitating." He grinned as he pulled out his flask. "Nothing whiskey can't put right."

The warrior's mouth twitched into an almost-smile. "Lachesis will be down soon. Mind you don't let your master catch you with that." He returned to sharpening his knife.

William took a pull from his flask and tucked it away under his burkheld. His fingers brushed against the belt-pouch he'd appropriated from the young knight. An urge to go outside itched beneath his skin—to breathe fresh air and explore its contents in privacy—but he feared revealing his freakish secret, now that one of the elite warriors was talking to him. Once Lachesis set, it would be safe to venture outdoors.

With a sigh, he flopped down on his pallet. Folding his hands over his stomach, he closed his eyes and let his consciousness drift. All nehmwights had internal clocks set to the suns' schedule, but he'd learned that his own was especially sensitive. Between one heartbeat and the next, he knew that the second sun would slip beneath the horizon in ten minutes. He lingered in a half-doze until a familiar tickle along his arkhabala intruded upon his awareness. The sound of rustling cloth and creaking leather brought him back to the present.

The guard had risen from his seat by the door, dagger gripped in one hand while the other hovered near the peep-hole cover in the wall. He slid the cover to one side to look out. The other three warriors stirred, hands slipping to grasp weapons. Their eyes gleamed in the lamp's glow.

William rolled to his feet. "It's only Zakaar Ravenos, Golor," he mumbled. *And the second sun is setting; he's right on time. I'll use this as an excuse to slip away before Tenebris awakens.* He rubbed his temples; his headache had worsened. "And Lachesis is down."

The warrior grunted and jerked his head in a confirming nod. He sheathed his dagger and stepped from the door as William approached. "I'll go see what Zakaar's caught for our breakfast." Formally, he dipped his head in a bow. "The daywatch is over, Golor. May your deeds bring you honor."

"Valeshka bless the falling of night, Arkhasuhl." Lips twitching, the warrior added, "My blooding-name is Khalad, youngling. I permit you to use it."

One hand on the door latch, William blinked at his companion, who, grinning outright, pressed the flat of the knife blade under William's chin and shut his mouth with a click. "My brothers and I shall delay your master," he murmured, tracing the sign of the war-god in the air between them. "Go. Enjoy the gloaming."

William nodded, schooling his expression to stillness. *Khalad may prove a valuable ally, but I should proceed with caution.* Doubtless, the warrior wanted something from him.

Outside, William set Zakaar to work preparing the meal and slipped into a nearby copse of trees before the harkhurz could argue. Once the shelter was hidden from view, he unfastened their captive's belt from his sakkhelt. The belt-pouch slid off easily. He settled against the trunk of a gnarled old tree with a smirk.

Let's see what Milord High-and-Mighty considered important enough to keep on his person.

A white linen handkerchief, neatly folded, took up the most space. William was about to crumple and discard it when something firmer than cloth gave between his fingers. He froze, then peeled aside layers of linen.

"What, in all the nether perditions ..." He blinked, staring at a rectangular card the size of his hand. It was some kind of portrait—albeit more realistic than any painting he'd ever seen before—featuring a blue-eyed, bespectacled kadorei maiden garbed in a dark green gown. She held a strange, black pipe with metal protrusions. A musical instrument? He shivered, then scowled. Why did musical instruments make him uneasy?

William furrowed his brow and focused on the portrait. "Who is she?" He ran his fingers over the smiling figure. He couldn't place the medium. The surface was glossy and smooth. Had Aethyric power created it—was that something wyldlings could do? The Dreadlord's scroll said nothing of such abilities. But who was the maiden in the portrait, and why did the young knight carry it around with him?

She looks a bit like Northward, come to think of it.

Suddenly, he recalled Northward's tantrum the prior evening—all the times he'd mentioned a name—and puzzle pieces clicked together. A grin spread across William's face. He stroked the portrait, running his fingers over the image's pale, smiling face and golden hair. "Hello, there," he purred. "It's a pleasure to meet you ... Annabelle."

A Much-Needed Bath

Before he rejoined the others, William tucked the portrait inside his sakkhelt. It rested close to his skin and weighed heavily on his mind. Tenebris hurried them along after the meal to resume their trek westward across the Herbmar Plains using the old Grivvensfel caravan route. Midway through Serpent Watch, Northward began calling for Annabelle. Oddly, Zakaar, who prowled alongside their little column, didn't react.

Am I hearing things? William called for a halt and ripped aside the curtain. "Well, Milord High-and-Mighty. I see the soporific wore off."

Northward writhed in his bonds, silver kythim rising like vapors around him. *"I can't see anything!"* He stared wide-eyed out of his prison. "Nehmwight," he grated, voice rough with disuse. "Where are you taking me?"

William frowned. Northward's voice timbre changed between the first and last bit.

"Like I'd tell you anything that might aid in your escape, ridiculous night-blind kadorei." William spoke the words of a cantrip, conjuring a blue-green werelight, and then sent it to hover over his right shoulder.

Squinting, the knight demanded, "At least tell me *why* you abducted me, you son of a goat."

William threw back his head and laughed. The little ball of blue-green light floating over his shoulder shook along with him. He leaned over, his face inches away from the captive. "Really? 'Son of a goat.' That's the best insult you can come up with?" He straightened, chuckling. "Addle-pated twit. Goats are intelligent. If you had half the brains of a goat, then you'd realize I'm not inclined to give away information."

Not that I'm privy to all the Dreadlord's plans. But Northward doesn't need to know that, does he? He doesn't need to know anything. He tapped his fingers against his chest, where the portrait nestled inside his sakkhelt. With an effort, he forced his hand down to his side.

"Like I'd trust the words of a cowardly poisoner and a child-murderer, anyway," Northward shot back. Black threads and bright red sparks twisted through his silver kythim.

"Suns burn you. I didn't kill any—" William stiffened, his mouth opening and closing without emitting a sound. The little ball of light shivered. *Outer darkness! Tenebris silenced us both this time.*

Northward's eyes bulged. He opened and closed his mouth like a fish, but no sound emerged. *"What's going on?"*

"Stop bickering!" Tenebris snapped in dialect. William flinched. How did his master sneak up behind him so often? "I tasked you to deal with him on our journey, William, not engage in verbal combat." He sniffed, wrinkling his nose. "Faugh! It is well we stopped here; the Golorum require rest and the prisoner needs a bath. And you should exercise him. There's a pond nearby. See to it." With a wave of his hand, he dismissed the spell as he strode away, and William's throat loosened.

Why'd you do that, Tenebris? William scowled at his back. He coughed. Heat rushed through him as he muttered, "Freezing void, I hate that spell."

Northward relaxed. "Praise Yshua." He glared at William. *"He should be the one imprisoned. There are three mothers grieving for their daughters while Ravenos and this son of a goat walk free."*

A strange twisting sensation burrowed through William's gut. Mothers. Mothers grieving. Surely, his mother hadn't wept for him when she placed him on the sacrificial altar. The only mother he'd known was Valeshka, the Mother of Outer Darkness from nehmwight legends. She wasn't even real. As his hand drifted toward his whiskey flask, he eyed the captive sidelong, then froze. His breath quickened.

Northward didn't speak aloud just then. And there were other times ... Was William reading his mind? If so, how was he doing it and why couldn't he read the minds of others? What he wouldn't give to read his master's mind.

"Shall we convey him to the pond, Arkhasuhl?" Khalad called from the far side of the palanquin. Like Tenebris, he spoke in their native tongue.

William averted his gaze. "Yes, Golor." He responded in the same language. "But only bring him so far as that oak tree. He can walk the rest of the way." He kept his eyes on Northward, observing his kythim—swarming with red and black sparks—and listening closely. *Can I catch him at it again?*

Jaw tensed, Northward simply glared at him as the Golorum lifted the palanquin and angled toward the oak tree. William walked alongside, the werelight bobbing in his wake like an oversized firefly. He didn't need it—there was plenty of starlight— but he wanted it ready for the clumsy, night-blind kadorei.

The algal, fishy scent of the pond filled his nostrils, and his thoughts drifted toward the strange portrait of the maiden. A smirk tugged at his lips as his fingers rested against where he kept it in his sakkhelt. This 'Annabelle' intrigued him. That she was important to Northward was obvious, but what was her significance? Could he use the Seeker's Web to locate her and somehow use her as leverage?

"*If this son of a goat even* thought *about touching Annabelle* ..."

William nearly jumped out of his skin. Burning suns and freezing void! If he could read Northward's mind, then did that mean Northward could read *his* mind? "Valkor's Scythe," he snapped, making fists. "You're noisier than a lumbering cave bear."

"What noise have I made, nehmwight?" Anger seethed in the youth's voice, but at least he spoke aloud this time. "I haven't said anything, and I'm tied up so tightly, I can't blustering move." They reached the oak tree, and the Golorum lowered the palanquin. Northward's eyes widened, and fear sparked along his kythim. "What's going on?"

"You need a bath, kadorei." He sneered as he said the word. "I'm going to loosen the snare around your arms and legs. Your old pal, Zakaar, is at my beck and call, so don't try anything stupid." He reached inside his robe, pulled out the triangular wyldling snare key. Casting his mind into the violet light at his core, he envisioned the snare falling away as he touched one point to the cords binding Northward's limbs.

The cords loosened and slithered like dark, metallic snakes. The captive shuddered again, watching the snare as it unraveled from around his legs and wriggled, of its own volition, to coil around the key.

"That's the key to my freedom. I must get it away from him. Somehow."

William snorted. *As if I'd ever let you.* He tucked the snare and its key inside his sakkhelt—beside the portrait—then stepped back, out of kicking or grappling range. "Don't even think about it, Northward." He pursed his lips, watching the prisoner. *I am reading his blazing mind. Careful ... can't let on.*

"That's a foolish statement," Northward muttered, flexing his arms and grimacing. "If you have to mention it, then you know

I've already thought about it." As the last of the cord slithered away, he pried at the collar around his neck.

William smirked. Northward couldn't get a finger between it and his skin, but that didn't stop him from trying—the stubborn fool. With a groan, the prisoner pushed himself into a sitting position, breathing deeply. The faintest of smiles flickered across his face.

Blessed relief…

Scowling, William yelled, "Oi! Zakaar, get your suns-charred tail over here." When the harkhurz sauntered over, he added, "Now, grab His Malodorous Highness and get him cleaned up while there's water available to dunk him in. He's been simmering in his own sweat for days and stinks worse than a dead skunk in a dung heap."

"With pleasure, Dulciber," the kaenhir responded. "So long as you do not expect me to go into the water with him."

Chafing his wrists, Northward glanced at him with a furrowed brow. "*'Dulciber?' That's the family name of the Count of Mirrors. What gives?*"

William suppressed the urge to backhand the other youth. "All I expect, harkhurz, is for you to keep him from escaping."

Hurriedly, the captive found his balance and—before Zakaar could seize him—slid from the palanquin. His bare feet struck the ground with a thud, and he swayed. "Give me a second," he said, holding on to the bed, "I can walk. And I'll bathe myself."

Zakaar snarled, reaching for him, but hesitated when William held up a hand. "Let him."

"Maybe I can run?"

Meeting the prisoner's defiant gaze, William grinned. "Just be ready to grab Northward if he tries to flee."

Zakaar bared his teeth. "Not to worry. I will relish chasing the warlock, should he run."

Northward straightened up and squared his shoulders. "I won't run. Not from you. Not from anyone." His glare settled on William. "*I'm not afraid of you—you son of a goat.*"

He needs to come up with a better insult. William scoffed. "Enough with the warrior bravado, Northward." He smirked. "I'm not the one you need to worry about." He beckoned, and Zakaar grabbed the captive's arms to dragged him closer. William leaned in and whispered, "Worry about the harkhurz."

Northward wrinkled his nose. *"Ugh, what sort of rot-gut spirits has he been drinking? And can I smash my forehead into his face hard enough to break it?"*

Not a chance! William stepped back with a frown and raised an admonitory finger. "Keep in mind, I'm the only thing standing between you and the toothy maw of oblivion, here." He patted Zakaar's shoulder, who tightened his grip on Northward. The prisoner sucked in air through his teeth with a hiss.

"Stop playing, Zakaar." William jerked his head to the left, toward the pond. "Now, come on. We haven't got all night."

Northward's lips thinned. *"Remain patient. Stay vigilant."*

William made a flicking gesture, which sent the glowing ball bobbing ahead of them to light their path. The ground was level, clear of stones or other obstacles. Cool air tickled William's face and grass swished around his legs. Crickets chirping and the voices of the Golorum drifted to his ears. Ahead, water lapped against a shoreline and the heady scent of honeysuckle tantalized him. The straggled silhouettes of trees blocked out a portion of the stars, part of the constellation called Villem's Scepter. The kadorei gave it a different name: the Sword of Gideon.

How do I know that? Rising from the bowels of his memory, the scent of honeysuckle wreathed him as a woman's voice sang the names of the stars: *"Konstant, Shafra, Albokar, the Rubies, Miqbid, Raman ... bright shines the sword of King Gideon ..."*

Who sang that to him? He knew no kadorei women. The Dreadlord's wife might have sung to him as a small child, but that hadn't been her voice. Was he going mad?

Northward's pace slowed as he gawked at the starry sky. *"The stars. Sir Rick taught me to navigate. If I can find Konstant, then I could—"*

Enough. William beckoned to Zakaar. In a pendulum motion, the harkhurz seized and lifted the captive, swung him back, and then sharply forward, launching him into the air. Northward plunged into the water with a splash and then sank like a stone.

"Valkor take you!" William snarled. "That's not what I meant. He'll get away, you benighted cockroach kisser!" He flung off his burkheld, ripped off his boots, and then dashed for the pond, wading in until cool water lapped at his knees. Pebbles and grit jabbed into his feet.

Outer darkness ... Tenebris will kill me! And then the Dreadlord will resurrect me, so he can have the pleasure of killing me, too!

Hands trembling, he dug the wyldling snare from his sakkhelt and sent two cords toward the turbulent, bubbling water at the center. He felt the snare catch hold of something. William concentrated, then reached for the gem-like, violet pool inside himself. Pain rippled through his arkhabala, and he grimaced. Cursed Aethyr. He needed to cast his thoughts into a different pattern. A descending spiral rather than a jagged line.

Finally, the power flowed through him, and he addressed the snare: *Return the prisoner to me.*

He held the key. It obeyed him. While the snare reeled in Northward like a prize catch, William glared over his shoulder. "I told you to clean him up, you jelly-brained oaf, not toss him into the deepest part of the pond!"

"I cannot enter the waters, Dulciber," the harkhurz replied, his amber eyes round. Anxiety flickered in his aura. He spread his hands. "The ways of the folken forbid it. And yet, the warlock must go in. How else was I to do as you command?"

What is he so afraid of? It's only water. Spitting out further invective against his companion in the names of various deities, William grabbed Northward's restraints and pulled him into the shallows.

Northward sagged in the wyldling snare harness. He vomited a trickle of bile and pond water. *"The snare's weakening me."* He slumped, his head dipping closer to the water. *"But why now? Why not before? Lord Yshua, please make it stop..."* White light flickered at the core of his kythim.

"Oi, that's just spectacular." William grabbed the captive's hair and yanked him upright. "Zakaar, where's the suns-burned soap?"

"The snare," Northward said through clenched teeth. He swallowed thickly. "It's making me sick. Unless you want me to keel over and drown, you'd better stop doing whatever you're doing with it."

William glowered. "You're pretending."

Northward met his gaze, unflinching. The silvery kythim swarmed with tiny ochre squiggles, like worms. An odd tone rang in his ears as his vision doubled, and then two Northwards glared at him. Their eyes widened, spinning sickeningly. The prisoner whimpered and closed his eyes. Nausea rolled through William. He felt as if Tenebris had cut his skull open, reached inside, and turned his brain inside out. He resisted the urge to vomit. The two faces merged into one again, snapping into focus.

What, by all that burned under the suns, was *that?*

William groaned. "Burn me to ash. You're *not* pretending."

"I have the soap," Zakaar said, coming up behind him and throwing a bar of coarse yellow soap at the prisoner. The bar struck his chest and plopped into the water. Northward stared at it. With an exasperated sigh, William released his hair and moved up on the shore, grimacing as his head swam and his stomach protested every movement.

"Watch him close, Zakaar," he snapped as he fidgeted with the mass of dark cords. He murmured a cantrip to steady himself, reached for the violet pool, and made winding gestures with his fingers. The snare retreated and coiled into his hand, leaving only the bit fused to the collar. The prisoner sighed.

As quickly as William's nausea lifted, new images and sensations flooded his mind, all glowing silver. *These are Northward's memories!* He bit back a cry. Such intimate knowledge of the prisoner made him gag, but after a moment of head-spinning disorientation, he fought to regain his identity, wrapping up Northward's silver memories in a package and then locking them away in a box crafted from the pool of violet light.

That ought to keep it contained. Now ... how do I use this to my advantage?

He took a deep breath while staring at the snare coiled and quiescent in his hands. A corner of the portrait jabbed into his chest. He stiffened, recalling that several of those stolen memories concerned the maiden. A grin spread across his face.

" What's made him so blustering cheerful?"

William's attention flicked to the captive. He scowled. "Oi, you've got your soap. What're you waiting for, Northward?"

"The Festival of Lights," the other youth muttered as he picked up the chunk of soap, worked up a lather, quickly scrubbed himself, and then rinsed off the suds.

At William's command, Zakaar grabbed Northward by his hair and one arm, then hauled him from the water. Fingers drumming along the hilt of his knife, William eyed Northward's dripping, straggled hair. A person's hair, when combined with their blood, had potential for many uses.

William drew his knife. "Don't move." The prisoner tensed, eyeing the approaching blade. Zakaar's grip tightened. Northward grimaced and bit his lip as blood trickled down his left arm.

"Sheathe those finger-daggers of yours, Zakaar. I'm ridding him of that rat's nest, not blooding him." While stepping aside to avoid being kicked, William slid the knife between Northward's head and Zakaar's hand. The blade parted sodden strands. He went round the prisoner's head quickly, grabbing wet hanks and slicing them off like a gardener pruning a bush. He stuffed one inside his sakkhelt. Waste not, want not.

The captive's expression grew mournful. *"Would Annabelle—would anyone—even recognize me now?"*

William grinned as he tossed aside a handful of damp hair. "You look like you've got mange. Your own mother wouldn't recognize you." Snickering, he wiped the flat of the blade against his leg, then sheathed it. He donned his robe and pulled on his boots. "Hold him, Zakaar. I need to clean up your mess. Again."

"My most abject apologies, Dulciber." Zakaar wrapped his arms around Northward, pinning both his arms and lifting him.

"The knife. I could take it from him. After dispatching Ravenos, I would—"

"Stop glaring bloody murder at me." Lips tight, William tended to the wounds Zakaar had inflicted, tucking away scraps of bloodied fabric with the lock of hair. "I hate this as much as you do, but it has to be done. Can't have you dying from some infection before—" *Idiot! Why tell him anything?* He swallowed the rest of his words. "Never you mind." The prisoner gasped as William tied the bandage, yanking the ends tight.

Once he finished, Zakaar set Northward on his feet and prodded him toward the palanquin. The prisoner stumbled ahead of them.

"Freezing void! You're slower than a lame-legged tortoise. Move faster."

"The ugly son of a goat wouldn't be so confident if he didn't have a vicious kaenhir for a henchman."

William smacked the back of his head.

Northward pivoted, did something with his leg, and William found himself staring up into the heavens, head throbbing and struggling to breathe. A hoarse laugh like a raven's harsh croak escaped Northward's throat. And then the captive went sprawling beside William with the kaenhir's boot planted in the small of his back.

William caught his breath and struggled to his feet. *Oh, you're in for it now, Milord High-and-Mighty.* "Carry him, Zakaar," he spat.

Zakaar chuckled as he hoisted Northward over his shoulder. "You will suffer, warlock. Have gratitude that you are needed, or I'd kill you."

"All right, that's enough freedom." William raised his hands with a wicked grin and reached for the Aethyr. Like serpents, twin lengths of the wyldling snare darted toward Northward and trapped his limbs, wrapping around him until none remained in William's hands. The harkhurz hoisted him up and then deposited him in the palanquin.

"I'd planned on leaving you awake to enjoy the night, but after your little stunt—" William narrowed his eyes as he bared his teeth in a grin— "I think you need an object lesson."

He brandished a glass vial. It glinted in the blue-green light. "This is something I whipped up while we were waiting for you to fall into our trap. I call it Shadow's Breath. It'll make you sleep for the next twelve hours. Unlike poppy-milk, it's sure to give you horrible nightmares." His grin broadened. "And you won't be able to wake from them."

"Even if he's lying, I don't want to be drugged into oblivion again. I must stay awake and lucid ... find out where they're taking me. Reach Annabelle—and escape."

"You'll never escape us, Milord High-and-Mighty," William gloated as the harkhurz pried the captive's jaws open. He poured the bitter brew down Northward's gullet. Zakaar held his mouth and nostrils closed to force him to swallow it all.

Laughing, William pulled the curtains closed on the prisoner's coughs and splutters. "Sweet dreams, Northward." As he walked away, he thought he heard the captive calling Annabelle's name.

He dismissed Zakaar, then glanced around to make sure his master wasn't nearby. In search of his whiskey flask, his fingers brushed the latest additions to his sakkhelt. Yes, he could find a use for those items. *One way or another, I'll gain enough power to get out from under Tenebris's thumb.* Flask in hand, he turned his face into a sudden cool breeze from the north.

Dreamscape

The Dark Tower

A cool breeze tickled Annabelle's cheek, as soft as a whisper. "Hello? Is anyone there?" She frowned. She could've sworn she heard a voice. *Could it be Enoch? It didn't sound quite like him, but ...* Right hand on the pommel of her short sword, she surveyed the silent forest in which she stood. Commander Storm should be satisfied; wherever she was, she had her weapon along and ready to draw.

Craggy-barked cedars loomed around her like somber giants. No birds sang in the trees. No insects made nuisances of themselves with their buzzing. A glowing blue mist surrounded her and shapes in her peripheral vision tended toward blurriness. Something about the experience seemed familiar. Despite the darkness under heavy evergreen boughs, the eldritch haze provided enough light to navigate the damp undergrowth. She continued cautiously in the direction she'd heard the voice, brushing away cobwebs—were there spiders here? —and pushing through wet bracken ferns. Water droplets splattered her face. Pausing to wipe off the moisture, she glanced down and drew in a sharp breath.

"I must be in the dreamscape." She examined the dark blue armor encasing her body from neck to toe. Its surface felt slick under her fingers, lacquered like her grandma's jewelry box. If she needed, she could also summon a helmet merely by concentrating. Enoch had worn similar armor, chased in silver, when they'd first met in their dreams.

Her heart raced with excitement, leaving her momentarily breathless. *Something* drew her onward. Nothing more than a feeling, but ... maybe Enoch was here, and she could finally see him. Scanning the bedewed forest, she whispered, "Please, God, let it be so."

She resumed her trek through the woods. The flora grew sparser and her path cleared, leading her uphill where young aspen and birch replaced the huge cedars, their ranks thinning as she climbed. When she reached the summit, she hugged a papery birch trunk and looked around.

While the haze clinging to her remained blue, ahead of her, the color changed to violet. No trees grew on the flattened top of the hill. Above, bright stars speckled the black sky—brighter stars than she'd ever seen on Earth—despite the fullness of the moon. A tower made of dark stone rose from the middle of the clearing with hydrangea bushes growing around an arched doorway. Could Enoch be inside?

She gripped Murder Stick's hilt. *Only one way to find out.*

Suddenly, she found herself inside the tower, where glowing violet mist drove away the darkness. Had she just teleported there? A stone staircase spiraled upward, and she hesitated at the bottom. Perhaps she could ...

The world blinked. Annabelle adjusted her stance for balance. She'd reached the top of the tower.

"Enoch?" No answer. She bit her lower lip. Bright stars glared down at her—myriad watchers accusing her of trespass. Her fingers tightened on the sword's grip. Why did she feel drawn to this place if he wasn't there?

A quick look and I'll leave. It's so quiet. Like the world's holding its breath. Waiting.

Annabelle took in her surroundings. A crenelated stone wall circled the space, which resembled an odd combination of library and laboratory. There was a telescope mounted between two crenels. Against the wall was a large desk or work table, an assortment of feathers, bones, pebbles, and other items placed around a design etched into its surface. Beside a large wooden cabinet decked with dried herbs and glass bottles containing liquids and powders stood an apparatus of glass tubes, flasks and retorts any chemist would covet. Further along was a bookcase and scroll depository showing evidence of extensive use.

It looks like a mad scientist's laboratory. All it needs are lightning rods and a table with manacles and restraints. She shuddered and moved on.

A tall drafting table with a technical-looking schematic pinned to its tilted surface drew her attention. Mathematical equations were scrawled in a spiky hand around a ... clockwork spider? Squinting and tilting her head, Annabelle moved toward the table for a closer look.

"Oi! Who're you? Get away from that."

A scream rising in her throat, Annabelle drew Murder Stick as she pivoted, falling into a stance Toad had taught her with the blade raised defensively. Her scream died, mangled into a squeak. A tall figure in brown robes backed away with a jerk, hands raised with palms toward her in a warding gesture. Her gaze rose to meet a pair of lambent orange eyes—opened wide as her own—set in a narrow, gray-skinned face. Dark dreadlocks were pulled back to reveal slightly pointed ears. A young man, however alien his appearance, was staring at her with his mouth hanging open, as if thunderstruck.

Annabelle stared back, heart hammering against her breastbone. *Is he some kind of Elf? Or an Orc? His irises are orange. And they're freaking glowing.*

"Merciful Valeshka, Mother of the Outer Darkness," a breathless voice whispered in her head. *"It's ... it's her."*

She blinked, her sword arm lowering. "Huh? Who are you?" A strange feeling built inside, an echo of the time she'd first encountered Enoch in the void place and their kythim had tangled together. *It's almost like I should know this guy. And did he just speak inside my mind, like Enoch used to?*

The gray-skinned youth exhaled. "Burning suns," he said. His voice was a baritone, like the one that spoke in her head. "This is *my* tower you've so blithely invaded. I believe I'm the one who should be asking the questions." He narrowed his gaze. "What are you doing here? And how in the nether perdition did you get past my wards?" Tight-lipped, he stepped closer, flexing his fingers. His eyes flared. Energy crackled around his hands, smoky blackness shot through with orange light that matched his irises.

Is he a mage? Will he zap me with lightning?

With a gasp, Annabelle raised her sword and edged backwards. "Stop. Please, don't come any closer." She winced. *I sound like a frightened little girl.*

Smirking, he loomed over her. Holy cow! He was tall—easily as tall as Raeden. She shrank under the youth's baleful glare. The dark energy crackled around him, and she smelled ozone. "Put that blistering thing away before you hurt some—" His voice cut off as Murder Stick's tip flicked up and touched his neck, and he froze, glowing eyes wide.

"Please," Annabelle said, strained. "I don't *want* to hurt you. I'm sorry; I didn't mean to invade your space, and I didn't see any wards. I came up here ..." She licked lips gone dry. "I was hoping to find my ..." she scrambled for a word to describe her relationship with Enoch. "My brother."

He blinked, as if surprised. "Your brother." Backing away slowly, he muttered a phrase in a consonant-rich language—it sounded like a curse—and lowered his hands. The energy flickering amid his fingers died away, and his irises dimmed. He regarded her warily. "I've dismissed my defensive spell. Your turn. Sheathe that ... thing, or I'll take it away."

Annabelle snorted nervous laughter and adjusted her stance. "I'd like to see you try."

Oh, dear, did that just come out of my mouth? I've no desire to harm anyone. I can't let Murder Stick's name become true.

The youth bared his teeth in a grin. His canines were more prominent than a normal person's—almost like a vampire's. "It wouldn't take much effort for me to disarm you—Milady Blue." His eyes narrowed. "Unless you're *him* in disguise."

"Him who?"

The grin shifted to a scowl. "First, put that thing away, and we'll have a nice, long ... talk." He raised his hands again, and the sleeves hung like brown wings around his elbows to reveal slender, pale lines and ridges along both his forearms. Someone had cut him, and some marks appeared to be recent.

Annabelle gasped, her sword tip descending. "Oh, my goodness. What cut you up like that? Were you attacked?"

His brow furrowed, then he scoffed. "No. I did this with my own knife."

"Oh, my." She blinked, sorrow welling up in her breast. "You cut yourself ... intentionally?"

Orange eyes intense, he shook out his sleeves to cover his arms. "Of course," he said, his tone brusque. "Hazards of my profession." A crooked smile twitched at his lips as he crossed his arms and hid his hands in opposite sleeves. "I'm not suicidal, if that's what you're asking. And I have no intention of harming you. Shall we call a truce? Put that thing away, and we'll start afresh." His smile twisted into a smirk, and he bent at the waist, his eyes never leaving hers. "Welcome to my tower, Milady Blue. You may address me as ... Varazslo."

Annabelle swallowed. What could it hurt, giving him her first name? She wasn't from Tehara. "I'm Annabelle," she replied, lowering the blade to her side. She wouldn't sheathe it—not until she was sure about this guy. "But you can call me 'Milady Blue.' That sounds cool." A nervous chuckle escaped her. "Varazslo. Interesting name. I'd like to say 'pleased to meet you,' but I'm not certain that's the case."

"Varazslo is the title I chose for myself." A grin that reminded her of a shark spread across his face. "For my part, *I* am very pleased to meet you, Annabelle. I didn't intend to frighten you. I'm just surprised that someone got into my tower."

Her grip tightened on her weapon. *I wish he wouldn't look at me like that—like a cat watching a mouse. Or like a mad scientist examining a new specimen.*

Forcing down her unease, she glanced past him at all the equipment. "Just what *is* your profession? It looks like you dabble in astronomy, chemistry, mechanical engineering with a bit of object art thrown in. I've never heard that any of those fields require arm-cutting."

"Er. Yes, I dabble. In those ... fields ... you mentioned." Varazslo cleared his throat and shifted from one foot to the other, averting his gaze, then looking back at her. "Well? You still haven't answered my questions. What sort of spell did you cast to make it through my wards?"

Annabelle frowned. "Spell? What are you talking about?" She snorted. "I don't know magic. I told you—I came up here looking for my brother, Enoch." Varazslo's eyes widened, then narrowed, and the corner of his mouth twitched into a half-smile. Her heart lurched. "Are you sure you haven't seen him around here?" She described Enoch, but Varazslo shook his head, frowning.

It was too much to hope for. Her shoulders drooped.

"That doesn't explain what you're doing. *Here.* In my tower ... Annabelle."

The way he'd said her name sounded almost gloating. She bit her lip. "I heard a voice, so I followed it here, thinking it might be Enoch." With trembling fingers, she tucked a lock of hair behind an ear. "Apparently, I was wrong." She squared her shoulders. *I will not cry.* Swallowing her disappointment, she forced a pleasant smile. "So, if you'll please excuse me, Varazslo, I won't trespass on your territory any longer. I'll be on my way."

She concentrated, imagining herself back in the blue-mist enshrouded cedar forest. Nothing happened. *Oh, dear Lord ...* Blinking rapidly, she forced her face to stillness. *Put up a strong front. You've still got Murder Stick, Ann. He doesn't know your sword skills suck.*

A faint smile quirking his lips, Varazslo observed her with his eyes aglow. "Anyone capable of penetrating my wards can leave whenever they wish." He stepped to one side, revealing an open trapdoor, and swept out one arm in invitation. "Milady Blue."

Eyes never leaving him, Annabelle sidled toward the exit with Murder Stick raised in a half-guard. As she drew abreast, Varazslo grabbed her left arm. She froze, fingers spasming on the sword's grip. She thought wildly: *Should I stab him?*

"Annabelle, wait." He sounded less like a mad scientist-mage and more like a teenage boy. At least his irises stopped glowing, and he seemed ... less sure of himself.

He's actually kind of cute.

Cheeks darkening, Varazslo glanced aside, then faced her once more. "I'll help you find your brother—if you'll tell me something in return."

Annabelle stared into his ember-colored eyes, a tiny stream of hope trickling through her. Would he help her find Enoch? *Can I trust him?* "What do you want to know?"

Still holding her arm, Varazslo leaned in, his lips parting. Annabelle's heart pounded. *What the heck?* Heat rose to her face, and she squeezed the sword's grip. *Is he going to ...? I should move away.*

Abruptly, purple light surrounded them both. Varazslo froze and his eyes widened. "Suns burn me to ash. It's *him.*"

"That's quite enough, nehmwight's get!" a resonant baritone boomed.

"Why does he keep *calling* me that?" Varazslo growled as he glanced around, his grasp tightening.

What's going on? Annabelle squinted into the light. *That sounds like the weird bard in the cloak.* Before she could do anything, strong hands seized her shoulders and wrested her from Varazslo's grip.

Dragon on a Pedestal

A scream froze in Annabelle's throat as she spun away into a void shot through with violet streaks. Up became down, and down became up. Murder Stick was gone from her hand. She curled into a ball and wrapped her arms around her legs, battling nausea. The cloaked bard was behind this—but where had he thrown her? Panic threatened to overwhelm her. No. She must try to control where she landed.

Oh, God, please save me! Send me somewhere safe.

In response, her mind conjured a vision of a blue dragon chained to a pedestal.

Yes ... there!

Annabelle plunged into water. For a moment, confusion reigned. Something was missing. But then warmth and well-being pooled within her core, as if she'd finished a mug of hot cocoa. The sick feeling vanished. Her body relaxed, unfurling like tea leaves. She opened her eyes. The darkness had retreated and a sourceless light she'd come to associate with the dreamworld revealed house-like structures covered with coral and seaweed. The dwellings and thoroughfares appeared large enough for people, but nothing moved within and the entire place had an empty, neglected feeling.

An underwater city? I wonder if it's Atlantis.

"Ahdmerel, come," a familiar, deep voice called.

Annabelle stiffened. *The blue dragon! I made it.*

Perhaps he could help her find Enoch. *Wait ... didn't I just talk to somebody about that?* A vague impression stirred of meeting someone with strange eyes who had offered to help, a flash of violet light then ... nothing. The memory was gone. She shook her head. Sating her curiosity about the city had to wait.

With a powerful kick, she lunged for the surface. Her head broke through, and she sucked in air ... she didn't need. A frown wrinkled her forehead. Her lungs hadn't screamed for air while she hung suspended in the water looking at the coral-encrusted buildings. *Oh, that's right. I can breathe underwater in the dreamworld.* Very odd. But convenient. And yet ... it felt like something was missing.

She treaded water. The pale flicker of an arm caught her eye, and she gasped. *That's what's wrong!* Her heart raced. In place of the dark blue armor, she wore her swimming suit from back home. Had the weird bard somehow taken her armor away? She let out a pent-up breath. At least she wasn't naked.

Shutting her eyes, she imagined the armor encasing her body. Nothing changed. She sighed. *Apparently, I must forgo the armor during this search. Maybe I need to earn it again, in some kind of trial.* A grim chuckle wracked her frame. Hopefully, she wouldn't need the armor when facing the dragon.

She turned in a slow circle. The sea rolled along, endless, beneath a sky as blue as a robin's egg. How could she miss a huge dragon chained to a pedestal?

"Come, little wyldling," a deep, kindly voice called.

Annabelle glanced around. The broad reaches of the gentle sea seemed empty. But the voice she recognized from before had called her. And that strange word. Wyldling. It had been in the book of legends. Enoch had spoken of it in a shared dream, but she couldn't recall the details. Dreams could be amazingly silly.

A flurry of kicks and a downstroke forced her higher above the water. She craned her neck. "Where are you, blue dragon?"

She grimaced. *Well, that sounded ridiculous. I have to learn his name.*

"This way, Ahdmerel."

Eyes wide, she reversed the direction of her spin. There—a blip on the horizon.

"I'm coming, blue dragon!" She concentrated on being *there.* Nothing happened. Annabelle groaned. *I must get there before I wake up. Let's try teleporting again.* She narrowed her eyes at the blip and *willed* herself there.

A pillar of dark blue stone decorated with carvings suddenly loomed over her, a tall, massive edifice rising from the waters. A thrill went through her. *I did it!* But then a twinge of doubt assailed her. Her heart quailed at the height; it was too tall to be the dragon's dais. Had she swum in the wrong direction? It was the only defining feature she'd seen. Where else could she have gone on this vast, wide sea?

She considered her situation. Despite the monolith looking different from the dragon's dais in a previous dream, it didn't feel as if she'd come to the wrong place.

Steady, even strokes brought her around the pillar, to where a broad staircase emerged from the water and ascended in a spiral. "How cool is that?" she murmured, hauling herself out of the water.

The stairs felt like marble under her bare feet, but the surface wasn't slick. Friezes depicting winged, serpentine dragons, people, and everyday objects stood out in bas-relief from the curved surface of the huge pillar on either side. Some were clearly scenes of battle, while others showed more peaceful and productive events: farming, building, dancing, even worship. Part of her wanted to stop and take it all in, but she forced her feet to carry her up the wide steps.

Annabelle swallowed. Her heart beat a nervous staccato against her breastbone.

How high is this thing? Panic fluttered on the edges of her awareness. *No. Don't you* dare *look down, Annabelle.*

Huffing a sigh of relief, she crawled from the edge after climbing the last step. Water dripped from her sopping hair and from her swimsuit. The smooth, dark blue rock had runes and geometric figures engraved on it, but her attention fixed on the blue-scaled, winged creature coiled up and chained to a broad dais in the center of the plateau. The dragon's head rested on his front limbs, eyes staring straight at her.

Relief washed over her like spring rain. A feeling akin to homecoming lifted her heart.

"Ahdmerel." He raised his head. Chain links rattled. "Come closer, little wyldling."

There were those words again. Ahdmerel. Wyldling. They felt like a part of her.

She tottered over to him. Upon reaching the dais, she stumbled. The dragon's tail uncoiled and supported her, the fleshy, spade-shaped end curving around her. She grabbed hold of the claw he extended, and he lifted her up on the dais.

"Rest, little one." The tail gently lowered her until she reclined in the crook of a scaly elbow. "You have come a long way. I thank you." Cinnamon-colored eyes with diamond-shaped pupils gazed at her with human warmth and welcome.

She stared into the reptilian visage. His scales were dark blue, like the stone of the pillar, fading to a lighter blue along his neck and chest. Fleshy tendrils similar to a catfish's barbels quivered around his jaws, a mustache of tentacles. Ears like truncated bat's wings fanned out from his head. Behind them, two pairs of dark blue horns swept back, as long as her arms and twice as thick at the base where they grew out of his skull. The pair on the outside were longer. Spines protruded from his neck and along his backbone, spaced out like the vertebrae beneath.

A thought rose, unbidden, to her mind. *The gap between the spines leaves just enough room for a person to sit. I wonder what it would be like to ride on him. Flying across the waves … No. Focus, Annabelle!*

"Who are you?" she whispered.

The dragon's cheeks lifted and his eyes crinkled at the corners. "History names me 'Rainblessed,' but I prefer the one affirmed at baptism. Please, address me as Hadrien."

Her heart leaped. Hadrien was a Sage from Enoch's book of legends! Questions tumbled out of her mouth before she could stop them. "Are you one of the seven Sages? Are all the Sages dragons like you? The book didn't say dragons were a thing on Tehara."

Hadrien blinked. "My brothers and I have been referred to as 'evaingynon,' which translates roughly as 'wise ones' into the trading language. Whether we deserved the title remains dubious." He tilted his head. "However, I am not familiar with the term 'dragon,' my dear." She opened her mouth to explain, but he continued speaking. "And how do you wish to be called, wyldling child?"

Annabelle blushed. *I've forgotten my manners—with a dragon, of all things!* Bowing her head, she replied, "I'm Annabelle. Or just Ann. Nice to meet you, Hadrien." He appeared even more reptilian than Commander Storm, although mammalian warmth radiated from his body. Were the twitching tendrils around his mouth squishy or firm? She reached out, then hesitated.

"Well-met, Annabelle." His exhalations wreathed her in a pleasant scent she couldn't name, and his brown eyes twinkled. "Perhaps you would like to ask another question?"

Heat rose into her face. "Can I ... pet you?" With a deep, vibrating chuckle, he nudged her hand, and she stroked his snout, smoothing her hands along the mouth-tendrils. They were stiffer than she expected, and his scales felt smooth and dry. Hadrien's eyelids descended, and he made a rumbling sound like a cat's purr.

Peace drifted over Annabelle as she put her arms around his head and rested her cheek against his jaw. Being with Hadrien brought back early childhood memories of her grandfather holding her in his lap while reading fairytales and Bible stories.

I feel ... safe. Like I can tell him anything. That everything will be all right afterwards. I must ask him how to find Enoch.

An urgency rose in her. "Please, Hadrien. Can you help me? I'm trying to find my brother, Enoch. But ..." She swallowed and leaned back into his tail-spade. "We used to meet in our dreams. But something happened, and our connection broke. I can't reach him."

The Sage eyed her sadly. "Indeed, I know of your quest. It is a difficult burden you bear, venturing to Tehara for the sake of the young knight. I have been praying for your well-being and safety. Your trials have only begun, I fear. Tell me of your trouble, Annabelle. It may help to lighten your burden."

Nestled in his elbow with his tail-spade cupped around her, Annabelle explained how she and Enoch used to interact, losing their bond after she went through the wormhole, about her nightmares with the gray, snakelike ropes, and the tribulations she'd undergone on the journey. Hadrien listened in silence with his sorrowful eyes fixed on her. As she finished her tale, she met his gaze. "Hadrien, do you know why I can't reach Enoch?"

"Oh, little one. I have been sensing your pain for an interminable period, and now I know why. From what you describe, the young knight's wyld has been bound, and your bond muted by wyldhar'ko'profides—that is, the wyldling snare." He sighed, lowering his huge head. "I hoped the Council would have destroyed it all, as Melkior demanded following the tragedy at Brume Hill, but this seems not to be so."

"Wyldling snare." She frowned. *That sounds familiar. Did I read about it in that book and not realize its significance?* "What's that?"

Hadrien lifted the ridges above his eyes. "You described the wyldling snare adequately when you retold your dreams. It often takes the form of dark gray, supple twine with metallic properties, but manacles and collars were also made. The main purpose of the snare is to impede the wyldling's access to the Aethyr." He lowered his head. "My brothers and I never discovered who created those abominations ... although we made use of them, to my shame."

Annabelle considered what Hadrien said. It sounded like something she'd read in the book of legends. "Is there some way to get through the impediment? How do I get our connection back?" Her pleading tone turned bitter. "Commander Storm plans to leave me in Treehome because I'm useless. And I'm beginning to agree. So, I must figure this out."

Chains rattled as the Sage shifted his limbs and raised his head. "You are far from useless, Ahdmerel. The cure to the malady you share with Skelsdaran can be found in Treehome. Whatever may come, Jethro's son does well in bringing you thence. The Dwelfnic Council will provide you with both aid and succor."

Jethro's son? He must be referring to Commander Storm. Huh. I suppose even the Commander has parents, somewhere. Although curious, she had more important topics to discuss with Hadrien before waking up.

"Hadrien, who—or what—is Skelsdaran? And you called me 'Ahdmerel.' It feels like a part of my name, somehow. Right here," Tapping her breastbone, she scrunched her forehead in thought. "Enoch's a wyldling. That much I know. It seems like 'Skelsdaran' is a part of his name. I've been wondering ... what does it all mean?" A cool wind buffeted her, and she shivered.

The flattened end of Hadrien's tail curved around her, shielding her from the freshening breeze. "Both Ahdmerel and Skelsdaran are High Dwelfnic titles for a specific type of wyldling." Eyes wide, Annabelle stared at him. *Is he saying what I think he's saying?*

The Sage continued, "Skelsdaran translates roughly to 'master of the wind blades.' My brother, Kaspar—if he yet lives—shall mentor him." He paused, meeting her gaze. "*My* wyldling—the scion of my Aethyric aspect—is Ahdmerel, the Weaver of Water."

Annabelle stared at her hands. *So ... I do have powers. Like Enoch, only with water instead of air.* Her heart raced. *Was that how I healed Simon—with water magic? And I found the spring by the pond. Things are starting to make sense now.*

"I'm a wyldling," she whispered. Slowly, she raised her eyes. "Your wyldling."

"Most assuredly," Hadrien replied. "And I am your evaingynon." The tendrils around his mouth quivered. "I shall aid you, Annabelle, as I am able." His great body shuddered, making the chains rattle as he bowed his head, eyes downcast.

Why was Hadrien imprisoned here? *That should've been one of my first questions.* Annabelle frowned, placing her hands on either side of his lower jaw. He didn't seem like a criminal. Well, no time like the present to ask. "Hadrien, why—"

Huge tears welled up in his brown eyes. He blinked, and they splashed into her lap. She cried out in shock. More tears fell to join it, faster and faster, and the liquid flowed down her legs and crept up her torso, along her arms, encasing her from feet to neck. Hadrien's tears darkened to dark blue like the stone beneath them and hardened.

Annabelle raised an arm. The dragon's tears formed gauntlets. "How ... why ..."

My armor ... it's back!

"Thank you!" Grinning, she tapped her fingers against her torso. It felt good wearing that armor. Like she'd found a missing piece of herself.

Hadrien settled back with a rattle of chain links. "You will need the sourekghar—and my vashryu—'ere the end of your journey, wyldling child."

"Those—those things you mentioned. Vash-ree-you. Soo-wreck-ga-har?"

His eyes crinkled with amusement. "You wear a representation of the sourekghar at this very moment—the armor crafted by my brethren and me for our wyldling allies. Vashryu are focus gems, used to channel, amplify, and contain Aethyric power. I attuned the sourekghar and vashryu you need to the water aspect. You will find both at Ynys Lloches. Doubtless, the gwerindawr will help you complete your quest to save Skelsdaran. However, they may ask for something in return."

Gwerindawr. Ynys Lloches. More names to search in the book of legends. But another matter concerned her now. "Something in return," she said, musingly. Brow furrowed, she searched the reptilian visage for signs of duplicity. She surveyed the fetters binding him. "Am I expected to free you from your chains, as payment for your help?"

He blinked, as if taken aback by her question. "My aid comes without a price—whether I remain shackled here or gain my freedom." Sorrow darkened his gaze. "Though I yearn for it, I fear I have earned these chains. As have all my brethren. Many monsters were created during the Oblivion Wars, and the Oblivion Wars made monsters of us all. I will ask you to not consider freeing me until after you have heard my tale in full. Then, may you be my judge. By the grace of the Threefold One, I am bound to you, Ahdmerel. My destiny is tied to yours and I will conceal nothing from you."

One of the mighty Sages of Legend---a dragon---bound to me?

Hadrien lowered his head, and, without hesitation, Annabelle put her arms around his neck in a hug. It seemed like he needed one. An icy wave of loneliness swept over her as dark, stormy waters tossed aside jagged icebergs. And then, the warm balm of love buoyed her in tropical waters beneath a bright blue sky. She gasped and drew away. *Those are his emotions.* Tears stung her eyes. "Hadrien, I would love to hear your story—"

Something shook her. Her vision blurred, and Hadrien turned to blue smoke. His tail no longer supported her, and she was falling again, falling ...

"Hadrien!"

Annabelle's entire body jerked as she awakened. "Hadrien," she cried, grasping for her dragon, but her hands found only air.

Dim, steely light met her gaze. She rubbed them to clear away the bleariness, then struggled to rise to her knees in the hollow between oak-root buttresses. Her body screamed its protest. She moaned. *Did I get hit by a truck?*

And then she remembered. Just a day and a night had passed since they fled the nightmare forest of Les Koshmarov. She'd hardly been able to train yesterday—although the Commander had insisted on it. Sleeping on the stone floor of a castle ruin yesterday, while a storm raged outside, hadn't helped matters any, despite the salves Raeden had given her.

Eyebrows raised, Raeden steadied her. "Good morrow, Freylin," he said gravely. "Your servant has been trying to wake you for some moments now."

"Oh, my goodness. The legends are real. The Sages are real," Annabelle gushed, then stifled a yawn. "Sorry."

"There is no reason for apology," the kaenhir said, furrowing his brow. "You need only to rise." His emerald gaze scanned her up and down. "And this you have done. Firstdawn has only just cracked. One wished to rouse you before the Lord Commander returned from his patrol."

Annabelle swallowed a laugh at an image of the sun cracking like an egg and spilling its contents across the horizon. She grimaced.

He tilted his head. "Freylin ... are you still in pain? There is no shame; you are not accustomed to travel. Or fleeing from danger."

Especially giant wolves, Annabelle added in her mind. *Or lykharim, as the Commander calls them.* Aloud, she said, "Yeah, I'm sore."

She suppressed a shudder, recalling the huge wolf-creatures snapping at their heels as they raced through Les Koshmarov toward the waystone. They'd made it, but only just. Commander Storm's fighting prowess, Peter's aerial attacks, and Raeden's archery played a large role in their escape. Tinker had gored a lykhar with his antlers. Even Toad had been helpful, calling out targets for Raeden and Peter.

Heat rose to Annabelle's cheeks. She stared at her hands. She'd contributed nothing to the battle. *All I did was hyperventilate and whack a wolf's snout with Murder Stick. Tinker was almost hamstrung. I should've acted faster.*

"Raeden," she said in a small voice. "Don't tell him I said so, but ..." She took a deep breath. "Commander Storm was right. About how unprepared I am for all of this." Heart pounding, she gazed into her companion's green eyes. "When you shot down all those lykharim—you were *amazing*. I don't know if I properly thanked you for saving my life back there. I was useless. Worse than useless." Her eyes stung. She swallowed and tasted salt. "Afterwards ... Yesterday ... I was a bit out of sorts. So, I'm thanking you now."

Still looking at her, the kaenhir tilted his head. Both his ears twitched and his whiskers quivered. "There is no need for thanks. It is your servant's duty and—how does one say it? Ah! — his privilege to protect you. He would gladly—" he hesitated, clearing his throat. He fiddled with his monocle. "Freylin, you are not useless. You are learning valuable skills."

"Oh! That reminds me." She clambered to her feet, and Raeden rose in one smooth movement, watching her intently. "Before I start breakfast, I should check Tinker's wound."

"Your servant will assist you." Raeden paced her as she trudged toward the fire-pit she'd helped dig the night before. "The cook pot and tea are already prepared." He touched her shoulder. "Freylin, what was the word you shouted as you awoke? About the Sages?"

Annabelle paused, biting her lower lip. *He's going to think I'm crazy.* She stared at the cook pot hanging over the fire-pit, filled with water just beginning to heat up for the farina. Then she turned to Raeden. "I dreamed I spoke with the Sage, Hadrien Rainblessed."

Some of the tension seemed to leave his frame. *"Ach so."* His eyes glittered and his whiskers twitched with humor. "Freylin, you have read so much of the legends and the Sages, the tales have crawled into your dreams."

"No, it wasn't like that. It was real—as real as any of the dreams I shared with Enoch."

Raeden hummed thoughtfully, but said nothing.

She frowned, rubbing her hands down her arms, then continued toward the edge of camp, where the two mounts dined on bright green, fern-like plants. The riding equipment and panniers rested against a nearby tree. Raeden pulled his medical kit from one while she coaxed Tinker away from his breakfast with a sprig of arborcress mixed with willowbark, leading him out from the shadowy undergrowth and into the clearing, where she'd have more light.

Annabelle stood to one side and pulled the bandages off Tinker's left haunch. He shifted position and grunted. She stroked his flank, murmuring encouragement, then sniffed the ragged and ugly-looking laceration. Thank God; it hadn't gone septic. Examining the place where the lykhar had attacked her mount sent shivers down her spine.

A wound. Here was her chance to figure out if she could heal someone with magic.

Gently, she placed her hands above and below the injury. *God, please help me. Don't let Simon's recovery be a fluke. Please let Tinker be healed.* She shut her eyes and concentrated, seeking the blue, liquid warmth she'd sensed rushing up from her core.

Nothing. She drooped with a sigh.

With a rattle of glass jars, the kaenhir placed the kit on the ground at her feet, startling her. "Freylin, is something the matter?" She shook her head. After casting her a concerned glance, he grasped Tinker's bridle, barking a command to stay still. The stag froze, and Raeden said, "Your servant will hold him steady. He knows pain is coming and will not harm you."

Okay, so the healing didn't work. There's no use fretting about it. Tinker needs you to focus. While murmuring soothingly to her mount, Annabelle pulled bottles from the kit, then held them up with a questioning glance at Raeden.

He nodded in approval at her choices, then arched an eyebrow. "Please explain what you mean, Freylin. About the Sage in your dreams being real."

Annabelle suppressed a sigh. The only way Raeden would believe her was if she told him everything. While she cleaned the ragged lykhar-bite—wincing every time Tinker flinched—she haltingly described her entire dream experience. The placid sea. Breathing underwater. Swimming to the huge azure pillar. Meeting the blue dragon and their conversation.

"I didn't realize the Sages were dragons. There wasn't anything in the book about that." To her chagrin, she had to explain to Raeden the concept of a dragon.

When she finished, Raeden shook his head, ears wilting. "You speak as if you truly believe you met with a Sage," he replied, his voice tight. "Your servant thought you formed these ideas from the stories you read. Now, he is not so certain."

"I couldn't have, because I dreamed about Hadrien before I even knew about the book. Before I knew he was a Sage." Looking at her companion, she frowned. "Raeden, is something wrong? Are you upset?"

Raeden handed her materials for a poultice, then curled his hands into fists. "Your servant is upset, Freylin, because it is very distressing to hear you say that you spoke with Hadrien Rainblessed."

"Why?"

"Because it is not possible, Freylin. All seven Sages fell in the Oblivion Wars, over an age ago." Ears quivering, he fixed her with a wide-eyed gaze. "They are all dead."

Mind-Fortress

Commander Storm strode into view. He paused beside a gnarled old oak tree, where Toad sat upon a root ball. The two exchanged words. Annabelle kept a surreptitious eye on them as she scooped steaming cereal into three bowls. She handed one to Raeden, who knelt beside her. He thanked her graciously and began eating, his eyes never leaving her. All the while she'd tended to Tinker, and then prepared breakfast, he'd stuck close and observed her carefully, refusing to speak further about the Sages until the Commander returned.

And now that he's back, maybe I'll get some answers. Hadrien can't be dead! Otherwise, who was I talking to in my dreams? Unease fluttered in her belly.

Finally, Toad hopped into the underbrush and the Commander approached the fire-pit, his expression inscrutable— as usual.

Annabelle's breath quickened as her heart raced. "Breakfast is ready," She announced, holding out a bowl.

With a grunted thanks, he accepted the bowl. "Anything to report?"

"Um. Yes. I talked with Hadrien Rainblessed in my dream. He told me I was a wyldling, like Enoch. Only, not like Enoch." She tittered, attempting to gauge the evainghir's mood, but an eyelid flicker was the Commander's only reaction. "Because he's air and I'm water, you know? And he called us by our titles, Ahdmerel and Skelsdaran. I've seen him in my dreams before, and he's calling to me. But always at a distance. This is the first time I actually—"

"You have dreamt of the Sage before," Commander Storm interjected. "How long has the Sage been appearing? Did the boy tell you about him—or any of the Sages?"

"Two months? Maybe three. Moons, I mean." Biting her lip, Annabelle stared longingly at her cereal. "Enoch didn't tell me anything about Sages or dragons, and I didn't even know Hadrien's name until after I read about him in the book of legends. Why?" She frowned. "You think I'm making this up?"

"No." Commander Storm's visage grew hard, his eyes as cold as basalt on the ocean floor. "Describe everything you can remember, womanchild. From past dreams. Leave out no detail, no matter how trifling."

In a rush of confusing babble, Annabelle told him all she recalled of her experience with Hadrien. Details from the dream were already fading; why hadn't she written it down as soon as she woke up? While she spoke, the underbrush beside her quivered, and Toad hopped out to perch on a root nearby. He met her eyes and then glanced away, shifting his front limbs. He looked troubled.

Raeden—who'd finished his breakfast and was clearing up the campsite during her summary—flinched at the word "wyldling." Toad made a slight noise as she described Hadrien's tears flowing over her and becoming the dark blue armor. The Commander's gaze seemed to sharpen at that detail, and he muttered something in a different tongue. Otherwise, his warrior's blank face gave away nothing. He held his bowl and observed her in silence while their untouched cereal cooled.

She paused, a frown wrinkling her brow at a memory of a mist-shrouded wood. There was something else—another dream right before she met the Sage. Something about looking for Enoch, orange eyes, purple light, and a dark tower ... And then it was gone, like vapor in the wind. Without details, she decided it wasn't worth mentioning.

"There is more," the Commander said. "Continue."

As if it held answers to all her questions, Annabelle searched the depths of the bowl she clutched, the cereal's warmth seeping into her ice-cold hands.

His tone sharpened. "We cannot tarry much longer, womanchild. Now, speak."

Annabelle blurted, "Hadrien told me the reason I can't sense Enoch is the wyldling snare." She stirred the cereal with her spoon, examining the bits of dried fruit and meat as if they were fossils she'd unearthed. Her throat constricted, and she forced out words. "He said there's a way I can get our connection back."

When the evainghir didn't reply, Annabelle looked up, glancing between him and Raeden. "Hadrien can't really be dead, can he? Was I talking to a ghost?" She recalled the love and acceptance she'd experienced in Hadrien's presence, and yearned to visit with him again. *I don't care if he is a ghost!*

Grasping his crucifix pendant, Raeden's eyes fixed on her as he mouthed a prayer.

Commander Storm regarded her in silence for several heartbeats. "Once you finish your porridge and we're underway, we begin your mental training." He turned to include the amphibian. "Both of you."

Toad puffed up. "Yes, sir," he cracked out, the odd expression clearing from his eyes.

"But ..." Staring at the Commander, Annabelle's mouth opened and closed. She spluttered, "What did Hadrien mean about the wyldling snare? Can Enoch and I get our connection back? *You* even told me there was a chance."

About to turn, the huge warrior hesitated. "Aye. There is a chance. However, if you cannot protect your mind—or recognize friend from foe—the point is moot."

Her throat tightened. "Commander, please don't leave me behind."

Commander Storm walked away without acknowledging her. "Let it go for now, kiddo," Toad said, eyeing her untouched bowl. "You gonna eat that?"

Annabelle's stomach clamored to be fed. "Yes!" With hot indignation rising within, she gulped down her lukewarm cereal.

Once she finished and sat in the saddle, the Commander led them down a narrow, twisty trail with trees looming alongside like somber sentinels. Peter returned and flew high above, scouting for danger. Raeden brought up the rear, riding on Lorun. Annabelle's insides squirmed, her breakfast not settling well as she mulled over her dreams and the Commander's reaction. He hadn't answered her questions at all, and what he had said only mystified her further.

Hadrien is supposed to be dead. If that's the case, then who was I talking to? And this "mental training" the Commander wants to put us through. Recognizing friend from foe ... She frowned, considering the implications. *Does he think the Sage is an imposter? But Hadrien didn't try to hurt me. He was nice, and he answered my questions. Gave me hope.* She scowled. *Why must everything be so difficult?*

"You look like someone just snatched the last cinnamon roll," Toad observed from his perch in front of her saddle. He snickered, his pale blue eyes gleaming. "Scowling doesn't suit you, kiddo. If you're not careful, your face will freeze like that."

Annabelle forced a grin and spoke sweetly through gritted teeth. "If you don't like the way I look, then why do you keep looking at me?"

Toad's throat sac pulsed rapidly. "Good point," he said, then turned to stare at the passing trees. "Ah! Much better!"

"Jerk," Annabelle muttered, shifting. Her leg muscles were still sore from sword training. She glanced at Toad, who faced the side of the trail with a vacant look. Frowning, she recalled the strange expression on Toad's face while she'd described her dream about Hadrien Rainblessed. And the Commander wanted to train Toad as well.

"Toad, have you been having weird dreams, too?"

He flinched, as if roused from a reverie, and pivoted to glare at her. "What's it to you?"

Pierced by his baleful regard, she leaned back and fidgeted with the reins. "No need to snap at me. I'm only asking. It would be good to compare notes."

Toad's glare softened as he settled down in his saddlebag, going from angry to troubled in a heartbeat. "Sorry, kiddo. I ... It's been a difficult past few days." He snorted. "Make that a difficult week and a half. Not that I can remember much from before I ran into the kid in the woods. And yes, by 'kid' I mean Enoch," he added in a sharper tone when she started to interrupt. "I wish I had known then what I know now. I could have guided him in his role as the Baron-Knight. All this talk of meeting folks in dreams ..." With a sigh, he lowered his head to rest on the rim of the saddlebag. "Come to think of it, I've been dreaming about the weirdest things for as long as I *can* remember."

Anticipation quivered along her nerves as Annabelle bent closer. *I wonder if Enoch dreamed about the Sage-dragons, too. What would it mean if Toad did—that we're all connected?*

Heart pounding, she whispered, "Are there any dragons in your dreams, like in mine?"

Light sparked in Toad's eyes, and his vocal sac pulsed faster as he stared at her, glanced aside, and then met her gaze. His mouth twitched, on the verge of speech, when a shadow fell over him.

"Time for your training," Commander Storm announced. He'd dropped back to walk beside Tinker. Annabelle jerked upright with a gasp. Here was an opportunity. *This skill involves the mind, which is where my strength lies. It should be easier for me to learn than the sword-dance.* Once she could protect her mind—and she fixed her connection to Enoch—the Commander wouldn't be so quick to leave her behind in Y'Dendordenelle!

Toad stiffened to attention. "Yes, sir. I'm ready to learn." He glanced sidelong at Annabelle. "What's the plan?"

"Protecting the mind is not something to be learned in a single lesson. Once begun, I must stay the course and continue training you. By the end of this first lesson, you should know how to isolate and barricade your mind behind impenetrable walls. I will then launch an assault to test your defenses, so that you will recognize an attack when it comes, and take stock of your own weaknesses. In the next lesson, I shall teach you how to camouflage this refuge, to ensure your enemy cannot find it. After that, I will teach a technique to suppress fear for a time."

Annabelle leaned toward the Commander. "But why would anyone want to invade my mind? It's not as if I know anything of real importance. I'm not even from this world."

"You have a connection to the lad," he replied. "Did you never consider how this might be exploited by his captors or others with malicious intent?"

She winced, his words too close to her earlier pondering for comfort. "But I only saw Enoch in my dreams, and the connection's gone now." She fussed with her skirt, smoothing it out as she struggled to push down her frustration and sorrow. "If it's such an awful risk, then why didn't you teach Enoch how to guard his mind?"

The Commander's lip curled. For a moment, she feared she'd pushed him too far, but then he answered. "Had circumstances differed, I would train him in like manner. No doubt, he would have voiced the same questions as you."

He shook his head and his expression turned wooden. "Given the insurrection in the Eastern Marches, my presence was required elsewhere. There simply was no opportunity to remedy his lack of experience. I ... regret that." His voice quieted and then he stiffened. His visage became granite and steel again. "I make no excuses; this is simply my assessment of the situation. I failed to protect my ward."

Annabelle's eyes widened. *Wow! The Commander— admitting to a fault?*

The evainghir cleared his throat. "Enough of that maudlin puling. To work. We'll begin with something simple. Close your eyes. Envision yourself within a secure barracks."

"Got it," said Toad.

Annabelle frowned. "Barracks. I don't know what that even looks like. Is that like a castle?"

The Commander harrumphed. "If it suffices, then envision yourself building a fortress around your mind."

As opposed to my heart, Annabelle thought as she hummed a few bars of a popular song. Toad gave her a strange look from the saddlebag.

"Attend to your lesson, womanchild," the Commander snapped.

Eyes wide, Annabelle gasped and straightened her spine. "Sorry," she said, ducking under the Commander's glare. "What you said reminded me of a song. I'll try to keep my mind from wandering off again."

His brows lowered. "See that you leash it tightly. Defending oneself against any kind of attack is a serious business." He gripped the pommel of a sword tightly. "Self-control and discipline are crucial. If you were one of my soldiers, I'd—" He broke off with a grunt and a shake of his head.

"With respect, Lord Commander," Raeden said, his voice hard and cold. He raised his chin. "Your servant warns you. Freylin is not your soldier. You will not lay a hand upon the heart-sister of Sir Enoch."

"Indeed, I shall not." He glanced from Annabelle to Raeden, and then back again. Amusement glinted in the Commander's eyes, and his mouth turned up at the corners in an almost-smile. It disappeared in a blink. Had she imagined it?

Commander Storm exhaled softly. "It helps to close your eyes for this task, womanchild. You must construct within your mind a fortified palace of your own devising—down to the tiniest detail. Exterior walls and battlements. Floor by floor, every chamber, wall, door, and window, any balconies, spires, or turrets. Decorate your home however you like. Fill it with furniture, sweetmeats, music, and books if you so desire for your own comfort. Model each chamber after a place where you feel safe. Protected." He paused. "Have you chosen a structure?"

"Yes, sir," Toad remarked. "I'll take your suggestion and use the barracks; it's defensible, and I can actually remember what they look like." He chuckled. "This is a cakewalk."

Annabelle licked her lips. *Mmmm, cake. No, Ann; focus.* She screwed her eyes shut. "I think I'll build my mind-palace as a cabin by Tippecanoe Lake. That's where my Nana and Papa live, and I always felt safe there. I suppose it doesn't have to be very fancy on the outside, so long as I believe it's an impregnable fortress, right?"

"Correct," the Commander rumbled. "Your mind-fortress can take any shape, but you must picture it in fine detail." Leather creaked beside her, and his voice sounded very close. "Begin with the foundation and build upward, as you would a real home."

"Good thing I watched the house being built," Annabelle replied. "Otherwise, I'd probably mess it up." She grimaced. *There's no guarantee I won't mess up, anyway.*

"Be confident. Impress your will upon it at every stage, declaring, 'none may pass,' before moving on to the next."

"Yes, sir," Toad said.

"Alrighty then." Annabelle concentrated.

First things first: mark the location. Then, dig a hole. And since it was all in her head, she could pretend she had magic powers and do everything herself instead of using heavy equipment. A memory of a grassy knoll above a lake coalesced, and she placed herself in the picture. She thought she smelled Nana's apple kuchen, but then the scent vanished, replaced by the algal and fishy odor of the lake. Distantly, water lapped along the shoreline. A bumblebee droned past.

Brow furrowed, she imagined a chunk cut out of the earth and piled it on one side. She excavated the basement and conjured cement for the foundation. Before it dried, she pressed her hand into the cement, like a seal, as she said the words. Blue light flared beneath her palm, then dispersed throughout the foundation.

"Whoa, that was cool." She tittered.

"Does she make the mind-palace out of ice?" Raeden asked. "Very peculiar."

Toad snorted, muttering something unintelligible.

"Quiet, Sir Thomas," the Commander replied. "Unless you have a question?"

"No, sir."

More gently, Commander Storm said, "Share your progress, womanchild."

Annabelle resisted the urge to open her eyes. "Just laid the foundation and impressed it with my will, like you said. I'm about to erect the framework for the house."

He grunted. "Go on. And describe all you do. I shall provide guidance, as necessary."

Annabelle built the house framework and infused it with her will. She paused, debating which type of building materials would be best for the exterior walls. Stone or wood? Ceramic? Bricks? Sticks? Straw?

"Use whatever you want," Toad said, as if she'd spoken aloud. "The material doesn't matter, kiddo. Just make sure you have something the Big Bad Wolf can't blow down."

I suppose I could make it out of ice, like Raeden said, if I wanted to. But that might be too weird. Maybe I'll save it for the outermost defenses, or the concealment step. Next lesson. And it'll be wonderful to be able to suppress fear.

Mentally shrugging, she made the exterior look just like her grandparent's home in the Wisconsin Northwoods, laid her hands upon it, and imbued it with her will. She envisioned herself walking through the door, into what would have been her grandmother's kitchen ...

"That'll do, womanchild."

Tinker had stopped moving. She opened her eyes and then shaded them; everything seemed too bright. Her head throbbed and then the pain dissipated. They'd halted in a sunny glade. Raeden held her mount's bridle. "Time for a rest," he said, his voice distant as he scanned the surrounding trees, where birds chirped enthusiastically.

Annabelle exhaled noisily. "Thank God."

Commander Storm stood beside Tinker. His eyes crinkled at the corners. "Do not celebrate yet. Dismount. I do not want you in the saddle when we continue the lesson."

She chuckled. "That doesn't sound ominous or anything." When Raeden approached to assist her, she held up a hand. "I want to try dismounting by myself."

"It's about time," Toad muttered.

The Commander glanced between her and Raeden. "Your Excellency, whilst I train them, scout the perimeter."

"Yes, Lord Commander." Fist to chest, the kaenhir bowed. His emerald gaze questioned her, but she shook her head. After he mounted Lorun and the stag bounded away, a yearning to call after him, to ask for help, quivered in her chest. But then she steeled herself and concentrated on getting down from Tinker's back. She did so without mishap.

The Commander said, "Well done."

Holy cow! Annabelle jumped as if he had goosed her and spun to face him. Had he just praised her? However, his gray eyes were as steely as ever. He waved at a flat-topped boulder. "Sit down, womanchild. We shall begin in a moment." Shifting his attention to Toad, still sitting in the saddlebag and watching her, he asked, "Sir Thomas, questions before we continue?"

Toad blinked, as if waking from a reverie, and hopped onto the saddle. Hind legs first, he slid down from the saddle, webbed toes feeling for the stirrup, and then to the ground. "Before we begin, sir, how far is the next waystone?"

Annabelle sat cross-legged on the stone, warmed by the suns, the heat seeping through her leather skirt and trousers. "Yeah, I want to know, too. Last time I asked, you didn't specify. And when will we get to Y'Dendordenelle?" Her heart clenched. If she didn't master this mind-fortress exercise, then that was where her journey ended.

Stop kidding yourself. The Commander plans to leave you there no matter what.

No. She must cling to hope. God had brought her to Tehara for a reason—to save Enoch. He would provide a way for her to continue on her quest.

The evainghir hunkered beside her boulder with forearms resting on his knees. His tail supported him from behind. "The next waystone is a day's journey from here at our current pace. Barring delays, we should reach it before it activates, at second-noon. And then, another day of travel shall bring us to another waystone, which will take us directly to Y'Dendordenelle at Klotho-set." He glanced at Toad, who hopped up beside Annabelle. His voice was neutral. "Yes? You have another question?"

"Sir, I've been thinking about what the kiddo said." Toad hesitated, his glance drifting to her. "About that Hadrien guy talking to her in her dreams. You've taught us how to block somebody out, but what if they're already in there? Is there a way to get rid of them—cast them out?"

"I don't want to stop dreaming about Hadrien," Annabelle blurted. She glanced at Toad, then added, "Hadrien was kind. I could tell he cared about me." Toad gawked at her as if she'd grown horns. What was his problem? She turned to face the Commander. "He didn't seem like he wanted anything; it was more like he was offering me information."

"A bit of advice, womanchild," the evainghir growled. "Beware those offering gifts. There is always a price."

"I suppose," she muttered, as if he dragged the words from her. "You make a valid point." *But I don't believe the adage is true, in this case.* And yet, her attempt at healing had failed. Was everything in the dream false? She looked down, half drawing her sword and then sliding it back into its sheath. "I *still* need to know why I'm having these dreams. What they mean."

Commander Storm grunted, a dark expression flickering across his visage. "Dreams are tricky at the best of times and their revelations are always suspect. When they touch upon the Aethyr, one must practice even greater caution. If you are a wyldling ..." He grimaced, as if something pained him. "Better to leave you in Y'Dendordenelle, rather than deliver you to those who took the boy."

"But—"

He raised an admonitory finger. "In this matter, womanchild, you must bow to those with greater expertise. We will address your questions and concerns in Y'Dendordenelle. For now, you must accept this. Learn these lessons as though your life depends upon it." His eyes hardened. "Because it may."

Annabelle hugged herself, chilled despite the heat of the day. Toad's warty hide brushed against her leg. His presence comforted her.

"I understand, sir."

"Good." The evainghir nodded. "Now. Take hold of your weapon, but keep it sheathed. It will help to ground you. I will mimic a forceful invasion, test your defenses. Envision yourself within your mind-fortress. Tell me when you are ready." His gaze settled on Toad. "Do you have reason to believe our mission has been compromised, Sir Thomas?"

Toad eyed Annabelle sidelong, his throat sac fluttering. "No, sir. Just wondered."

"A mind invasion is unlikely to be of any duration that would require a forcible eviction," Commander Storm rumbled. "The exercise is incredibly taxing, and even an untrained mind unconsciously and naturally repulses any intrusion after a few moments. However, a skilled invader will well use those few moments. Sir Thomas?"

"I'm ready, sir."

While Toad strained and cursed, Annabelle detached the scabbard and laid it across her lap. Grasping both the scabbard and hilt as if about to unsheathe the blade, she closed her eyes and concentrated, picturing the familiar scene by the lake, then the surrounding walls. She covered the windows with steel shutters and barricaded the door, then sat down at the kitchen table. The ghost of Nana's apple kuchen haunted her nostrils before evaporating. The room was eerily empty. Toad had gone silent. The birds still twittered, and she blocked out their senseless chatter.

I have an excellent imagination. There's no reason I shouldn't pass his test.

"Okay." She inhaled deeply. "I'm ready."

Something slammed into the nearest wall and the entire building shook. Annabelle cried out in alarm. Sword in hand, she threw her arms up around her head. She peeked between her elbows at the window. The steel shutter had a crack. *Oh, no* ... Another heavy blow, and the side of the house shattered like glass. Pain battered her temples and everything fell into ruin. She screamed.

Peter squawked. "Annie!"

When did he come back?

Strong hands grabbed her shoulders, bracing her upright. The pain vanished. She hugged Murder Stick against her chest, took a shuddering breath, and opened eyes streaming with tears.

Commander Storm's face was inches from her own. She ducked her head. "Look at me." He grabbed her chin and forced her head up. She met his steely gaze. Violet sparks danced in his gray eyes. "You are unharmed," he said, letting go and leaning back on his tail. He heaved a sigh and ran a hand over his visage.

Peter nosed his way between them. He placed a taloned forepaw on her shoulder, tilted his head, and peered at her with one eye. "You okay, Annie-O?"

No. I'm not okay. That. Freaking. Hurt!

With a whimper, she threw her arms around him and buried her face in his ruff. She breathed in the dusty scent of fur and feathers until her heart slowed. "There, there," he crooned as he patted her back, awkward with taloned paws.

After a moment, she lifted her throbbing head. "I'll be fine in a bit."

Peter bent and plucked a purple flower with a bruised stalk out of his harness. "I brung ya a crown iris. One day, I'll find ya some more."

With a shaky smile, Annabelle took the blossom and inhaled the citrus-mint scent. The pounding in her head briefly subsided. *It's shaped like the irises in my mom's garden, even if it doesn't smell like one.* "Thank you, Peter."

A weight settled on her right thigh. Toad peered up in her face. "Commander. What did you do to her, sir?"

"I launched a minor assault on her mind-fortress."

"Minor, my warty backside!" Toad retorted, jumping out of her lap to glower at his superior officer. "What did you do—drop an asteroid on her mental castle?"

Annabelle scowled. *That's certainly what it felt like!*

Commander Storm examined her grimly. "No; I used the equivalent of a battering ram against her front door. A small one. Much less force than I used on yours." His eyes narrowed. "Her defenses should have held longer."

Annabelle's shoulders slumped as she stroked the flower petals. "So, I didn't do it right." Raising a hand to her aching head, she held the Commander's gaze. "But I'll keep trying." *I have to master this skill! Once this headache goes away, I'll try again.*

Toad snorted. "Mine didn't last, either, kiddo. But I see what I need to fix."

Peter nuzzled her cheek. "Don't worry, Annie-O. You're bright as brass buttons. You'll figure it out."

Shadows and Stars

William's head pounded a familiar rhythm called pain. Practicing with the Aethyr didn't hurt him as much as before, but it still exacted its toll. Aside from that, it had been a week since he'd had anything like a decent day's sleep. There was only so much his potions and the occasional dip into kaiber powder could mitigate.

However, insomnia held compensations. Neither the cloaked bard with the violet aura nor the flayed knight with the flaming sword could harass him outside of dreams. William put that wakeful time to good use. Perusing his master's notes while he slept had unearthed a glamourie that suited his needs.

And what did Tenebris want with such a powerful illusion spell?

With his satchel clutched under his arm, William crossed the brow of the hill. *It's Tenebris; he probably wants it for the sake of knowing a powerful spell.* He kicked a loose rock. A smile twitched at his lips. The sleepless days and painstaking research had paid its dividends. After five failed attempts, William—lowly Second Circle apprentice that he was—could perform a glamourie no Arkhasuhl even *witnessed* until he attained acolyte status!

The body-memory and mannerisms siphoned from the captive by the wyldling snare—and those had been an unexpected boon—would cover a multitude of errors. From those stolen impressions, he'd crafted a convincing Northward persona. Zakaar nearly taking William's head off proved its efficacy. It had taken an extra measure of elixir to calm the harkhurz.

William had a plan. Nine potential scenarios plotted out and diagrammed. Now he needed the ideal location and he could set his scheme into motion. For example, a defunct wardspell circle with enough residual energy to fuel a complicated spellform. Several in the Contested Lands might suit his purpose. That evening, they reached one. Tenebris excused him from camp chores to practice the Seeker's Web and attempt to locate any sign of pursuit across the plains. After using the spell himself to determine there was none, no doubt Tenebris believed William would fail at his task.

Tenebris hasn't the slightest inkling what I'm capable of. Why is he holding me back?

William kicked another rock, scowling. Coarse grass and weeds adorned the hilltop. A lone oak tree crowned it with spreading boughs, and a jumble of stones nearby looked like it had once been part of a waystone ring. When he passed between them, a prickle of energy danced over him and excited his arkhabala. The tattoos stirred and stretched across his shoulders like an awakening beast. William's scowl turned into a grin.

It's still a place of power.

One of the larger stones possessed a level, flat surface—another reason William considered this location ideal. He unrolled a leather sheet with the spellform painted on it with ink mixed with his own blood and spread it over the stone. Then he unpacked the anchor items and placed them in the proper pattern. He lifted the memory anchor—a crystalline statuette of a woman with a dark inclusion inside—from its padded compartment with great care.

Eyes darting around, William reached inside his burkheld and pulled out his whiskey flask. He took a sip and then put it away. He needed to ration it until they reached Fastness.

"If I can get out from under Tenebris's eye long enough to *find* more whiskey," he muttered as he unsheathed his bone knife. The blade shone blue-white under the starlight as he set it against the scarred skin of his left wrist. He paused, recalling the maiden's horrified look when she saw his scars. The pity in her eyes.

His mouth tightened. *I'll show you who needs to be pitied, Milady Blue. And it isn't me.*

With a grimace, he sliced a shallow cut—a slight stinging sensation—and then turned his arm so the blood spattered down on the leather, beading up on the water-proofed material.

He intoned a cantrip to prime the spellform. Blood droplets disappeared as the energized leather drank it up. Energy hummed along the spellform's lines and vibrated through his marrow. Making a face, he skimmed all his blood from the blade onto the spellform, then sheathed it before binding the cut. *Good, no nausea this time.*

"Now for the fun part." He brought out Northward's belt-pouch and extracted the portrait. "Annabelle," he murmured, staring at the maiden's smiling face. "Milady Blue. I'll find you and ferret out whatever secret you're hiding." Reverently, he set the portrait in the center of the spellform, then took out the poppet he'd prepared using Northward's hair and blood.

Tenebris had taught him the art of making poppets—a crude doll that fit in the palm of one's hand—how to construct them from twigs, clay, and cloth with hair and blood worked into its frame. Poppets were handy as a focus in Seeker's Webs. Because Annabelle's portrait served as the focus, William planned to put the poppet to a different use. A cantrip would activate the glamourie he'd set into the construct, but he'd wait until he found his quarry. Better not to blend the two spells. According to his calculations, doing so divided the probability of success in half.

Clutching the poppet, he shut his eyelids and concentrated on the spellform. Energy rippled through his arkhabala. It quivered, shifting, flexing across his skin. A delicious agony.

Seek, seek, seek …

A falling sensation, and then … His fatigue and headache were gone. William opened his eyes. He stood in a forest of shadows and tall trees. A violet mist surrounded him and a chill pervaded the area. He was in the world of dreams. A grin spread across his face. Excellent. His quarry slept now—wherever she was in the flesh. His fingers curled around the poppet.

Oh, how the tables have turned, Annabelle. Sword or no sword, I'll have the advantage during this encounter.

Then he tensed, his grin fading. That suns-cursed cloaked bard might be around. Last time, he'd ruined everything. Better to stay on guard. Carefully, William extended his kythim in a network of shining purple and orange strands and strained all his senses. No sign of anyone, let alone the cloaked bard with the violet aura. But in the past, there hadn't been any warning— he'd simply appeared.

Burning suns! He needed to move. As Tenebris would say, he got nowhere by standing around like a dithering dullard.

William began walking, pushing aside the brush while pondering what he already knew. The strange bard ripped Annabelle away from him the last time, just as he was making headway with her—at least, she'd seemed inclined to talk, rather than stab him. He clenched his jaw. Doubtless, the bard didn't want William tapping into whatever power the maiden possessed. Because this was about power. What else was there?

His kythim trembled like a spider's web. A thrill wracked his frame as the orange strands shifted to violet. And then, the violet tendrils pulsed *blue* and retracted with a *snap*. William panted, hairs from the poppet sticking to his clammy palms. That was close. Had she sensed him? Softly as a soot panther, he crept forward.

Beyond a stand of trees, running water burbled its liquid music. A human voice harmonized with its melody. *Is she singing?* Frowning, he followed a twisting path through the trees. The mist retreated to his peripheral vision, and the singing grew louder as he descended the trail. *Is it some kind of spell?* She'd denied having magic, but ... her voice was beautiful.

His heart pounded in his chest and stole his breath. It reminded him of the moment before the bard had torn the maiden from his grasp, as William leaned closer to ask her a question he couldn't even recall anymore. Her widening blue eyes, her unnatural paleness growing rosy ...

With a grimace, he rubbed his forehead. It *had* to be a spell.

The trees fell away, and the path opened up into a meadow, where stars looked down on the figure of a maiden limned in sapphire light, wearing dark blue armor with a sword at her hip. She knelt before a stream with her back to William. Halting behind the brush at the edge of the clearing, he stared while thoughts chased one another through his head.

That armor, he mused, forcing a hand from the lapels of his robe and the flask hidden within. He dared not sip whiskey here. *She wore that armor last time. The sword is the same as well. Are they something she conjured up in her dreams, or does she possess them in the waking world?* While he turned the poppet over in his hands, her lovely voice switched to a different tune. She sang about a strong word cleaving the darkness. *Ah. She must know magic, then—the lying little tesseramint.* A frisson ran through him, and his awareness fragmented, overlaying the present with a memory. Arms rocked him, and a feminine voice crooned a lullaby with a similar melody. He shook his head, dispelling the anachronistic sensations. He had a goal to accomplish.

Time to learn how convincing a glamourie I've wrought. Whispering the cantrip, William activated the poppet. His arkhabala hummed. Memories that weren't his own flashed in rapid succession—what the wyldling snare had stolen from Northward and then bestowed upon William—imbuing a familiarity with the form he was about to assume. He concentrated on an image held in his mind, envisioning himself as a shorter young man with almond-brown skin and cobalt blue eyes. His burkheld morphed into the silver brocade jacket, buckskin trousers, and boots he'd gained from the captive. The poppet evaporated into a purple mist.

Vertigo struck him. He braced himself on a tree and closed his eyes until it passed. Once everything settled, he examined his disguise. His hands were smaller and brown instead of gray. Even his face felt different to his probing fingers. The spectacles were convincingly real. Straight, fine hair bound in a tail had replaced dark brown dreadlocks. Borrowed lips spread in a crooked grin that had never graced the features he'd stolen. To make certain, he concentrated, and a looking glass appeared before him. It lingered long enough to show him Northward's face before vanishing again.

It worked!

Composing himself, William stepped out into the glade. Now, what did that kadorei oaf's voice sound like? He took a deep breath. "Annabelle?"

Well, that wasn't half bad. A little raspy, but it would do, in a pinch.

The maiden's song cut off, and she whipped around, her long hair flaring out to the side like a skein of silk. Her eyes looked huge in her milk-pale face, widening as they settled on him. She wasn't wearing the spectacles he'd seen in the portrait, though. "Enoch," she gasped, her hands flying up to her mouth. "Is it really you?" She rose, hastily pushing hair behind her ears. Her sapphire aura flared as she beamed at him. The opalescent brightness he'd noticed in Northward's silver kythim was even more pronounced in hers.

An answering smile took over his face. It felt ... odd. William hoped it didn't look odd. "Of course," he replied. Perfect. Just like in Scenario No. 1. Burrowing through his captive's mind had unearthed one shared memory with Annabelle that William planned to use as a proof. "Uh ... we drank chocolatl together, the day you gifted me your portrait. Who else would it be?" He spread out his arms.

Feast your eyes, Milady Blue. If you can find a flaw, then I may let you eviscerate me with that sword.

"Enoch!" Crying out, she charged across the meadow. Before William understood what was happening, the armored maiden pressed against his borrowed form, embracing him.

He stiffened, with arms still held out on either side. Outer darkness! Was this a form of attack? What was he supposed to do? None of his scenarios had predicted this. All his senses spun like a top. He clenched his jaws together. It took every scrap of his concentration to maintain the Northward persona and *not scream curses.*

"Thank God," she said, voice muffled in the jacket. "I've been so worried! It's good to see you. We're all looking for you—Commander Storm, Raeden, and ..."

Oh. This is a ... hug. Vaguely, William recalled being hugged as a small child. It had been Cycles ago. He'd forgotten that it felt so ... good. Warmth spread through him and a flush rose to his cheeks as she clung to him, prattling away.

"... Commander Storm's leading us from waystone to waystone. Just one more to go—someplace called Kherberos, in the Eastern Marches—and then we'll arrive at Ee-den-dor-den-elle." She sang the word. "Treehome. Raeden says you've visited there before, and the people there will help us find you ..."

Wait, did she just say Commander Storm?

William's eyes widened. Villem's spear! The evainghir single-handedly exterminated Arkhadahns by the hundreds. William realized the Commander would pursue them, but to have it verified shot him through with arrows of unreasoning, gibbering terror. In a similar fashion to the corpses of the children Zakaar killed, he pushed it down deep and buried it under a pile of rocks. He needed his wits about him—

His breath caught. Freezing void! The twittering little riverlark had just revealed where they're headed!

"... praying for something like this to—" Annabelle let go and backed away, eyes wide and looking bewildered. "What's wrong? Did I hurt you? I'm so sorry." She wrung her hands.

William released a pent-up breath. "No. I mean, you didn't hurt me." His mind raced, embellishing the story he'd invented in Scenario No. 5. It was best that he stuck close to the truth, though. "Ravenos beat me. Nearly broke my bur— my ribs." He hesitated, fishing for a boring insult. The sort Northward would use. "The b-blackguard."

Annabelle gasped. "That's horrible! Ravenos is the one who kidnapped you, right?" She squinted. "Enoch, are you feeling okay? You're acting weird. You look ... feverish." Pursing her lips, she reached toward his face.

He grabbed her hand before she touched it. Her fingers were like ice. "Uh ... I was sick. But I'm okay now. Mostly. I feel strange sometimes. Like I'm not ... myself. They make me drink sleeping drafts. Potions and ... things."

Ha! Exactly as I predicted in Scenario No. 7. Hopefully, now she'll attribute any discrepancies in the persona to the effects of drugs.

She twined her fingers with his, and he experienced a frisson. "I'm so sorry. Are you suffering?" Her eyes were huge and dark in her pale face.

How deep they go, like scrying pools. I could look into them for an Age.

An alien, uncomfortable feeling squirmed inside William, and he wrenched his gaze away. What was the matter with him? It was that cursed Northward she was so concerned about, not *him.* If she figured out he wasn't Northward, then she'd have that suns-burnt sword at his throat quicker than he could say "bloody decapitation." He cast a surreptitious look at the blade riding at her hip. In Scenario No. 8, she attacked him, but he'd deemed it an unlikely outcome based on her reluctance to harm him the first time they'd met.

Suddenly, he craved a pull of whiskey. No, a whole barrel of whiskey. He cleared his throat. "It's not so bad," he said gruffly. "I'm fine."

Why are you still holding her hand? Yes, this feels nice, but—argh! This game is perilous. Release. Her. Hand. And yet, he hesitated.

"Don't act all macho; you're obviously uncomfortable." Glancing down, she gave his hand a squeeze and fretted at her lower lip. "Maybe I could try to heal you like I healed Si—" A slight frown wrinkled her brow. "Wait a sec ..." Her gaze rose to meet his. "Enoch, where's your armor?"

"My armor?" Nervous energy jolted William. He was still processing "try to heal you." Could she heal? Could she reach inside him and winkle out the truth? *If only I had some wyldling snare with me.* But he'd needed it all to bind Northward—just in case.

"Is it because of the wyldling snare?" she asked, her eyes all wide and innocent.

He flinched, yanking his hand from hers, and blinked, his mind racing. "The wyldling snare!" he gasped. *She knows about the snare? Can she read my mind? I must be more cautious. Time to switch over to Scenario No. 3.*

"Yes, the wyldling snare. That has to be it. How'd you know about that?"

"Hadrien told me in my dreams." Grabbing his arms, she grinned. "Oh, Enoch, one of the Sages—just like in your book, *Fortulles Evaingynon Seprima!* Raeden brought it along for me, so I could learn about Tehara." Her gaze intensified. "Are you seeing any of the Sages in your dreams? Apparently, they're all dead, so now Commander Storm's teaching me how to block my mind. He seems to think it's been invaded by an imposter. He didn't say as much, but I—"

"The wyr-um, e-evaingynon?" William's voice came out strangled-sounding. "N-no, can't say that I've seen any of them."

What she says is impossible. The wyrmkin are supposed to be dead.

"Oh." Her face fell. Her fingers dropped from his arms. "It's probably the wyldling snare. Hadrien says it's stifling our connection, but ... how is it we're able to meet now?"

Despite his unease, William couldn't conceal a grin. He'd planned for this question in Scenario No. 2, eager to expound on his own theories about the wyldling snare, even if his audience couldn't follow. But she seemed clever enough. "My bindings have been relaxed. Apparently, the resistance necessary to break through the snare's interdiction is directly proportional to the amount of snare in contact with my skin. So, here we are." He raised his arms and let them fall.

Annabelle snorted as she stood akimbo and raised her eyebrows. "How technical, Enoch. I didn't realize you collected polysyllabic words as well."

William braced himself for an attack, but she only laughed and patted his arm. She was smiling again, and her eyes sparkled. What was that strange twisting in his gut and the heat rising inside him? He swallowed and cleared his expression, although his heart was pounding so hard he feared she'd hear it.

He should leave. Now. She'd revealed where Northward's rescue party was going. There'd be other opportunities to study her ... so long as he didn't muck this up.

Annabelle's smile faded. "Enoch, can you tell me anything about the people who kidnapped you? We already know about Ravenos, but who was he working for? Raeden said witchcraft was involved, somehow." She glanced aside, biting her lower lip. "Magic, anyway."

Okay, excellent. Scenario No. 1 had this covered. Instead of answering, William found himself staring at her mouth. *That's a highly distracting habit she has.* Everything about her was distracting. She must be casting some type of beguilement on him. However, the cadence of her speech didn't suggest this. But what did he know about manipulators of the Aethyr? He should have prepared a shield. At the very least, he shouldn't have allowed her to touch him.

"Enoch?" She frowned and waved a hand in front of his face. "Are you okay?"

"I can't tell you about my abductors," he blurted. "Something won't let me, even though I want to." He cleared his throat. "They must've placed some foul enchantment on me." *Like the one you're casting on me, Milady Blue.*

She tilted her head. "I can't put my finger on it, but there's something different about you." Color rose in her cheeks as she hugged herself and averted her gaze. "The way you act. The way you're looking at me. It's ... strange."

Suns burn me to ash, I've mucked it up! William stiffened. It was as if his brain had stopped functioning. None of his scenarios accounted for her muddling his thoughts. All nine danced about in his head, blurring together into nonsense.

To gain space to breathe, he turned away and crossed his arms, digging his nails into silk. Into his skin. He stared in horror. The sleeves of the fancy jacket rippled and his burkheld returned from the elbows down. After a moment of concentration, the coarse brown cloth shifted to the embroidered silk of Northward's jacket.

Is she doing this? Eroding my glamourie while pretending to be fooled? Perhaps she's not so guileless after all ...

Annabelle slipped around him and took his right hand in both of hers, those blue eyes as wide and innocent-looking as ever. William managed—just barely—to not yank it out of her grip. *Quick, say something—anything!*

"It's the wyldling snare," he said in a rush. "It's been messing with my head, and I fear it's changing my personality."

Annabelle gasped and stared at him. "Oh, no! We need to find you as soon as possible." Lowering her gaze, she rubbed her thumbs along the back of his hands. "I'm not sure exactly how Commander Storm plans to rescue you. He's so close-mouthed about it—" a scowl contorted her features, "—and he says he's going to leave me at Treehome because I can't fight and I lost my connection with you." She brightened. "But now he'll let me come, for sure. Maybe if I told him I saw you—"

"You can't tell him anything," he blurted as he pulled his hand from hers. Her touch distracted him. "You meeting me here must remain our secret, Mil—Annabelle."

Annabelle stared at him with her brow furrowed. "Why?"

Panic swirled like a tempest, sweeping away his well-laid plans like embers on the wind. Wait. Scenario No. 9 provided a contingency for this. "My captors," he began, "I didn't want to tell you ..." He turned away to hide his crooked grin and made fists at his sides. "I heard them talking. You know they've put a spell on me, but there's more to it. They know about you, Annabelle. They know we meet in the dreamscape. The instant they suspect the Commander knows how to locate us—them ..." He paused for effect. "They'll drain my blood and extract my power. And then they'll use it to find you and do the same to you."

Oh, that's a brilliant idea! Why didn't I think of making threats like that before? Northward will be putty in my hands once I'm done—

Arms slid around his chest and Annabelle pressed against him. William froze. Why had he turned his back on her? Why hadn't he left already? The glamourie wouldn't last much longer; Those strange twistings in his gut probably meant it was unraveling. That's why his stomach felt unsettled. And if Annabelle saw who he really was—recognized him as Varazslo—she'd draw her sword and eviscerate him for all this trickery. With that armor on, she could crush him. She could make ...

She made weird hiccoughing sounds. Her hands fisted in the borrowed jacket, body shaking like Tenebris had cast the Pain Hex on her. "Oh, Enoch," she choked out. "I'm sorry."

She's ... weeping?

How did he make it stop? Discomfort writhed inside him like a nest of serpents. That had to be the spell failing. *Leave, now!*

Wrenching himself from her embrace, he turned and grabbed her shoulders. She stared up at him, all shimmering eyes, blotchy face, and trembling lips. "I'll keep praying for you, Enoch. And don't forget, we're coming to get you."

The twisting in his gut worsened. He had to use the defense cantrip—now! William readied his arkhabala and opened his mouth to speak words that would sear her to the bone. "I'll try to see you again," he blurted instead. Villem's chained flail! Why had he said that? He hadn't meant to say that!

I must flee.

William blurred away to his tower before she could launch another assault. Releasing the glamourie sent a ripple of relief through his arkhabala, similar to a cramped muscle finally relaxing. Himself again, William slammed down his wards—he'd constructed them to be more powerful than ever—and rested his forehead against cool stones. How could she still be affecting him? It took some time to wrestle his emotions back under control.

Once recovered, he leaned over the drafting table and the diagram he'd drawn for the Northward disguise. A smirk tugged at his lips. What an excellent way to gather intelligence on their pursuers' movements. Despite some ... miscalculations, he'd fooled Annabelle. All the spellform required was a stronger defense element to block out whatever she'd done to him. Messing with his emotions ... How in blazes had Northward spent time in her company and retained any vestige of sanity? Taking up his pen, he dipped it in ink and began scribing new elements in the diagram.

As he worked, he tried to ignore the persistent echo of gut-twisting discomfort.

An icicle poked his cheek. William shook his head. *Go away.* The icicle returned, prodding him insistently.

Hands raised to fend off the irritant, William jolted awake and stared into a pair of luminous amber eyes. A brown-furred hand withdrew a three-pronged sword-breaker, the longest middle prong glinting in the starlight.

Blazing harkhurz had been sticking a weapon in his face!

He snarled a vicious oath as he pushed himself up. "Zakaar, scorch your ears! What are you on about? And where's Tenebris?" Knowledge of his discoveries weighed upon his mind even as giddiness made his heart race. He must report what he'd learned about the rescue mission.

The harkhurz hunkered beside him. Whiskers twitched and amber eyes glinted as he sheathed the sword-breaker in a scabbard strapped to one thigh. Suppressed laughter colored his reply. "I find you asleep on the job, Dulciber. Milord," he added, stressing the title, "eats his supper by the fire. I am thinking he will not be pleased to see laziness, so I awaken you."

"You didn't have to shove blistering steel in my face," William grumbled. "I would've woken on my own soon enough. And I wasn't being lazy, you ignorant mudpuppy; I was *working.*" He surveyed the spellform he'd set up. The candle had gone out, but everything else remained the same. He was relieved to see the glass woman figurine still undamaged and upright. Tenebris would kill him if he broke it. He opened his satchel and began placing items inside.

"I saw no work being done," Ravenos said, chuckling. "You were curled up like a baby. And snoring. Loudly. I have heard saws cut wood more quietly."

William paused in the act of wrapping the female figure and turned to examine his companion. Ravenos sounded almost ... jocular. Like he had before the Blood Rage sickness contaminated his mind. William's annoyance faded as he broke into a grin. Day by day, Ravenos improved. The elixir was working.

Also, he'd woven a convincing illusion of Northward, found and fooled Annabelle, and learned details of the evainghir's plan to reclaim the knight. William knew their destination. Either Tenebris or the Dreadlord could devise a plan to intercept them.

Doubtless, the Dreadlord would reward William for his part—perhaps even allow him to study the wyldlings.

Hmm. That idea he'd come up with to terrify Annabelle, about extracting Enoch's power ... intriguing. Would draining a wyldling's blood make their power available to him? Perhaps he could experiment on Northward—if he could repress his queasiness at the sight of another's blood.

Something to consider.

Tilting his head back, William gazed into the sky. The constellation Valeshka's Eye had risen. Witnessing his triumph. *My stars*, he thought. *And they are surely rising.* He released the laughter building inside him.

Ravenos eyed him askance. "Dulciber, are you well? That was not such a funny joke."

As he nestled the figurine in its place, William allowed his mirth to subside. "I wasn't laughing at what you said. Not everything is about you." He closed the satchel and turned to the harkhurz. With a smirk, he added, "I'm pleased because my spell was an absolute success. Through the Seeking, I've learned something of vital importance about the location of our enemies. I must tell Ten—I mean, Master Tenebris."

The harkhurz's ears lifted, and he rose in one fluid motion. He bared his teeth in an approximation of a grin. "Surely this will bring you great honor, my friend."

William snorted, shouldering the satchel. "It had better." He strode down the hill, the hem of his robe whisking through the grass. If this didn't satisfy his master concerning his competence with the Arkhabadh, then nothing would.

William stood with his master a little apart from the fire-pit where the six Golorum enjoyed their after-dinner drinks. Freezing void! He craved whiskey. His arkhabala prickled under his master's intense gaze. Face unreadable, Tenebris stared at him while stroking his beard. William swallowed thickly and refused to lower his eyes. After sending Ravenos away, he'd told his master much of what Annabelle divulged to him, while making it seem as if all the details arose from his deft and inspired handling of the Seeker's Web. Tension built in him like a coiled spring while he waited.

Tenebris broke the silence. "You claim to have eavesdropped on a conversation," he said, arching an eyebrow. "A conversation between the Commander and another. Yet, how did you acquire a link to the evainghir?" William made a sound of protest and the Arkhadahn raised a hand. "I'm not saying I don't believe your account, William; I'm trying to understand the process you used. At your level, the Seeker's Web is not so versatile a tool that one constructs merely based on the desire to follow a specific individual. You need hair, skin, and blood linking him to a poppet. And the evainghir is too canny to leave bits of himself lying about for bumbling apprentices to pick up."

Eyes glowing, he leaned closer. Gray kythim flared into existence around him, sparks of turquoise rising along paths of lavender. William stared. He'd never seen that before in his master's kythim. What emotions were those?

Iron-hard fingers grasped his chin and forced him to meet his master's gaze. "Stop gaping like an imbecile, William. I'm talking to you. Now, explain yourself. And for Valeshka's sake, speak clearly. Don't mumble."

He wouldn't tell Tenebris about Annabelle. No. This was *his* discovery. He'd snared Milord High-and-Mighty without his master's help; he'd snare Milady Blue in a like manner. Half his work was done. She was already en route. Soon, he'd have her.

Once I stand before the Dreadlord, I will reap all the glory of capturing the wyldlings.

William forced himself to hold his master's gaze. His throat worked at producing sound. "I, uh ... collected specimens from that clearing where we captured Northward." He shrugged. "Must've got lucky and found someone close to the Commander. Their trail led to him."

Valkor's Scythe! I can't believe I said something so daft. The tesseramint's beguilement has muddled my brain for certain. There's no way Tenebris will believe that load of dung.

Tenebris's eyes burned into him for another heartbeat. And then he released William's chin and straightened. His kythim faded from view. "It is a most unorthodox use of the spell. For a Second Circle apprentice, sound is the least of the sensory impressions. And—you say—sound was all you received."

Second Circle, indeed! Mixed blood or not, he ought to have gained the Third Circle a season ago. When would Tenebris admit he was ready to advance? William worked the ache of Tenebris's fingers from his jaw. Anger heated his words. "Who cares about orthodoxy, so long as I achieved the desired results?" Ice-water flushed through his veins. Heart pounding, he awaited the blow in response to his audacity.

Tenebris looked at him. Then he threw back his head and laughed.

William blinked at the light-hearted, carefree sound of amusement. *Unorthodoxy seems to be going around tonight,* he mused. He'd never heard Tenebris laugh like that.

With a fierce grin, the Arkhadahn grabbed William's shoulders and shook him. Was that pride glowing in his eyes? "Well done, William. It's about time you showed initiative. Despite all your bumbling, I knew you'd prove your worth as my apprentice." He let go and stepped back, the reserved and grave Arkhadahn once more. "You've come far in the past few weeks, William. Further than I anticipated. I'm of a mind to advance you beyond the Third Circle."

What? William gaped. This had to be a trick—a prelude to another beating. It had to be. But his heart raced and his breath caught as hope surged within him. He'd done the calculations. *With a third circle etched into my arkhabala ... that would more than double the potency of my spells. But ... beyond the Third? How many more circles?*

Better not show eagerness. Or ask for clarification. His master had been known to offer him something he wanted and then yank it from his grasp—to teach him patience and keep him hungry. Or so he said.

While tucking his hands inside his sleeves, William composed himself. "When, Master?"

"Once we arrive at the Dreadlord's stronghold." Tenebris glanced at him sidelong. His master didn't seem fooled by his calm facade. "However, you must prove you can master Sixth Circle spells. I know you've been preparing."

William started. Did Tenebris plan to raise him to the *Sixth* Circle? No, surely not. Six Circles denoted acolyte status.

Tenebris's smile widened. "You believe me unaware of your activities, but I can tell you've been rummaging through my spells. How else could your Seeker Web have been so fruitful? And I know all about your silly treasure trove of items stolen from that knight you transformed, and the scrolls you study on the sly. You've fooled no one with your little charade."

William licked his lips. He needed a drink. Did Tenebris know about the whiskey flask? Was his master leaving that out on purpose, to give William an opportunity to confess? "Master, I can ex—"

Tenebris held up a hand. "Spare me your excuses. I'm not angry, William. Neither am I ... pleased with you, precisely. However, our journey has provided time in which to pursue new avenues of thought. Consider things in a different light. You took the knight's effects as spoils by right of conquest. The Dreadlord honored you with his gift of knowledge—even if it was of the unclean Aethyr." Crossing his arms, Tenebris raised an eyebrow. "Which I know you've used to fuel your spells, to have had such success. It explains that knight's transformation. Don't deny it."

William stiffened as a shock went through him. "Master, I ... I didn't do it on purpose." *Wait, am I in trouble? He's not yelling or beating me. What gives? Is Tenebris ill?*

His master smirked. "Of course you did. Why do you think I revealed your sire and then forced you to claim that ridiculous kadorei name 'Dulciber' as your own?"

You didn't force me to do anything, Tenebris. If it's truly my name, then I claim it because I want to. The flames of anger stirred within him, but he tamped them down and told his master what he wanted to hear. "To shame me."

"True, but not only for that." Tenebris grinned, the old familiar cruelty glinting in his eyes. He chuckled. "It appears your studies on the Aethyr and its practitioners were not as in depth as I'd hoped. Ah, well ... a pity you aren't as clever as you believe."

There's the insult and the cryptic statement I was expecting. But why wasn't Tenebris angry about his use of Aethyr? He'd always insisted it was an "unclean" power.

William swallowed his exasperation. "What do you mean, Master?"

Retaining the shark-like smile, Tenebris tilted his head and shook a finger at him. "Ah, ah, William. Puzzle it out for yourself. Information obtained without cost lacks value."

Ducking his head, William clenched his jaw. *I will, Tenebris.*

His master chuckled again. "Prepare yourself, Arkhasuhl. Upon our arrival at Fastness, I shall test your readiness to advance to the Sixth Circle."

William eyed his master warily. *Suns burn and blister me. He's serious!* "T-thank you, Master. I'll be ready."

Tenebris waved a hand. "Now we've settled that ... time to inform the Dreadlord about what you found. Come." He whirled, robes flapping around his legs as he stalked toward the hulking silhouette of the wagon, where the components of the Farspeaker array awaited. Tenebris—inept where devices were concerned— would require his help.

Be it to the Third or Sixth, Tenebris truly plans to promote me. As an acolyte, it won't be long before I'm able to challenge him. William smothered a grin as he hurried after his master. It wouldn't do to betray his excitement. *My stars really are rising.*

Battlecrows

Reprimands

"What are you so happy about?" Toad's voice broke the expectant stillness of the predawn air. "Get your head in the game, kiddo."

Annabelle's elation shattered like a glass goblet. She sucked her lips between her teeth to stifle her smile. Although her head felt grainy and half-asleep, part of her was still giddy over meeting Enoch. Their connection had returned! Commander Storm *had* to let her continue. True, there had been some rather unsettling bits she couldn't quite recall—and Enoch had behaved rather oddly—but she'd wanted to share her joy. Work through what she'd learned with Toad and get his opinion.

Unfortunately, Toad was even grumpier this morning than he'd been yesterday. Perhaps he hadn't slept well, but, as usual, he refused to discuss his problems with her, and shut down every attempt to broach the subject of her dream.

I need to tell Toad about meeting Enoch—tell him he's still alive. Maybe then he'd be in a better mood. He can help me work out the bits I can't recall, and we can present the good news to Commander Storm together. But now isn't the time.

Toad's eyes narrowed. "Maybe I'm not pushing you hard enough. Your stance is sloppy. One decent shove, and you'll fall over. Bend those knees more and straighten your shoulders."

She rolled her eyes. "Yes, sir." Huffing out a sigh, she adjusted her stance and grudgingly admitted that this improved her balance. She clutched her weapon, one hand grasping the hilt, and the other wrapped around the scabbard, ready to draw. Memory stirred, sluggish. Something from her dream. Something important. Unease slithered through her. She examined Murder Stick's simple crossguard as if it was the most fascinating object in the world, willing the memory to surface.

"Well?" Toad's voice cracked through her musings. "Quit making faces at the blasted thing and use it."

"Sorry." Annabelle winced. "Gimme a sec. I'm still waking up."

Toad's throat sac fluttered. "As if a real opponent would be so accommodating." In a lisping falsetto, he said, "Oh, excuse me, Mr. Enemy, sir. I'm a bit indisposed. Could you please wait a sec?" He deepened his tone. "Of course! I see you're distracted. Shall I stand aside until you're ready? No rush; take your time." He groaned, then spoke in his normal voice, "In a real fight, you won't have the luxury of time, kiddo. There's a reason a warrior's mantra is: 'Momentum is life. Inertia means death.' Your enemy won't hesitate. Don't you remember what Commander Storm said yesterday about freezing up in battle?"

"Yeah," she muttered, pushing aside her unease. She needed to focus on the present. *Murder Stick practice now, worry about dreams later.*

Indeed, Commander Storm had mentioned the warrior's mantra yesterday. He'd pulled her aside after they passed through the waystone at second-noon. "It's time to begin your sword training in earnest," he'd said. "You must ingrain the sequences to muscle memory. This requires regular and consistent practice." While their lunch simmered over the fire, he showed her several sword forms. The three stances were the most rudimentary, the very first a novice learned. His demonstration made the sword forms look so easy, and his movements were graceful despite his height and bulk.

Annabelle swallowed a groan. No way she'd ever be half that good.

Toad's eye ridges lifted. "Ready when you are, kiddo."

Inhale through the nose, then exhale through the mouth. Odors filled her nostrils—of burnt firewood and a heady, floral scent reminiscent of hyacinths that reminded her of Easter. *Nothing exists but the air entering and leaving my lungs.*

Centered, she took another deep breath. "Alrighty then." Drawing Murder Stick, she began the opening sequence.

"Kiddo, stop! Your stance is all wrong."

Annabelle grimaced. She recalled yesterday's lesson. *I have to focus.* She repositioned herself and launched into the first form. Mirroring the memory of the Commander's dance, she flowed through to the end of the sequence, and then sheathed her sword.

"Much better. That's more like it. Do it again."

With a faint groan, she drew her blade and did as he directed. Enoch had been through all this. One of these days, it was going to click. What she wouldn't give to carry the forms through correctly to completion.

Toad's criticism broke into her musings. "You're overreaching. Keep it tight. It's vital you keep your guard up."

Irritation spiked through her. "I'm trying."

"Yes, very," Toad remarked in a wry tone. "You're doing okay, really. All things considered. Because of your height, you have a distinct disadvantage when it comes to reach. When you extend your arm like that, your opponent could slip past your guard and skewer you. Focus on the defense, for now."

Great. Now he's patronizing me. "Yes, sir," she hissed through gritted teeth, and moved on to the second form.

"No. Do the first one again. I want to see your improvements."

Toad demanded she go through the first sword form several more times before he muttered, "Good enough," and allowed her to move on to the second. When she messed up, he made her go back to the beginning of the first sword form and do both over again.

With the image firmly in mind of Commander Storm executing the sword forms, she forced her trembling limbs into action. As a faint glow lightened the forest, she went through the sequence of movements. Thoughts of her dream kept intruding, and she remembered a detail that chilled her blood.

I must tell Commander Storm about that spell on Enoch. The Commander could kill him by trying to rescue him! That means he can't go ... I have to be the one to do it. With or without others' help. Whether the Commander likes it or not.

Annabelle's muscles were burning when she completed the first two stances and flowed into the third form.

"Stop," Commander Storm's voice cracked like a whip. "I've seen enough."

Yikes! He's back from his patrol.

Annabelle crashed to a halt, groaning. Her palm was slick with sweat. She gasped for breath. Her muscles screamed, and her right arm dropped, trembling, to her side. She tightened her grip on Murder Stick's hilt until her fingers ached.

I won't let go. My weapon must always be at hand.

"Well," her amphibian trainer remarked dryly, "that was ... something."

"Womanchild." Briefly, Commander Storm measured her with his steely gaze. "At ease. Sir Thomas, with me." He jerked his head toward the fire-pit.

Head bowed, Toad sighed. "Yes, sir."

Annabelle sheathed Murder Stick, almost missing the scabbard. *Fudge! That could've been bad.* She staggered over to the nearest tree and leaned against it, catching her breath while watching her companions.

Over by the campfire, the Commander and Toad spoke too low for her to hear. The huge warrior gripped his swords, his reptilian visage tight. At one point, Toad cringed.

Is he being reprimanded?

When they finished, the Commander dismissed Toad. He hopped away into the bracken ferns surrounding the glade. Annabelle straightened as Commander Storm strode over to her. He loomed between her and the rising sun, his shadowy form filling her vision. "Proficiency will come with time and practice. However, you must take this training seriously. You cannot—I repeat—cannot allow your mind to wander with cold steel in your hand."

Face burning, she lowered her gaze to his sturdy leather boots. His feet were three times the size of her own. A finger under her chin forced her to look up into his narrowed eyes.

The Commander tapped her forehead. "Focus, womanchild. Your mind must become an arrow aimed at its target. A blade thrown with deadly accuracy. Without focus, you shall never progress." He let go of her chin. "Now," he continued, more gently, "clean up. I'll expect your report whilst we travel."

His massive figure wavered in her vision as he walked away.

"For the love of Jeremiah Bullfrog!" Toad groused.

There's that classic rock song reference again!

"I didn't sign up for this when I became a knight. Mule-headed kids and moody girls ..." Bracken rustled, and Toad's grumbling drew closer, practically at her feet. In the gathering light, she made out his dark brown, warty body as he hopped on a stone nestled between two raised roots.

"Toad," she said. "I've been wondering. This Jeremiah Bullfrog you mentioned ... is he a friend of yours?"

"No clue." Toad looked confused. "I never understood a single word he said."

Annabelle barked a laugh. *Just like in the song! But how could Toad know about that?*

Eyes like electric blue fire glowered up at her. "Kind of like you, kiddo."

He looks angry. Is he going to yell at me? The last thing she needed was another scolding. She wished she knew whether he cared about her, or just put up with her out of a sense of duty. She trembled as emotions she couldn't parse or pigeonhole—something like pity, exasperation, and a tingly warmth—surged through her in a maelstrom. "What do you mean?"

Gaze fixed on hers, Toad took a deep breath. "What I mean, is ..." He ducked his head and groaned. "I'm sorry, kiddo. For being impatient. I got frustrated, seeing you need help and not being able to *do* anything in this ... body." His vocal sac pulsed. "Shouldn't've taken it out on you like that." Blinking, he glanced at her. "You did good, all things considered."

He did care! With a hoarse cry, Annabelle scooped up Toad as if he were a twenty-pound cat and kissed him between the eyes. He stiffened and—like the first time—spasmed and squalled.

"Oh! I'm so sorry!" She let him slip out of her arms, and he crouched in the dirt looking pole-axed. "I keep forgetting you're a knight, not my pet. I'm sorry." She sniffled, wiping her nose. "Commander Storm's right; I need to learn how to focus. It's just ... so *hard*. I've never been good at athletic stuff, and whenever I try, my mind goes careening off on random trajectories."

She nibbled her lower lip. Maybe Toad would be open to discussing her dream now. "Speaking of which ... My dream last night. It's really important. I'm confused about what happened, and I want to piece it all together with you before I report anything to the Commander. Can we please discuss it now?"

Toad shook his head; she feared he'd brush her off again, like he always did. Then he sighed. "If it's important, then I suppose we should. Before I—"

With a harsh cry, Peter burst through the canopy in a scattering of leaves and stray feathers. He landed in a crouch, wild-eyed and tail lashing, then bounded to the Commander, who listened to his report, his attention honed like a razor.

Now what? Annabelle exchanged a look with Toad. They went over to hear the news.

"... don't know what they're doing there," Peter was saying. "But it can't mean no good, them bein' where they are."

"It is not for you to speculate," Commander Storm snapped, one hand resting on the pommel of a sword. "Your task is to relay your observations. Were you seen?"

Peter ducked his head, ears drooping. "I ... no. Any messenger-spy worth his giblets knows the tricks of the trade."

Glance shifting to Annabelle, he perked up. The Commander stared to the north, frowning and fingering his sword hilts.

Toad hopped in front of Annabelle. She pulled up short rather than trip over him. "What's going on, sir?" he asked.

"There's a big company of soldiers between us and the waystone," Peter burst out just as the Commander opened his mouth. "Looks like a caravan, but I couldn't get close enough to be sure." The syrax cringed. "Sorry, Dukey."

Annabelle clapped her hands over her mouth to hide a grin. Commander Storm would dump more training on her if he saw her laughing at Peter's silly rendering of his ducal title.

The evainghir bared his teeth. "Enough, buzzard. Return—"

Just then, Raeden rode Lorun into camp, his quiver bristling with new arrows he'd acquired from a weapons cache. He regarded Annabelle, then looked from Peter to the Commander as he dismounted. "Lord Commander. Is something wrong?"

"Your Excellency," the Commander said. "You served as a caravan guard for a season. I require your assessment of a potential threat. The buzzard shall lead you. Reconnoiter and then report back at the first rendezvous point."

Peter flicked his ears back, but he nodded. "Will do." With a mischievous glint in his eyes, he added, "Will do ... *Dukey*. Ha!" With a squawk, Peter sprang backwards and then launched himself to the far side of camp in a flurry of flapping wings, beyond the Commander's reach.

Raeden dipped his head. "Yes, Lord Commander." He glanced at Annabelle.

Commander Storm's mouth twitched. "I will remain with the womanchild." He sounded amused as he rummaged through one of Tinker's panniers. "Nothing will get by me. Not even a pack of lykharim."

Raeden stepped back, eyes widening. "Of course." He shot one final look at her, swung up on his mount, and cantered off, melting into the forest in Peter's wake.

Annabelle's eyes followed him until he disappeared. She twisted the reins in her hands and glanced at the Commander. She shuddered. Seeing the bladed tail-rings he removed from the pannier sent a chill down her spine. He'd worn those when they'd fled the beasts in the nightmare forest. "C-Commander. Is this going to be like ... like before? With the lykharim."

Commander Storm glanced up from strapping on his tail-blades to regard her with an inscrutable expression. "No. It's likely to be worse. Our foes are even greater in number and possess human intelligence. However, we must continue as planned." He tightened the final buckle. "Your report on the dreamscape must wait. Going forward, we travel in silence."

A Familiar Standard

Atropos was rising when Raeden met them on the trail, ears drooping and eyes dark. Tension radiated off him as he drew Lorun up beside Tinker, where Annabelle sat, paging through Enoch's book, searching for more information on the wyldling snare. After a glance at her, he spoke softly in a clipped tone. "Lord Commander, your servant regrets he finds not a merchant caravan. It is a mercenary company under a banner one has not seen before. They make no sign of moving."

Commander Storm nodded, his face hardening. "It is as I suspected. Describe their standard."

Raeden's eyes glazed. He stared into the middle distance, and his tone was stilted, as if he recited from memory. "A great black bird, like a raven, on a field of bloody red." He spread the fingers of both hands. "Wings outstretched and beak pointed to the sky. Swords and arrows lie broken beneath its claws."

The evainghir's lips rose to bare his teeth. "Battlecrows," he snarled. "It seems Captain Wuya survived that skirmish, after all. No one else would dare carry that standard."

Annabelle flinched at his sharp teeth and the rage in his visage; she'd never seen him betray such potent emotion. *Whoa. Whoever this Captain Wuya is, they sure made him mad.*

Quick as lightning, the Commander composed his features to a trooper's wooden blankness. His tone was ... calm. "Are they still deployed as the buzzard claimed?"

"Yes, Lord Commander." Raeden's ears quivered and his regard settled on Annabelle. "They stand direct in our path."

Annabelle's heart hammered, squeezing out her breath. The kaenhir eased Lorun close enough to brush against Tinker. "Your orders?"

Toad's eyes gleamed from the saddlebag. He poked his head out and watched the evainghir, waiting.

Commander Storm stood tall, his face implacable as a bluff of sheer granite. "We continue on, albeit with more caution than before. The tree should screen us. Our troop is small. We may slip past them unseen, if we take care." He looked at Annabelle. "Remain vigilant, womanchild."

She swallowed. "Yes, sir. With my weapon in hand." She grasped Murder Stick's hilt and offered him a wan smile.

He nodded, a grin twitching at his mouth before disappearing. "Stay close," he turned and set out, prowling through the trees, leather armor dappled with sunslight and leaf shadows—one hand always near a blade. His matte black tail-blades reflected no light.

The scent of pepper, cardamom, and a hint of stale sweat filled her nostrils. "Even if you cannot see him, your servant will stay near you." Raeden's breath tickled her ear. "He gives his solemn vow. No man—no enemy—shall touch you." Words jammed in her throat, so she nodded. He clicked his tongue. Tinker moved forward.

Images of war and bloodshed from movies and television filled her mind. She shivered and her breath faltered. Her eyes dropped to find Toad staring at her.

"It'll be all right, kiddo," he whispered without a trace of sarcasm. "We'll get through this." He swiveled, pale eyes taking in their surroundings. Oddly, his blunt reassurance and alert reconnaissance soothed as much as Raeden's.

Annabelle chewed on her lower lip. *He didn't say "don't be afraid," I notice.* Her heart thudded against her breastbone. Not like she could simply switch off her fear, anyway. Commander Storm hadn't taught her that yet. *But I can practice my breathing and slow my heart rate.* There wasn't much else for her to do—besides fret and worry.

Nothing seemed amiss as they traversed the rough terrain. Having made an arrangement with Toad, Annabelle studied the book in half-hour chunks while he kept watch. She'd reached another story about King Gideon going on a quest to rescue his sister, who'd been enslaved by the harrowdwelfnim and forced to work in an opal mine. The dwelfnim were eager to help him against their enemies.

Long ago, a terrible curse separated the harrowdwelfnim from the dwelfnim, causing the former to despise the light of the suns and retreat to the arctic regions or underground, where they embraced a culture of bloody violence. The tale confused her. Who did the cursing? Why did the two races—closely related before the curse—despise one another? The narrative didn't say. Perhaps the author assumed the reader already knew.

Occasionally, Peter descended to report to the commander. Then she and Raeden drew close for the evainghir's murmured counsel and instruction. Toad also listened intently; the commander's orders for him were simply: "You know what to do." And he would nod as if given a solemn charge.

But what could Toad do if the mercenaries attacked? Despite being a knight with all Enoch's training—and more—he was a man trapped in a toad's body, for goodness' sake.

The Commander dropped back to take Tinker's bridle. Raeden, as promised, lingered nearby. He held an arrow nocked and ready on his war bow as green eyes scanned their environment, ever wary and diligent.

Concerned she would miss an impending attack, she paid attention to her environs. The forest slid by uneventfully. Birds sang in the trees. Insects hummed in the summer air. Leaves rustled in a faint breeze. The sunslight changed angles through the canopy. Strain as she did to hear them, Lorun and Tinker's hoof-falls remained silent. No sign of danger, and the breeze was pleasantly fragrant with floral scents.

She suppressed the sigh building in her lungs. *It's not that I want something to happen ... but I want something to happen. Either that, or a rest. I could do with a break.*

Beside her, Raeden tensed and looked at the canopy. He still held the bow and arrow resting against his knee. Commander Storm slowed, one hand on Tinker's bridle, the other on his sword hilt. Annabelle's breath caught in her throat as she grabbed Murder Stick's hilt.

Is this it?

Peter drifted down from the branches above, his hazel eyes taking them in. The syrax furled his wings. "They still haven't moved," he whispered to the Commander while looking at her. "And they don't look like they're gonna move anytime soon. Have their cook-pots over the fire, setting up camp, tending their weapons, and all that."

"Aye," Commander Storm rumbled. "I had foreseen this." He glanced sidelong at Annabelle. "They're waiting."

Toad's head poked out of the saddlebag. "Enemy scouts?"

Peter shook his head. "Haven't seen none leave. Still the same number in their group as before. They's all just hangin' around, like for a picnic."

"I doubt a picnic's what they have in mind," Toad said.

"Hmmm." Commander Storm surveyed the area. "Then we shall have an hour's rest." He looked at Raeden. "Tend to the womanchild whilst I walk the perimeter. Come, buzzard. I have orders for you."

Annabelle blew out a pent-up breath, watching the Commander stride away. The syrax padded alongside with his tail and ears drooping. *Poor Peter. He looks worn out.*

"It'll be nice to take a break," she murmured as they halted just beyond earshot. Hers, anyway. "The Commander seems indefatigable. He just keeps going and going. Like the Energizer Bunny." She let go of her sword and shook out her fingers.

Toad chuckled. "He needs a drum."

"And what did he mean, 'tend to the womanchild?'" She deepened her voice to mimic the Commander. "I'm not a potted plant."

Toad laughed outright. "Well spotted, kiddo."

She rolled her eyes as she slid from the saddle, then grinned. *I'm getting better at this.*

Raeden replaced the arrow in his quiver and dismounted. "Of course you are not a potted plant. Your servant believes the Lord Commander meant nothing particular by it."

Annabelle smoothed her hand over Tinker's flank. He nuzzled her cheek while she checked his bridle, raising another smile. She scratched under his chin and around his ears. He grunted happily, leaning into her touch. Tinker seemed to have no worries about the mercenary band. *Why can't I be more like him?* She leaned against her mount's muscled neck and put her arms around him.

"I wish there was something I could do."

"Come, Freylin." Raeden offered her his arm. "There is something you can do during the waiting times."

Something other than worry, you mean?

She tucked her hand in the crook of his elbow, and he led her to a rounded stone, where she sat. He knelt beside her and pulled a small book from inside his vest, its well-worn cover the color of dark wine. A golden cross adorned the front.

"Oh." She lowered her head sheepishly. "Of course. We can pray."

Raeden opened his prayer book and flipped to the page he sought. He glanced at her, and then began, "The LORD is my light and my salvation—whom shall I fear?"

"The LORD is the stronghold of my life," Annabelle read, "of whom shall I be afraid?" *A very appropriate choice*, she mused as they took turns reading verses of Psalm Twenty-Seven.

Commander Storm returned just as they were finishing. "Mount up," he said, his expression unreadable as Raeden closed the prayer book and slipped it inside his vest. "We have three hours until the waystone activates."

"Come, Freylin." Raeden offered her a hand. She was grateful for his help; her body seemed reluctant to move. The sunslit glade, with its chirping birds and peaceful air, would've been an excellent place to set up camp and cook their supper.

Commander Storm sent Raeden ahead to scout the safest path and took hold of Tinker's bridle. Before they set out, he said, "Unless it is an emergency—silence from here on out, womanchild. And keep one hand near your sword."

"Yes, sir." Wetting her lips, she touched its pommel.

He stepped closer, his gaze on a level with hers. "If we get separated, you will follow Sir Thomas's orders. This is no time for your adolescent obstinacy and petty arguments. If he tells you to do something, you will do it."

She met his stare before glancing at Toad. "Okay."

Commander Storm narrowed his eyes at Toad. "And you, Sir Thomas. No needling her."

Toad perched on the saddlebag with his head raised proudly, like the knight he was, inside the amphibian. "Yes, sir," he replied. "I remember my duty. I'll protect her."

How is he supposed to do that? Annabelle suppressed a snort. The Commander was leaving her with someone she could pick up and carry. It should be the other way around. Warmth rose from her chest to mantle her face as she imagined a young man—who looked a bit like Neal MacReady—carrying her like a princess in his strong arms.

Pursing her lips, she shifted in the saddle. *Gah! That's* never *happening. Stop thinking about that jerk from school. It's not like we ever dated.*

Toad regarded her soberly, head tilted. "Don't worry, kiddo. It won't come to that. But if it should ... I have a plan."

How comforting. Annabelle swallowed, then grimaced. *Stop that, Ann; this isn't Neal, and Toad's not being sarcastic right now.* This was Sir Thomas, the knight, speaking. If he said he had a plan, then he meant it.

She cast her mind back to Raeden's prayer and the refrain of the Psalm they'd read together. "Be strong and take heart," she said. Thank God her voice was steady.

"Aye." Commander Storm gave her a curt nod. "That's the spirit." With a tug on Tinker's halter, he led them from the glade.

The Commander Versus an Army

She'd seen more people gathered together, but it had been at an REO Speedwagon concert during the Wisconsin State Fair. And this was supposed to be the least-guarded flank. Commander Storm had told her the soldiers were deployed as if their captain expected an enemy to approach from the west.

Annabelle breathed shallowly, her heart in her throat, watching through a screen of bushes as hundreds of armed and armored men assembled into ranks on a broad field. Toad also observed them from his leather nest, his throat sac pulsing.

Despite the mismatched armor, the soldiers appeared both deadly and disciplined. All had a black bird emblazoned on red shields and breastplates. All appeared to be human—kadorei, she reminded herself. On Tehara, every person was considered human, regardless of what they looked like.

Her eyes lifted to the stone ring on top of the hill beyond the mass of soldiers. *We need to be there within an hour.* She fretted at her lower lip and glanced at the evainghir, who stood at his ease and watched the soldiers as if they were on parade. How would Commander Storm get them past these mercenaries?

Tinker shifted beneath her, no doubt agitated by her own nervousness. Patting his neck, she took a deep, calming breath and flexed fingers stiff from grasping her sword hilt. She wiped her damp palm on her trousers as cold unease slithered through her bowels. Neither Raeden nor Peter had joined them; she assumed Commander Storm had given them tasks.

Please God, help them, she prayed. *Help us all.*

Lachesis slipped closer to the eastern horizon. Annabelle squinted. What were those men doing? Ranks shifted, and they milled about before reforming their lines—this time facing away from the forest. Her heart sped up, and she held her breath as the soldiers half-marched, half-jogged to the west. They were leaving the field! But why? She didn't dare ask.

Suddenly, Commander Storm was beside her. "Time to move," he rumbled. He grasped Tinker's bridle and led the stag along the forest's edge. Annabelle kept watching the mercenaries as they moved away. She gasped. "They're not all leaving."

"Enough for our purposes," he growled. "Keep quiet if you love your own skin."

Annabelle grimaced. Soon, they left the cover of the trees. The hill loomed over them, dark and brooding as Lachesis fell behind it. A man shouted, far away. Another took up the cry.

The Commander released the bridle, both hands blurring as he drew his scimitars. "Hyah!" he bellowed as he slapped Tinker's rump with the flat of a blade. "Ride for the waystone!"

He sprinted toward a cadre of men running around the bend. They hesitated, as if taking in the juggernaut charging at them. The figures diminished as Tinker bolted up the hill.

Trembling, Annabelle faced forward and clung to the saddle horn with both hands. The standing stones grew larger. Commander Storm could take care of himself. He'd survived a pack of lykharim with barely a scratch. He could beat eight men.

Couldn't he?

Annabelle grabbed the reins and leaned back. Tinker's gait faltered several paces shy of the stone ring. She turned his head. Dancing, he maneuvered to face back the way they'd come.

"What are you doing?" Toad protested. "Go on, kiddo!"

"I can't," she replied, her voice sounding high and strange in her ears. "Not without the others. Besides, there's no light. The waystone should be glowing."

Toad grumbled. "We're early. It hasn't activated yet." He made an exasperated sound. "At least get inside the ring and hide behind the stones. *Now*, kiddo."

To her shame, that was exactly what she wanted to do. And Toad had given an order. She urged Tinker past the standing stones and into the ring proper. Then she dismounted, bracing herself against the stag. The waystone in the center was an oblong, colorless crystal shot through with multiple inclusions that rendered it opaque. Sunslight refracted in its depths, but no other light shone. With an effort, she turned away and peeked around a tall, dark gray menhir.

Down the hill and around the bend, five armored figures lay scattered on the ground, sprawled in awkward positions like rag dolls. Commander Storm, a whirling dynamo with blades in hand and on his tail, faced three remaining opponents. Soldiers approached from the west at a steady jog—a larger group, this time. Her heart plunged.

"That's twenty men," Toad observed from his perch on Tinker's neck. "An entire platoon." He gulped. "Criminy."

Her right hand cramped. She'd drawn her weapon without being aware of it. The blade shook, along with her knees. Annabelle loosened her grip on Murder Stick; the Commander would tell her she must ration her strength.

Commander Storm's tail whipped a man across the face while he drove the other two back with his blade-work. The one he'd struck tumbled, boneless, to the ground. A sword flashed, and crimson sprayed from another's neck. The last man broke and ran toward a second platoon approaching from the northwest. Commander Storm didn't pursue; he prowled the small rise dividing his attention between both threats.

Annabelle's eyes widened. "What is he doing? He can't hold off—" she swiftly estimated, "— forty mercenaries at once."

"Looks like he's gonna try." Awe filled Toad's voice.

Her voice emerged as a squeak. "That's suicide!" Clutching her sword, she mouthed a silent plea. *Please, God, protect the Commander. Don't let him die. Get him away from those soldiers. Please bring all my—* She froze, her heart knocking against her ribcage. "Where's Raeden? And Peter? Why aren't they back yet?"

"Couldn't say, kiddo," Toad replied. "Sorry." He actually *sounded* sorry. "Wait. Look, kiddo. Up in the sky."

With difficulty, she tore her gaze from the Commander and lifted it to the sky. Something rose-colored shone in the dying rays of Lachesis against a backdrop of whitish gray clouds, growing larger every second. "Peter," she gasped. "Thank God!"

The syrax descended in a flurry of pink feathers. She ran over and threw her left arm around his neck. He nuzzled her cheek. "Annie-O," he said. "Praise Yshua, you're okay."

"Hey," Toad called. "Cat-vulture. Glad you made it."

Annabelle stepped back. "Where's Raeden?" Her heart pounded, and ice coated her insides. *Please tell me he's okay!* She felt brittle at the thought of anything happening to him. Commander Storm fighting forty men was bad enough; she'd shatter like an icicle if they left Raeden behind.

Toad peered down from the saddle. "Have you seen His Excellentness?"

Peter shook his head. "But that don't mean nothin'. If Reddy don't wanna be seen, then nobody'll see him." The syrax turned to Annabelle. "Don't you worry, Annie-O. Sure as the suns rise in the west, he'll be here soon." He shook out his wings with a savage glint in his eyes. "Stand back. Imma go help Dukey egg-strick-you-late hisself."

After Peter launched himself into the sky, Annabelle dashed to the menhir to check on Commander Storm. He still stood on the rise, arms dangling at his sides with swords in hand, seemingly at his ease. The wave of black and red mercenaries was much closer now. Another platoon had joined them. A chill raced down her spine. Sixty men, now.

Shouting drifted to her ears. A soldier in the nearest platoon fell and those coming up behind trampled him. And then another stiffened and dropped. And another.

"What in the world ..."

With an avian shriek, a pink missile plunged from the sky and snatched up a soldier. Peter lifted him, kicking and screaming, into the air above the height of the nearby trees—and then dropped him unceremoniously on top of several others. Commander Storm waited, swords held at the ready.

Peter stooped on another target. Three more soldiers in the front line fell for no apparent reason. Annabelle leaned further around the stone and squinted. One soldier broke away and got within several strides of the Commander. As she watched, his neck sprouted a feathered shaft, and he dropped in his tracks, clutching at his throat and spasming.

Annabelle's heart skipped a beat. A skilled archer was firing arrows at them from the cover of the forest. It had to be Raeden. She realized she was whooping and screaming her friend's name and clapped a hand over her mouth. Hopefully, the battle drowned out her voice.

The mercenaries were in disarray now. Ranks broken and in confusion, soldiers from all three platoons milled about, wiser ones retreating while others continued plowing toward the lone man on the knoll. Several more fell, both arrow-shot and syrax-dropped. This time, the arrows came from a different angle. A mounted figure broke cover. Bow raised and firing arrows, Raeden's upper body remained steady even as Lorun charged up the hill. Four more soldiers fell, targeted with pin-point accuracy.

No way, Annabelle mused. That only happened in the movies. And yet, hadn't he done the same miraculous shooting in Les Koshmarov?

Raeden was halfway to them when he ran out of arrows. He slung the bow over a shoulder and rode into the circle, sliding from the saddle when Lorun halted. He swayed, then steadied himself with eyes locked on hers. "Freylin, are you hurt?"

"N-no," she replied in a tiny voice. Her heart was beating so hard she found it difficult to draw enough air for breath. "Are *you* hurt?"

"*Nich.*" His ears drooped and trembled as he approached. "Your servant is weary. He heard you cry out for him and feared you'd been injured."

"I'm okay."

No, I'm not! Her mind gibbered. *I want to help, but I can't!*

"Kiddo!" Toad stared at the waystone. "Look." An opalescent glow built in its center.

"Freylin," Raeden began, reaching for her.

"Not without Commander Storm." She peered down the hill. The Commander had put down another five soldiers, but more kept coming. As he separated limbs from bodies, Annabelle winced. What if one of her companions lost an arm like that? She eyed Lorun's pannier where Raeden kept the medical supplies. *Somehow, I don't think a poultice would suffice for severed limbs. I need to figure out how I healed Simon.*

Above, Peter dodged black bolts; the new group had archers, as well. *Oh, crud.* Her grip tightened on Murder Stick's hilt. She sucked her teeth as she watched his aerial dance draw closer to the stone ring. "Hurry, Peter," she murmured. Raeden touched her shoulder.

As if he sensed her concern, Peter's eyes fastened on her and his beak parted in a piercing cry. It seemed like he grinned. He flared his wings wide, stalling his flight, and then tucked them in to dive toward a gap between two standing stones. Toad shouted, "Cat-vulture!" A black bolt struck a wing. Peter shrieked and tumbled from the sky, his trajectory going wide. Pink feathers flew as he struck a menhir and then slid to the ground.

The pressure of Raeden's hand increased. "Freylin—"

Annabelle screamed. "Peter!" She shrugged off the restraining hand and ran toward the downed syrax. "Please, God." She reached for the blue light she knew dwelled inside her somewhere. "Another miracle. Please." Nothing. Teeth gritted, she swallowed a sob.

Raeden hauled her back. "You cannot help him now."

"No," she wailed, straining. Even if she couldn't replicate what had happened with Simon, she had to get to Peter. There must be something she could do. "The medicine!" She whirled and collided with Raeden on her way to Lorun.

The kaenhir grabbed her arms, his gaze intent on her own. "Your servant will fetch Peter. Stay here." Annabelle froze at the command in his voice, then nodded. In a few strides, Raeden reached the syrax. He didn't flinch when a crossbow bolt struck the menhir inches from his head. Jaw clenched, he seized Peter's harness, dragged him inside the ring, and left him at the foot of the glowing waystone.

Eyes slitted, Peter twitched, and his beak parted in a mewling cry. Blood seeped from around the crossbow bolt buried where his wing merged with his back, staining rosy feathers a dark crimson. Her fingers itched to pull it out, to staunch the bleeding, but her feet remained stuck to the ground. Tears stung her eyes. *What if he's dying, and I can't help him?*

"Stupid deer," Toad croaked as Tinker sidled, snorting, across the hilltop. "If I had hands, I'd teach you who's boss. Kiddo! Stop monkeying around and get over by the waystone."

Raeden trudged over, his breathing rough as he set a hand on her shoulder. "Freylin. Come to the waystone." He glanced behind her, and his eyes widened.

Annabelle turned. Nearing the base of the hill, Commander Storm put down the final pair of soldiers from the first platoon, their heads tumbling free from necks spouting gore. Annabelle shrieked, and Raeden's grip tightened.

Teeth bared, the evainghir whirled and met her gaze. "Go, child!"

"Freylin." Raeden tugged on her shoulder. "Come. Remember, the crossbows."

"Sir Thomas," the evainghir roared as he jogged to the base of the hill, "Raeden, by the Great Below, get her through, or I'll slice off your—" His voice cut off. He jerked and went stiff, his eyes wide, as a black bolt punched through his shoulder. And then another sprouted below it.

Annabelle screamed in wordless anguish.

This can't be happening. Commander Storm is invincible. He can't—

A third black bolt slammed into his side, and he staggered.

No!

Shouting, Raeden tugged again, but she pulled away, blinking tears and choking back sobs. With a snarl, Commander Storm yanked out the black bolts and then labored up the hill. The new platoon was at the base with several mercenaries at his heels. One raised a crossbow.

Toad's voice was cold. "Oh, no, you don't."

The man with the crossbow burst into flames and ran, screaming, a human torch.

"What was that?" Annabelle gasped, whirling in time to see Toad collapse—*what the heck?*—and slide from Tinker's saddle. With a cry, she caught him before he struck the ground.

The light from the waystone intensified, backlighting Peter's crumpled form to a silhouette.

She hugged Toad and stared down at the Commander and his pursuers. Blood streamed from holes in his armor. Grimacing, he fell to his knees. The two remaining Battlecrows approached while brandishing knives like stilettos.

Annabelle trembled as rage boiled over inside her. *God, wash our enemies away, like the Egyptians who chased the Israelites.* Hot liquid surged and the world took on a blue haze.

Behind the Commander, water shot forth from the ground as if from a firehose, driving his two assailants back. Similar to a venting dam, countless lateral geysers burst forth in a row across the hillside, and water slammed into soldiers. The resulting flood swept away screaming mercenaries and turned the lower half of the slope into a mudslide.

Did I do that? The world spun vertiginously as a great weariness hit her like a hammer.

"Freylin!" Raeden was pulling her back.

Cradling Toad, she staggered over the ground, which refused to stay still. Menhirs danced overhead. Her vision flickered, growing dim despite the brightness of the waystone.

Arms caught her and hoisted her aloft. Cardamom and pepper mingled with sweat-smell, and she wrinkled her nose. "Raeden?" *The Commander,* she wanted to ask, but the words wouldn't form.

"This will not do, Freylin." The kaenhir's arms were strong and solid around her. "You are made too weary by the trials and the tribulations. No matter. Your servant will gladly carry you."

His voice faded as he carried her into the waystone's glare. It sounded as if he was speaking from another room. And then his arms no longer supported her. Toad was gone, too. She stood on her own in a white space surrounded by light.

Where are Raeden, Toad, and Peter? And Commander Storm ...

Breath choppy, Annabelle looked around, but she could see nothing aside from a blank, pearly sheen. She couldn't find the star-streaked tunnel she went through last time.

Calm down, Ann. You can't afford to freak out now.

Annabelle rested a hand on Murder Stick and fought a rising panic that replaced the fatigue and dizziness she'd experienced in the stone ring after ... whatever she'd done with the water on the hill. Yes. She had done something. No denying it.

She circled back and stared at a set of double doors hewn from soot-gray stone. Her eyes widened, and she stepped back. The doorway had not been there before.

The twin doors stood at least twenty feet high, and each one was easily as wide as Commander Storm was tall. A bas-relief sculpture with several serpentine, winged figures took up the entire surface. Jewels and precious metals were set in place of the creatures' eyes—ruby, emerald, sapphire, jet, gold, and silver. The beast rearing up in the center had opals ringed by pale moonstones for eyes.

"Dragons," she murmured. She reached out tentatively with her right hand to touch the carvings, but jerked it back before she made contact. *Stop being such a chicken. How are you supposed to get anywhere if you don't open the door?*

Annabelle placed a hand on the central dragon carving. Of the seven figures, only that one faced her. Her fingers stroked the reptilian muzzle as she peered into the opal eyes.

"Please," she whispered. "Please, let this be a safe place."

The stone figure warmed beneath her hand and the entire sculpture glowed. The opals flared brightly with rainbow fragments, as if someone had switched on a light bulb behind them. She backed away as a translucent white dragon's head emerged from the center of the door. Kindness emanated from its noble visage.

"Wyldling child," a male voice spoke in her mind. "Welcome to Y'Dendordenelle. We have been expecting you, Ahdmerel—Weaver of Water."

"That's me," she said, touching her collarbone. "Who ... who are you?" *One of the Sages?* she thought but did not ask.

"I am called Evanrudhe, and I am your host."

Not a Sage, then. Annabelle sniffled. Tears traced hot paths down her cheeks. "Please, sir, I've lost my ... my friends. Do you know where they are?" She swallowed. "Commander Storm. Peter. Are they okay?"

"Your companions are alive, and safe," the voice soothed. The ghostly dragon's head sank back into the sculpture. "Enter, child, and find rest."

As the voice faded, the doorway split open wide of its own accord. Annabelle crossed the threshold, her lips parted in awe. Beyond, all was white light and a choir of human voices lifted in joyful song. It felt like coming home.

Treehome

Waking Up

Someone shook her. "Miss Wells?"

"No ... no ..." Head tossing, Annabelle surfaced from the murky waters of sleep. A melange of floral scents both soothed and refreshed, towing her toward wakefulness.

Unfamiliar birdsong replaced the roar of floodwaters, screaming children, and howling lykharim. Fingers brushed hair from her brow, and a woman's voice murmured. "Fear not, Annabelle Leigh Wells." Her name sounded like music. "You are sheltered by the Threefold One under the boughs of Treehome. Wake, now."

With a gasp, Annabelle opened her eyes and struggled to sit up. A strong arm supported her shoulders. She stared into compassionate eyes the color of citrine. Relief washed over her; she knew that beautiful face. "Dinah," Annabelle said, rubbing her grainy eyes as she scooted into a more comfortable position. "I had a bad dream again." Her throat felt raw.

"Hmmm." Dinah rose from sitting on the edge of the sunken bed and crossed the spherical room to a little fountain grown from the curved wall. The fringes of her rust-colored sash and belt swayed with her movements. She tucked long, black hair behind a pointed ear. Annabelle had received quite a start, the first time she'd seen the tall, willowy young woman's ears. She'd asked if she was an Elf. Dinah, brows furrowed in confusion, replied that they were a race of humans called "dwelfnim."

I wish Enoch's book was better at giving physical descriptions of all the different people. Just once, I'd like to avoid sounding like an idiot.

"This is the fifth time your sleep has been interrupted in twenty-eight hours." Sighing, Dinah filled a large, wooden bowl from the ever-flowing spout of the fountain and then brought it to Annabelle. "You need to replenish your reserves. Dehydration is no small thing for a water Aspect wyldling. The Master Healer says you should drink at least ninety drachms of water a day—more if you exert yourself beyond normal limits. This is even more critical for you than it is for your companions."

She smiled, amusement lighting up her golden-brown eyes. "And before you ask, yes, Commander Storm survived his injuries, the messenger is recovering, Sir Thomas has revived, and His Excellency is faring well."

"Thank you." Eagerly, Annabelle took the bowl. It was more water than she'd been accustomed to drinking all at once before arriving at Treehome, but after her fit of exhaustion and vertigo two days ago, she'd learned that she needed every drop her hostess provided.

Dinah shook her head as she settled cross-legged beside the sunken bed with her flowing white skirt draped modestly over her knees. "I lament the dreamcatcher ward cannot banish nightmares, only keep out intruders."

Annabelle paused after her first refreshing gulp. "Intruders? You mean, no one here can visit each other in their dreams?"

"No one outside of Y'Dendordenelle can enter the dreams of our residents. Those here who have the ability can share dreams with those within the bounds of the dreamcatcher ward." Dinah picked up a blue-green froth of yarn the color of sea foam and resumed her knitting. "Frightening as they may be, your dreams are quite safe here, Annabelle Leigh Wells."

Annabelle frowned, then resumed drinking. That explained why she hadn't seen Enoch in the dreamscape again. Some kind of protective spell over Treehome kept out everyone. So far, Dinah had answered Annabelle's questions without reservation.

These dwelfnim seem nice. I hope they can help us. I've wasted so much time lying here with this stupid sickness from doing ... She shuddered. *Whatever it was I did.*

She'd spent the previous day in and out of delirium; crying out for her parents, for Enoch, and her traveling companions while tended to by strangers—tall, beautiful, and kind young women with vividly colored eyes. They called themselves dwelfnhadrim. She couldn't remember all their names, but Dinah, as the eldest of them, was her most frequent attendant. She'd told her that the men couldn't visit her in the Women's Quarters; the sexes had separate dormitories and Annabelle had been too ill to move. She found herself thinking about Toad.

Why did Toad collapse like that? Raeden said he was knocked out for hours.

Raeden had sent her a note written in blocky, all-caps that verified Dinah's assurances that they were all well. A female syrax named Sophie delivered his message, and Annabelle recalled admiring her indigo feathers and fur stippled with black and silver rosettes. Sophie rested her head in Annabelle's lap for ear-scratches while Annabelle perused Raeden's note during two hours of lucidity. Vaguely, she remembered the syrax curling up beside her for a while that restless night, her rumbling purr lulling Annabelle into a deeper sleep.

Annabelle paused, breathed, then resumed drinking. The water was fresh and clean with a hint of floral after-taste. A rainbow profusion of flowers spilling from trough-like shelves embedded—or grown from—the wooden walls may have had something to do with that. Their delicate scents blended, filling the air with the fragrance Annabelle could only call "morning." The specter of troubled sleep and nightmares receded.

Click, click, click.

Black brows furrowed, Dinah watched her drink while her nimble fingers wielded wooden knitting needles lacquered in a red that contrasted with the yarn she used. "You seem much better today. How are you feeling?"

"Oh, after drinking the water, I feel great." Annabelle set down the empty bowl. "I've never been prone to dizzy spells, but ever since I came to Tehara, I get exhausted whenever I tap into whatever it is I have inside me." She placed a hand over her heart. "What was wrong with me, anyway? Is it because I'm a wyldling?"

"Yes, Annabelle Leigh Wells," Dinah replied. "Your affliction is called malsourenfalkh. That's 'overextension sickness' in the trading language. Wyldlings often overextend themselves—drain their reservoir—before they learn their limits. From now on, you must always have a source of water at hand."

Annabelle snapped her fingers. "So that's why I couldn't heal Tinker's bite wound." At Dinah's quizzical look, she explained about her role in the guardsman's miraculous recovery when she first arrived on Tehara, and her failed attempt to heal her injured mount in the same way. It was a relief, knowing the healing power was real. "With Tinker, I didn't have any water," she summed up. "The ground was soaking wet when I healed Simon."

Dinah's eyes sparkled. "Healing with water. How remarkable!"

Annabelle shrugged. "It makes sense. The human body is over seventy-five percent water. Unfortunately, I didn't have the power to fix Simon's broken bones. I wonder if it's because there're minerals involved, like calcium and magnesium."

"Hmm. You may have a point. While the versatility of a wyldling's skills within his or her aspect is limited only by imagination, the act of healing involves aspects aside from water. With bones, that would be stone, or earth." Lowering her knitting, the dwelfnhad frowned. "Commander Storm ought to have warned you about all this."

"Yeah, well, he didn't." Annabelle hunched her shoulders and picked at the hem of her nightgown. She added, biting off the words, "Not about power reservoirs or wyldling limits. There's a lot of pertinent information he failed to share with me. Answering questions isn't exactly one of his strong points."

Commander Storm didn't bother to warn Enoch, either. Did he know Enoch was a wyldling? Everything might've been different if he had told him upfront.

"That is unfortunate," Dinah mused, her needles clicking away again. "But don't be discouraged, Annabelle Leigh Wells. I'm happy to answer your questions, to the best of my ability."

"Thank you." Annabelle smiled back, then cleared her throat. "Um, Dinah? Not to be rude or anything ..." She squirmed a little. "Could you please call me Ann?"

Dinah's black eyebrows shot up. "You honor me," she replied. She kissed the first two fingers of her right hand and then touched Annabelle's forehead. "So shall it be, Ann, my sister in

Yshua Khristos. You may continue to call me Dinah, but among my kin, my use-name is 'Dee.' Please address me as either, as it pleases you." With a smile, she returned to her knitting, and the soothing clickety-click resumed.

Did I just swear to something I'm unaware of?

Annabelle chewed on her lip. "That sounds like some sort of ritual. Am I supposed to say something back, um ... Dee?" She hunched her shoulders. "Please forgive me if I mess up; I don't know the customs or etiquette of this world very well."

As much as I'm learning from Enoch's book, there's so many things it doesn't tell me.

"There is nothing to forgive," Dinah replied, still knitting. "We dwelfnim can be formal regarding the relaxing of formalities." She chuckled. "And you need not be concerned about making mistakes, because others will understand. I've just completed my training as an ambassador to the kadorei. I will help guide you. There are many cultures on Tehara that—" The dwelfnhad's eyes widened and she lowered her knitting needles. "Gilgamesh's toenails! I'd nearly forgotten. This morning at firstmeal, Lord Evanrudhe inquired about your recovery. He invited us to join him and your companions for mainmeal, provided you feel up to it."

"Lord Evanrudhe. Who's that? The name sounds familiar. Is he the one in charge?"

"In a manner of speaking, yes. Our people are governed by a council of seven members. Lord Evanrudhe is the First Councilor."

Annabelle winced. "I'm meeting a lord—another lord? Will I need to curtsy? Is there some special way I'm supposed to address him? We don't have lords where I live." She laughed nervously. "The Commander is supposedly a Duke, but just wants to be called 'Commander,' and Raeden doesn't seem to care about me using his title ... so I'm kinda at a loss here."

Dinah grinned. "You may address him as 'Lord Evanrudhe,' and since you are meeting him in an informal setting, he won't expect you to curtsy. And he'll most likely request you to eschew his title, as well. He's eager to meet you and discuss the next phase of your mission."

Eyes wide, Annabelle straightened. "Finally! Commander Storm hardly told me anything about where we're going, how we'd find Enoch, or what we'll do when we get there. He claims to have a plan, but ... honestly?" She threw up her hands with a noise of disgust. "I think he's just making it all up as we go along."

Not that it matters. Unless I can convince him my connection to Enoch has returned, he's just going to leave me here. Too bad there's a ward to prevent dream-sharing, or I could prove it.

Dinah laughed. "My experience with His Grace has taught me he *always* has a plan, as well as plans within plans. During my service in the army, I saw him carry a campaign through, even when his reasonings remain mysterious. He's sworn an oath to uphold the Council."

Annabelle bit her lip to stifle a snort. *"His Grace," indeed. I can't picture Commander Storm in the civil office as a Duke, wearing fancy clothes. He's strictly military. But I could picture him swearing an oath.* "What does this oath entail?"

"In essence, to serve as the Commander of Armies and protect the four baronies. However, you'll need to ask him about any details. He may even tell you." The dwelfnhad raised an eyebrow. "All that aside, I'm sure you're eager to see the Commander and your other companions again."

"Yeah. All you said and Raeden's note are fine, but ..." She looked down and fiddled with the hem of her nightgown. "I've been worried. Raeden writes so matter-of-factly, but he seemed overly interested in my health. Like he thought I was dying. He mentioned praying for my recovery three times in a single paragraph."

Dinah's coral lips curved in a smile and her eyes sparkled as she set aside her knitting. "They've all been concerned and were asking after you—each in his own way." Her nod indicated the eight rolls of parchment displayed on the short-legged lap table beside the sunken bed, and Annabelle's eyes widened. She hadn't noticed that Raeden had sent more than one note.

"I imagine His Excellency also wished to keep you informed of matters," Dinah continued, her slender brown fingers toying with the reddish-orange cross pendant she wore on a necklace of intricately woven fibers. "Yesterday, he sent you a message at the beginning of every Watch on the hour, like clockwork. And two others arrived just this morning. Now," she added with a smile, "I'm not well-versed in the moods and mannerisms of the wensallen-kaenim, but he appears to be growing quite agitated."

Baobabs

Once washed and dressed in a choupla—a simple gown with a scoop neck that fastened at the shoulders—Annabelle followed Dinah through a round opening wide enough for three to walk abreast. She shivered as she passed through a chilly field of slight resistance, and then choked on the warm, moisture-laden air outside. Perspiration beaded on her forehead. The cacophony of life was loud in her ears; insects hummed and buzzed everywhere and strange creatures—some of them might even be birds—called and screamed from the depths of alien foliage a mere stone's throw away.

"It's a jungle out there," she said, gazing at lush and verdant surroundings. "Ack!" She jerked backward as a large iridescent green beetle droned past her face, its jewel-like wings a blur.

"There is no reason to fear," Dinah said, waving the beetle away. "The warding posts keep the dangerous beasts away. Also, the soaps and lotions we use repel insects that spread disease."

"That's definitely useful," Annabelle replied. She peered into a cluster of giant ferns. "And I'm not afraid. Just surprised, that's all."

She turned, her gaze traveling up and up and up the tan-colored and bulbous trunk of the giant tree. The gnarled and rootlike branches were not above the clouds, but the tree towered high enough to rival a ten-story apartment building.

And this is where I've been sleeping?

"Holy cow. That's got to be the biggest tree I've ever seen."

"It's called a baobab," Dinah said. "Many of us make our homes in the vacuoles and vesicles of the baobabs. Treespeakers—dwelfnim who can manipulate wood—use their ability to encourage the baobabs to form these bubbles for our dwelling places as they grow." Smiling, she patted the beige trunk as she would a favorite pet.

"That's so ... incredible!"

Dinah chuckled. "Wait until you see the Worship and Fellowship Halls. Both can accommodate the entire population of Y'Dendordenelle, at need. The community usually gathers for a meal in the Fellowship Hall following the evening worship service."

A gray-stoned foot path led them from the dormitory into the jungle. Dinah was happy to point out anything she might find interesting; her voice blended pleasantly with the natural noises. Stunted palms and squat bromeliads soon gave way to taller trees. Green vines thick enough to support a swinging Tarzan's weight draped across limbs and dangled down to the forest floor while brightly colored birds flitted from tree to tree and brown-masked lemurs leaped through the understory. The lemurs often interrupted their acrobatic games to perch along the vines, their dark-banded tails hanging like the ends of striped scarves as they watched them pass by.

"They're so cute!" Head swiveling every which way, Annabelle didn't know where to look as they walked. Yellow trumpet flowers competed with the weird-shaped waxy petals of purple orchids and the flaring red hibiscus for the most eye-catching blossoms.

Memory fragments of Enoch's younger self playing in the jungle with dwelfnic children cast brief, ghostly images over the present-day scenery. This reminder of her purpose curbed her enthusiasm. She wasn't here to sight-see; she was here to request the dwelfnim's aid in rescuing Enoch. Hadrien had told her she'd find what she needed here, and despite Commander Storm's skepticism, she wanted to believe Hadrien.

Dinah pointed ahead. "See where the path splits four ways? That's the boundary between the Women's Quarters, the Family Quarters, and the Men's Quarters, where your traveling companions are staying. The larger path leads toward The Fellowship and Worship Halls, the Great Library, and other community buildings."

As they approached the crossroads, a lithe figure plummeted from the green dimness above to land in a crouch on the mossy earth beside the path leading to the Men's Quarters. Annabelle gasped, and then relief swept over her.

Raeden straightened, blinking. "Good morrow," he said, bowing with his right fist over his chest. "Apologies if your servant caused a fright." He clasped his hands behind his back, emerald gaze fixed on Annabelle. "He has been waiting for Freylin and found he could not stay in the Men's Quarters any longer."

Dinah dipped her chin. "Good morrow, Your Excellency." She placed a hand on Annabelle's shoulder. "As you can see, she has recovered from the overextension sickness."

"Very good. Your servant is most pleased to see her." His ears quivered, and his voice took on an uncertain note. "You are well, Freylin?"

She grinned, suppressing the urge to throw her arms around him. "I feel fine. How are—" Narrowing her eyes, she noticed the rumpled state of his clothing and his disheveled hair. "Raeden, how long were you sitting up in that tree?"

"Since mid-Heron Watch, when he awoke." Raeden took out his watch, clicking it open. "Wren Watch is nearly over."

"Over six hours then," Dinah murmured. sounding amused.

Annabelle gaped, and Raeden leaned toward her, adding, "It is no great hardship, Freylin. Your servant is accustomed to keeping much longer watches than this on scouting missions."

"Were you planning to join us, Your Excellency?" Dinah asked. "We're meeting the others in the Fellowship Hall. Here, Ann, let me get that," she added, plucking out a leaf stuck in Annabelle's hair.

"*Shach.* Your servant will join you," Raeden replied, his gaze fixed on Annabelle as he put away his watch. "He will also escort Freylin anywhere else she wishes to go."

Dinah looked at her questioningly. Annabelle shrugged. "Fine by me."

As if I could stop him—even if I wanted to. Which I don't. Being around Raeden made her feel safe, like having a large, friendly, and over-protective dog at her side.

Eyebrows arched, Raeden leaned forward. "This was not a—how does one say it? —a suggestion. It is what shall be done." His whiskers quivered and his eyes twinkled. From her experience with him, she knew he teased her.

Annabelle laughed and took his offered arm, resting her head against it instead of hugging him. "I'm glad to see you, too. I missed you." They continued on their way, Raeden answering her questions regarding their companions, with Dinah occasionally chiming in. Before long, the wide gray path branched seven ways, each new path a different color.

"Prepare yourself, Ann," Dinah said as the surrounding jungle thinned and grew lighter. "You'll see the Worship and Fellowship Halls soon."

Presently, the pearl-stoned path brought them around a thick stand of fern-like foliage, and a different vista spread out before them. The flora dwindled to sparse patches of tufted grass scattered over dusty brown soil, and the blue sky vaulted overhead.

Annabelle's jaw dropped, and she squeezed Raeden's arm. Rising from the surrounding jungle were two enormous trees, their bulging trunks merged at the base by a raised ridge of living wood. Lined by flowering shrubs and exotic plants, the pearl stone path led across the dirt clearing straight to them. People walked along other paved trails snaking through the hard-packed earth, seemingly the size of ants as they approached conjoined baobabs with girths rivaling entire city blocks.

Wyldlings, Plural

After entering a set of doors carved with bas-relief dragons—which Raeden held open for her and Dinah—they turned left down high-ceilinged, curved corridors wide enough for ten people to walk abreast, illuminated by glowing globes embedded high in the interior walls and small, round windows on the exterior wall. Occasionally they passed other people, all of them dwelfnim—tall and slender with pointed ears—who greeted them with smiles and nods.

Before long, the corridor opened into a huge room with sunlight filtering down from large windows. Colorful murals, tapestries, and sculptures were displayed on all the walls and benches. Several people walked out as they entered, leaving it almost empty.

Annabelle glimpsed a tall, broad-shouldered man with braided, shoulder-length black hair standing with his back to them before a colorful tapestry the size of an Olympic swimming pool. His hands rested on a waist-level divider grown out of the floor that formed the backs of several individual seats with spaces between them. Beside the man, Toad crouched on the table-like top of the divider. He also faced the tapestry, which depicted a collage of warlike scenes and natural disasters.

"Indeed, Sir Thomas," the dwelfnhir was saying as they entered. "The Battle of Brume Hill is one of only three tapestries to survive the fall of Kellindashelle. And it is the one in the best condition." He had a pleasant baritone well-suited for speaking. Annabelle could envision him delivering sermons; perhaps it was the mantled robe and rust-red cloth belt he wore that brought a clergyman to mind. However, the tapestry snared her attention.

Wide-eyed, she stared at the montage of violent scenes all woven together in a swirl of color and power, as realistic as a photograph screen-printed on a blanket. Scenes depicting the earth splitting open into great chasms to swallow an entire village, an army destroyed by a line of tornadoes, and croplands consumed by a blazing inferno while figures armored in black crashed together in a flurry of colorful sparks and crackling light.

Toad asked a question she couldn't make out, and his companion answered, "Kellindashelle was already in decline when the typhoon hit and sent the kingdom into the sea. Although the reigning king perished, the king's brother and his wife evacuated much of the populace before the storm made landfall. Legends tell that both prayed to the Threefold One and pleaded with Him to hold off the tempest long enough for the people to flee."

Annabelle's eyes were drawn to a black-clad figure standing on a hill with arms raised in a V while waters roared and foamed around it, sweeping away other human figures like broken dolls. A chill raced down her spine, and she shivered. The scene was too close to her nightmares for comfort.

Raeden peered into her face. "Freylin?" he said, just as Dinah called with laughter in her voice, "Giving history lessons again, David?"

The man turned, eyebrows raised. "We can learn much from the mistakes of the past, Dee." Eyes the same hue as Dinah's swept over them as a faint smile curved his lips. "I see you've brought our other wyldling guest and an old acquaintance." Nodding at Raeden, his gaze settled on Annabelle as they drew near, and she felt breathless. Her grip on Raeden's arm went slack. She was growing accustomed to Dinah's beauty, but this man, who looked like her new friend, was even handsomer than both guys in that popular vampire movie.

Wait a minute. Did he say "other" wyldling? Is he talking about Enoch?

Raeden pulled away from her and stepped aside. After exchanging a look with the kaenhir, who nodded, Dinah took Annabelle's right hand and the handsome man's left hand. "Annabelle Leigh Wells," she pronounced, squeezing Annabelle's hand. "May I present my cousin, Degalaevid, Shepherd and warrior of the enlightened faction? David, this is my sister in Yshua Khristos, Annabelle Leigh Wells."

Holding her gaze—indeed, she found it difficult to look away, or even breathe—the dwelfnhir placed his right fist on his chest. "I am honored to meet you, Annabelle Leigh Wells. Sir Thomas and Lord Raeden have both spoken of you with high regard." He glanced aside at the divider, where Toad sat, staring at her.

Electricity zinged through her, and her heart palpitated. *What did Toad say about me?*

Annabelle found her voice. "I-it's very nice to meet you—" she struggled to remember how Dinah said his name, "—um, sir. And there's no reason to be formal. Please, call me Ann."

The man's eyes widened. With a grin, Dinah raised their hands and brought them together. "I consider us all well-met. What say you, cousin?"

He took her hand, his grip warm and gentle. Annabelle made a squeaking sound in her throat as heat rose to her cheeks. As if they were at a funeral, he murmured, "Well-met ... Ann. You may call me David." After pressing her fingers, he let go, and Annabelle lowered her arm. *I half-expected him to kiss my hand, but I suppose they don't do that here.*

Rolling his eyes, Toad snorted and muttered something under his breath.

Humor and affection danced in Dinah's eyes. "Do not allow his stoic mien to fool you, Ann; he becomes quite impassioned when preaching his sermons."

"So, you *are* a pastor," she blurted. "Do you have a church? I mean, um, worship here?"

One black eyebrow raised, David replied, "My pardon, Ann, but I don't know the word 'pastor.' I serve as a captain in the armed forces and was recently ordained as a Shepherd. And yes, we have worship services every day at Klotho-rise and Lachesis-set in our sanctuary. I am leading worship tonight."

"Your servant is glad for this, Freylin," Raeden put in, stepping up beside her. "He has read and prayed with you, but he cannot administer the sacraments."

"Yes, Your Excellency," Dinah said, "it would be good for the wyldlings to share in the Agape Feast while they are here."

There it is again: wyldlings, plural. Annabelle shot a questioning glance at Toad. *Did* he *know there are other wyldlings?*

"Sir Thomas," David asked, "have you been instructed in the Way of Yshua?"

"Uh ..." Toad shrank into himself.

Annabelle's heart raced. "Wait a sec. I thought Enoch and I were the only wyldlings—but there are others? Who are they?"

As one, Dinah, David, and Raeden turned to Toad. *What the heck?* Annabelle's eyes widened as puzzle pieces connected—Toad helping her with the fire. The lykhar burnt by sparks. The mercenary bursting into flames.

Toad sighed heavily. "You're looking at him, kiddo."

"Toad ... *you* set that man on fire?" Something wrenched inside Annabelle's chest. She blinked to dispel the sudden burning in her eyes. "So. You're a wyldling. Like me and Enoch." Toad's figure blurred, and then cleared. She shook her head. *All this time ... I can't believe he never told me.*

"Freylin?" Raeden touched her arm.

Disappointment seared like a hot knife. Fingers curling into fists, she whirled to face him. "You knew all along that Toad was like me. Why didn't you tell me?"

Raeden's ears wilted, then lifted as his gaze hardened. "Though he suspected for days, it was not for your servant to tell. Sir Thomas told him the truth only this morning."

Dinah, beside her, rubbed between her shoulder blades. "Ann, I can see you have much to discuss with Sir Thomas. Come, take a seat. We have time before the meeting begins."

Raeden checked his watch. "A quarter of an hour."

With a gentle push, Dinah steered her toward the divider, its attached benches, and Toad. An oppressive warmth rose inside Annabelle, and she pursed her lips. *I will not cry!*

As they approached, Toad narrowed eyes as blue as a winter sky. She sat on the little bench farthest from Toad, and the dwelfnim drew away to one side near another doorway.

Annabelle looked at Toad and spoke, her tone seething with venom. "So. How long have you been having weird dreams?"

Toad glanced down and shuffled his front legs. "Three weeks, maybe. I've had weird dreams off and on for as long as I can remember."

"Tell me about them." She squinted. "All of it."

Scoffing, he shot her an annoyed glance. "I can't remember them *all*, kiddo. Sometimes, I dream I'm chasing a criminal I'm trying to bring to justice, and other times these tigers made of fire showed up ... I'm not sure if they were part of a 'normal' dream." He snorted. "If such a thing as 'normal' exists here. Dreams are just weird by nature."

"True." Annabelle softened toward him. "Flaming tigers are pretty neat. Like something out of a poem. 'Tiger, tiger, burning bright,' as Blake wrote." She chuckled. "But do you remember seeing any dragons in your dream, like I did?"

"I was getting to that, kiddo." His gaze became unfocused. "Always, there was a caldera filled with lava, surrounded by trees with flaming leaves. Lightning flashed everywhere without thunder. I walked across it all without a mark." He shuddered. "In the center, I mounted a pedestal to speak with a golden dragon chained at the top."

Her eyes widened, and a grin spread across her face. "You met a Sage, too! Did he tell you who he was?"

"He claimed he was Balthazar Phoenixheart." Toad rolled his eyes. "Called me Helzarvenn, the Caster of Flames. Like something from a fairy tale. What a crock of bull—"

Annabelle groaned loudly as she threw up her hands. "Toad, for goodness' sake. We're both wyldlings. We both have," she wriggled her fingers, "magic powers that we've used. You heard me mention *my* dreams about the Sage." She rubbed her forehead as she contemplated her dreams about Hadrien. "You could've just ..."

She recalled the helpless horror in her nightmare, watching the water wash away a horde of children dressed up as black-feathered soldiers. Had Toad dreamed something similar? *Doesn't he realize we can help each other?* She swallowed. "You could have told me, Toad."

"I didn't tell you," Toad snapped, "because my memories are suspect at the best of times. And then, some talking, mythical beast shows up in my dreams ...” His vocal sac fluttered faster than normal. “I thought either someone was invading my mind—or I was going crazy.”

“Even after I said I was dreaming about Hadrien?” Tears bubbled up into her voice. “Did you think *I* was insane? I thought we were becoming friends, and all this time, you let me bear this—this *burden* alone.”

Toad swelled and raised himself to his tallest extent. He was just opening his mouth when David raised a hand and said, “Sir Thomas, before you say something you might regret, I counsel a bit of reflection on your next words.”

Toad’s gaze locked with Annabelle’s. “Oh, I’ve reflected, all right.” Eyes blazing with golden sparks, he hopped along the divider until he sat snout to nose with her. It was all she could do to keep herself from cringing.

Her anger evaporated. She swallowed past a lump in her throat. Raeden growled, softly. Lips parted, Dinah exchanged a look with David, but the dwelfnhir shook his head.

“So, kiddo,” Toad said in a low, fierce tone. “You think you’re the only one here with problems? Well, now...” He barked a humorless laugh. “In my dreams, I can almost remember who I was before. I’m myself, and I’m wielding a sword made of fire. Sometimes I’m wearing amazing armor.” He paused; his eyes shone with wonder. “It gave me hope I could be a man again.”

Annabelle regarded him. *What does Sir Thomas look like? I wish I could see him in the dreamscape.* Her brow furrowed. *Why haven’t we ever met there?*

Toad looked down, flexing his front toes. “But then I’d wake up, still in this ridiculous, weak toad-body.” He made a squeaky, gulping noise. Trembling, he continued, “I came here believing

I'd get my body back, but then I heard they can do nothing for me." He cast a heated glare at David, then leaned closer to level his burning gaze at her.

With a whimper, Annabelle shrank away, her shoulder pressing against the divider. *Oh, God help me. I've never seen Toad so angry before ... Is he mad at* me? A blend of emotions she couldn't parse—something akin to heated excitement mingled with fear—roiled behind her breastbone. Suddenly, Raeden stood beside her, growls rumbling in his chest.

Toad snarled, "According to the powers-that-be here, I have to wait until this curse or whatnot fades on its own—and nobody knows how long that'll take. Couple that with this weird mind-power where I can apparently *set things on fire—*"

"Sir Thomas," Commander Storm thundered. The evainghir had entered the gallery from a separate doorway. "Desist. You are out of line."

Toad swelled up, turning his glare on his superior officer. He hissed, "With all due respect—*sir*—I disagree. I'll decide when I'm out of line. You might want to take cover. Remember, I'm the one who can flambé things with my mind." His eyes blazed with golden light.

Was that his power? Annabelle gasped. *He wouldn't ... would he?* She glanced between Toad and the Commander, who stared back impassively with his arms folded.

"Please, Toad. Stop it," she whispered, hugging herself.

Growling, Raeden stepped into view and thrust an arm between her and Toad.

"Sir Thomas," Commander Storm said in an even tone. "Rein in your temper. You are frightening the womanchild."

Toad's eyes dimmed, and he settled back on his haunches. "Sorry, sir." He glanced from the evainghir to Annabelle, half-hidden behind Raeden's arm. "Kiddo. I ... I apologize." His gaze traveled from the two dwelfnim, who had both stood by silently watching the exchange with blank expressions, to the kaenhir. "Sorry about that. I'm not gonna hurt her, Your Excellentness."

"This remains to be seen," Raeden replied stiffly, but he stepped aside.

Toad deflated. Annabelle's fear trickled away like water down the drain. He looked so forlorn; she suppressed an impulse to cuddle him. He'd never let that slide—and how much control he had over his wyldling fire ability wasn't clear.

With a sigh, Toad grumbled, "It's not easy opening up to people."

Annabelle bit her lip. "But you told the Commander." *Why not me?* Cold loneliness hollowed her gut.

"I ordered him to tell me," The evainghir interjected as he strode across the gallery. "Are you quite finished with your conversation? We can revisit that topic when the First Councilor joins us." He halted, looming over them, wearing new armor and seeming every bit as formidable and solid as she remembered. A memory of black crossbow bolts penetrating the leather scales flashed through her mind, and a shudder wracked her frame. She glanced first at his side and shoulder, then up into his visage.

"Are you ..."

Lips twitching and humor glinting in his eyes, Commander Storm grunted. "Merely flesh wounds, womanchild. The healers here have mended them."

"Oh." She stared at her fingers twisting the fabric in her lap. *First time I've heard deep punctures referred to as "flesh wounds." I wonder ... could I have healed the Commander, like I did for Simon?*

Raeden shifted his position. "Freylin." Her gaze lifted to the kaenhir, who watched her with concern, hand extended. She grasped his wrist, and he hauled her to her feet. Under his breath, Toad muttered as he hopped from the divider to her seat, and then to the floor. He headed toward the doorway where Dinah and David awaited them.

As Raeden took her elbow and led her to the door, Annabelle asked the Commander, "How much of that did you hear?"

"I heard Sir Thomas mention possessing the sourekghar in his dreams."

"Soo-wreck ... what? I think I heard Hadrien use that word."

"Sourekghar. Armor for wyldlings." He raised his eyebrows. "Seeing as circumstances prevented it earlier, you will now deliver your own report on your dreams the night before we arrived."

Oh, that's right ...

Annabelle's heart hammered against her breastbone. "Holy cow, do I have a report for you, Commander." She licked her lips. "Remember when we came here through the waystone?"

Commander Storm harrumphed. "I could hardly forget, womanchild; I have fresh scars as a standing testament of that day." Slowly, he turned and walked down the corridor, beckoning them to follow. "Walk with me. I am listening."

With Raeden as her silent shadow, Annabelle scurried to catch up. "Well ..." She brushed imaginary lint from her choupla, then gauged his mood from his scaly profile. "What with all that's happened, I didn't get the chance to tell you, and I needed a little time to evaluate everything, but ..."

"Spit it out, womanchild," he growled through his teeth.

Taking a deep breath, she spoke in a rush. "Please don't be mad. I met Enoch in the dreamscape that morning."

Lord Evanrudhe

Mainmeal

Sunslight streamed through round openings in the ceiling and curved walls, bathing the room with golden light. Birdsong drifted in along with a fragrant breeze. Annabelle couldn't enjoy any of it. She felt like she was about to take an exam for which she hadn't prepared.

Throat tight, she traced whorls on the grain of the dark polished wooden table in the Four Knights Vesicle, where they waited for David and Dinah to return with Lord Evanrudhe. The vesicle's door-curtain was a martial tapestry featuring four armored men, one leaping out of each corner toward the middle with their swords raised over their heads so that the points met in the center. Purple flower spikes and golden swords against a field of black bordered the scene. Before she left them to arrange for the mainmeal, Dinah explained the men represented the four Baron-Knights.

Commander Storm had bombarded her with questions about her dream—most of which she couldn't answer—while they walked to the Four Knights Vesicle. Apparently, learning that she'd connected with Enoch and discovered more about the wyldling snare binding him wasn't enough to placate him. She would remain behind in Treehome. For her own safety, of course.

The Commander loomed at the head of the table. "You are not ready for what lies beyond Y'Dendordenelle, and I have no time to prepare you adequately. The risk is too great, womanchild." His shadow fell over her like clouds covering the suns. "Do you understand?"

"Yes, sir." She kept her voice steady despite the tears stinging her eyes. "I understand all too well. I'm a burden to you."

"Lord Commander," Raeden said, his monocle glinting in the sunslight as he turned toward them. Like a sentinel keeping watch, he stood at a round window with hands clasped behind his back. "Would you dishonor Freylin so, in denying her this quest? Much as your servant has, she has sworn to bring her heart-brother home. The Threefold One wills it. She must take part in it."

Commander Storm's voice softened while retaining a deadly edge. "What the Threefold One wills is immaterial. I have sworn to uphold the security of the Enlightened Faction, which supersedes the sentimental whims of this womanchild. No doubt the boy was abducted for the power—the threat—he represents. Allowing the womanchild to continue increases the risk of a second wyldling falling into enemy hands."

Annabelle gasped. *Why would he say that? Rescuing Enoch isn't a whim! And he makes it sound like he views me and Enoch as ... weapons.* She shivered, recalling how she'd called the water. Used it to attack.

Ears flattened, Raeden lifted his chin and stared down the evainghir. "Your servant will protect Freylin wherever she goes. While he draws breath, he will let no one take her."

Commander Storm spoke in a level tone. "Can you protect her in the dreamscape, Your Excellency?"

Raeden held his gaze for a heartbeat, then lowered his head. "*Nich,*" he replied bitterly. "That place is beyond his reach."

Crouched on the table across from her, Toad cleared his throat. "Uh ... Commander?" He hopped closer to her. "I could protect the kiddo in that dream place." He huffed a laugh. "Criminy, I can even train her to use a sword there."

She gaped at him. "Really, Toad? You'd do that for me?"

Toad glanced at her sidelong. "Well, yeah. I just said I would."

With a half-strangled sob, Annabelle reached for him, and then hesitated. *I shouldn't. He doesn't like when I pick him up.*

He rolled his eyes. "Go ahead, kiddo."

Joy filled her. *He really is my friend—even if he is grumpy.* She gathered Toad into her arms and kissed him between the eyes. He made a squeaky, croaking noise. Eyes closed, she rested her cheek on his warty back for a moment as his throat sac fluttered against her arm. It was less satisfying than nuzzling something fuzzy, such as a cat or dog, but she took comfort from his warmth.

Commander Storm cleared his throat. "Sir Thomas. Recently, you expressed a lack of confidence with your ... proficiency in certain aspects of the dreamscape. Are you resolved on this course?"

"Yes, sir." Toad's voice quavered at first, then strengthened. "Like I said, I can wield a sword there. I can protect her. Once I figure out how to find her," he muttered, then cleared his throat. "K-kiddo, could you please put me down?"

Her cheeks heated. "Sorry," Annabelle set him down on the table. He shifted position but remained nearby. Steeling herself, she met the Commander's gaze. "Raeden and Toad said they'd protect me." From his place by the window, the kaenhir voiced his assent. "And I can still learn to defend myself better."

The reptilian warrior grunted. "This does not ensure further participation in the journey, womanchild. By your own account, your mind may be compromised."

"That remains to be seen," a new voice said.

"First Councilor," the Commander said without a trace of surprise, his voice sober. He bowed his head and held his right fist to his chest. Raeden had circled around the table and gone down on one knee like a man waiting to be knighted.

With a start, Annabelle scrambled to her feet.

A tall, silver-haired man wearing a long, beige tunic belted with white cloth had pulled aside the tapestry curtain that served as a door and stepped into the sunslight. David and Dinah entered behind him, bearing large trays containing covered dishes they brought to the table.

"Greetings, my friends," the newcomer said. "Please forgive my tardiness; I would have been here a quarter of an hour since, but a fresh wave of refugees arrived this morning from Rang Shadah. They required immediate attention and care." His voice brought to mind a sense of peace, welcome, and a memory of carved dragons bathed in an opalescent glow.

Annabelle's eyes fixed on the new arrival. *It's him. Our host. The one who'll check me and Toad for mind invasion. And maybe ... send me home.* Her heart pounded furiously as he held her gaze. *I wonder why he looks so sad.*

Lord Evanrudhe's solemn expression lightened. He glanced at the evainghir. "We shall discuss the second stage of your journey later, Commander." Smiling, he raised his hands, resembling a pastor giving the benediction. "There is no need for this formality. Be at ease."

Beckoning her, Commander Storm strode toward their host. "First Councilor," the evainghir said as she joined them, "this is the wyldling I spoke of, from the realm called Earth across the Void-Bridge."

Annabelle raised her eyebrows. *Oh, so I've gone from "womanchild" to "wyldling?" Now we're making progress.*

Dinah tsked and took her hand. "First Councilor," she said, "may I present Annabelle Leigh Wells?"

Hazel eyes settled on Annabelle, and Lord Evanrudhe smiled. "Ah, Miss Wells. Glad to see you up and about. I've been looking forward to making your acquaintance in the physical realm." He placed a hand on her shoulder and favored her with a kind smile that she could not help but return. "I am called Evanrudhe, and have the honor of serving the Enlightened Faction as First of the Dwelfnic Council. Pray, let us be seated."

"What's the Enlightened Faction?" she asked as Dinah ushered her back to her seat.

"All those who serve Yshua's kingdom here on Tehara, my dear." Lord Evanrudhe allowed her to take her seat before occupying the bench at the head of the table. It seemed Toad was already acquainted with the First Councilor; they exchanged nods. The Commander moved to the foot of the table, where he stood with hands clasped behind his back. Once David and Dinah set out mugs of chilled juice that tasted of mango mixed into mint tea, and distributed the covered dishes—Toad received a shallow bowl filled with mealworms—the two dwelfnim and the Commander sat.

After leading them in a prayer of thanksgiving for the food, they uncovered bowls of a hearty stew served with hot, flaky rolls.

An aroma like chicken soup made Annabelle's mouth water, and she dug right in. *What I wouldn't give for some beer-boiled bratwurst slathered in brown mustard right now. But this stew is great.* They ate in silence for several moments, passing around an ewer with the mango-mint drink.

Lord Evanrudhe turned to Raeden in the seat across from Annabelle. "Your Excellency, Shepherd Degalaevid—" he nodded at David, "—advised me of your request for his sponsorship, and the Council approved it. A weighty decision and a difficult path." His glance flickered toward Annabelle. "Albeit a commendable one."

Setting his spoon beside the empty bowl, Raeden bowed his head. "One serves as the Almighty has called him."

Annabelle was about to ask what they were talking about when Lord Evanrudhe spoke again, as if musing aloud. "I understand you two have been experiencing visitations in your dreams." Toad glanced up with an inquiring hum and a mouth filled with mealworms.

"That is the case," Commander Storm put in before Annabelle could respond. "I have begun a mind-protection regimen for both Sir Thomas and the womanchild. Both claim to have spoken with one of the Sages in the dreamscape."

Annabelle pursed her lips. *"The womanchild" is right here and can darn well speak for herself, Commander Storm.*

A smile quivered on Lord Evanrudhe's lips. "You must forgive the Commander, Miss Wells. As your guardian, he is accustomed to speaking for you."

Startled, Annabelle gaped. "Did you just read my mind?"

Toad snorted. "Your face, more like."

Lord Evanrudhe's smile broadened as he nodded. "Sir Thomas speaks true; you possess a rather expressive countenance, my dear."

Shoulders slumping, Annabelle fussed with her empty mug. "Am I just an open book to everyone?" On her left, Dinah took her mug and refilled it.

Raeden tilted his head. "Freylin, one does not see how you can be a book, but you often place your heart upon the tunic."

What the heck? Annabelle scrunched her brow.

Toad groaned. "Not another messed up idiom."

The Commander grimaced. "We wander far afield from the matter at hand." His steely regard took in Toad and then settled on Annabelle. "Let us address the issue of these children wandering about in the dreamscape without proper shielding, and conversing with beings long since presumed dead."

"Hey." Toad's eyes flashed. "Sir—with all due respect—I'm a knight. That makes me at least nineteen or twenty. I might not know my exact age, but I know I'm not a kid anymore."

Commander Storm snorted. "To me, you both are children."

Annabelle blinked. *Weird. Toad isn't much older than me.*

Visions

After the meal, Annabelle and Toad, with Commander Storm shadowing them, followed Lord Evanrudhe toward a tapestry. Its dark blue expanse featured rainbow-hued merpeople. Raeden's reaction when he'd first seen the curtain had perplexed her; his ears went back, and he growled something about "enemies of the folken." But then his face settled into a dour mask and he'd refused to speak of it.

"The gwerindawr and the wensallen-kaen are ancestral enemies," Dinah murmured in her ear as she hugged her.

"Wow! Really?" Annabelle turned from the kaenhir back to the tapestry. "I was wondering what gwerindawr looked like. So far, my book hasn't said."

Dinah glanced at Raeden's flattened ears and forbidding visage as he glared at the tapestry. "Better not speak of it now. My apologies, but I must see to my responsibilities. I'll return as soon as I can. Courage, Ann." After clearing the dirty dishes off the table, she left.

When Raeden moved toward Annabelle, David suggested they visit the Rainbow Garden and discuss "the ceremony." Whatever that meant. Gravely, the kaenhir said he would pray for her, bowed, and went with David.

Lord Evanrudhe pulled aside the gwerindawr tapestry to reveal a hemispherical space about the size of Annabelle's bedroom. Ten large cushions of various colored patterns awaited them. Sunslight streamed through an oval window, dappling colorful rag rugs scattered about the small area. On the cushions lay smaller pillows, skillfully embroidered with plants and animals, and just the right size for hugging.

"Whoa!" Annabelle chuckled. "Looks cozy. Do people take naps in here?"

"We use the Four Knights Vesicle for deliberations," Lord Evanrudhe explained. "These alcoves are a space apart for relaxation and contemplation in between debates. Please, recline wherever you wish. Make yourselves comfortable."

Annabelle chose a dark blue cushion with swirls of lighter blue, green, and traces of purple. *Like a seascape,* she mused, squeezing a pillow decorated with an axolotl as she gazed at the merfolk decorating the door-curtain.

Toad surveyed his options, hesitated, and then hopped on the plain, dark gold cushion to her left. Commander Storm stood beside the entrance in the ready stance, with knees bent and feet shoulder width apart. Resting her chin on the pillow, Annabelle frowned. *Does he think he needs to guard us?*

Lord Evanrudhe knelt on a rug between Annabelle and Toad. "Before we begin, my conscience drives me to confess: I am neither Dreamspinner nor Mindreaver. My talents lie elsewhere." With hands braced on his thighs, he leaned forward, glancing back and forth between them as he spoke. "However, I am the closest thing to an expert here in Y'Dendordenelle. I would not entrust an undertaking requiring such delicacy to anyone else. I say this not to frighten you, but to impress upon you the gravity of the situation. I do not relish delving into others' minds. It has been nearly an epoch since I have done so."

"What'll you be looking for in our heads?" Toad asked. He glanced at Annabelle. "And what's the significance of us seeing ghosts in our dreams?"

The dwelfnhir's lips twitched. "Based on your descriptions, these ... visitors cannot be apparitions. My primary concern is to verify the presence of the Sages and to discount other sources as having meddled in your minds." His sorrowful eyes took on a hopeful gleam. "Since hearing of these visitations, I have been fervently praying the former is true. That I need not mourn my dear friends Hadrien and Balthazar any longer."

Annabelle's eyes widened. "Wow, you were friends with the Sages? Does that mean—"

"It could mean nothing." Commander Storm's expression was even stonier than usual. "However, I would rather err on the side of caution. First Councilor, if we could please begin the examination?"

How rude! Annabelle squinted at the Commander. *Why doesn't he ever want to talk about the Sages?*

Lord Evanrudhe was frowning. "You wish for me to ascertain whether the wyldlings' minds have been invaded, Commander Storm. To do so, I must, perforce, invade their minds. This is not something I embark upon lightly, and I prefer them to understand the process insofar as it can be understood. I will have their informed consent."

Annabelle exchanged a look with Toad, then nodded. "I agree whole-heartedly."

"They know enough to decide," the Commander replied, narrowing his eyes. "Anything else is a matter of curiosity. Sir Thomas, I shall allow to make his own choice, whether to stay here until his curse fades—if it does—or to continue with me to Y'Vasheirdenelle and then to Y'Pohlzardenelle. Although I harbor misgivings on that account, he is a man grown, if just barely. Regardless, we must inspect his mind before he continues on this mission."

Annabelle recalled what she'd learned about the different colonies from Enoch's book of legendary tales. She recognized Y'Vasheirdenelle as the colony founded by Gilgamesh

Earthshaker, the Sage most gifted in the Aethyric aspect of stone. The other name, Y'Pohlzardenelle, also sounded vaguely familiar. *It's probably Balthazar Phoenixheart's special place, because Toad's the fire wyldling.*

"'If' the curse fades," Toad muttered. "Gee, thanks. Way to boost my morale."

Sadly, she glanced at her fellow wyldling. *Poor Toad. Remember, Annabelle: you're not the only one here with problems.*

"Enough about me," Toad said gruffly. "I'm going. I have business at this Ee-pole-zar-wherever. Sir, what about the kiddo? If her mind is clear, then I think she should go along. You, me, and the dog-man can protect her just fine."

Commander Storm clenched his jaw. "As the womanchild's guardian," he replied with special emphasis, "I have deemed this the proper course for her own well-being. Her mind shielding lessons progress poorly. When I depart, she will remain here in Y'Dendordenelle, where she can be kept from the dreamscape, her mind protected from future incursions, and no one will abduct her."

No! I won't be left behind. Annabelle cast a pleading look at Lord Evanrudhe; the Commander seemed to defer to him. Perhaps she could convince the dwelfnhir to order Commander Storm to take her along. "Please, Lord Evanrudhe," she blurted. "I want to help rescue Enoch, and I need to meet him in the dreamscape. Toad and Raeden said they'll protect me. And if Hadrien is really who he says he is, then I think he'll help me learn what it means to be a wyldling."

A smile flickered on Lord Evanrudhe's face. "Indeed, he would. And so will I, once our business here is concluded."

Relief coursed through her. "Oh, thank you, Lord Evanrudhe! I have so many questions."

"You are welcome, child. You need only ask." He raised his eyebrows, his expression kind. "Do you have anything to add to the argument on your own behalf, Miss Wells?"

Licking her lips, Annabelle hugged the pillow tighter. "No. Yes. Um. Just ... is there anything you can do to make it safer for me to continue on my quest? Commander Storm hinted there was a way, but he wouldn't tell me anything, that I needed to wait until we arrived at Treehome. So, now we're here, and ...." Her voice petered out, and she hunched her shoulders helplessly.

Commander Storm tensed and shot a narrow glance at the First Councilor, but the dwelfnhir's attention remained on Annabelle. "My dear," he replied, "Commander Storm spoke truly. There is an artifact here that may aid you. However, traveling that route possesses trials and perils all its own. We shall speak of it after the examination. Do you wish to move forward?"

Though her stomach knotted at the thought of someone poking around in her head, Annabelle forced a smile and nodded. "Okay. Yes, Lord Evanrudhe. Read my mind. Probe my brain." She swallowed. "You have my consent."

"And mine," Toad said, shuffling around on his cushion. "My dreams are the only place I'm *me*."

"The womanchild first," Commander Storm rumbled. "She is the greater risk."

"No, wait!" Toad puffed himself up. "With all due respect, First Councilor, you said this mind magic isn't in your wheelhouse. So, practice it on me first. That way, any potential brain-scrambling happens to me instead of the kiddo."

Warmth blossomed in Annabelle's chest. She grinned. "Oh, Toad. That's the sweetest thing—"

"Oh, can it," he snapped, squinting at her. "Right now, I'm less than half the man I used to be. You're more or less able-bodied. It's the sensible thing to do, and you know it." He turned to their host and added, "No offense, Your Lordship."

"None is taken," Lord Evanrudhe replied with a faint smile. He arched an eyebrow. "If your superior officer agrees?"

Commander Storm's steely gaze shifted from Annabelle to Toad, to whom he gave a nod. "I concur."

Annabelle opened her mouth, saw Toad's resolute look, and then shut it again.

As he met her gaze, Lord Evanrudhe seemed on the verge of a smile. "I shall administer only the lightest of touches." His expression grew serious. "Very well, Sir Thomas. If you choose to go first, then I shall honor your request. Before we begin, let us pray."

Annabelle bowed her head. The prayer was a long one, asking for wisdom and strength. Her mind wandered halfway through. She barely registered the petitions Lord Evanrudhe addressed to the Almighty Threefold One as her thoughts careened down first one pathway, and then another.

I have so many questions—about wyldlings, the dreamscape, and this 'artifact' he mentioned. Once this mind-probe thing is done, I'll talk to Lord Evanrudhe. He's so down-to-earth. He'll answer my questions—if Commander Storm doesn't butt in!

Following the "amen," Toad closed his eyes and Lord Evanrudhe placed a hand along Toad's back. With the axolotl pillow clutched to her chest, Annabelle watched them both sit there, tension humming through her. Occasionally, Toad's eye ridges twitched and his throat sac pulsed faster. Lord Evanrudhe muttered something.

Hmm. That doesn't look so bad. I expected something a bit more ... flashy. She frowned.

Commander Storm hunkered beside her cushion. "There is nothing to fear, womanchild," he rumbled. "I would not permit this if I did not trust the First Councilor. Despite what he claims, he is the most competent sourethol in the Enlightened Faction."

"Sourethol?" Another word that sounded familiar.

"Also referred to as the Aethyr-touched. Many dwelfnim possess an affinity for one aspect of the Aethyr. Very few—" he nodded at Lord Evanrudhe, "—are gifted in more than one."

"I read a bit about them in the legends book," Annabelle mused aloud. *This must be Commander Storm trying to distract me? Comfort me? Heaven forbid!* "Are Dinah and David sooreth-alls? Um." She made a face. *That can't be right.*

"Souretholim," he corrected. "Aye. The Shepherd and the Ambassador are both Stonesingers, and are bound for Y'Vasheirdenelle—the Fortress of Living Stone—as soon as the waystone activates. They shall accompany me there to consult with the Eldest." He averted his gaze, expression darkening, then turning bland as he faced her.

With her chin resting on the pillow, she glanced at him sidelong. "Commander, if I pass this 'examination,' and it turns out there *is* an artifact that can protect me ..." She bit her lip. *Forge ahead, Annabelle!* She gathered her courage. "Will you let me come along with you?"

He looked at her, expression unreadable. She watched him with bated breath and prayed. *Please, please, please, God!*

His mouth twitched, and he said, "Aye. Provided you pass the trials."

Eyes wide, Annabelle waited for him to elucidate, but he raised his eyebrows and jerked his chin toward Lord Evanrudhe.

I guess that subject is closed, for now. She turned her concern to Toad, who sat blinking at her, looking dazed. "I'm fine, kiddo. A little tired, but ... okay."

"I found no sign of outside incursion, Commander," the dwelfnhir said, smiling. His eyes shone, and he seemed to contain a great excitement. "It appears ... although I cannot reach him ... Balthazar lives." Clearing his throat, he turned to regard her. "Lie down, Miss Wells."

She lay on the cushion, resting her cheek on the axolotl pillow. His gentle smile crinkling the corners of his hazel eyes into crow's-feet, the silver-haired dwelfnhir took Annabelle's hands. Suddenly, a jolt ran through her, and her vision doubled, then tripled. His expression concerned, Lord Evanrudhe said something, but it sounded garbled. She drifted away in flickering opalescent light. She saw ...

Shadows creep around the edges of a deep and lonely cavern where the cloaked bard sits before a pipe organ. Wearing a mask that looks like a face, he turns, eyes glowing violet, and holds out a glowing sapphire orb with a mocking half-smile. "We meet again, Ahdmerel," he says. "If you desire Rainblessed's vashryu, then you will face me."

Flicker.

A green aura shines around a shifting figure—first a wolf, then a woman, then an eagle— watching her from a hilltop. Only the blue-green eyes remain the same. An echo of rage and great loss surrounds the woman, and an aching kinship tugs at Annabelle's heartstrings.

Flicker.

From within a blazing inferno like molten gold, a red-haired man with pale blue eyes reaches out to Annabelle. His strong features remind her of Neal, but she had never seen such bleakness in her friend's face. Nor was Neal's chest ridged with scars. An electric thrill mingled with tender exasperation leaves her perplexed.

Flicker.

A gray-skinned youth with fierce orange eyes places a helmet with curling ram's horns on his head. Black ink tattoos on his bare torso writhe like spiny tentacles, growing larger and darker until his entire body is consumed by shadow. Recognition slams through Annabelle like an incorporeal spear, but is gone before she can grasp hold of it.

Flicker.

Enoch, bearing a silver diadem upon his brow, stands tall in his silver-chased armor. His eyes widen. "Run, Annabelle!" He turns away as a transparent sword appears in his hand and settles into a battle stance against a dark figure she can't make out.

She strained, her kythim blazing sapphire as it streamed toward him. "Enoch!"

Flicker ...

And then she spiraled into a chaos of prismatic light.

"Kiddo!"

Annabelle opened her eyes, panting. Concerned, wide-eyed faces hovered over her. Lord Evanrudhe peered at her. Opalescent light like that of the waystones swirled around dilated pupils as black as night. Commander Storm hovered on her other side. Violet sparks flared in the steel-gray depths of his irises. She'd never seen the Commander with such bald-faced emotion on his scaled visage. Their mouths moved, but she heard nothing but a keening whine.

Toad pushed into view, pale eyes huge and throat sac fluttering like a flag in a stiff breeze. He raised a front paw and touched her cheek. A ghostly image of the red-haired man surrounded by fire from her vision briefly overlaid the form of the oversized amphibian she knew.

"Kiddo, please be okay. They took the kid; I can't fail her, too. Oh, God, don't let her be harmed ..." He moved back, and the voice faded away.

Blinking, she struggled to rise on her elbows. "What. Was. That?" she asked, her heart hammering. At first, her voice seemed muffled, as if underwater, but then her ears popped and sounds came rushing in—birdsong, the creak of leather, men's voices raised in consternation. She winced, collapsing back on the cushion.

Lord Evanrudhe's arm encircled her, and he helped her sit. She leaned into him, her cheek resting against the cool linen draping his shoulder as he smoothed a hand down her hair. Just as her father did. After so long, being held comforted her, even though the dwelfnhir smelled like musty books and rain instead of aftershave. Moisture pricked her eyelids.

While murmuring reassurances, Lord Evanrudhe rubbed her shoulder and then braced her upright. Annabelle sniffed and blinked back tears. Commander Storm knelt at her feet, hands braced on his thighs, gray eyes narrowed and cold as the steel strapped at his hips.

I must have imagined the concern I saw in his expression.

"I apologize, my dear," the dwelfnhir said. "There was a ... resonance. Sometimes, there are echoes carried across from the Aethyr in this place. Are you feeling well?"

"I'm okay," Annabelle said as she exhaled. She rubbed her forehead.

Toad crawled on her cushion, brushing against her leg. "You sure?" His voice and gaze were both steady. Doubtless, she'd also imagined the panic in his voice earlier. She frowned with her fingers resting on the furrowed skin of her forehead. *Had* Toad spoken aloud?

"The womanchild is well, Sir Thomas," the Commander said, briskly. "Let us focus on essentials. First Councilor, did you detect aught of invasion in her mind? Is she compromised?"

Lord Evanrudhe shook his head. "I did not, Commander. I found no trace of invasion. No trace of another's meddling. She is not compromised."

"I didn't react like that when you probed my brain," Toad said, an edge to his voice. "Did you push harder because the Commander thinks someone messed with her head?"

"Sir Thomas," the evainghir snapped. "Show more respect."

Lord Evanrudhe raised a hand. "Let it go, Commander." He favored Toad with a tight smile. "I did nothing differently with Miss Wells, Sir Thomas, but all minds are unique. My touch was as delicate as I could make it. As I said, I am no Mindreaver; I dare not delve deeper into her memories." Blinking heavily, he sighed. "Before we speak further of my findings, allow me to assure myself that I have done no harm." He raised a silver eyebrow. "In the meantime, make yourself useful, Commander. Would you mind fetching her some water?"

With an assenting rumble, the evainghir cast her one final glance before he rose and stalked from the alcove. Toad remained pressed against her leg, looking between her and the dwelfnhir. "Lord Evanrudhe, what about the Sage in her head?"

Lord Evanrudhe's fingers were gentle and warm on her cheeks. Annabelle was struck by the unfathomable sorrow behind the man's eyes, as vast and deep as the outer reaches of space between the stars. His lips parted to speak, and then he hesitated. "I did not sense other presences," he finally said, "but as it was with you, Sir Thomas, there are echoes that remind me of the evaingynon."

"The chains," Toad said. "Maybe they can't be 'present' in our heads because they're trapped wherever they are in the dream place. Thank God," he muttered, shuddering.

"Dreamscape," Annabelle corrected Toad, and he cast her a nonplussed look.

"The vashryu," Lord Evanrudhe murmured, as if to himself. "Could it be? The essence preserved therein ... hmmm."

Vashryu! I've heard that word before. Aloud, she said, "Hadrien told me I needed to seek his vashryu."

"So he did, Miss Wells," the dwelfnhir replied with a weary smile. "And the fact that he did lends credibility to your recounting. It gives me hope. Each evaingynon possessed a vashryu—a focus-gem of extraordinary power and capacity attuned to his chosen aspect."

He leaned closer, peering into her eyes. There was a moment of confusion—her mind spinning through a void and her vision doubling before returning to normal. His brow pinched, and then his expression cleared. "Praise Yshua; your mind remains sound. Do you wish to speak of your experience?"

Annabelle blinked. "I saw ... Enoch." Her glance went to Toad, then to her hands playing with the skirts pooled in her lap. "I think I had a vision."

Commander Storm returned with ewer and mug in either hand. She considered asking him questions, but his eyes were like augers as he knelt at her feet. Maybe later.

His voice was cold and implacable. "You saw the lad?" He filled the mug from the ewer and thrust it into her hands, its blue-glazed clay chill against her palms. "Elaborate." Lord Evanrudhe shot him a glance with arched eyebrows, and he added, "After you drink."

Annabelle took a long gulp and then rested the mug against her forehead, relishing its coolness. Suddenly, energy surged through her and she felt as if she could take on the world.

"Wow," she said, turning the mug around in her hands. She glanced between it and the Commander. "Thank you. That really hits the spot."

Toad snorted. "Good thing His Excellentness isn't here."

Commander Storm regarded Annabelle with his usual wooden expression. "You are welcome, womanchild. Now, tell us of your ... vision."

"Okay." As she considered the odd images, she grew confused, because they faded like vapor in the sun and eluded rendering into words. All she remembered clearly was the last one: Enoch wearing a silver crown, and carrying that strange, transparent sword. While the men debated her description, she wracked her brain trying to recall the other visions.

Lord Evanrudhe spoke her name. She emerged from her contemplation with a muted yelp. Observing her soberly, he shook his head. "After all you've endured, I fear putting you through another ordeal. Are you well enough for the ceremony?"

Annabelle nodded. "Sure, I'll be fine—" She froze, staring at him. "What ceremony?"

Defender's Oath

Following the worship service, Annabelle stood rigid at one end of the platform, staring down at her bare feet while the Council members assembled. The scent of the altar flowers grew heady in her nostrils. Despite the tropical heat outside, the polished wooden floorboards felt cool.

Movement caught her eye as Toad hopped over to the opposite end of the platform, near the edge. He crouched there, watching her with his mouth closed and throat sac beating. During the service he'd maintained a stony silence and seemed distracted. She'd asked him what was wrong, but all he'd said was, "It's nothing, kiddo," and refused to elaborate.

I don't buy that, Toad. She fretted at her lip. Why wouldn't he just *talk* to her?

Wood creaked, and she glanced surreptitiously at Commander Storm, who stood to her left, this time without his armor and signature weapons. Clad in a black, double-breasted uniform jacket with gold buttons and matching trousers, he looked ... odd, and seemed almost as ill-at-ease as Annabelle felt. His fingers kept drifting toward the swords that weren't there.

Lord Evanrudhe had explained a little about the symbolism surrounding the ceremony. Because Annabelle had not yet attained her majority, the Commander served as her primary guardian on Tehara. Part of his role was to stand in for her father. *Commander Storm as my dad—what a horrible thought! He's so ... remote. And cold.* She suppressed a shudder. A sudden yearning for her parents overwhelmed her. She swallowed past a thickness in her throat.

The seven councilors stood between her and the tree growing out of the dais, three women lined up on the side closest to her and three men on the other end. Lord Evanrudhe stood a few steps before the other six. When she looked at him, she found him watching her, eyebrows arched inquiringly.

Annabelle managed a wan smile and a slight nod. She would go through with this ceremony. It was important to Raeden, who had been her friend from the beginning. And it would smooth the way toward continuing the quest to find Enoch.

At the far end of the platform, Shepherd David and Raeden—both clad in uniforms like the Commander's—stepped up to the raised floor. She glimpsed Toad sidling closer to the edge to avoid them, his mouth moving as if he muttered to himself.

Their eyes met. Toad's filled with a cold fire that sent her heart racing. Her stomach did a flip-flop. What was *wrong* with him? *Is he mad at me? I feel like I'm on trial, somehow.* Toad jerked his gaze toward David and Raeden. Rubbing her arms, she shifted her weight from one foot to the other.

A warm breath fanned her hair. "Steady, womanchild," the evainghir rumbled, like thunder on the horizon.

Annabelle took a deep breath, then looked up. Raeden was down on one knee before the councilors with his head bowed. Beside him, David stood with hands clasped in the small of his back, as handsome and serious as ever.

The man on the far end spoke. "Who have you brought before us, Shepherd Degalaevid?"

"Raeden von Bleistaff, hereditary Count of the Blackwood Forest, and head of the clan."

Annabelle's eyes widened. *I knew he had a lordly title, but ... why isn't he home, ruling his clan? Not that I know where the Blackwood Forest is, or anything.*

"Why have you brought him?" the second man asked.

"I stand as sponsor to his desire to swear the defender's oath and serve as champion to an innocent requiring protection."

The third male councilor spoke. "And who is the innocent he desires to serve?"

Commander Storm stepped forward, the wood creaking beneath his weight. "My ward, Miss Annabelle Leigh Wells," he said, "is an innocent without adequate battle-training."

Wow, he spoke my name and his head didn't explode. She sucked her lips between her teeth to prevent the thoughts in her head from bubbling out. *How am I an innocent? According to the Bible, no one is truly innocent. And as for battle-training, I suppose a few days of sword practice don't count—*

One woman said, "Your Grace, present the child to us."

Heart hammering against her breastbone, Annabelle straightened her back. Commander Storm's hand engulfed her right shoulder. He ushered her to stand three paces short of where Raeden knelt, still as a stone aside from his ears and his quivering tail. Once he released her, the Commander's hands hovered near his hips, as if seeking his swords, then he fell back to stand with his hands folded before him.

Another woman spoke. "Annabelle Leigh Wells, your guardian has determined that you lack the skill to defend yourself and stand in need of a champion. Do you agree with his assessment?"

Yeah, I suck at swordplay, but doesn't being a wyldling make me less helpless? Not that I know how to control it ...

Her cheeks flamed as she uttered the words Dinah coached her to say. "Yes, I agree with his assessment. I lack the skill to defend myself." She forced herself to scan the assembled councilors. Although their faces betrayed little emotion, compassion shone in their jewel-toned eyes. The woman who spoke first gave her a tiny smile and an infinitesimal nod.

The third woman, the one on the end, said, "Commander Storm, this man, Raeden von Bleistaff, has offered himself in service as your ward's avowed champion and protector. Know you any reason he would be unfit for this duty?"

Annabelle shot a look at the evainghir towering at her left shoulder to find his steely gaze upon her. Her heart stuttered. Quickly, she looked down at her toes. She wriggled them. Man, her feet were like ice. Why did she have to go barefoot? Something to do with her "innocence."

"His Excellency is of sound mind and heart," the Commander said. "He is a man of upright morals and firmly held principles. I do not object to him serving my ward."

Annabelle bit her lip, praying. *Please, God, let this work so I can go with him when he leaves Treehome.*

"Very well," Lord Evanrudhe said. "Rise, Your Excellency."

Taut as a strung bow, the kaenhir pushed himself up in one smooth motion. He clasped his hands behind his back with his eyes fixed on the cruciform tree behind the councilors. She wished to know his thoughts. There hadn't been time to talk with him before the ceremony. He'd already promised that he'd protect her. Why swear an oath?

Don't worry about it now. If this fulfills one condition for me to leave with Commander Storm, then that's what matters.

The First Councilor was still addressing Raeden; she'd missed what he'd said about the Oath and all it entailed. "... and do you intend to swear in the name of the Almighty Threefold One to serve as this maiden's champion, to defend her honor and her person from harm, and to ensure her spiritual well-being as the beloved child of Lord Yshua?"

Raeden stared at the tree. "Yes, he intends to swear the oath."

Lord Evanrudhe nodded. "Then swear your oath before the council, Raeden von Bleistaff, of the Blackwood Forest clan."

With his right fist over his heart, the bright-eyed kaenhir turned to face Annabelle. "This one swears in the name of the Almighty Threefold One to be your servant all of his days."

Annabelle narrowed her eyes. *Wait ... this doesn't sound like the same oath Dinah described to me. I thought it would only bind him for the duration of our quest.* She wasn't the only one who noticed; several Council members were frowning and glancing sidelong at one another. One woman openly gaped before smoothing over her expression. Commander Storm stirred. His eyelids fluttered, and he rocked back on his heels. However, Lord Evanrudhe's face never changed.

Raeden continued, "He will be the mighty oak to shelter you from the raging tempest. He will provide you succor when you faint. He will be the strong right arm to uphold you during trials. He will be the last defense against all your foes and the wrathful blade to cut down all those who mean you harm. His sword he lays at your feet until the end of his days."

Annabelle's heart banged so hard against her ribs she feared they would shatter. No one had ever spoken such beautiful, poetic words to her before. But why make the oath so much stronger? And then a strange thought surfaced. *Raeden doesn't even have a sword!*

"... If it takes his life to keep you whole, then so be it." His throat bobbed and his voice roughened as he traced the sign of the cross from his forehead to his chest. "Thus has he already sworn before Lord Yshua in his heart."

"No." Annabelle blurted. "We can't go through with this." Her voice hitched. "Not your entire life. I'd never ask you to *die* for me."

Raeden's eyes softened. "You do not have to, Freylin. And your servant has sworn his oath. It is done." He turned to Lord Evanrudhe. "He is her champion."

Lord Evanrudhe blinked, then replied, "Verily; may it be so," and the councilors echoed him. "In the name of the Almighty Threefold One, Yaweh, Yshua, and Ruach Hakodesh—" he traced the sign of the cross upon Raeden's brow, "—this man is now consecrated in his purpose." He paused, looking the kaenhir in the eye. Raeden nodded.

Lord Evanrudhe turned to Annabelle and addressed her by name, saying, "This man, Raeden von Bleistaff, is now bound into your service. Forsaking the world and all others, he shall pursue neither worldly position, wealth, or wife so long as he is bound to you. Only his death shall release him from the vow he has sworn."

Annabelle swallowed a gasp. That hadn't been in the script either. She'd planned to release Raeden from her service as soon as they rescued Enoch. Dinah hadn't told her the Oath was irrevocable by anything save death! Why had her friend chosen to give up so much in becoming her champion?

It's unfair ... nothing is required of me in exchange!

She glanced at Toad; he was staring at Raeden with his mouth hanging open. Noticing her attention, he shut his mouth and quivered, his eyes dancing. What? Was Toad *laughing* at her?

Raeden went down on one knee beside her—like a knight paying obeisance to a queen—with his left hand braced against the floor and his right fist pressed against his chest. She wished she could see his face, but his head remained lowered.

Lord Evanrudhe looked down into her wide eyes and asked, "Do you accept this brave warrior's sacrifice to serve as your champion unto death?"

Tongue-tied, she stared down at her traveling companion and friend, who remained down on one knee. His black-tipped ears pricked up and swiveled toward her. Their deep interiors were quite pink, almost as pink as Peter's fur—*or my face right now.* She had never been so tempted to touch his ears.

Not unto death, she thought. *I don't want him to die for me. It wouldn't be right.* She hesitated with her lips parted to respond, thoughts racing. *He's doing this for Enoch. And if this clears the way for me continuing on the search for Enoch...*

Raeden was willing to lay down his life for his captive friend if it bought Enoch his freedom. It was his choice as an adult and a warrior. Who was she to deny him that?

But I won't let him die because of me. That's my *Oath, before God.*

Just as Dinah had instructed, she placed her hand upon Raeden's head, between his quivering ears. Beneath the silken copper strands, she could feel strength and power in the tremor of his muscles. Lord Evanrudhe covered her hand with his own, large, warm, and calloused. Around hers, his long, brown fingers sank into the kaenhir's hair.

"Miss Wells?"

Annabelle glanced up into Lord Evanrudhe's kind, yet sorrowful eyes. He'd warned her about what would happen next. A connection would form—like, but unlike the one she'd shared with Enoch. Steeling herself, she declared, "I do accept him as my champion." Internally, she swore: *And I will protect Raeden, even as he protects me. This oath is a two-way street.*

As her voice rang out in the evening air, power like an electric shock jolted through her, and she felt Raeden flinch. Tingling like pins and needles spread from her palm to the rest of her body while he shivered beneath her hand.

"It is done," Lord Evanrudhe whispered, lifting his hand.

Annabelle clenched her jaw until the tingling subsided. In its place, a knotted cord of sensations tightened in her chest. *Those aren't mine. That must be our bond!*

Gasping, she withdrew her hand and placed it over her heart, rubbing. "Raeden? I can feel you ..." But what was he feeling? She wetted her lips. "Are you okay?"

Trembling, Raeden's wide eyes rose to meet hers. "Freylin. Your servant is well. He is blessed. He finally understands." A warm glow filled Annabelle's chest as the cord unknotted and relaxed. Raeden's ears lifted as he smiled, tenderness filling his emerald gaze. "He would die to assure the light he sees inside you does not go out."

Annabelle swallowed. *Oh, Raeden. I never should've agreed to this oath. What have I done to you?*

Grivvensfel

Dreadlord

Night swaddled the travelers in its dark, warm cloak as they approached Grivvensfel. Bored, William had extended his kythim to explore the surroundings when he experienced a frisson. Anxiety surged through him. *That's not my emotion. Is something amiss with the harkhurz?*

He came to a halt as Zakaar slid through the gnarled bushes lining the path, wide-eyed and breathless, and fell into step beside his master.

William quickly retracted his kythim, and the knotted tension dissipated. What in the freezing void was that? Had he sensed the harkhurz's feelings as if they were his own?

Orange spirals of apprehension fizzled in Zakaar's aura as he reported to Tenebris. "Grivvensfel is occupied, Milord. It is the Dreadlord. And he has brought nightstalkers."

Astonishment crackled through William like lightning and seared away his musings. *Burning suns! What is the Dreadlord doing here?* He glanced at the Golorum, whose hard expressions went even stonier. Unease churned in his gut. Would there be an altercation? Pure-blooded Golorum loathed nightstalkers, often killing them on sight.

William swallowed. Concerns regarding how the warriors would respond if they discovered *he* was half kadorei occasionally surprised him and brought stirrings of alarm.

But I'm not like the nightstalkers. Sunslight doesn't burn or blind me even though I can pass as a true nehmwight. So, I must be ... something else.

Tenebris muttered an oath and barked out an order to stop. Shaking himself from his thoughts, William grasped the nearest post of the palanquin as it came to a halt. From inside, the captive began wondering what was going on. It was Northward's mental voice; William recognized the distinction.

Lips tight, his master whirled on the harkhurz and fingered the locket he rarely removed. "How many Rakt-nasala?" When Zakaar blinked in confusion, Tenebris pinched the bridge of his nose, grumbling. "I am surrounded by blithering imbeciles." Piercing Zakaar with a fiery glare, he spoke slowly and clearly. "How many *nightstalkers* accompany the Dreadlord? Where are they and how are they deployed? Tell me exactly what you saw, harkhurz, or I shall flay you where you stand."

With a shudder, Zakaar explained that the Dreadlord and six nightstalkers occupied a large building on what had once been Grivvensfel's main road. The nightstalkers didn't appear to be armed, but that meant little. William listened and considered their employer and benefactor. He'd known the man for as long as he could remember. Doubtless, the Dreadlord's companions served as an honor guard and were there only for show. Formidable warriors as nightstalkers were, the Dreadlord possessed his own means of protecting himself.

William's heart raced. Anticipation and fear warred for dominance as he considered the implications. Perhaps the Dreadlord brought urgent tidings. Had plans changed? He glanced at the palanquin. They'd brought the wyldling, as directed. Were they to be punished for some perceived wrongdoing known only to the Dreadlord? He licked his lips and forced his hands to remain at his sides instead of seeking his flask. No whiskey. Not in front of Tenebris.

He glanced sidelong at his master. "Do you think we're in trouble, Master?"

"I can't think of a reason." Tenebris frowned and stroked his beard. "Just keep your mouth shut. And your eyes and ears open. Make sure the kadorei behaves himself," he added under his breath. "If you can handle the mute-spell?"

He bit back a scathing response, settling for: "You showed it to me several times, Master." And on many other occasions, when Tenebris had used it on him. "I practiced it on Zakaar and Northward. It only takes me five seconds now."

Tenebris grunted, his eyes fixed on their destination.

The Dreadlord awaited them beside a stone building festooned with ivy, a tall figure with noble bearing flanked by his nightstalker escorts. He was clad in form-fitting dark gray armor and a matched pair of scimitars sheathed in tooled black leather scabbards hung from his weapons-belt. Eyes the color of amethysts surveyed their party, softening in a smile as they settled on William, then hardening again as they passed over Tenebris, Zakaar, and the Golorum. He arched a black eyebrow. "Good evening, gentlemen. So good of you to join me. Yvres Tenebris, a pleasant night to visit the local tavern, is it not?"

"O-of course, Your Eminence," Tenebris replied, hands fisted at his sides. "As you—"

"William Dulciber," the Dreadlord interjected, lifting a gauntleted hand to indicate the palanquin. "If you would please show me what you have brought?"

He's singling me out. Why? To cause problems with Tenebris?

No time for idle speculation. Avoiding his master's gaze, William squared his shoulders. "Of course, Your Eminence." He activated his arkhabala, prepared the mute-spell as he pulled aside the palanquin curtains, then cast it on the captive.

Northward's eyes bulged. He stared out of his prison with his kythim flaring the bright green of utter shock. His mind spewed forth a stream of horrified babble. *"A dwelfnhir! What in perdition is a dwelfnhir doing here—is this Grivvensfel? —in the company of his ancestral enemies? And escorted by nightstalkers! How can he trust them? Nightstalkers are notorious for being unstable and killing without restraint."*

Standing at the palanquin corner closest to Northward's head, William twisted the edge of the curtain behind his back and shifted his balance. His arkhabala prickled. Why, oh why, couldn't the mute-spell be used to silence thoughts? So what if the Dreadlord was a dwelfnhir? William had never thought much about it, because the Dreadlord ... was the Dreadlord.

William's stomach felt tied in knots and Northward's terrified confusion wasn't helping. He had no reason to fear the Dreadlord. The man seemed to take an interest in his progress and had steered his education along a certain vein. And yet ...

Too much is riding on the Dreadlord's approval. William touched the place where the portrait rested in his sakkhelt. *I'll need his help to capture Milady Blue. But what can I give him in return? Perhaps he would be grateful enough to have another wyldling to allow me access to study her power. It's ... intriguing.*

His breath quickened as he recalled the sensation of her arms around him, the way she'd smiled, and her shimmering blue eyes. Heat rose to his face, and a strange feeling stirred inside him, something akin to the longing he sometimes experienced when looking at the stars.

Mother of the Outer darkness! Her confounded spell was still affecting him. He'd tried many cantrips, sunderings, and even a charm-binding. Nothing worked. Why couldn't he break it? Was she that powerful? With that sort of strength, he could put Tenebris in his place. He forced his hand from the lapel of his burkheld before it dove inside in search of his whiskey flask, while his eyes sought his master.

Tenebris faced their patron with shoulders back and chin lifted. "Honored Dreadlord, you see I brought the wyldling. I planned to deliver him to you. There was no need to interrupt your research to meet us here in Grivvensfel."

Northward's mental voice babbled again. *"That dwelfnhir is a dreadlord? But that's a nehmwight title! What in nether perdition is going on?"*

"Plans change, Yvres Tenebris," the Dreadlord replied. "But first, tell me about your travels since we last spoke."

While his master updated the Dreadlord, William eyed the two nightstalkers flanking the door and standing in a rigid military posture. Their pale gray skin looked even more washed out against the black uniforms in the Eastern Marches garrison style. Why did the Dreadlord insist they dress as kadorei soldiers? As he habitually did when in the company of nightstalkers, William cataloged the kadorei features—stockier build, wider face, and more rounded ear-tips.

As long as nobody looks too closely at my ears, I could pass for a full-blooded nehmwight. He glanced at Northward, who was still gawking at the Dreadlord. *And I'm neither unstable nor a crazed killer.* Perhaps the Dreadlord used Aethyric magic to control his nightstalkers. Yes, that tracked. He had the raw power. Tenebris respected and feared the Dreadlord above all, and Tenebris only admired those more powerful than himself.

A grin tugged at his mouth. *And someday, that'll be me.* The grin faded. *If I can convince the Dreadlord to teach me.*

"... and now, despite delays—" Tenebris shot an annoyed glance at William, "—we have made it here to Grivvensfel, as per the original plan."

William pursed his lips. *Oh, so now the delays are* my *fault?*

"Very good," the Dreadlord replied, his expression neutral. "My timetable has moved up. The Commander eluded my first trap, and now ..." His eyes narrowed. "My sources recently informed me that your father—" his lip curled, "—has scented blood in the water and sets his own ambush for the evainghir's party. This leads me to wonder, Yvres Tenebris. How did Vespyrahl learn of all this?"

William's breath caught in his throat. A shiver raced through him as he glanced between his master and the dwelfnhir. Warlord Vespyrahl was Tenebris's *father?*

The Arkhadahn twitched. "Dreadlord," he rasped, "of what do you accuse me? You know I have no dealings with Warlord Vespyrahl. My sire never truly held my allegiance. I cut all ties with his faction when I joined yours."

Master Tenebris has many secrets, indeed! William twisted the palanquin curtain behind his back, wringing it like a chicken's neck as he held on to the mute-spell. All he'd known was that Tenebris hated Vespyrahl above and beyond other warlords. Apparently, his loathing was personal. No matter. The Dreadlord would deal with Warlord Vespyrahl.

A bloom of bright yellow terror infused Northward's kythim. *"Is Annabelle in danger from a nehmwight warlord? I believed she was safe! No, Yshua, please, no. Protect her."* He shook with the effort of trying to speak, his face darkening. White tongues of flame erupted in his silver kythim as he repeated: *"Protect her, Lord Yshua."*

William grimaced. It felt like someone was pummeling the inside of his skull. Northward was fighting the spell. It was all William could do to hold on to it and prevent an outburst.

Meanwhile, the Dreadlord had resumed speaking. "Thus, I must bring you to Fastness via waystone. Now that I possess the last of the wyldling bloodline, the next phase of my plan shall begin." He looked past Tenebris and measured the prisoner with a cool gaze. A faint smile curved his lips, but it didn't reach his gem-hard eyes. "Greetings, Enoch Northward Sel Drayven. I have looked forward to this. Tis a pleasure to meet you."

To Capture a Wyldling

Zakaar's earlier hunting foray provided them with a meal of terror bird meat supplemented with greens and delicacies brought by the Dreadlord. At the Dreadlord's behest, William, Zakaar, and Northward dined together at the smallest of the three upright tables in what used to be Grivvensfel's tavern.

William would have enjoyed the food more, but his head still reeled from the double blow of learning that his master was the son of Warlord Vespyrahl, and that Vespyrahl planned to waylay the evainghir. The first revelation he pushed aside in favor of examining the second, which carried more dire implications. While he shoveled sweetmeats into his mouth—before Northward and Zakaar snatched them all—questions consumed his thoughts.

Forget *how* Vespyrahl found out. That was a mystery to solve later. *Why* did the warlord seek Northward's rescuers? For vengeance? It could be personal. All knew of the antipathy between Vespyrahl and Commander Storm, who made it his business to destroy every warlord and Arkhadahn who rose to authority in the nehmwight factions.

William grabbed his tea, considering another possibility. Perhaps the most powerful warlord on the continent knew the Commander harbored a suspected wyldling.

In the midst of drinking, he inhaled and choked on his tea. With Annabelle in Vespyrahl's hands, William would lose his chance to study her. Freezing void! She was supposed to be *his* wyldling. A surge of strange emotion twisted his gut. He spluttered until his throat cleared. A bitter laugh made him look up to meet Northward's cold gaze.

"Careful, pig." Their prisoner sneered. "Wouldn't want you to keel over before I brought you to justice."

Seated beside him, Zakaar growled and smacked Northward upside the head. The youth grimaced but made no outcry. His kythim sparked with vermilion rage. As he turned back to his food, the harkhurz grumbled, "You are in no position to bring anyone anywhere, warlock."

A pig, am I? Northward ought to expand his insults beyond the barnyard references. It was too bad the Dreadlord insisted he remove the mute-spell from Northward. Wiping his mouth on his sleeve, William bought time to compose himself. He brought out his flask and took a hearty swig while regarding his two companions through narrowed eyes.

Northward sat across the small round table from William, dressed in his fancy silver jacket, tunic, and trousers. His feet remained bare, but the Dreadlord insisted they allow him to eat while unencumbered by the snare, save for the collar, two lengths wound around his ankles, and the strands connected to them. For now, William held his leash. That would change once they arrived at the Dreadlord's stronghold. Northward was the Dreadlord's property now, he mused as he put away his flask.

But the Dreadlord gave me the treatise on the Aethyr, so he obviously wants me to study it. Perhaps he'll allow me to assist him in his research involving the wyldling. Maybe, if I ask, he'll allow me to observe Northward on my own. If Annabelle is taken or killed by the warlord ...

He squashed a twinge of regret; the squirming in his gut was because of scarfing all those sweetmeats. He took a long slurp of his tea, hoping the mint would settle his stomach. Surely, one wyldling in the snare would compensate for the two out wandering the wilderness. And he wanted nothing to do with that cursed knight and his flaming sword.

William slammed down his empty mug and snapped, "If I were you, kadorei, I'd watch my burning mouth."

Northward glared at him. "If I were you, I'd beg for the Threefold One's forgiveness."

What was the blistering fool nattering about? William snorted. "You only wish you could be me. I don't require anyone's forgiveness." He picked up a drumstick and sank his teeth into the greasy meat, tearing it from the bone and chewing furiously while scanning the room.

The Dreadlord's two men stood on guard outside the door, to William's relief. He shifted in his seat. Being in the presence of nightstalkers made his skin crawl. They tended toward mental instability. Prone to murderous rages. He couldn't fathom why the Dreadlord trusted their ilk.

Merciful Valeshka! At least the Golorum are ignoring them instead of fighting.

He looked past the six elite warriors, who ate their meal at a large table between them and the door to a private room, where the Dreadlord conferred with Tenebris. A ward against eavesdropping shimmered silver through the cracks. Were they discussing the Dreadlord's plans for Northward? William licked grease off his fingers, but hardly noticed the rich flavor. *He* wasn't privy to those plans.

But he would be. As soon as his meat was gone, and he'd had a fortifying swig from his flask, he'd speak to the Dreadlord. Alone. *He'll be interested in what I have to say about another wyldling. By Villem's spear! When he learns about Annabelle, he'll need to act to prevent her capture. If nothing else, a wyldling in Vespyrahl's hands spells disaster for the Dreadlord's faction.*

While he brooded, Zakaar finished his meal, leaving a pile of well-gnawed bones on his plate. "Dulciber," he said as he rose, "I go to walk the perimeter now." He glared at Northward, who eyed him sidelong while chewing on a wing. "You want me to hold him down while you give him his medicine at the end of the watch?" His whiskers quivered and lavender eagerness spiraled in his aura. So far, he restrained his murderous impulses—no doubt a testament to William's fine potion brewing.

"No," he replied. "The Dreadlord won't like that." He dismissed the harkhurz with a wave. Once Zakaar left, William sneered and jabbed a finger at his captive. "Lucky for you, he wants you of sound mind."

Northward snorted a laugh. "What for? If this Dreadlord doesn't plan to kill me, then he's going to harness me like an ox and use me somehow. A beast of burden has no need for brains." His tone sounded resigned, but the shrewd glint in his eye and the indigo triangles of calculation in his kythim betrayed him. Northward was fishing for information again. Well, he wouldn't get any. Not that William had much to give, were he so inclined.

"I reckon it's part of your torture—being aware of everything." William shrugged. "It's all the same to me."

Just then, he sensed a change in air pressure as the ward went down. The door opened and Tenebris came out. His expression gave away nothing of his mood and his kythim remained invisible even when William strained to read him. How did Tenebris manage that? One day, William would figure it out and then his master would be an open book to him.

And then I'll defeat him.

"William," his master said, beckoning. "Quit stuffing your face. It's unbecoming of an Arkhadahn to wallow like a pig. The Dreadlord wishes to speak with you now. Bring the prisoner."

Scowling, William pushed himself to his feet. "I wasn't wallowing," he muttered. The other youth sniggered. "Oi! Shut it, Northward. You're the one leashed like an animal." He yanked at the snare, sending a mental impetus along its strands as he did so. Northward gasped and he fell out of his seat. "Come along, you clumsy ox." An ox, indeed. A dense and irritating beast of burden. That was Northward, for certain. He grinned.

Ox. I like that image for you, Milord High-and-Mighty.

William led his captive toward the open door. After the first stumble, Northward came quickly enough. Tenebris moved aside so they could enter, but didn't follow. "Don't embarrass me," he hissed. "Prove yourself worthy of six circles."

"Yes, Master," he replied as Tenebris stalked away. *I am worthy of six circles, Tenebris. You even said so yourself!*

"Six circles. What are these sons of goats talking about?"

He whirled to glare at the other youth. "None of your business. Just keep your blazing mouth shut and don't speak until spoken to."

Northward frowned, blinking. He held up his hands as if to ward off a blow. "Um. I didn't say anything."

William scoffed. "Likely story." Inwardly, he flinched. *Did I read Northward's blazing mind again? This is growing more annoying than helpful.*

He peered across the threshold. Beyond lay an office where the erstwhile proprietor had conducted business or did their accounting. Hung from a ceiling hook, a lantern cast a warm glow throughout the room. A regina moth circled the light, its large fluttering wings sending weird shadows across broken, cobwebbed shelving, water-stained walls, and the black-haired dwelfnhir seated behind a shabby desk with peeling lacquer.

William bowed. "Your Eminence."

"Enter, youngling. And bring our guest."

"Come on." He tugged on the snare, compelling Northward to follow him inside.

Busy scribing rows of figures on an unrolled parchment, the Dreadlord glanced up with a tight smile and gestured at a long, padded bench along one wall. "Have a seat, lads." He set down his pen and sanded the parchment.

William shut the door and eyed the bench dubiously. The pad was a faded maroon and its stuffing was coming out, no doubt raided by vermin for nest material. He'd sat on worse, but why not test it? He made a mocking bow to the other youth. "After you, Milord High-and-Mighty."

Chin lifted, Northward lowered himself on the bench with the ease of a knight in his own court, though his eyes darted between William and the Dreadlord. He clasped his hands in his lap. William waited for three heartbeats, and then gingerly sat on the end nearest the door. Wood creaked and groaned like a tree about to fall. He flinched, on the verge of jumping up again, but settled when nothing else happened.

Northward snorted, his lips pressed firmly together as he stared at the moth orbiting the lantern. His kythim danced with silent laughter.

The Dreadlord raised his black eyebrows. "Comfortable?" William swallowed his embarrassment and nodded. *Here's another person whose aura I can't read.* Gaze shifting to the prisoner, the Dreadlord took his time in rolling up the parchment and then slid it into a messenger tube. "Enoch Northward Sel Drayven?"

Northward tightened his lips and kept watching the moth.

William scoffed. Regina moths were pretty enough, but what was so interesting about this one that he'd risk alienating the man who held his fate in his hands?

With a sigh, the Dreadlord made a twisting movement, curling his fingers, and a silver shimmer infused the door, walls, ceiling, and floor. He steepled his hands before him on the desk and turned to survey the youths. "We are now warded. Enoch Northward Sel Drayven."

The prisoner flinched, then made fists. *"How could he know my family name? Commander Storm said nobody knew about my family. But he lied ..."*

William stared at him. *Well, this is interesting. I didn't know Northward's real surname, either. Now I wonder—*

"Forgive me," the Dreadlord continued, "but I must ask you to endure the indignity of being muffled for the span of a conversation." He turned to William. "If you would?"

He started. "Who, me?"

The Dreadlord nodded. "If this is within your skill?"

He's testing me. That's what Tenebris meant about proving myself worthy.

"Of course." Swallowing with difficulty, William faced Northward, who steadfastly refused to look at anything aside from the moth.

Let's see ... muffling spell. Similar to the mute-spell. Renders the target blind, deaf, and dumb. He'd studied it and seen Tenebris do it. *Should only take a pinch of effort.*

Could he do it as Tenebris did, without shedding blood? Only one way to find out. He intoned the cantrip and his arkhabala hummed as he strained to pull energy into his palms. Nothing happened. Mouthing an obscenity, he stared down at his empty hands.

I memorized the cantrip and uttered it perfectly. That should have worked.

"Any time now," he heard Northward jeer. "Not only does he eat like a pig, but he's slow as a slug. A slug-pig. Slig."

His eyes snapped up. "Suns burn your tongue, Northward! Be quiet. I'm working here." The other youth's eyes widened as he gave William a probing look, and his kythim flared with complex shapes and colors William couldn't decipher. The Dreadlord's face held an expression of amused interest.

Grimacing, William tried the spell again, sweat popping out on his forehead, but to no avail. Mortification heated him. Without bloodshed, his arkhabala was insufficient.

Blistering agonies, I don't want to cut myself for a measly third order spell! I should've practiced this on Zakaar when I first considered it, then I would've known.

He sighed and shut his eyelids. There was another way—the Aethyr. With each use, it became easier to tap into and no longer hurt when he melded the Aethyr with the spells he wrought through his arkhabala. Did other Arkhadahns ever do the same, despite the common belief that the Aethyr was unclean? Pursing his lips, he concentrated on the spell.

This time, as he spoke the cantrip, he extended his kythim and dragged in skeins of power, glittering like jewels. His arkhabala prickled as violet-tinged energy poured into his palms.

Yes! I did it. William turned his palms out to face Northward and hurled twisting coils of glittering amethyst. The other youth stiffened and grunted as the violet strands spread out to engulf him inside a continuous field.

Chest heaving, Northward gripped the shabby bench beneath him. His lips moved. *"What's happening? Make it stop!"* Turning, his glazed eyes flickered past William's, then fastened on them. *"Perdition take you—you son of a goat!"*

A horrible cacophony—a voice screaming for help—filled William's mind, and he reeled, falling off the bench and clutching at his skull to keep it from shattering.

The Dreadlord eclipsed the lantern's light. A hand touched him. His arkhabala flexed, shuddered, and then his grip on the spell snapped. Suddenly, the barrage of mental sound faded to a distant keening, and then a gorgeous silence fell. The Dreadlord bent over him, one hand on his shoulder and the other on Northward's. No longer covered by the muffling spell, the other youth's head drooped down to his chest. The Dreadlord eased him down until he lay on his side, eyes closed and breathing peacefully. William was struck by Northward's resemblance to Annabelle, all the tension and rage having fled from his face.

"I sent him to sleep," The Dreadlord said in a gentle tone. He peered at William, frowning. "Any damage?"

William groaned as his arkhabala shivered into quiescence, then hauled himself to his feet. Don't show weakness! "No." He grinned. "Save your concern for Northward, here."

The Dreadlord straightened, his frown deepening. "It was a cruel thing I did," he murmured, "asking you to inflict him with blindness and deafness. Cruel to both of you. But necessity compels, when the Evil One mans the helm—or so my brother claimed. The lad shall recover." With a nod, he turned and strode back to his chair behind the desk. He folded his hands on the desk's surface. "Tell me, William Dulciber. How long have you been able to sense others' thoughts?"

William went still, gaping at his host. "How ..." *I don't dare defy this man. The Dreadlord has powers I know nothing of. He put Northward to sleep with just a touch. He cut me off from the*

Aethyr and stopped my spell. What else might he have done to me? Can he read my thoughts?

"How did I know?" Smiling thinly, the Dreadlord quirked an eyebrow and leaned forward. "Come, now, lad. Do you expect me to divulge my secrets so easily? However, I shall tell you this: demanding silence from a person who has not spoken is a sign either of madness or telepathic ability. And I do not believe you are a madman."

William found himself reaching for his flask and forced his hand down. Warily, he said, "Sometimes, I'm able to hear what Northward is thinking, like part of a conversation." He licked his lips. That's how he'd found out about Annabelle. "But I haven't been able to replicate this with anyone else." At least, not in the waking world. He'd sensed a few of Annabelle's thoughts. No need to give everything away, though.

"Fascinating," the Dreadlord murmured. "Earlier, your master informed me you accessed the Aethyr; manipulated it to gather valuable information regarding Commander Storm's whereabouts. Captain Wuya recently confirmed contact with his party. And now, I have witnessed you use the Aethyr to fuel that muffling spell, blending it with your sorcery. I am ... impressed." He narrowed his eyes. "It would be a waste to not cultivate your talent, William Dulciber."

"Are you ... offering to teach me?" His heart raced. A hunger filled him to know all the Dreadlord knew—to sit at his feet and learn—seasoned with the iron tang of fear.

A chance to learn Aethyric principles from the Dreadlord himself!

The Dreadlord's smile broadened. "Indeed, I am. I have spoken with your master. This would not break your covenant with him as his apprentice. Any training you receive from me will not impede your progress in … that art." He winced, as if tasting something sour, and then his expression cleared. "Now, we shall discuss your forays into the dreamscape."

"Burning suns!" William blurted as he leaped to his feet. *It's as if all my secrets are laid bare to this man!* "You know about that, too?" *By all the impotent godlings and the Outer Darkness—I just shouted at the Dreadlord!* He resisted the urge to cringe and abase himself. Mustn't show weakness. He fisted his hands at his sides, driving his nails into his palms. "I beg your pardon, Your Eminence, for my outburst."

The Dreadlord chuckled, his violet eyes gleaming. He waved away William's apology. "Twas understandable. I would react the same, had another revealed they knew things I desired to keep hidden. Given my wealth of experience and the skills I've honed over the epochs, I possess a certain advantage over a callow youth. Matters of the mind are within the purview of my family. In a manner of speaking."

He paused as all humor fled from him. The Dreadlord's sorrowful and bleak gaze made William question his age. He spoke in terms of epochs. What skills could one gain during the extended lifespan of the dwelfnim? Most nehmwights didn't live beyond their first epoch, let alone two. Precious few attained two hundred Turnings.

"Although I rarely visit the world of dreams," the Dreadlord continued, "I can sense a certain resonance when untrained younglings are blundering around, manipulating and warding off areas in the dreamscape." He smiled faintly, as if to take the sting from his words. "I also have other sources of intelligence, William Dulciber, and one has informed me you are a suitable candidate for training in the art of traveling dreams. Which segues nicely into our next topic." The smile faded. "Tell me about the pale maiden you encountered. The one bearing Rainblessed's sourekghar."

Suns burn me to ash! William drew in an extended breath to calm himself and sort his thoughts, while trying *not* to think about the flask tucked inside his burkheld. He'd already planned to tell the Dreadlord about Annabelle and her armor. It was uncanny how he'd plunged right to the point. The fluttering moth drew his attention. An impulse swept over him to conjure a werelight and entice it from the golden glow.

Instead, he glanced at the slumbering youth while flexing cramped fingers. "The maiden—I call her Milady Blue—claims to be Northward's sister," he rasped. Clearing his throat, he added, "They have the same eyes, so perhaps it's true. I'm fairly certain she's a wyldling. Though she denies knowing any magic, she claims to have healed someone." He grimaced. "And she throws about beguilement spells rather liberally, seemingly without knowing what she does."

Heat rushed into his face, and he drew in a sharp breath as he recalled meeting Annabelle in his guise as Northward. His insides still twisted when he pictured her as he'd last seen her—with blue eyes filled with tears.

Lying little tesseramint. You'll pay for muddling my mind, Milady Blue.

He concentrated, his arkhabala purred, and an orange werelight popped into existence. One of the first spells he'd learned. Calm settled over him and his breathing evened out.

The Dreadlord's laughter startled him from his reverie. "I ... see. And do you have much contact with this 'Milady Blue?' Does she trust you?"

William nodded, passing the werelight back and forth between his hands. "I've made headway in that direction, Your

Eminence." At least, as long as he had his Northward disguise, she would continue to speak with him. He'd already made adjustments based on that first meeting. "The gullible little riverlark blathered on about being on a mission to rescue Northward, who she was with, and where they were going."

"Very good." The Dreadlord steepled his fingers. "So, this was the source of your intelligence; I shall keep that in strict confidence. Your master would not be pleased, but I am impressed with your ingenuity. First, you capture young Sel Drayven, and now another wyldling is within our grasp. Although I was not aware that others of that bloodline survived ..." He frowned, then shook his head. "A matter to consider later. First, we must secure this maiden. Do you know her current companions and whereabouts?" The Dreadlord's violet eyes glinted, hard as the amethysts they resembled.

Violet. The same color as his kythim was now. William's insides chilled. What did that mean? Had he tapped into the Aethyr so often that he was losing touch with the Arkhabadh? No. Outer Darkness forfend! He would have his six circles once they reached Fastness.

William inhaled, then exhaled. Looking at his werelight calmed him. That was still orange. All was well; his flask could stay where it was, for now. And he hadn't missed the Dreadlord's use of "our" and "we."

"I know exactly where Milady Blue is, Your Eminence." William sent the little werelight bobbing up toward the lantern and its mesmerized moth. He took a deep breath. "She's under the evainghir's protection; traveling with him and several others."

"Indeed." The Dreadlord's tone was flat. Cold calculation replaced the mirth in his gaze. He tapped his fingertips together. "Well played, lad. Training you shall be interesting. Assuredly, I can make good use of you and your crooked mind." Chuckling, he murmured, "What delicious irony. I wonder ..."

Was now the time to ask the Dreadlord for his help in capturing Annabelle in exchange for a chance to study her? He fed more energy into his orange orb. It brightened. Yes! The regina moth now seemed more interested in his werelight than the lantern.

William swallowed, then leaned against the wall and tucked his arms in opposite sleeves. "Your Eminence, I will happily deliver Milady Blue to you—like I did Northward—but would it be possible ..." He licked his lips. "You gave me the scroll on Aethyric power. I would like to study the wyldlings." He tugged the werelight back toward himself, and the moth followed.

The Dreadlord chuckled, and this time the humor reached his eyes. "How fortuitous. Our minds are aligned. My plans were to involve you in my research once you'd passed whatever trial your master had in store for you."

William's breath caught in his throat. "I ... I'm honored." This seemed too easy. He counseled himself to be cautious. If something sounded too good to be true, then it probably was.

But I don't care. This is my chance! Sometimes, one must take risks to reap benefits.

Holding out both hands for the werelight, he maintained its luminosity while decreasing its size. A faint warmth and orange light bathed his palms. The moth followed and landed on his left thumb, a furry insect the size of a small bird. Its pale eyes glistened in the orange glow as it folded dark blue wings traced with delicate silver and long trailing ends on its hindwings, while twitching its fluffy antennae. He moved the werelight, and the moth crawled into his hand.

No wonder Northward was so entranced. She really is a splendid moth.

"Of course," the Dreadlord said, "you must first convince the wyldling maiden you are her friend. Cultivate her trust. Warn her about the dangers threatening her." He rose and strode toward the bench where Northward lay, then stood looking down at him. "You will provide her with information as I direct. And then, your Milady Blue shall play right into our hands."

"Yes, Your Eminence," William replied. A shark-like grin spread across his face. "I already have some ideas." After extinguishing his werelight, he cupped both hands around the moth. Trapping it.

Now you're mine.

Moonlight Trial

Contemplation Garden

Annabelle closed Enoch's book of legends with a sigh. Her eyes kept drifting to the shadows cast by the flickering candle as they danced along the concave walls. She smiled at the huge, white moth fluttering around the light source, admiring the opalescent sheen of its wings as she shooed the insect away from the flame. Concentration on her studies came with difficulty, but sleep had been impossible to find. She *should* be sleeping. Dinah had told her as much when she sought her own bed two hours earlier, after they finished discussing the events of the day and tomorrow's plans.

Tomorrow at third-noon, Commander Storm planned to depart. Toad, Peter, Dinah, and David would leave, too. Annabelle set aside the book and drank from her canteen, attempting to dilute the bitterness churning in her stomach. Time was running out. Whether she traveled with the Commander or stayed in Treehome remained to be seen.

At least Raeden will be with me either way.

Absently, she rubbed her chest where emotions not her own curled and trembled like a puppy uncertain of his welcome. Lord Evanrudhe had promised the discomfort and intense emotions would lessen as they both adjusted to the Oathbond. The Councilors had all seemed surprised that they'd formed such a powerful connection.

The moth went after the flame again. Should she catch it and take it outside before it got burned? She scrutinized the insect as she mulled over her earlier conversation with Dinah and Raeden as he escorted them to the boundary between the Men's and Women's Quarters. Blowing out the candle, she imagined glowing globes hung like lanterns from trees lining the path, lighting their way while huge moths fluttered everywhere ...

"... then again," Dinah informed her as they walked to the dormitory baobab, "this is the first time in history that a kaenhir has sworn the Defender's Oath—let alone to a wyldling." Because of some peculiarity of their physiology, she explained, wensallen-kaen reacted adversely to people and items touched strongly by the Aethyr. No harm would have come to Annabelle, but apparently, Raeden had taken a deadly risk in swearing the oath.

Annabelle gaped at her friend. "What are you saying—that he could have died?" She'd dragged her new champion to a halt and stood in front of him. "Did you know about this?"

Raeden nodded gravely. "He did, Freylin. Forgiveness." His ears twitched. "Lord Evanrudhe said none of it would affect you." He reached out to take her arm.

She spluttered. "'Wouldn't affect me?' You ... you nimrod!" Tears burning her eyes, she evaded his grasp, pounding her fists on his chest to emphasize her words. "Bond or no bond, your freaking death would've affected me!" With a choked-off sob, she gripped his uniform jacket and buried her face in his chest. "After Enoch ... you're my best friend here. I can't lose you."

"I shall go on ahead, Your Excellency," Dinah said. A warm hand touched her shoulder. "Ann, I'll see you at the crossroad."

Gently—as if she were made of spun glass—Raeden held her and stroked her hair. Annabelle wept herself empty. As her wrenching sobs quieted, she let the warmth of the Oathbond fill her. He truly cares for me; I won't let him throw his life away.

His chest rumbled beneath her ear. "Your servant offers his most abject apologies, Freylin. He did not mean to cause pain. The trading language is the devil's tongue, and he sometimes confuses the words." His arms loosened.

"It's okay." Sniffling and wiping her eyes, Annabelle stepped out of his embrace before he ended it. "But ... now, it seems such a waste for you to go through all that." Irritation spiked through her, and she lifted her chin. "Risking your life, and all for what? Commander Storm's clarified that my further participation on this quest is contingent on acquiring an artifact and Lord Evanrudhe hasn't given me a straight answer about how to do it."

"A waste?" Heat and cold prickled along the bond as Raeden bent to peer into her face. "Freylin, this is a great distance from all your servant holds true. Your servant can ... feel you ... here." Eyes narrowed and ears back, he slammed his right fist over his heart. "No matter what happens, if you are anywhere on Tehara, then he will find you."

"But ... why?" She blinked. "You're giving up too much for me. A life."

His ears flattened, and he glanced away. "He does not give up so much as you believe," he murmured. A dark, searing heat she couldn't identify pulsed through the steady, warm glow of the Oathbond, but was quickly gone. "Your servant felt he must do this thing. His shame at losing the young knight is great. You have a desire to find him, and the Lord Commander declares you need a protector as a condition to continue. Your servant must help you to do this."

"I see." She frowned. "You're just doing it for Enoch, then." Why did that disappoint her?

"Nich," he replied, turning to her. "Not all. He does it to break his shame." His ears lifted and his whiskers quivered. Something like laughter sang along their bond. "As you know, he also does it for you, Freylin. So that you can accomplish the purpose the Almighty Threefold One has planned for you." He offered her his arm. "And now you must go to your rest. This day has been very full of the tributaries and tomorrow promises more of the same."

Annabelle snorted as she tucked her hand in the crook of his elbow. "Tributaries? You mean tribulations."

"Your servant has said what he has said," he replied stiffly, but she felt the quiver of humor in the Oathbond. By then, they'd reached the boundary, where Dinah awaited her under the mellow light of a globe. Raeden relinquished her arm to the dwelfinhad only reluctantly. He sank to his knees, bracing his hands on his thighs. "Sleep well, Freylin."

As Dinah led her away, Annabelle glanced back. Raeden stared after her, his green eyes shining under the eaves of the dense canopy ...

Dismissing the memory, Annabelle rubbed her forehead. Now, if only the matter of this special artifact could be settled so neatly. When did Lord Evanrudhe plan to present it to her? Commander Storm was leaving tomorrow!

Annabelle gazed around the dormitory room and listened intently while her eyes adjusted to the faint light filtering down through a net stretched across an opening above her. She categorized the nightly noises into the buzzing whine of cicadas, the chirping of crickets, and the bird-like calls of frogs. No human voices broke the nocturnal symphony.

With an inarticulate grumble, Annabelle settled back down into the oblong, nest-like declivity that was her bed. She stared up at the skylight and the pallid gleam of the gibbous moon trickling through the baobab's intervening branches. *I should get to sleep. I need my rest.*

She tried breathing exercises to calm her mind. It didn't work. She tried praying, but her thoughts swirled and crashed like a maelstrom. Making fists, she drew in a deep, shuddering breath. *I need to move.* Earlier, Lord Evanrudhe had mentioned that walking in the gardens at night when he was restless helped calm his mind enough to sleep. Maybe she should do that.

Annabelle slipped out of bed and into the choupla she'd worn earlier, leaving the blue sash and belt. She debated bringing Murder Stick along; Commander Storm had told her to always have her weapon at hand. *But he didn't wear his at the ceremony, so why should I take mine now? Ack! I'd better take it along.*

With a groan, she fastened the sword-belt around her waist. Before she left, she drank from the canteen at her bedside. She imagined Dinah's voice, urging her to stay hydrated.

Annabelle glanced at the canteen in her hands, then drank until it emptied. With a maximum capacity of twenty-five drachms—roughly a quart—that meant she'd fill it four times daily to reach her goal. Oddly, her stomach didn't feel sloshy after drinking so much so quickly. Yet another quirk of being the Weaver of Water.

She set down the empty canteen, then pushed aside the sleeping vesicle's partition drape. The smoothed-over roots of the floor were cool beneath her bare feet as she padded through the vacuole and past the bubbling fountain. Phosphorescent spheres set into the curved walls lit her way to the latrine. Typical human bodily functions still applied to wyldlings.

Taking a different path than she'd used before upon leaving the latrine, she exited the dormitory through a small, round opening and entered the courtyard of the Women's Quarters. Floral scents greeted her like old friends, hanging heavy in the still, warm air, even if she couldn't put a name to them.

Doubtless, her new champion sat vigil in the jungle on the opposite side of the baobab. *Right now, he's probably lurking up in that tree, again, waiting for me.* He wouldn't come into the Women's Quarters, though—not unless she called. She hesitated. Should she call Raeden?

She concentrated on the Oathbond. Despite his weariness, her champion was still awake. *No, I won't call him. He needs to rest. If he wants to come after me, then he'll find me.*

Annabelle padded through the courtyard, alone with her thoughts, and bathed in the light of the gibbous moon. She stopped to gawk at it. Although it looked similar to Earth's moon, Tehara's moon was larger or in a closer orbit, and mottled with green-gray patches.

Leaving the Women's Quarters, she walked past the gardens and orchards and onto a path that wended its way through ornamental hedges. A jasmine-like scent hung heavy in the air. The shirring "ree-ree" of a cricket symphony pulsed around her. Rustling like the flapping of feathery wings intruded, then subsided, but she couldn't locate its source. After a while—she wasn't sure how long—a tugging at her gut alerted her to the presence of water.

My wyld's talking to me, like it did when I found that spring. Is this all instinct? How do I bring it under conscious control?

Both Lord Evanrudhe and Dinah had told her a wyldling's ability was limited only by imagination. He'd taught her the three-step wyldling's mantra: "Calm. Concentrate. Commit." How to focus her mind and draw upon her wyld. She'd even levitated a bathtub-sized blob of water and formed it into a sphere—until it exploded, drenching her companions. Luckily, there'd been time to change clothing before the worship service. Although Lord Evanrudhe seemed pleased with her progress, Commander Storm's bleak expression told her he deemed her skills inadequate in the face of the dangers they'd face out in the wide world.

She grinned. Despite the evainghir's disapproval, it had been gratifying to see him soaked to the skin and dripping everywhere. *Well-deserved revenge for every time he's made me sweat.*

The liquid babble of a fountain beckoned her. Rounding a curve, she passed through an opening in the floral hedges and into a pale-stoned courtyard with a fountain at its center. Water trickled from the mouths of stone fish leaping from a pillar carved like a rippling geyser. Perched at the top, where the water flattened out like an umbrella, a stone dragon spread its wings, frozen in the act of leaping toward the sky. The tendrils around his open jaws and the shape of his ears identified him. Water streaming from his eyes made it look as though he wept.

Annabelle gasped. "It's Hadrien!" She ran to the fountain and stared up at the Sage from her dream. An urge to jump into the basin and examine the statue more closely swept over her.

No, it's unhygienic.

She paced around the basin, thumb stroking the pommel of her sword, and focused on her breathing. Maybe she could practice using her wyld once she felt more settled. Listening to the trickling and bubbling of the fountain calmed her mind.

The catechism verse she'd chosen for her confirmation rose to the surface. "Trust in the LORD with all your heart," she murmured as she made another circuit. "Lean not on your own understanding. In every way, acknowledge him, and he will make your paths straight."

She laughed at the irony. *Here I am, walking in circles around a water fountain.*

"Miss Wells, is that you?"

Annabelle flinched, gasping as a dwelfnhir wearing a plain, ankle-length tunic with a white cloth belt entered the courtyard. His silver hair seemed to glow in the moonlight.

Lord Evanrudhe's eyes widened. "Ah! Please accept my apology for startling you, my dear." He arched an eyebrow. "Couldn't sleep?"

She bit her lip. "My thoughts are too loud for sleeping."

"You are not the only one." Lord Evanrudhe adjusted his hold on a bundle under one arm. "I was heading to my Contemplation Garden to gaze upon the moon and pray concerning you, and here you are. The Threefold One moves in mysterious ways." He shook his head, smiling. "You have wandered far from the Women's Quarters, child."

With a glance at the fountain, she hunched her shoulders. "Being here is ... soothing." She sidled over to the basin, rearranged her sword, and sat on the wide stone ledge. "Um. I think the water called me. Or my wyld brought me here." Her brows pinched together. "At least, I think that's what happened."

"Indeed, it is," Lord Evanrudhe replied. "Your sensitivity to the Aethyr is growing apace. Our session earlier proved as much." He cleared his throat. "If something is troubling you, I can lend an ear ... if I am not intruding." The dwelfnhir raised his brows in question. His fathomless eyes seemed less sorrowful in the moonlight.

I wonder why he always looks so sad.

"No, you aren't intruding," she stammered, clasping her hands before her. "I wanted to talk to you, actually."

Lord Evanrudhe sat down and peered at her. "Miss Wells, I am here. Is there something you wish to ask of me?"

I wish Enoch was here to look at the moon with me, but I don't think you can give me that, Lord Evanrudhe.

Meeting his gaze, she said, "Please, Lord Evanrudhe. Commander Storm leaves tomorrow. You said there was an artifact ..." She averted her eyes and smoothed out her skirt. "I'm sorry. You must think I'm ungrateful for being demanding. Everything you've done for me already is wonderful."

"Child, there is no need for apology. I do not think you are ungrateful. You are anxious for our young Enoch. But you must be patient. The Threefold One holds all of us in his hands, and we wait upon his pleasure. All things are accomplished in their seasons." He raised an arm and swept it around, taking in the entire gardens. "Before you plunge into danger again, Miss Wells, take time to appreciate the blessings he has given us."

She reexamined her surroundings, then looked up at the moon. "The moon ... this place is so beautiful," she murmured. "If it weren't for Enoch ... I'd love to stay."

Lord Evanrudhe's voice warmed with a smile. "Mora always cherished this place. She claimed dwelling here in meditation helped her to cast the veils from her eyes, so to speak."

"Mora?" Annabelle turned to the dwelfnhir. "Who's she?"

"Long ago, she was baptized as Altaariz Morannen." His eyes grew misty, and he tipped his head with a melancholy smile. "I loved her as I would my own child. She had an inner light few could match. I remember her flitting about these gardens like the hummingbird she was named for. She also enjoyed gazing at the moon—Lûsin, as it is called in High Dwelfnic."

He uses the past tense. Is Mora dead, then? Maybe that's why he looks so sad.

Sympathy welled up in her. "Is Mora ... is she ...?" She swallowed, unable to finish.

With a sad smile, Lord Evanrudhe stared up at the moon. "Yes. Mora joined the Almighty in His heavenly courts an Age ago. Her trials are long over. Yours have only begun, my dear."

An Age? Oh, my gosh. He's been in mourning for over a thousand years!

"I'm sorry for your loss." Annabelle knuckled moisture from her eyelashes. After a moment, she blurted, "All I want is to rescue Enoch, but whenever I turn around, there's another obstacle." She heaved a sigh. "Everything has been so difficult."

Lord Evanrudhe tilted his head. "Were you expecting it to be easy?" He spoke in a neutral tone, his expression open and curious, but Annabelle felt the sting of an accusation all the same.

"Well, no," she replied, hunching her shoulders. "I just wasn't expecting all of this to be such a ..." She struggled to find the correct word. "Such a trial."

The dwelfnhir smiled gently. "Dear child, when the Almighty allows us to undergo hardships and trials in our lives, it is not to punish us or to make us suffer. It means he is shaping us to serve his purpose." He leaned forward and arched an eyebrow. "Lord Yshua wants us to call upon him and ask for his help in facing these trials. He is faithful and will give you strength."

Something I haven't done enough. Heat growing in her face, Annabelle looked down, smoothing out the skirt of her choupla. "You're right," she whispered.

"Miss Wells, you asked for my help in reconnecting that which was sundered and protecting your mind. I would gladly give it. I have spoken with Commander Storm regarding your quest, and we have come to an agreement." His expression resolute, Lord Evanrudhe picked up the white bundle between them. It was the length of her forearm. He looked at it wistfully and then unwrapped it. "Here is the artifact."

Eyes wide, Annabelle gasped at the vision of beauty revealed: a mirror-bright silver dagger with an opalescent gemstone set in place of a fuller. Shorter than the weapon Commander Storm had given her, its edges were strangely dull, and it seemed to glow in the moon's light. Beside it lay its sheath, an unprepossessing thing made of black leather. Recognition sent a frisson down her spine. She'd seen this blade before ... in a dream? There'd been a cloaked figure with a mandolin, playing melancholy music ...

"It's beautiful," she whispered. "I feel ... drawn to it. Like, when my wyld led me to the fountain, but not as strongly." *Should I take it? No. This is probably some sort of test.* Her eyes rose to Lord Evanrudhe's face. "What can it do?"

He pulled it back and sheathed the blade. "I will tell you a little about the relic. Mora would have wanted you to have this, Miss Wells. It was she who named it Daar-Lûsin. Or 'dagger of moonlight,' as we clumsily render its name into Trade-speak. She helped to consecrate and dedicate this dagger to protect younglings from the darkness."

Her brow furrowed. "How will it protect me? Is it a magical weapon?"

"Oh, eminently magical." Lord Evanrudhe chuckled. "Melkior, the Sage called Voidbinder, created this blade and imbued it with the light of the moon. However, his purpose in forging the dagger was not to make another weapon. It is intended to aid those who do not desire to fight, but wish to pierce through barriers, dispel illusions, and flee from danger. Although moonlight is weak when compared to the radiance of the suns, even reflected light serves the will of the Almighty."

"I wonder what Melkior would think of me carrying around his dagger," she murmured. "I'm not *his* wyldling, after all."

"That would not matter to him." Lord Evanrudhe patted the relic. "Most assuredly, this artifact's creator would want you to have it, Miss Wells. In its own way, Daar-Lûsin will serve you as faithfully as your avowed champion on the perilous journey ahead of you."

"Can it really restore my bond with Enoch?" she asked, her voice thick.

"That all depends on you, my dear," he replied soberly. "Daar-Lûsin will help you penetrate the fog created by the wyldling snare. But first, you must become acquainted with one another, and the dagger must approve of you. Artifacts constructed by the Sages choose their own wielders."

He talks about it like it's a sentient being. She chewed on her lip, staring at the blade. "How does that work?"

"Daar-Lûsin will test you, child. Set challenges before you. Seek to know your quality. And then the artifact may choose to accompany you. Only after that will it attempt to reforge the connection that was sundered."

She peered at the relic in his hand, then glanced into his face with a hopeful grin. "Um, are you going to give it to me so we can start getting acquainted?"

Lord Evanrudhe smiled sadly as he unsheathed the opalescent blade and gazed upon it. "I would very much like to give it to you, Miss Wells. But ..." Before Annabelle could reach for it, he tossed it into the fountain. It hardly made so much as a ripple as it plunged into the water.

What the heck?

She cried out in protest, and he met her bewildered eyes. "Daar-Lûsin chooses its wielder. To become better acquainted, you must face the Moonlight Trial. Earn the artifact's allegiance, Miss Wells."

Moonlight Trial. Allegiance. Déjà vu rippled over her as she stared at the place where the dagger had vanished. "How?"

"You must go wherever it takes you, Weaver of Water. Enter the fountain."

She licked lips gone dry, composing herself. "It's okay to get inside? I thought maybe that would be forbidden. Unhygienic."

Lord Evanrudhe chuckled. "Nothing forbids you from entering the fountain, child." Solemnity chased away his mirth as he traced the sign of the cross on her forehead, intoning:

"The LORD bless you and keep you. The LORD make his face shine on you and be gracious to you. The LORD look on you with favor and give you peace."

"The Aaronic Blessing! Our pastor says that at the end of every service." Annabelle gave him a smile. "Thank you, Lord Evanrudhe."

He bowed his head. "You are welcome. Go, and face the Moonlight Trial, with my blessing. I will pray for your success."

She hesitated, her heart racing. "You mean ... I could fail?"

Lord Evanrudhe quirked an eyebrow. "With the Almighty behind you, child, how could you fail?"

"Right." Taking a deep breath, Annabelle swung her legs around and lowered them into the fountain basin. Murder Stick bumped against her thigh. The cool water embraced her calves and dampened the hem of her choupla. She shut her eyes.

Alrighty then. Here goes nothing. Please, God, be with me.
She slid off the ledge, expecting her feet to contact the basin floor. Instead, she plummeted into a darkness colder than death.

Arches

Annabelle tumbled about like flotsam tossed by the waves of the ocean. She was falling, falling, falling ...

... until her feet contacted a solid surface. The water disappeared. She shuddered, hugging herself, and opened her eyes. The moon shone down, full and bright, taking up a tenth of the sky and eclipsing the surrounding stars. She stood on a garden path fenced in on either side by wild, overgrown shrubs and flowers of velvety texture. Most of the blooms were a dark hue, but the largest had white, waxy petals, like magnolias. The flat stones were cool beneath her bare feet, and water trickled somewhere ahead and off to her right. Other than that, no sound emerged from anywhere in the wild tangle of vegetation.

"Oh, gosh. Where am I?" Gooseflesh pebbled her skin. Breath fast and rough, she hunkered, searching the ground for the opalescent cruciform shape. "Where's the dagger?" Her voice came out high-pitched and thready. She felt along the ground and in the foliage. No dagger met her grasping hands. "Oh, God, that can't be good. Please, please, help me."

"I can help you, Annabelle," a sweet voice piped from behind her.

Annabelle spun, jumping to her feet, her right hand flying to her sword. Several yards away, a freestanding arch rose from the path, its soot-gray lintels engraved with intricate symbols that seemed to writhe and twist of their own volition. The same path—or one identical to it—continued beyond the arch. A tall, dark-haired woman stood upon the threshold of the stone, her choupla of flowing white shot through with opalescent panels that gleamed in the moonlight and accentuated her umber skin.

Laughing weakly, Annabelle said, "Um, hello. I'm afraid you have me at a disadvantage. I don't know you." And yet, she felt she knew this beautiful apparition; even felt comforted by her presence. "Are you an angel of the LORD?"

The dark-haired woman's laughter was like chimes ringing. "No, dear child. I am as human as you are." She clasped her long-fingered hands at her trim waist. "You may call me Khinjara. As my friends do." Her smile reminded Annabelle of Lord Evanrudhe.

"And mine call me Ann," she replied, unable to tear her eyes from the woman's shiny presence. Her grip on Murder Stick loosened. She brushed off the skirt and smoothed down the fabric of her choupla, feeling silly. With her pointed ears and slender features, the woman could only be a dwelfnhad. Not an angel. Didn't the angels usually say "do not be afraid" whenever they appeared to people in the Bible?

"Well-met, Ann," Khinjara said. With a smile, she held out a hand. "Are you ready?"

Annabelle bit her lip. "For the trial, you mean? But ... I don't feel prepared at all. I can't find the Dagger of Moonlight." She stepped forward, tentatively placed her hand in the dwelfnhad's, and looked pleadingly into her beautiful face. "Please, help me find it. I don't want to fail the test before I even begin."

Khinjara's fingers were warm as they closed over hers, gentle as butterflies' wings. The scent of Easter lilies wreathed around her. "Do not worry about failure, Ann. The Almighty Threefold One is with us. He will provide for all your needs. Come."

The two walked side by side along the flagstones of the garden path. Wide-eyed, Annabelle clung to Khinjara's hand as she took in her surroundings. Apart from the water noise, the silence was brooding, as if someone or something watched and waited. The dwelfnhad's expression remained placid, revealing nothing, although she squeezed her hand in reassurance.

"What is this place?" Annabelle whispered.

"Melkior's Garden," Khinjara replied in subdued tones. She smiled, but there was a deep sorrow behind her eyes. "This is where he came to meditate. I played here, as a child."

He's the one who made the dagger! "You knew the dragon—I mean, Sages?"

The dwelfnhad nodded, humor and light returning to her exquisite features. "Quite well. I knew all seven of them."

I thought no dwelfnim alive remembers the Sages, aside from Lord Evanrudhe. But it'd be rude to ask her age.

Annabelle's heart beat faster. "What was Melkior like?"

Khinjara stopped and stared up into the sky at the giant moon, and her smile faded. Her voice shook. "Melkior was the gentlest of the Sages, contemplative and slow to anger—but terrible once roused. He often saw the complete picture and brought the others to a consensus. More than anything, he wanted peace ... for the world, and in his own mind. Melkior, he ...." A tear slid down her cheek. Her grip on Annabelle's hand tightened and her other hand clenched into a fist.

"I'm sorry," Annabelle said in a rush. "I didn't mean to dredge up bad memories."

Shaking her head, Khinjara let go of Annabelle's hand. She smiled. "You are not to blame for my feelings, Ann. And not all the memories are bad. I praise the Threefold One for the happiness I experienced—even if those I experienced it with have long faded into dust. I will always have the Almighty to lean on."

Annabelle shifted uncomfortably. "I know God is always with me," she replied, speaking slowly. "But sometimes it's really hard to feel his presence."

Khinjara nodded. "I understand. 'Tis difficult to trust that which we cannot see or touch. Lean on his promises, Ann. Do not rely upon your own understanding where the Almighty is concerned." She took her hand. "Shall we continue?"

"Can you tell me what to expect with this trial?"

The dwelfnhad smiled sadly. "Only that a trial of three parts lies before you."

How portentous. Annabelle snorted a nervous laugh. "Why a trial of three parts?"

Khinjara chuckled. "As my father used to say: 'Like the suns, trouble always comes in threes, but so do opportunities to escape it.' More than that, I cannot tell you."

"Okay." Annabelle inhaled deeply and then exhaled. Perhaps Khinjara's remark was a hint that she should expect danger. Her fingers brushed Murder Stick's pommel. Was this place like the dreamscape? It felt similar, yet differences could prove fatal. Would her meager sword and wyld training be enough to protect herself here?

She imagined Toad's voice speaking in the silence of her mind. *"Don't worry about what you can't change, kiddo. Pay attention to your surroundings. Focus on succeeding in this trial. That's all you can do."*

She sucked on her teeth. *Enoch's depending on me.*

"Alrighty then," she said aloud. "Let's go." She squeezed Khinjara's hand, and the dwelfnhad squeezed back.

They walked for a while, and then Khinjara gestured ahead. Six soot-gray arches emerged from the greenery, the lintels partially obscured by foliage wrapped about half of their height. The path went straight toward them and then ended at a round courtyard. Flowering vines straggled up through cracked paving stones to twine around the freestanding doorways arrayed before them. The lily-like blossoms poured out a sweet fragrance, a blend of cinnamon, vanilla, and honey. *What gorgeous flowers!*

Annabelle stopped to survey the six structures. So did her companion, who released her hand and stood beside her in silence. Instead of the garden beyond, the arches framed identical views of a flat gray void. The arches had inscriptions engraved on their apexes, all looking a little different. As she watched, the words glowed a different color for each arch—red, yellow, green, blue, silver, or violet.

"I can't decipher the inscriptions."

"The Almighty is with you, Ann. Pray for guidance." Her fingers brushed Annabelle's shoulder.

"Okay." Annabelle bowed her head in prayer. She looked up when she finished. "So, I just pick one of these doors and go through?"

The dwelfnhad nodded and folded her hands at her waist.

Annabelle licked dry lips as she surveyed her six options. "But how will I know which is the right one? Will you help me?"

Khinjara shook her head, her brown eyes soft with regret. "I must not influence the decision you make, Ann."

"That figures," Annabelle muttered, turning to the arches. As she watched, the blue script on one arch writhed and reformed into words she could read.

"Trust in the LORD with all your heart, and do not lean on your own understanding."

Wide-eyed, she faced the dwelfnhad. "That's my confirmation verse. It must be a sign. I need to trust God to lead me where he wants me to go."

Khinjara nodded. "A wise decision in any situation."

Heart racing, Annabelle raised her chin and stepped toward the arch with glowing blue script. The sweet perfume of the floral vines surrounded her. She hesitated at the threshold, heart thrashing like a fish in a net as she stared into the void. Could she step blindly into that nothingness?

If it'll help me find Enoch ... then yes. Yes, I can. And will.

"Please, God, let this be the right one," she murmured.

"Is this your choice, Ann?"

Don't you dare second-guess yourself, now!

Annabelle swallowed noisily and tore her gaze from the matte gray surface. She regarded her companion, then nodded. "Yes," she spoke aloud, for good measure. Her lips quivered into a smile. "Even though green is my favorite color."

Khinjara smiled back. "I am not partial to any one color. I love them all equally." She plucked a bloom from the vine climbing the lintel, then offered it to Annabelle. "This is a Trumpet-lily. Breathe in its essence. Its fragrance will sustain you beyond the arch."

Why—is my next challenge in a garbage dump?

Biting back nervous laughter, Annabelle accepted the lily. It was the size of the musical instrument it resembled. "Thank you! It's beautiful—just like you." She inhaled its sweet, vanilla-cinnamon scent.

"Place it in your bodice. It will sprout vines and cling to your garment, leaving your hands free."

Annabelle balanced the flower in the scoop neck and watched as green tendrils sprang forth, rooting and twining in the fabric. "Whoa, that's cool. A living necklace."

Khinjara chuckled. "Are you ready, Ann?"

Nodding, she gripped Murder Stick's hilt. *Trust God, trust God, trust God ...*

"Then I shall open the way for you," Khinjara said, placing one slender hand upon the lintel. The other, she pressed between Annabelle's shoulder blades. The doorway flared with opalescent brilliance, like the waystones. Khinjara's eyes glowed with the same radiance. "Go with Lord Yshua," she said and then ushered Annabelle into the incandescent vortex.

Murder Stick

Cold prickled against her face. Annabelle stared up at evergreen boughs, her breath puffing out in icy clouds. A full moon shone down from a dark sky beyond crisscrossed branches. White patches stood out against the black. Snow? Nearby, a persistent whirring hum faded in and out of earshot.

"Now where am I?" she breathed out in a rush, watching the vapor rise and then disappear. *It's winter here—wherever this is!* She'd been talking to Khinjara beside the arch, and now ...

She was lying on the ground in a copse of conifers with an annoying huge insect she couldn't see buzzing around. Hopefully, it wouldn't land on her. *A bug in winter?* Raising her head, she peered down the length of her body. The Trumpet-lily blocked her view as it exuded its vanilla-cinnamon scent. She inhaled, and the fragrance settled her. *Poor thing. I hope it doesn't wither.* Carefully, she moved it to one side, and then stared at thermal black gloves on her hands, the dark blue snowmobile suit encasing her form, and a pair of black and gray moon boots. Her winter clothes.

What's going on? At least I'm appropriately clad for the weather; no wonder I'm warm. I'd freeze to death in that choupla.

She frowned. Where was Khinjara?

Annabelle struggled to sit up, bracing herself against the crooked trunk of a cedar that seemed oddly familiar. Overhead, disturbed limbs creaked and shivered, then cold whiteness slithered to plop down on her head and into her lap. "Gah!" Brushing heavy snow from her stocking cap, she blinked at a small pile of snow spread across the nylon of her snowmobile suit, then brushed it away with gloved hands. It was then that she noticed she wore her sword-belt with Murder Stick buried in snow at her side.

"How incongruous," she muttered. "Too bad it's not the Dagger of Moonlight." She ran a hand over her hair, trying to think. Whatever made that whirring sound was driving her batty. "Khinjara?" she called tentatively.

"I am here, Ann," Khinjara said into her mind. The source of the humming noise darted into view and hovered before her face—a hummingbird with opalescent wings, a bib of umber feathers, and familiar dark eyes.

Annabelle gasped. "Holy cow! You can switch forms? Totally cool! But why a hummingbird?" She held out a hand and the little bird alit on a gloved finger. It felt like holding an insect.

Khinjara cocked her head and peered at her with one eye. "I have not chosen this form; tis a surprise to me, as well." She puffed out her feathers. "Unfortunately, this form is better suited for tropical climes. This realm is quite ... chilly."

"Yeah. I suppose this place is part of my trial." Annabelle grimaced as she clambered to her feet. "Well, first things first: I have to find the dagger!"

"Do not concern yourself with the dagger, Ann. Seeking the dagger is not your trial."

"What? But I thought—"

"Should you win Daar-Lûsin's approval, the dagger will present itself after the challenge is complete."

Annabelle huffed a laugh as relief swept over her. "Thanks for giving me a straight answer." Gently, she stroked Khinjara's back. "I need to figure out where we are. It seems familiar."

Khinjara launched herself into the air, bobbing like a miniature helicopter. "As for our location ... There is a dwelling beyond this little woodland, and young people frolicking in the snow. Perhaps you can inquire of them? Brr!" She fluffed her feathers.

"Will you be warm enough, Khinjara? Here." Annabelle unzipped the suit partway. Underneath, she still wore the choupla with the Trumpet-lily's vine-like growth woven throughout the bodice. "Why don't you perch on me and conserve your energy?"

"Thank you!" Khinjara darted inside the flower. Her mental voice sounded sheepish. "Forgive me, Ann. I find I am ravenously hungry."

She smiled. "That's okay. I understand. Hummingbirds have a really high metabolism. They need to eat almost constantly. Thank God we have the Trumpet-lily to feed you." As she watched, all signs of the flower faded from view. Her breath caught as she touched the place where it had been. "Khinjara?"

"Fear not. Although you cannot see or touch me, I am still with you."

Voices floated through the chill air as she pushed through springy conifer limbs. She knew them. Annabelle moved faster. Her heart pounded so hard that it strangled her voice. When the trees opened up, she emerged into the snow-shrouded expanse of her backyard. Although it was nighttime, the light of the full moon reflecting off snow made everything seem bright as day.

Snowballs in hand, three figures dressed in winter gear turned from their play to stare at her with the same blue eyes as her own. The two smaller ones—a young boy and an even younger girl—wore snowsuits, boots, caps, and gloves like hers. The tallest one was clad in an old-fashioned dark jacket resembling a trench coat, and thick leather boots that reached his knees. Around his neck, a pewter band glinted in the sunlight. Warmth rushed through Annabelle and she trembled as she stood frozen, surveying all three, her mind buzzing like Khinjara's hummingbird wings.

How can this be? He's here, before my eyes. He's safe. He even looks well—better than he did the last time. Has he been on Earth all this while? Oh, please, God, let it be real.

Her heart went cold. What form would this trial take? Khinjara had hinted at danger ...

"It's Ann," the little girl cried, beaming. "She came back. Wake up, Drew!" She smashed her snowball against the boy's cheek, and he left off gaping at Annabelle to squawk, "Stop it, Amy!" and dug melting snow out of his collar.

The tallest one's shock dissolved into a grin, teeth a bright flash contrasting with almond-brown skin. "Ann? Praise Yshua! You're alive!" He brushed snow from his gloved hands and plowed through the drifts toward her.

An answering smile spread across her face. "Enoch!"

Annabelle managed a single step before he crashed into her. Laughing, he lifted her up, twirled her around, and then set her back on her feet. "I've no idea how I'm here, but ..." He stared at her, still grinning. "Kaspar's breath, I *missed* you."

Roughly, he gathered her into a hug. She rested her cheek against his shoulder and closed her eyes. He smelled like leather and wool. "I missed you, too."

She grunted as a second body and then a third crashed into her. Enoch let go and stepped back. Two young voices spoke over one another, and she scrambled to parse out what they said.

"Ann, are you home for good?" Amy's voice was muffled by the snowsuit. "Enoch said you went to a place called Teh-har-rah." She squeezed tighter. "I think you should stay here."

"Mom and Dad are *pissed off,*" Drew crowed, even as he held her tight. "I bet you're grounded for a year. Sneak attack!"

And then, something cold and wet slithered down the back of her neck, and she shrieked. Cackling, her little brother scampered away to duck behind a lopsided snowman.

"That's against the rules," Amy hollered. She let go of Annabelle and tore after him.

Annabelle smiled as her siblings squabbled, pelting snowballs at one another. Enoch took her hand. Gripping it tightly, she gazed at him, marveling that he was *here*, no matter how or why. *I won't let him disappear into purple mist—not this time.*

Suddenly somber, Enoch jerked a chin in the kids' direction. "They seem like good children. You're blessed to have a family."

A lump formed in her throat. "I know." *Should I tell him what I've learned?* Everything she wanted to say or ask him jammed up inside like logs in a river. "You have a family, too, Enoch. You have me, Verbena, and Simon. Not to mention, I'm still with Raeden, Peter, Toad, and Commander Storm." She gathered her breath to tell him about Y'Dendordenelle and her wyldling abilities.

Enoch moved in front of her. Gaze intense, he grabbed her shoulders. "Simon's okay?"

She nodded. "His legs are broken, but he's on the mend. Actually, I heal—"

"Praise Yshua!" Enoch cut her off. "And you're with Red and the Commander? Safe?"

"Yeah. We made it to Treehome and we're coming to rescue you." She narrowed her eyes. *I've told him all this before.*

Enoch exhaled, puffing out his cheeks. "Thanks be to the Almighty, for his mercy endures forever. When I couldn't find you by the Wall, I was worried something awful had happened."

He glanced at her weapon. "I notice you have a sword. Who gave you that?"

Chuckling, she stepped back and drew her weapon. "Commander Storm. I barely know how to use it, but Toad, Raeden, and the Commander are training me to defend myself."

Enoch raised his eyebrows and whistled. "Nice blade. I'm surprised he gave you that; he doesn't believe women should train as warriors." He grinned. "Did you name it yet?"

"Yep." A smile twitched at her lips as she sheathed it. "I call it 'Murder Stick.'"

Enoch burst out laughing, and she laughed with him. "That suits you, Annabelle. Lord knows, I needed a laugh." He knuckled away a tear. "I'm glad they're training you. It takes years to master the sword-dance—I haven't yet—but some training is better than none. If I had my sword, then we could've had a bit of practice." He sighed. "You have Commander Storm, Peter, and Red to protect you, so you probably won't need to use it." Smiling, he lifted his chin, and moonlight glinted off the dull gray encircling the base of his throat.

Annabelle shivered. "That thing around your neck. Is it the wyldling snare?"

Eyes widening, he looked at her. "You know about the wyldling snare?"

She frowned. *Doesn't he remember what we talked about last time? The drugs his captors gave him must be doing a number on his memory.* "Well, I know it's how Ravenos trapped you. Toad told us everything he remembered. And you said—"

"Annabelle," Enoch choked out. He tugged her close and wrapped an arm around her shoulder, resting his cheek on the crown of her head. "I'm just so glad to see you alive and well. And safe with my friends and allies. Free of the wyldling snare."

"I am," she replied, confusion swirling in her gut. "But how did you get here? Doesn't the wyldling snare prevent you from entering the dreamscape—from finding *me?*"

Her breath caught. *Is this how Daar-Lûsin restores our connection?*

Enoch growled a curse under his breath. "I don't know if it's the snare, or whatever potion that son of a goat, William, has been giving me that keeps me from finding you." He paused and shook his head, frowning, but before Annabelle could ask if William was one of his captors, he was speaking again.

"Annabelle, I don't know how we're together here right now. Or how long I can stay. Maybe it's all because of the Threefold One's mercy." His arm tightened around her. "So, I'll tell you this much to pass along to Commander Storm. I'm deep in the Contested Lands right now, in Grivvensfel, and heading into the Western Marches toward someplace called 'Fastness.'"

Annabelle's eyes widened. "I'll tell him. But can you share any details about your captors?" *He couldn't before. But maybe circumstances have changed.*

Enoch drew in breath, as if to speak, then tensed. "Wait." His arm slid away from her shoulder, leaving her bereft. "Something's wrong." He pointed at an orange obelisk twice her height across the yard, behind the place where her siblings worked together building another snowman. Light swirled on the surface facing them, like it had in the portal she'd stepped through. "That wasn't there a second ago." Pivoting, he pointed out another orange obelisk by the deck. "Nor was that."

Turning with him, Annabelle saw a third orange obelisk on the other end of her backyard. Why did that color make her think of a giant moon and dark gray snakes? And a youth with glowing eyes ...

Enoch's tone grew dark. "Send the children indoors, Annabelle. And draw your sword."

She shook herself. "Amanda! Andrew!" As one, her siblings looked up, brows pinched in puzzlement. "Time to—"

The swirling light flared, and a tall, helmeted figure in black leather armor with dark gray rope coiled over one shoulder sprang out of the nearest obelisk. Its face was veiled. Movement from her peripheral vision and Enoch's harsh cry informed her that the other obelisks had each disgorged two armored intruders into her backyard. "Annabelle, protect the children! I'm trained in hand-to-hand combat. I'll hold off the others." Cold air fanned her back as he left.

Her mouth went dry. *Is this my trial—a battle? God, help me!*

"They've all got wyldling snare." Enoch grunted, and a stranger's voice made similar sounds. A loud *thunk*. "One down. They're here for all of us—the children, too."

Annabelle ripped Murder Stick from its sheath. She charged at the faceless warrior now shaking loose a coil of rope and stepping toward Amy. *No. I won't let you take her.*

"Don't let the snare touch you." Enoch groaned with effort. "Hyah!" The sound of flesh hitting flesh was followed by a death rattle. *Dear God, not Enoch.* Annabelle's heart clenched, but she couldn't spare a glance.

Swerving around where her sister crouched, she slashed the reaching hand with her sword. The glove made her clumsy. "Leave them alone!" The veiled warrior stepped back, chin raised at a contemptuous angle.

Behind her, Enoch unleashed a war cry, and Annabelle felt a knot of tension release as she stood between her siblings and the masked intruder. Something crashed as metal met metal. "Two down," Enoch gasped.

Face blanched, Drew pulled Amy up. "Who are these guys?"

"I don't know," Annabelle rasped. "But they're bad news. If you see an opening, run for the house." She glared at the helmeted warrior, who appeared to be sizing her up. She held her sword in the Number Two Guard position and tried to ignore the jelly-like condition of her knees. *No time to be afraid. I have to protect Amy and Drew.*

Another crash, and a meaty thud as a blunt object connected with a body. Enoch's voice sounded more strained. "Three down." More grunting and smacking noises ensued. *How is he taking them out barehanded?* But she didn't dare look—she didn't dare tear her gaze from her current opponent, who came toward her again. Shrieking, she backpedaled, lashing out with her blade. It didn't faze the masked warrior, who swatted her aside like a bundle of rags. She fell on her backside with an "oof!"

When she tried to rise, her legs shook so badly she slipped in the snow and dropped Murder Stick. A black sabaton kicked her weapon out of reach. Her gaze traveled up the armored length of the body to the veiled and helmeted head. The coil of dark gray rope seemed to writhe on its own, an end wriggling toward her. "Oh, no ..."

Her sister screamed. Behind the man looming before her, she saw another veiled warrior grab Amy. Red-faced and howling, Drew whaled on the masked warrior with a stick, but it appeared to have no effect. Beyond them, three of the warriors sprawled in the snow, unmoving. Several of her mother's landscaping rocks lay beside them.

His long coat gone, Enoch battled a fourth warrior, who was attempting to lasso the youth with the wyldling snare. Enoch ducked a loop of the gray rope. His movements were slowing. Blood dripped from his knuckles as his chest heaved.

He won't last much longer. Annabelle's breath quickened in sympathy. *God, help me! How do I keep these thugs from taking Amy and Drew? I lost my sword!*

Vanilla and cinnamon wreathed her with their spicy, sweet scents. Time slowed to a molasses crawl. "You still have a weapon, Ann," Khinjara's voice trilled in her mind.

"And where have you been?" she snapped. "I could've used some help earlier."

"I have always been with you, but this trial is yours to complete. You must *act.*"

Anger flared as the gray rope inched toward her. "And what am I supposed to do?" A sob ripped free from her throat. "I lost my sword, and I can't fight!"

Khinjara didn't reply.

Annabelle swallowed her tears and scanned her backyard. Moving in slow motion, Enoch battled the warrior by an obelisk.

Stop thinking, *Ann, and* do *something.*

Her eyes fixed on the nearest obelisk and its swirling portal. Streaks of sapphire spiraled amid the white and orange light. She recalled a dragon on a pedestal, surrounded by an ocean in which she could not drown. In her mind, Hadrien's voice echoed: "You are Ahdmerel—the Weaver of Water."

Annabelle's eyes widened.

A wyldling's weapon is her Aspect. There's frozen water all around me ...

"That's what Khinjara meant."

Time resumed its normal speed. Annabelle ripped off her gloves and threw them at the black warrior and his vile snare. Skidding backward, she buried her hands in the snow, grimacing at the icy pain. *Calm down and concentrate!* Liquid warmth rose from deep inside and everything in sight gleamed blue. *Stay calm, stay calm. You need to be calm and focus!* As the rope darted toward her, she flung up her hands and screamed.

Keep it away from me!

Ice and snow shot from the ground, shielding her from the snare. *Get him out of here!* As quick as thought, the sheet plowed into the warrior. It drove him back, smashing him into the obelisk by the fence, imprisoning him in ice.

She stared at her hands, shaking. *I wasn't calm. How the heck did I manage that?*

Heart thudding at an allegro pace, she scooted up on her knees and sought her next target. The other warrior was dragging Amy and Drew toward the obelisk on the far end of the yard. "Not on my watch," Annabelle growled. She slapped reddened and aching hands on the compacted snow and tried to recall everything Lord Evanrudhe had told her. She concentrated on the sapphire pool inside her.

I need an ice ball ... something to chuck at that guy's head.

Her head swam and black spots danced in her vision as she summoned more ice and a sloppy wave of snow rolled after the warrior. What the heck? That was supposed to be a ball of ice! The snow swept the warrior's feet out from under him, and he fell, releasing her siblings. Sobbing, Drew picked up a rock and hammered it into the warrior's helmet until he went still. Then both kids scrambled away.

Whatever works, I guess.

With tears streaming down his face, Drew ran past her, toward the deck. Hopefully, he'd go inside the house and stay there. And where were her parents during all this? *It may be night, but we're making enough noise to wake the dead!* Crying, Amy ran straight for her and into her arms. Annabelle rocked her, saying, "Shh. It's okay, you're okay."

Enoch shouted, "No!"

Drew screamed.

The world swayed as Annabelle turned around, one arm around her sister. Blue eyes huge in his white and red mottled face, the rest of her brother's body was cocooned in the dark gray snare like a bug in a spider's web. Enoch struggled on the ground, wheezing, also wrapped in wyldling snare. The remaining warrior was reeling Drew in as if he were a fish in a trawler's net.

"Ann," Amy cried. "The bad guys got Drew and Enoch!" Lips quivering, she stared with tear-filled eyes into Annabelle's face. "You have to save them."

But I'm so tired.

"I will." Annabelle licked her lips. She gave Amy a little push toward the house. "Go inside and dial nine-one-one."

Wide-eyed, Amy nodded, then ran for the deck and the sliding glass doors. Annabelle watched as she safely entered the house and then collapsed on her hands and knees. One hand fell on something cold, metallic, and half-buried in snow. Murder Stick. She grasped the sword with fingers going numb and rose, feeling like a creaky old woman, and tottered toward the prisoners. The masked warrior had Enoch trussed up at his feet. Behind him, the obelisk's portal glowed. Drew whimpered as the veiled warrior pulled him closer.

Please, God, give me the strength to save them.

Her grip tightened on the hilt. She inhaled the vanilla-cinnamon scent of the Trumpet-lily and then charged across the snow. As she ran, ice coated her blade. When she reached the midway point between Drew's cocooned form and his captor, she raised Murder Stick and brought the edge down on the wyldling snare. The dark gray cord snapped in two, one end recoiling back to the warrior, who fell back and disappeared into the portal. The snare around Drew shriveled and turned to dust.

Face pale, the boy gawked at her like she was an alien. She hissed, "Get in the house."

Nodding, he ran to where Amy stood framed in the doorway with the cordless telephone receiver. Drew took it from her and then turned toward Annabelle with a stricken expression.

Where are our parents? Why hasn't anyone come out to investigate?

Wordlessly, Drew pointed, and Annabelle spun to see the faceless warrior dragging Enoch into the obelisk. He thrashed against his captor, who had one leg inside the shining brilliance. As he strained away from the portal, Enoch screamed, "Annabelle—behind you!"

"*Guard six,*" the memory of Toad's voice cracked out.

She whirled, awkwardly thrusting Murder Stick. Her eyes widened when it met resistance. With a sickening squelch, the point slid into the tiny slit between the helmet's veil and the gorget. A man's voice gargled. Blood spurted, and she turned her head to avoid getting any in her face. Wet heat struck her anyway. The warrior stiffened, and then fell toward her, sliding down the blade. Crying out in horror, Annabelle jumped back, jerking her weapon free. The obelisk disappeared, and the snare turned to ash. Her stomach roiled.

I just killed a man.

She turned aside and vomited.

Her siblings were screaming again. "Hurry, Ann!"

Have to rescue Enoch.

Annabelle staggered toward the obelisk, bloody blade in hand, in time to meet Enoch's fierce gaze— "*be free, Annabelle,*" his voice whispered in her mind—and then watched him disappear into a swirling silver vortex.

"No!" she wailed, reaching out with her free hand.

I'm too late. He's gone. Again.

Numbly, she went to sheathe her weapon, then imagined Toad's voice scolding her. *"Whoa, whoa, whoa! You need to clean that blade, kiddo. Wipe off the blood."* Grabbing a handful of snow, she scrubbed it along Murder Stick's length until the crimson went away. In her mind's eye, the blade would always be blood-stained. Murder Stick had earned its name.

"Good. Now, put it away."

No. I should throw the awful thing away! She almost did, but the thought of Toad's disappointment stopped her. Hands shaking, she sheathed the sword.

Khinjara flitted out of the Trumpet-lily, trailing sparkling dust. Her tone was somber. "Ann. Time to choose a portal."

She choked back a sob. "Choose a portal?" She scoffed. "What choice do I have? There were three portals here, and now there's only one left."

"There is another." Turning, the hummingbird bobbed her head at where Amy and Drew stood in the open doorway, silent and watching her. Waiting for her.

Annabelle blinked. "I could ... go home? Just like that. Leave Tehara and my quest."

"If that is your choice."

She swallowed, looking between her siblings and the portal. "Where are Mom and Dad? Why are the kids home alone? They're too young to be all by themselves. Someone needs to take care of them. Khinjara, is everything that happens here ... for real?"

"I do not know the answers to those questions, Ann."

Annabelle closed her eyes and saw Enoch's brave expression as he vanished into the portal. She couldn't back out and leave him to an unknown fate—not now that she'd come this far. No. She was going to continue her quest.

Leaving Amy and Drew behind. Without supervision. I'm the world's worst big sister.

"Ann, are you coming?" Drew called.

"I'm sorry. I have to go. Enoch needs me." Opening her eyes, Annabelle forced herself to gaze at her little brother and sister. "I love you both," she said.

And then she deliberately turned away from her home and walked toward the unknown. She took a shaky breath. "Please, God, protect them."

She pressed a hand to the glowing obelisk. Its surface was slick beneath her palm. Nothing happened. "No!" She beat it with her fists. "Let me in! I have to save him!" Sobs wracked her body as she sagged against the chill stone.

Wings buzzed by her left ear. Tears burning her eyes, she turned to her guide. Her voice came out raw and wild. "Open the way!"

Khinjara bobbed. "As you wish." Without another word, the hummingbird plunged beak-first into the obelisk and disappeared. Ripples spread out from the point of contact, shimmering silver engulfing Annabelle and sucking her into a tunnel of blinding light.

Suddenly, she was elsewhere, and her winter clothes were gone. A silent garden beneath an enormous moon had popped into existence around her. Shuddering uncontrollably, she pivoted in a slow circle and took in the summer landscape.

There was no sign of dwelfnhad or hummingbird.

"K-Khinjara?" Annabelle rubbed her bare arms. It wasn't winter here. Why was it so cold? "Where are you?" She stepped forward, and her toe struck something. "Ouch." Glancing down, a caw of bitter laughter escaped her throat. She swallowed before it became sobs.

Daar-Lûsin lay in the grass at her feet. Trembling, she picked up the dagger. Tingling spread through her like a crackle of static charge. She stared at it. *Does this mean it accepts me? How could it? I killed a man, lost Enoch again, and left my siblings unsupervised! Poor Enoch ... I have to find him.* She reached out for Enoch, straining her senses, mentally screaming his name ... into nothingness.

Does this mean I failed? But Daar-Lûsin is here.

Tears streamed down her face. "I thought this would reforge my connection with Enoch. I still can't sense him. Why? Did I mess up ... do the wrong thing?" Her breath hitched as she stared at the opalescent blade in her shaking hands.

White light pulsed along its length and a voice—Khinjara's voice—spoke inside her head. "You did nothing wrong in defending your loved ones, Ann. And the children you left behind are not without resources. I am so sorry you endured such hardship during these trials. No matter what comes, I shall be your helpmeet. However, mending a sundered alarimet bond requires time. All wounds heal, in time. I ... need time."

As the final word echoed in her mind, a blinding flash, like lightning, surrounded her, and she was rushing through cold darkness, then into fragrant, humid air. Feelings not her own—until then, she hadn't noticed the Oathbond's absence—flared to life and ran riot in her chest.

Strong arms cradled her. Cardamom and pepper tickled her nostrils, mingling with the ghost of the Trumpet-lily's vanilla-cinnamon fragrance.

"Freylin?"

With the dagger clutched in her hands, Annabelle opened her eyes to a star-crazed sky. Green eyes lambent, her champion's head hung over her like a second moon. She was lying in his lap. Lord Evanrudhe knelt beside them, his silver hair glowing in a halo around his head.

"Well done." He greeted her with a sad smile and ineffable sorrow in his eyes—mirroring the sorrow she'd seen in Khinjara's gaze. "You passed through the trial, little wyldling. Daar-Lûsin has chosen a new wielder."

Burying her face in Raeden's chest, Annabelle burst into tears.

Ramble On

Good Practice

When it came, the mental attack struck Annabelle like a battering ram.

I must overcome this. How do I block him?

Seated at a laminate kitchen table, Annabelle clenched her jaw and held on to her defenses with all her might. Her energy waned, and it grew more and more difficult to repel the incursion. She should tap into the Aethyr to reinforce her barriers. Raeden had, inadvertently, given her the idea to use ice the first time she'd constructed her mind-fortress. Perhaps ice would keep out the invader.

Glacial ice is incredibly dense because of compaction, Annabelle mused. *However, glaciers arise from layers of snow under great pressure and over time. Lots and lots of time. Could I speed up that process?*

Lord Evanrudhe had given her brief instruction in using her wyld before they'd left Treehome a week earlier. Recalling what he'd taught her, Annabelle did a breathing exercise to calm herself, and then concentrated on the pool of sapphire light at her core. It reminded her of blue raspberry Kool-aid.

With a surge of her kythim, she sucked up power as through a straw, and shields of snow and ice coated the walls and windows of her grandparent's cabin. She piled on layers of snow, steadily pressing them until the crystalline structure compacted into ice, then kept adding to them. The pounding in her head diminished, then died away. Relieved, she sighed, but didn't let down her guard. Her opponent was both sneaky and tenacious. He wouldn't relent so easily.

During the brief respite, she layered ice on ice until Nana's kitchen resembled an igloo more than a room filled with modern appliances. She settled down to wait, clinging to Daar-Lûsin as to a lifeline. Lord Evanrudhe had told her the artifact's passive function would protect her mind from all but the most powerful and persistent invasions. Commander Storm warned her she must build her strength in the meantime and not rely on the dagger as a crutch lest she become complacent.

Hence the sustained battering of her mind. He called it "good practice." Yesterday, Annabelle had voiced a less polite name for it. The memory brought a smile to her lips. Toad had laughed uproariously when he'd heard her muttering it aloud. "It's about time you descended from your moral high ground and holier-than-thou attitude," he'd said, smirking.

Annabelle's smile turned to a frown as she coated the picture window with another layer of ice. That had been one of the few times her fellow wyldling had shown any sort of pleasant humor since they'd left Y'Dendordenelle three days ago. Mostly, he'd been a grump—lying on top of the saddlebag and ignoring her for much of their travels. Especially when the suns were out.

She toyed with the dagger, spinning it like a board game arrow. *You'd think he'd worry about drying up, being an amphibian.* She snorted a laugh, remembering. Out of concern for his health, she poured water from her canteen on Toad while he snoozed in the sunlight. He'd spluttered and cursed, puffed up and eyes flashing as the liquid boiled and hissed steam. "How am I supposed to charge up my batteries when you keep dousing my flame?" Before she could ask Toad how he knew about batteries, he'd hopped away, muttering curses.

Annabelle felt a nudge and envisioned a shark circling and bumping its snout against her barrier. Searching for weaknesses. She swallowed her laughter. With her bottom lip between her teeth, she bolstered the walls with more sapphire-infused ice. Defenses complete, she considered her mentor's latest mind-protection lesson.

"Once your fortress is impregnable," Commander Storm had told her, "You should go on the offensive and cast out the invader. Take hold of your blade, womanchild, and lean on what you know of the sword-dance to drive him back."

David had taken on most of the burden of training her in the sword-dance since they'd left Treehome. An able warrior, the handsome dwelfnhir had no need of Toad's directions—although it didn't prevent the cursed knight from commenting on *her* form. When he wasn't passed out and soaking up the suns' energy, that was.

Often, the cousins worked together, with Dinah serving as her sparring partner while David instructed. Annabelle had confided in Dinah that she never wanted to draw Murder Stick again. "I understand your fear, Ann," she had replied. "But you need to keep training in the sword-dance. Learning control will make it easier to disarm opponents instead of killing them. David is concerned you're not putting forth your best effort."

Shivers wracked Annabelle's frame as she glanced at the short sword. Murder Stick's round pommel—glowering like the blood-red giant sun, Atropos—seemed to glare accusingly at her. In the mundane world, the pommel was the same blank steel as always, but in her mindscape, it shone crimson as the blood spraying from the man she'd ... killed.

The first time she'd unsheathed her blade after the trials, when Commander Storm insisted she check her gear the morning they departed Treehome, a frisson shook her when she glimpsed the dried blood caked around the guard and in the blade's fuller. She'd hoped the veiled warriors, at least, hadn't been real people.

His expression grim, the evainghir handed her a vial of cleaning solvent, an oil jar, and a rag, then watched as she cleaned it. Her stomach roiled the entire time she scrubbed the blade while solvents stung her nostrils. Tears blurred her eyes by the end. She'd blamed the cleaning agent.

Commander Storm hadn't commented aside from a mild: "The blade must be kept clean, womanchild. Tomorrow, you resume your training."

I don't want to draw Murder Stick here. I won't!

Instead, Annabelle picked up the dagger, its handle fitting into her palm like it belonged there. The blade shimmered like mother-of-pearl and generated its own subtle glow like Khinjara's eyes when she'd opened the portal. Her fingers curled around the dull edges. It felt more like stone than metal. As always, when she handled Daar-Lûsin, a sense of peace buffeted her, but she resisted sinking into it. A small part of her still wondered whether another's life was a price worth paying to gain the relic and what it promised.

Maybe not, but good came of that trial. I saw Enoch. I know he's still alive. She'd told the Commander about 'Fastness,' a name he didn't recognize, which galled him. After they consulted with someone called the Caretaker at the Fortress of Living Stone—he did not appear to relish this impending visit—Commander Storm planned to assemble and lead an army to whatever location the Caretaker divined for Enoch.

And even though our alarimet bond isn't fixed, having the Dagger of Moonlight convinced the Commander to let me—

Her mind-fortress shattered like a Christmas ornament. Ice exploded, taking her grandparents' cabin with it. Pain radiated throughout her skull. She grimaced, curling into a ball as she returned to awareness of her physical body.

Darn it! I missed something.

Concern—not her own—flared hot in her chest. "I'm okay, Raeden," she murmured, and the feeling subsided to a dull throb; it never went away while her champion touched her. The scent of cardamom laced with pepper and the fur tickling her nose made her feel like sneezing. Nose wrinkled, she turned her head. Strong arms maneuvered her upright. She clutched the dagger to keep it from falling. *My weapon must always be at hand. Even if it isn't a weapon in the strictest sense of the word.*

Annabelle opened her eyes, flinching against the glare of late morning sunshine. Raeden's hand shaded her eyes, and Commander Storm's reptilian visage swam into focus. As usual, he was frowning. "I took advantage of your inattention to launch an assault. You must maintain constant vigilance, womanchild."

She forced herself to meet the cold steel of his gaze. *No matter what I do, it's never enough. What must I do to gain Commander Storm's approval?*

He squinted. "Next time, have a conventional blade in hand. Daar-Lûsin's purpose is defense, not attack."

Annabelle's heart clenched. *No. I won't use Murder Stick, never again.* Memories threatened to resurface. Quickly, she employed a trick the Commander had taught her, and wrapped her mind in an ice bubble to keep the horror at bay for a time.

After staring into her eyes, he rose from a crouch. "Shepherd," he said, glancing at the armored dwelfnhir leaning against a nearby tree. "I would have your opinion on our approach to Y'Vasheirdenelle." He frowned at Annabelle, then added, "Privately."

The giant warrior strode away, and Annabelle permitted herself the luxury of a shudder. Raeden drew her closer to his warmth. She rested her cheek against his chest and swallowed bile. The Commander was still hiding things from her.

"Well done, Annabelle." Kneeling beside her, Dinah smiled warmly and patted her hand. "Come. I have tea steeping by the fire." Annabelle managed a grin for her friend.

David echoed his cousin's praise. "Admirable work. You held out longer that time." He saluted Annabelle with a nod, then followed the Commander.

Admirable. Whatever. Still not good enough for the Commander. I suppose I should be grateful that he's allowing me to continue on the quest to rescue Enoch.

No longer under their scrutiny, Annabelle groaned and massaged her forehead. "If it weren't for Daar-Lûsin, I wouldn't have held out as long as I did." She swallowed with difficulty; her throat was parched.

"Do not fret, Freylin." Raeden helped her up. "You improve, day by day." Until he let go of her arm, the warmth in her chest mirrored the warmth in his eyes. "What worries distract you so?"

She tucked the dagger in the black leather sheath strapped to her right thigh and turned to her champion. Eyebrows arched, he offered her the canteen she'd left on the ground.

Over the past week, the Oathbond's weirdly intense emotional intimacy had subsided to a sense of Raeden's location. Unless they were very strong, she only experienced his feelings when he touched her. The kaenhir didn't seem so freaked out about making physical contact, although he limited it for when she most needed his support. He seemed more at ease in her presence rather than away from it. Based on what she'd gleaned from their conversations, his sense of her location and emotional state was much stronger than hers of his.

The Oathbond was no substitute for her connection with Enoch. In fact, sometimes it proved a nagging annoyance, like an itch she couldn't scratch. But it also comforted her to actually *know* how much someone cared.

After what happened during the trial ...

A pang lanced through her. She gulped water from the canteen to wash away the bitterness and push down self-loathing. They wouldn't go away, but her vitality returned.

Evanrudhe said what happened during the trials was between her and the Threefold One. However, he encouraged her to speak with the others while they traveled, particularly Dinah, David, and Raeden. With his unwavering support, her champion remained her rock, and the dwelfnim both counseled her, helping her to work through her emotions.

But I don't want to talk--or even think--about that right now.

"I'm concerned about Toad," Annabelle said in a rush. "He won't talk to me about what's bothering him. I thought he was my friend. He'd opened up to me at Treehome, but now all he wants to do is lie in the suns, suck up solar energy, and sulk." She drank, and energy flowed through her.

How much power does Toad need? If he collects anymore, he may spontaneously combust! Annabelle frowned as she examined her canteen, turning it over in her hands. *I wonder, could I drink too much water and explode? Is that a thing?*

With his head to one side, Raeden clasped his hands behind his back. He stared toward the campsite, where the person they discussed, doubtless, lay basking in the suns' rays. "Sir Thomas is a man of much pride, Freylin," he said. "It disappointed him that his man's body has not returned, but your servant does not believe he sulks."

Annabelle sighed and leaned against Raeden. Expression softening, he looked down at her. "Do not grasp overmuch for his friendship. A warrior who has suffered what he has is not a comfortable friend for a little maiden. Be content that he, like your servant, wishes to teach and protect you."

The water refused to do what she told it. Annabelle glared at the stubbornly empty canteen before her. Her rest break was over. Postponing the inevitable, she fussed with Tinker's reins, clenching them in fists. She'd wedged her open canteen between the saddle horn and the saddlebag to prop it up. Toad lay in the saddlebag with eyes closed, flap pulled back so the sunslight could play over him as they rode along an exposed ridge. He appeared to be asleep.

At least I don't have to listen to his snarky commentary on my attempts to use my wyld.

A slender brown hand patted her white-knuckled fingers. "Try again, Ann," Dinah coaxed. She rode beside her on a doe called Clover. Another doe, Jessamy, carried supplies behind them. "You almost had it that time. Would you like me to walk you through the steps?"

Annabelle shook out her stiff fingers. She knew the steps by heart, but verbal prompts couldn't hurt. "Yes, please."

I'm so glad I have Dinah here to guide me. The book of legends contains many examples of wyldlings manifesting their power, but nothing about how they use their wyld.

"Close your eyes." Annabelle did. "Take three deep, cleansing breaths," the dwelfnhad continued. "Envision yourself beside a placid river. Everything is calm. You are calm. Centered. In control of yourself and your mindscape."

While Dinah droned on, Annabelle did the breathing exercise. She imagined herself in Oak Park, seated on the bank of the Wisconsin River, which ran through her hometown. Across the way, she glimpsed the Isle of Ferns Park. She'd often hiked there with her friends and fed stale bread to greedy mallards. Reminded of Kensi, she experienced a pang. Was her best friend worried about her? She screwed her eyes shut tighter. *Not important right now. I'm supposed to be clearing my head of extraneous thoughts, not dredging up memories of home to distract myself.*

"Are you centered?"

Annabelle clung to the peaceful image of the river flowing through a park devoid of people, the sound of the water, its algal scent, its coolness against her bare feet. "Yes."

"Good. Now, holding to the calmness of that scene, focus on all the water sources around you while tapping into your reservoir. Concentrate, and visualize drawing it to you."

Mentally embracing moisture in the air, Annabelle simultaneously reached for the pool of sapphire light at her core. That second bit was easy enough, after Lord Evanrudhe's tutelage and her frequent practice while supervised by either Dinah or David during their travels. She'd drunk plenty of water and could tap into her reservoir at will. Pulling tiny droplets from the humid air also wasn't difficult. Compelling the water into her canteen remained the trickiest part of water-weaving. Rather than forming crystalline ribbons like Annabelle wanted, the water preferred to fall as a light drizzle around her once she pulled it from the air.

Focus, Ann. Don't recall past failures. Make the water obey.

She concentrated, extending her kythim, and pictured moisture gathering around a nucleus, coalescing from the air into droplets but *not* falling as rain. *Stay suspended*, she scolded the water. The droplets held, quivering. Thank God for water's strong cohesive tendency. She manipulated them with her kythim, painstakingly sticking droplets together and rolling them into a blue snake, like play-dough. She focused on that image.

"Got it," she said.

"Good," Dinah replied. "Now, open your eyes. Commit your wyld to undertake what you've visualized." Her voice softened. "Try not to gesture with your hands this time."

With a grimace, Annabelle flattened her palms against her thighs. She stared at the canteen. *That's your home*, she told the quivering water droplets. *Go inside. You're not too good for your home, now, are you?* Gathering her will, she mentally pulled the blue play-dough snake. A ribbon of water appeared and dribbled into the container.

Elation filled her. "I did it!"

The stream flew apart. Most of it splashed Toad. She cringed, half expecting him to explode, but he grunted and squirmed deeper into the saddlebag.

Dinah chuckled. "Well done, Ann! See? You *can* consciously use your wyld."

She sighed. "Not very well. That was *weak*."

"Strength will come, in time. As a sourethol, I can't know exactly how a wyldling grows in strength, but I assume it's like exercising a muscle."

"Oh." Annabelle shuddered. "I'm not sure I want to get *stronger*."

Dinah frowned. "Why are you so reluctant to gain in strength? Just as with sword-dancing, all you need is more practice to become proficient."

Annabelle glanced sidelong at her sword. Sucking in her lips, she looked up into Dinah's topaz eyes, so warm and caring. She ducked her head, wishing her hair was loose instead of in a braid, so that she could hide her face. "Don't you see? I k-killed someone. With my wyld. I encased a guy in ice. He probably froze to death. I'm a monster, just like those wyldlings in the tapestry. Where they're causing natural disasters."

Sorrow filled Dinah's beautiful face. "Oh, Ann ... Is that what you fear? Is that what's blocking you?"

A ripping snort came from the saddlebag. "You—a monster?" Toad's head emerged and his eyes blazed with cold fire. "I cry baloney. And whatever happened in that trial was all in your head, kiddo. How many *real* people have you stabbed?"

"Well, I ..." Her stomach lurched as she recalled the hot spray of blood, the coppery stench as it spattered her snowsuit. She gulped, tasting bile. "The dried blood on my sword was real, Toad. The warriors were real. At least one died on my blade."

Dead by my hand.

"In defense of yourself and two innocents," he snapped. "And I don't think it counts, because that jab sounded unintentional. Now, guess how many I've *intentionally* killed? Never mind. I'll tell you. At my last count, I dispatched fourteen men during my tour of duty. With my sword. Mainly in self-defense, but there were these six bandits I hunted down—"

"Sir Thomas," Dinah interrupted in a clipped tone, looking queasy. "Thank you, but we do not require further details of bloodshed." Under her breath, she muttered, "This is why I opted to become an ambassador instead of continuing with battle-training."

Shocked from her self-pity, Annabelle met his wintry gaze. "Toad," she said, slowly. "Did you just remember something from when you were ... a man?"

"Maybe," he drawled. "Or maybe I just made that up to make you feel better."

"*Toad.*"

"Jeremiah ever-lovin' Bullfrog!" He rolled his eyes. "Kiddo. I'm pulling your leg. Not sure how, but those are my actual memories. Too bad it wasn't anything pleasant, like a fishing trip with my dad. Eh. I'll take it. Better than nothing."

"An auspicious sign, Sir Thomas." Dinah forced a smile. "Even though it's rather ..." her smile changed to a grimace, "macabre, it shows that you're returning to your former self."

"This is awesome," Annabelle said, fixing a grin on her face. Anything to get away from that uncomfortable retelling. "Maybe if you talk to me more often, you'll remember more from your past and be able to transform soon."

And maybe then you can explain about the Earth references you make.

"Lord Evanrudhe suggested it was only a matter of time," Dinah agreed. She narrowed her eyes. "But you are attempting to change the subject, Ann. I cannot allow you to persist in this belief—that you are a monster simply because you have power at your disposal. As a follower of the Way of Yshua, you can resist the temptation to misuse it."

Annabelle's shoulders slumped. "You're right, Dee. I was just feeling sorry for myself. Leaving the kids. Failing Enoch ..."

Dinah's brow furrowed, looking troubled. "Continue on ahead. I must consult with my cousin. We'll speak more when we stop for the mainmeal." She pulled back on her reins and her mount slowed. Glancing over her shoulder, Annabelle observed as the white-tailed doe fell in beside the massive red elk. David bent from his seat to listen to whatever Dinah was saying.

What are they talking about? I suppose it's arrogant to assume it's about me, but—

"Hey, kiddo."

Startled, Annabelle whipped around. "What?"

Toad grunted. "So, now that I've given you perspective—and all your self-loathing's been squared away—how about you bring out the sword and do some lifting exercises?"

Annabelle's hand dropped to her weapon. Gingerly, she grasped the hilt and pulled the blade from its scabbard.

"Okay, now hold your sword in guard six—"

"It's Murder Stick," she whispered.

"Who the what now?"

"My sword." A sheepish grin tugged at her lips. "I named it Murder Stick."

Toad stared, deadpanning, "You named the sword 'Murder Stick.'" He burst out laughing. "Kiddo. That is so ... *you.*"

Annabelle blushed. "Yeah, that was Enoch's response, as well. But the darn thing's earned the name." Her smile faded. Then, after a moment, she chuckled. "At least the Dagger of Moonlight already has a perfectly suitable name." She eyed Daar-

Lûsin affectionately, recalling patches of rainbow colors flashing in its opalescent blade. "Otherwise, I'd probably call her Princess Sparkles."

Crown Irises

Klotho attained her zenith as the travelers climbed a hillock. At its summit, Commander Storm called a halt to prepare the mainmeal. Peter flew down to give his report, but Raeden had not yet returned from scouting. Why was it taking him so long?

Annabelle slid from the saddle. The Oathbond reassured her the kaenhir was in the northwest. As she tended to the mounts and the pack-deer, she crooned a classic rock song about rambling on to keep from worrying about her champion. Over the past week, Annabelle had assumed responsibility for the mounts and pack-deer, including Shepherd David's: a huge, red elk bred for warfare.

Anything to be useful and necessary for this mission.

Occasionally, she glanced over at the small fire-pit where David and Toad conversed quietly while the dwelfnhir laid out kindling. The Commander stood on the north side of the hill, hearing Peter's report.

Dinah was pulling rations from the pack-deer's panniers. "Would you like some tea?"

"Yes, please," Annabelle replied. "The travel teapot Lahni gave me is in Clover's left pannier." David's massive elk nudged her shoulder, and she scratched along both sides of his lower jaw. "Who's a sweet boy with death-antlers?" she cooed as the stag grunted with his eyelids drooping in bliss. "Who's a big softy and wants chin-scratches?" An insistent nose prodded her other shoulder. She turned to find Tinker bobbing his head and peering at her with glistening brown eyes.

Dinah laughed. "Looks like somebody's rather jealous of your attention, Ann."

Grinning, Annabelle rubbed her mount's nose. "I already gave you scritches, Tinker. But I suppose you can have more."

Dinah extracted a packet of tea and a small, blue-lacquered teapot decorated with stylistic waves. "When you finish with the deer, there's a lovely prospect on the southern exposure of this ridge. The Heaven's Breath is in bloom, and there could be ripe huckleberries, if we're blessed."

Annabelle was opening her mouth to respond when Toad shouted a blistering oath. With a loud *crack* of super-heated air, a pillar of flame erupted from the fire-pit. Peter squawked something unintelligible. She flinched, and Tinker sidled further into the woods. The other mounts stamped restively, bunching up further from the fire. Just as suddenly as it erupted, the fire sputtered out until only orange embers remained.

Holy cow!

"Goodness gracious," Dinah gasped. "David!" Setting down the teapot, she ran over to check on her cousin.

The dwelfnhir had fallen back on his elbows and scuttled away from the fire. He was laughing as Dinah knelt beside him. "Excellent control, Sir Thomas! I can barely feel the heat."

Annabelle stared. *Wow! I don't think I've ever seen David show so much emotion.*

"What control?" Toad squeaked, eyes wide and throat sac fluttering. "Criminy! I've no idea what I just did."

David sobered. "You channeled the heat in a rising column, did you not? I'm unharmed, Dee." He waved aside his cousin's concern. "How are you feeling, Sir Thomas? Drained?"

"Er ... not really?" He glanced aside at Annabelle, looking sheepish. "Sorry, kiddo. Didn't mean to scare you."

She laughed shakily. "I'm not scared."

Commander Storm strode into the clearing, his expression thunderous. "What is the meaning of this, Sir Thomas? When I gave you leave to practice, this did not include signaling all and sundry regarding our position." Toad closed his eyes and bowed his head, muttering. The Commander turned his flinty gaze on the dwelfnhir. "And I would have believed better of a former military leader, Shepherd."

David murmured his apologies, but the Commander apparently wasn't finished, and lectured Toad, David—and the hapless Dinah, who looked too scared to move—about maintaining secrecy on this mission. His scaly visage grew even more forbidding as he spoke, and the glade filled with an oppressive energy.

Peter nudged Annabelle's hand, breaking her fascination. The syrax must have slipped over by her when Toad's flare distracted the Commander. His hazel eyes danced, and he held what appeared to be a large white iris by its bruised stalk in his beak. He laid the flower at her feet, then nosed it closer.

Her eyes widened. "Is that ..." She picked up the iris. The bloom was huge and would just fit in a cup formed of both hands. She raised it to her face and sniffed, the petals tickling her lips. A subtle scent of sweet citrus and sunshine wafted in her nostrils. As she turned the flower this way and that, delicate peach shimmered at the base of its petals.

It's the same coloring as Trumpet-lily, she mused, stroking its silken, yet rigid petals. She'd pressed the other souvenir from her trials between the pages of Enoch's tome of legends, where it served as a bookmark.

She diverted her attention to her companion, who was vibrating with the effort of remaining silent. Grinning, she said, "Thank you, Peter. It's so pretty!"

His pink-feathered crest lifted as he puffed out his chest. "Yup. Before I went a-scouting, I found you some crown irises, Annie-O. Like I promised. They're only two miles away, as the syrax flies. There's a bunch of different colors. Wanna go see?" Amusement glittered in his eyes as he bobbed his head toward the campfire. "Dukey's gonna be yelling at them for a while."

And I sure as heck don't want the Commander to remember I'm here and start carping at me next. Twirling the flower, Annabelle smiled at the syrax. "Sure!"

Peter led her from the campsite. Commander Storm's basso rumble dwindled as they trotted a little way down the narrow game-trail to another spot where the canopy opened up. He paused and hunkered beside her. "Climb aboard, Annie-O."

Her stomach tightened as she tucked the flower's stalk inside her vest. The blossom rested on her chest. Like the Trumpet-lily had. *Too bad this one won't grow tendrils and root into my tunic.* She licked her lips. "You mean, we're flying?"

"Don't you worry none, Annie-O. It ain't too high, and I won't letcha fall. You'll be safe as houses, I swears before Lord Yshua." He tipped his head and eyed her in a bird-like fashion.

Annabelle took a deep breath. *I've been facing so many challenges lately. Maybe it's time to confront my fear of heights.* She glanced at the flower, stroking a petal. *I'd like to see these crown irises in their natural habitat.*

"Okay." Gingerly, she straddled Peter's back with her legs behind his wing joints and lowered herself to sit. "Are you sure you can take my weight?"

Peter scoffed. "I can take Eenie's weight with armor on; I can for sure take yours. But you'll wanna lean forward on your tummy more. Grab hold'a my harness straps."

Annabelle did as he directed, hoping she wouldn't crush the crown iris. She wrinkled her nose against the syrax's warm cat-musk and dusty-feather scent. Peter crouched, and then sprang into the air, flapping his powerful wings. Squeezing her eyes shut, she clasped her legs tighter as wind whistled around her ears. For a moment, it felt as if she'd left her stomach behind. Her tensed muscles trembled, and her breath grew choppy.

Oh, dear God, please don't let me fall.

"Not so tight!" Peter squawked. "I needs to breathe. Relax, Annie-O. I won't drop ya."

Enoch would have no problem with this. I'd better calm down. Use the breathing exercises. Pretend you're safe inside an airplane cabin.

Head on one side to avoid a mouthful of pink feathers and fur, Annabelle inhaled through her mouth and exhaled through her nose, matching the rhythm of Peter's steady wingbeat. Wind buffeted her, and tendrils of loose hair whipped like snakes around her face. She couldn't hold the image of herself seated in an airline seat; she'd only been four when she'd flown on a plane to visit her grandparents in New Jersey. Picturing Enoch astride Peter—confident and carefree—seemed to do the trick. The tension in her muscles eased.

Stop being a coward, Annabelle. Open your eyes.

She was treated to the swiftly alternating view of a pink wing, followed by blue sky. With controlled breaths, she raised her head and looked around. Straggled clumps of green drifted by on either side below them. Her knuckles whitened as she squeezed Peter's harness.

Her heart hammered in her chest. The experience was both terrifying and exhilarating. Like, and yet unlike, flying with Enoch in their dreams before she'd come to Tehara. In the dreamscape, one could describe flying as floating. Here in the waking world, gravity was very much in evidence.

But Peter won't let me fall. I trust him. This is like learning to ride Tinker. A random thought crossed her mind. *I wish Toad was here to see this, even if he'd tease me the entire time.* A smile quirked her lips. She could imagine it: Toad calling her a scaredy-cat, concocting ridiculous scenarios of her falling, and distracting her until Peter landed.

Even though he's not here, I should put on a brave face. I made it through those trials. I can overcome my fear of heights.

Carefully, she loosened her death-grip on Peter's harness straps before her fingers cramped. Sunslight warmed her back, countering the chill rush of wind. Klotho, Lachesis, and Atropos shone down, their light dimmed as small, cottony clouds passed and cast shadows on the lumpy, green patchwork of the forest canopy below. Now that she felt calmer, the Oathbond informed her that Peter brought her ever closer to her champion.

I wonder what Raeden's doing down there. Hunting?

Squinting, Annabelle peered ahead. Peter's flight aimed for a massive tree with large, spreading branches and bark that appeared black from her perspective. A rival for the sequoias of Earth, and the baobabs of Treehome, it rose head and shoulders above the forest—a leafy, green mountain that grew only larger as they drew near. How big *was* that tree?

Her jaw dropped and her eyes widened as new details and colors resolved in her vision. Blotches of white, purple, pink, and other hues dotted the viridian of the gargantuan tree's canopy. Were those crown irises? Now, she saw that the craggy bark wasn't black, but dark gray. Streaks of crimson, blue-green, violet, and orange-yellow gleamed through narrow cracks.

Like someone dumped cans of paint down the tree's trunk. What kind of tree is that? It's not a baobab. It makes me think of Yggdrasil from the Nordic myths. A World-tree?

The Oathbond thrummed like a plucked string, and she strained to pierce the gloom beneath sprawled limbs like giants' arms. Anticipation—and something like fear—tightened behind her breastbone and prickled throughout her body.

No. It couldn't be. Could he climb such an enormous tree?

With a piercing eagle's cry, Peter glided between branches. Annabelle ducked her head. Dim coolness replaced bright sunslight and subtle floral scents tickled her nose. Blinking, she stared as a figure, dwarfed to insect size in comparison with the World-tree's proportions, raced along a natural platform ringing the tree where every huge limb merged with the trunk.

"Raeden!" she called. He raised an arm and shouted something she couldn't make out.

"He's all excited to see ya, Annie-O!" Peter shrieked, sounding gleeful, as he flew to the broad base of the limb—as wide as a two-lane street back home. With a back-flap, he landed on the branch and lowered himself. "We made it." Chuckling, he added, "I *told* you I'd get you to the crown irises. Didn't I?" He cast a triumphant, sidelong glance at her and waggled his brow.

"Y-yeah." Annabelle laughed, her heart still pounding a nervous allegro against her ribs. Near the edges of the limb, where moss grew in shallow depressions, large irises of every hue bobbed in a persistent breeze on hardy stalks. Cracks in the gray bark oozed with orange sap.

The kaenhir approached at a jog, several blooms gripped in one hand. His clothing was stained with the tree's colorful sap. That almost-fear sense tightened in her chest, growing stronger as he drew near. Annabelle frowned. Something was wrong.

Peter chortled. "Reddy-boy musta come here to pick some flowers for you. Only the best and rarest for our sweet Annie-O."

"Maybe." Annabelle rubbed her chest. Peter's jabbering was little more than noise in her ears. It was bad enough, knowing she was so far above the solid ground. The high and wild sensation coming from the Oathbond made her want to jump out of her skin.

"Lawks!" Peter cackled. "Here he comes, wound up tighter than that watch of his. I betcha he's gonna ask—"

Raeden hunkered beside them. His ears drooped. "Freylin," he gasped, his voice as tight as the Oathbond. "*Liebstelichtl.* Why do you come here?"

Despite the anxiety singing its threnody inside her, Annabelle examined the colorful blossoms trembling in his grip. Burgundy, peach, and a turquoise one with pink streaks. Had her champion climbed the World-tree just to pick them for her? *If so, then no wonder he's been gone so long. But surely not!*

Her champion was glaring at the syrax. "Peter, how is it you bring Freylin? *Gefarern dracht.* Return to the Lord Commander *sovertzu*—curse this devil's language—with all haste." Wide-eyed like a spooked deer, his breath rasped in his throat. He placed a trembling hand on her shoulder. Gasping at the urgency sizzling along the bond, she stared at rigid fingers and nails lengthened into claws. Colorful tree sap stained their tips and his white fur.

Tensing, Peter tilted his head. "How do ye figure? I didn't see no danger on my patrol. Annie wanted to see the crown irises, so I brung her—"

"Peter," Raeden growled. "You patrolled in the wrong direction, on the wrong side of the ylber tree. This one has come from the north side. Just now. He has seen what approaches. The Battlecrow army, straight on the path for the waystone."

"What?" Annabelle gasped. "Not them again! How did they find us?"

Crest rippling, the syrax rose. "No worries. We got away from the likes o' them before. Almighty knows we'll do it again."

"Peter, it will not be so easy this time. Those in veiled helms march alongside the kadorei soldiers." Raeden's fingers spasmed and a red ribbon of rage and terror pulsed through the Oathbond. "This time, they have nightstalkers."

A Plague of Nightstalkers

Despite their significant lead, Annabelle's stomach remained in knots. David had explained nightstalkers to her; he referred to them as a cross of harrowdwelfnim with kadorei who were especially sensitive to the light of Klotho and Lachesis. They sounded like vampires, dark elves, and ninjas all rolled into one deadly package.

Please, God, don't let us run into them!

Their group had ascended a ridge for the final leg and found themselves on a plateau. Grasslands stretched out on either side as far as she could see, an idyllic mockery. Dinah's mount bounded on her right and Raeden, astride Tinker, kept pace on her left. He'd insisted they switch mounts because Lorun was the stronger runner.

Lorun's muscles surged as she fixed her gaze on the dark line of trees ahead. Commander Storm ran before her, and she marveled at his speed and stamina. The suns beat down against her bent head. Beneath the plain, leather cuirass Dinah had given her, sweat trickled along her spine.

Atropos was a glaring eye overhead, its imaginary voice a derisive hiss. *"Your defenders will fall in the battle to come. You are no fighter. You will fail in your mission."*

No! Her fingers tightened painfully on the reins. Why must there be a fight? Commander Storm believed they'd reach the waystone before the mercenaries. And her companions wouldn't fall in battle. *I'll help defend them with my wyld—like I did before—this time without killing anybody. Somehow. Failure isn't an option, because who'd save Enoch then?* A sob ripped free from her throat.

Dinah's mount pulled up beside Lorun. "Worry not, Ann," she said. Compassionate tears filled her topaz eyes. "Pray for deliverance. What will be, will be."

David's massive elk cantered up from the rearguard position. "Trust in the Threefold One. He will provide." A smile cracked the stern expression on his face as he patted the sword at his hip. "We are strong warriors. Do not count us as defeated yet."

How did he know my thoughts? Throat tight, Annabelle nodded, then returned her attention to the trees ahead of them, which grew steadily larger. She didn't want to talk. Talking wouldn't make her fear go away.

Before long, they passed into the cool shade beneath the spreading limbs of oak and other tree species for which she had no names. The terrain went from flat to gently rising. Commander Storm's pace slackened, and they reined in their mounts as he led them through the forest.

Annabelle shook her canteen. Empty. She sighed.

The dwelfnim dropped back and Raeden drew Tinker close. Wordlessly, he handed her a full waterskin. "Thanks," she rasped, then tilted her head back and drank. Through the Oathbond, she felt her champion's focus on her, like a bowstring pulled taut. He didn't seem worried. She bent to inhale the fragrance of her crown iris bouquet sticking out of the saddlebag, where Toad crouched with his eyes closed and throat sac pulsing slowly. One webbed hind-foot twitched, jostling her flowers.

My first bouquet. It was nice of Raeden to pick them for me. I don't believe he climbed that giant tree for that sole purpose, though. Peter's just being silly.

He held up a hand and shook his head when she offered to return the waterskin. She looped the strap over the saddle horn, then sat staring at it. She could practice tapping into her wyld with this water. Try to move it around, or something. Eyeing Raeden's bow and quiver full of arrows, she pondered her options. If he ran out of arrows, then she could make icicles and shoot them at the people who attacked them. Maybe aim at their legs, to slow them down instead of killing them. She had her waterskin; and moisture abounded in the plants, air, and soil.

Or I could make *the soldiers stop. After all, the human body is over seventy percent water …*

Commander Storm picked up the pace again, and Raeden stayed beside her. The surrounding shade deepened as the day grew old and the light pinkened. A shudder ran through Annabelle. Lachesis had sunk below the eastern horizon, leaving them to Atropos's nonexistent mercy.

"Freylin?" her champion asked. "Are you cold?"

"How could she be?" Toad cracked open an eye. "It's summer and hot as blazes." Pale blue eyes appraised her, and his voice softened. "You okay, kiddo?"

"I'm fine," she said, biting her lip and looking away. The odd gentleness in his voice made her want to cry. Why didn't he tease her, call her a worrywart? "We can't keep running forever," she blurted out. "What are we gonna do now?"

Toad braced his front toes on the rim of the saddlebag. "Find a place to make a stand and hold out until the waystone activates." His vocal sac pulsed. "At least, that's what I would do, if I were in the Commander's boots." He made a face. "Yuck. That would stink. I don't think he ever takes them off."

A ghost of a smile curved Annabelle's lips. The evainghir jogged ahead of them, seemingly indefatigable. She frowned. After running so far, would he have the energy to fight off their pursuers? If nightstalkers were faster and stronger than the regular kadorei warriors, what chance did they have against them? But the mercenaries had been running, too, so maybe it was an even match. She licked her dry lips. *I sure hope so. We need every advantage we can get.*

"Peter returns," Raeden said, his voice clipped. A moment later, the syrax descended through the canopy. Commander Storm crashed to a halt, cursing. The rest of them reined in their mounts as they drew abreast.

"They're a'coming," Peter said, ears and tail drooping. "Roundabouts a hunnert Battlecrows and fifteen, mebbe twenty nightstalkers. But the kadorei mercs are hangin' back."

"Lachesis set," David observed in a detached tone. "Any mercenary worth his salt knows the nightstalkers have the advantage in darkness."

Raeden sucked in air through his teeth. "Twenty nightstalkers." He gripped his war bow and glanced at Annabelle. "Formidable enemies. Swift and agile beyond the kadorei abilities. Worse than lykharim. Your servant has not so many arrows in his quiver. He could take down three, maybe five, before they overrun a defensive line."

Commander Storm narrowed his eyes. "I would not allow so many to pass me by, your Excellency." He wiped sweat from his brow. "We push on for the last mile. Into the forest, up another ridge, and across another terrace. The waystone lies at the eastern end, and there's naught but a sheer cliff beyond. There, we shall have the high ground, and there we make our stand. Come, make haste; we have not a moment to lose."

The saddle of a moving deer in a forest at twilight did not provide ideal conditions for a first attempt at conjuring icicles. Annabelle clung to the saddle horn with one hand and clutched the neck of her open waterskin with the other, squinting at the narrow stream of water rising from the spout. "You *will* turn into ice," she growled. Enoch's book of legends contained an account of a wyldling who used icicles in battle.

I should be able to make icicles too!

Lorun bounded over a fallen tree, she lost her mental grip on the tiny trickle, and the water sank into the waterskin, droplets splashing her hand. She tamped down an impulse to weep.

"You're concentrating *too* hard, kiddo," Toad remarked as he scanned the dark trees as they passed. The sanguine light of Atropos made it seem as if the forest burned somewhere in the distance. She kept expecting to smell smoke.

When Lorun's gait leveled out, she drank some water. "I need to figure this out. In case those nightstalkers catch up to us." She slung the waterskin's strap crosswise over her shoulder, then patted the bag. *There, now I'll have both fuel and ammunition.*

"Wait until we get to the waystone." Toad's voice shook at another jarring thud. "And we aren't moving. We'll have time. Our pursuers have no choice but to approach over the ridge."

His confidence lifted Annabelle's sinking spirits. Commander Storm, David, and Dinah were setting up a line of defense half-a-mile back. Apparently booby-traps were involved, and both dwelfnim's Stonesinger abilities would aid in that. Peter would serve aerial support. They would engage the enemy while falling back toward the waystone ... or something to that effect. Annabelle knew next to nothing about military tactics.

Meanwhile, Toad and Raeden would defend her from any foes that slipped past. A glance cast over her shoulder provided confirmation of what the Oathbond told her—that her champion rode at Lorun's heels. Something black and rootlike protruded from his mouth as he chewed. His lambent green gaze was grim and fraught with meaning. He'd told her that fears were best laid to rest—his words: "sent to the grave"—in continual prayer.

Thanks for reminding me. I should pray.

Annabelle turned and closed her eyes. "Please, God," she whispered. "Protect us from our enemies." She thought of Dinah, who, though battle-trained, hated fighting as much as she did. "Grant us courage." Recalling David's encouragement brought warmth to her cold insides. "Support and sustain us with your Spirit, LORD."

She considered their stalwart leader. "Give Commander Storm wisdom and strength." In her mind's eye, she relived the syrax's excitement as he told her about the crown irises. "Thank you for Peter's cheerfulness. Bless his vision and wings. Keep him safe." She smiled as the Oathbond thrummed approval. "Don't let Raeden run out of arrows or allow us to get separated." She paused for a breath. "And please, God. Help me harness my powers so I can help my friends."

Toad muttered. "Not sure what good that'll do. You should focus on trusting in yourself and your abilities."

Her eyes flew open. She stared at him, incredulous. "Don't you trust in God?"

"Look at me." Toad glowered at the passing trees. "I've got no reason to."

There's no point in arguing with him. Annabelle looked at him for a heartbeat and then concluded her prayer. "And save Toad—Sir Thomas—from his unbelief. Amen."

Toad grunted. "I appreciate the sentiment, kiddo—" He raised himself and his eyes widened. "Movement, nine o'clock!" The Oathbond tightened in Annabelle's chest. She leaned back, and Lorun slowed to a walk. She peered into the woods. *It's growing dark. How could Toad see anything?*

"Don't slow down." Toad sounded disgusted.

Arrow nocked, Raeden drew Tinker beside her. His nostrils flared as he pricked up his ears, his attention fixed on the south side of the trail. "Freylin, something is not right. You must keep moving—" He flinched, grunting.

A ghost of sensation—a tiny needle of pain—pierced her right shoulder, and she cried, "Raeden!"

Eyes wild, he yanked something long and black from his upper right arm. He turned to her and snarled through clenched jaws: "*Nachtjagger!*"

"What the—"

"*Schutz ihr!*" The kaenhir smacked Lorun's rump, and the stag bounded forward.

No! I can't leave him! Terror spiking, Annabelle clung to the saddle. Toad shouted. Suddenly three black silhouettes with glowing eyes stood directly in their path. Bugling, Lorun shook his antlers, lowered his head, and charged.

Oh, fudge!

She dropped low in the saddle, bracing for impact. Her mount struck his target, sending a great jolt through her body. A man cried out. Lorun uttered a horrible, grunting squeal. The coppery stench of blood assaulted her nostrils as the world tilted sideways. And then rough hands yanked her from Lorun.

Squirming, Annabelle drew in breath to scream. Iron fingers clamped over her mouth hard enough to make her whimper. "None of that, sweetling," said a harshly accented voice. Hot, sour-smelling breath puffed against her cheek. "Calling for help will bring death to your companions."

She looked into a pair of blazing orange eyes like the gates of hell yawning open, set in a too-pale, handsome face framed by dark hair. What the heck? Was this a nightstalker? Her heart plummeted into her stomach. A thread of confused recognition wove through the terror. Orange eyes. Where else had she seen a man with orange eyes?

Her captor chuckled. "Don't worry, little sweetling," he said, almost tenderly. "I won't harm you. Captain Wuya shall reward me richly for your safe del—"

"Kiddo, get down!"

Annabelle inhaled sharply. *Like I can move, Toad!*

Yellow light blinded her. An intense heat flared from above and she smelled burnt hair. The nightstalker hollered in pain, and the arms loosened enough for her to wriggle free and crab-crawl off the trail. She had to get away. Twigs, needles, and stones jabbed at her palms. The waterskin flopped and burbled under her arm. Heart hammering, she slipped under a prickly evergreen branch and was wreathed in pine scent. *Like Christmas trees.* The incongruity upended her mind. Back braced against the tree, she drew Murder Stick and surveyed the nightmarish scene lit by flickering firelight.

Lorun sprawled on the ground with his head twisted at an unnatural angle. His antlers were embedded in the abdomen of man curled on his side with flames dancing along his length. Both lay still. The ground under them glistened black and wet.

Beyond her fallen mount, a tall, dark figure ran around, head on fire and shrieking. The air wavered with smoke, and its acrid reek made her gag. *And here we are, surrounded by highly flammable conifers. Where is Toad?*

Her erstwhile captor finished beating out a tongue of flame on his shoulder and whipped around, holding out his right arm toward his shrieking companion. Something went "*Snick*." The human torch cut off mid-shriek, its body jerked, then collapsed like a puppet with cut strings.

Oh, please, God. Help. She tried to hide her mind from the emotions assaulting her, but the shield kept shattering.

"Ann..." a sweet voice chimed. She shook her head. Now she was imagining voices.

The orange-eyed fiend turned, removed an angular contraption from his right arm, and then hung it from his belt. "Sweetling," he crooned. "You cannot hide from me. I hear your heart beating. So fast it goes. Pitter-pat. Pitter-pat. Pitter-pat." Backlit by the fire and the crimson gloaming, his tall frame expanded to fill her vision as he approached.

Oh, God, please. Where'd Toad go? Where's Raeden? Am I all alone?

Her captor was a mere three strides away. Annabelle grimaced. It appeared she must save herself. But her limbs refused to obey her commands. Even if she wanted to, she couldn't raise Murder Stick an inch. And the thought of sticking it into another person ... Her breaths came quick and fast. The stench of charred cloth and cooked flesh grew unbearable. She coughed and choked. *Stop hyperventilating and do something!*

"Hello, sweetling." The black-clad man hunkered before her, eyes smoldering. He seized her right wrist. "A little warrior maiden, eh? Can't have you skewering me." He twisted, and her hand went numb. With teeth bared in a shark-like grin—were those *vampire fangs?*— he disarmed her. "Too bad about your deer and pet toad; they made such a pretty splat."

Annabelle gasped. *Lorun ... Toad!* Staring into those gloating, burning eyes, her insides went cold. The world froze. Everything glowed blue. Arctic wrath howled up her throat in a rising column, giving birth to an inarticulate cry. The waterskin burst and expelled jagged shards of ice toward her captor.

He tumbled back with a crow-like noise, shielding his face too late. Dark lines split pale flesh. He shrieked, "Wyldling!" A searing thread of rage and bloodlust stitched through the Oathbond, and then his form jerked. There was a snap, a crack, and then a bubbling sigh.

What just happened?

"Freylin!" Suddenly, Raeden was lifting her, his warm scent mingling hideously with a charnel house reek. He held her close, the Oathbond quivering with relief, anxiety, and an undercurrent of dark spikiness that terrified her. Trembling, she clutched at him, burying her face in his chest, cardamom and pepper chasing away the stench of death. He carried her a short distance and then set her on Tinker's saddle. He handed her Murder Stick, and she sheathed it mechanically.

Her eyes stung. *Toad ... have to find Toad.* She tried to speak, but words wouldn't come.

"Atropos will set soon." His white fur tinted rose and splattered with darkness, Raeden nodded toward the east. "Ride for the waystone, Freylin. More nightstalkers are abroad." His eyes gleamed and the thread of bloodlust in the Oathbond thickened. "Your servant will end them."

Wait, isn't Raeden hurt? We need to stop, check for wounds. Once more, her voice wouldn't work.

He leaped up into the saddle behind her, and Tinker bounded forward. Annabelle clutched the familiar saddle horn, her eyes drawn to the saddlebag gaping open, slack and empty like a dead man's mouth. She swallowed a sob.

Toad ...

Raeden's bow sang as ember-eyed fiends crept out of the shadows, felling them. Dizzy and thirsty, Annabelle huddled against his warmth. A sweet, chiming voice spoke in her head. It sounded familiar, like a friend, but it was all noise. She squeezed her eyes shut. *Too many voices in my head.*

Tinker stumbled. Annabelle shrieked. Her champion curled around her, pressing her close. There was a jarring thud. Raeden's agony ripped a jagged line along the Oathbond and he yelped like an injured dog. Everything spun, flinging her about until her stomach lurched. Then she was upright again, arms encircling Raeden's neck as he jogged toward the setting sun.

Breath rattling in his throat, he staggered to a halt and carefully slid her to the ground. The Oathbond seethed with rage and pain. Between them and the ring of stones bathed in the lurid rays stood two more fiery-eyed nightstalkers, wearing black cloaks, but there was something different about these. Their skin was darker, and they radiated an austere nobility—a focused menace the pale ones had lacked.

Annabelle's heart clenched and fluttered as Raeden stepped in front of her, blocking her view of the nightstalkers. Blood soaked his right sleeve. He *had* been injured.

"Ann..." the sweet voice whispered. *"Flee."*

No. I won't leave Raeden. Her trembling hand drifted toward Murder Stick's hilt.

One of the nightstalkers, the taller one on the left, spoke in an urbane manner, his tone conversational. "Hand over the wyldling, harkhurz, and your death will be both merciful and swift. I give you my word as one of the Valkyr Golorum: the maiden will not be harmed."

Annabelle wanted to ask why the heck they wanted her, but her throat was too dry.

Raeden growled, hackles rising. "No. A *Durkwohnter's* word is not to be trusted."

Durkwohnter? That's not the same word he used before.

"Ah, that is ... an unfortunate attitude," the spokesman replied, for all the world as if they were discussing the weather. "However, we must take the wyldling from you. Kahntark Vespyrahl demands it."

Underneath seething rage, the Oathbond assumed a steady hum that felt like resignation. She wanted to weep. "Run, Freylin." He drew his hunting knife. "Do not trust them. They worship blood-thirsty gods. They will use you, then kill you. Your servant will buy you time."

She grabbed his left arm. His muscles felt like rocks. "No," she rasped. "No. Together."

"Please, Freylin," Raeden growled. A feral gleam shone in his eye and the Oathbond felt ... wild. Wolfish. "Flee. Allow your servant to keep what honor remains to him."

They have two blades. I must help ... Murder Stick!

Her knees shook as she offered him the hilt. "Take it." She swallowed with difficulty. "I have my magic to fight with."

The leader's voice hardened. "Revchek, kill the harkhurz. Secure the maiden. She's exhausted her wyld and is powerless."

Annabelle gasped. Looking inward, she summoned the sapphire light. Nothing. Pain spider-webbed through her skull. *Crud, he's right. How does he know my condition?*

"Aye, Tarkmada." The other nightstalker ducked and reached over his head with both hands. Steel hissed as he drew two swords, one longer than the other. "Come peacefully, little wyldling maiden. We mean you no harm." His tone seemed friendly, but the menace radiating from him chilled her marrow.

"Run, Freylin!" Grasping Murder Stick and his knife, Raeden darted to intercept both nightstalkers. The leader hung back. With a roar, Raeden hurled himself at the swordsman, ducking and weaving, blocking lightning-fast blows with the short sword and his hunting knife.

Annabelle gaped. *He says he doesn't know the sword-dance!*

"You will come with me, wyldling." The leader now stood a stone's throw away. Another stride, and he could grab her. What the heck? She hadn't seen him move!

Ack! Raeden told me to run!

She stumbled backward, then whirled and ran. Away. She had to get away. Feet pounded behind her. She sobbed.

A heavy hand clapped down on her shoulder, steel gauntlets digging into her leather cuirass. The nightstalker jerked her to a halt and said, "You will come with me."

She screamed. "Raeden, Toad, anyone—help!"

"Ann! Draw Daar-Lûsin!"

Khinjara?

Annabelle gripped the dagger's hilt as a strong arm snaked around her middle. She drew Daar-Lûsin. Light flashed and then spread in an arc, lining bushes and tree trunks in pale moonlight against the darkness. The nightstalker shouted, and his restraining arm fell away.

Suddenly free, Annabelle tumbled through cold nothingness until she landed and sprawled in a shivering heap. The noises coming from her throat ashamed her. Cowardly, little baby noises. She pulled her arms closer to her torso and then froze. Something solid pulsed with energy in her hands. For a moment she stared at it, glowing faintly with its own pearlescent radiance, not recognizing it for what it was until the light faded and the Dagger of Moonlight vanished.

"Daar-Lûsin!" she screamed, staring at her empty hands. Where had the relic gone? Darn it! She'd earned its allegiance. It was supposed to protect her! Panic gripped her heart with icy claws. Cold emptiness like an extinguished candle occupied the space behind her breastbone where her sense of Raeden had dwelled. Did that mean he was dead? A shudder wracked her frame. "No. God, please help me."

Light bloomed as a giant moon shone on a familiar landscape. She lay on a garden path lined with tangled, overgrown shrubs and velvety flowers with huge petals. A gray stone arch loomed nearby, draped with Trumpet-lily vines. Their cinnamon-vanilla aroma filled the air.

Shaking, Annabelle stood up. "Melkior's Garden." Despite aching loneliness, hope flickered in her chest. Maybe she could return to her friends after all. She staggered toward the arch. In a tremulous voice, she called, "Khinjara?"

Soft, opalescent light flared beneath the arch like a tiny, muted star being born, and she drew up short, observing it warily. She gaped as a silent shockwave rippled from the point of light, then dissipated to reveal a gleaming white creature with huge, feathered wings and a crystalline horn spiraling from its forehead. A snowy mane tumbled down one side of an arched neck, which sparkled with opalescent scales peeking out from the white fur.

Whickering, the creature bobbed its head and pawed the ground with a cloven hoof.

"What are you?" Annabelle whispered. "An Alicorn?" Her paralysis broke, and she extended a hand to the winged unicorn.

It stepped forward to nuzzle her, and she stroked a long jaw lined with tiny scales. Weird, but beautiful. A familiar pair of brown eyes regarded her warmly from beneath a tousled forelock. "Ann." Khinjara's voice piped in Annabelle's head as the horn pulsed with light. "I have taken the form of a hisanabyad. Forgive me. I did not intend to frighten you. I brought you here to protect you from the nehmwight."

"Nehmwight? Hisanabyad?" Annabelle's voice went up an octave. "Cripes, I don't even know what those are!"

"This form is a hisanabyad," Khinjara replied. "To my knowledge, they exist only in myths and legends. Nehmwights are another matter. They are quite real and are also known as harrowdwelfnim---cursed to become creatures of the night who revel in blood and violence."

"Like the book said." Annabelle licked her lips. "And I left Raeden to fight two of them." Her eyes widened as she touched the cuirass in the spot over her heart. "The Oathbond is ... gone. I don't even know if he's still alive."

Khinjara's horn pulsed. "Your champion lives."

Annabelle's breath quickened. "I have to help him, Khinjara. Can you send me back?"

"If that is your wish, Ann."

Annabelle leaned against the hisanabyad's warmth and caressed her silken mane. In this form, Khinjara would be a formidable ally. She could charge into battle and skewer one of those nehmwights with her horn. "Will you come with me?"

Humor colored Khinjara's voice. "Not in this form, but I will be with you, Ann. Where you go, I go."

Understanding dawned. She hadn't lost Daar-Lûsin after all. Somehow—at least in this strange dreamscape-like dimension—Khinjara *was* Daar-Lûsin. Annabelle put her arms around the hisanabyad's neck. "Thank you."

Her horn flared, and Melkior's Garden faded to white.

Sounds of clashing forces roared in Annabelle's ears as she staggered to her feet. The wild-fire of the Oathbond tugged her eastward. Raeden was still alive. *Thank you, God!* The dagger in her hand dimmed, but she could still see. Strange.

At least I have the Dagger of Moonlight.

Annabelle crept around the copse on trembling legs. *I could take a shortcut through this.* When she came to a place where she could squeeze between trees, she froze, remembering the blazing eyes boring into hers.

Come on, Annabelle, stop being a coward.

She tightened her grip on the relic. *God, be with me.* Her breath came in shuddering gasps as she pushed through the low-hanging branches. Pine-scent was strong in her nose, but a sewer-smell underlaid it, along with an acrid odor that made her gag. The stench grew as she peered into the little clearing. A haze of smoke rose from smoldering bits concentrated around several shapes huddled on the ground. No doubt the reek of bowel and blood came from them.

No, no, no. Lorun. Toad. Dead. Killed by nightstalkers.

She clapped a hand over her mouth and fought clinging branches to escape the stink of death. Tears blinded her as she fled, following the battle-noise and pull of the Oathbond to her champion. Names rose to her lips, but her voice choked off.

God, help me, she prayed. *Help me.*

Her steps faltered, and she leaned against a tree, panting. Blood rushed in her ears with the frenzied beat of her heart, drowning out other sounds. Daar-Lûsin was still in her shaking hand. Gleaming in an unseen source of light, the dagger's opalescent blade and hilt possessed a beauty that took her breath away. But it was dull. Could she use it to defend herself?

No. A feeling of revulsion rose like bile in her throat. She couldn't use Daar-Lûsin that way. Like the hisanabyad's horn, it looked like a weapon—it had a point—but she knew with a certainty as inexorable as death that the blade wasn't meant to maim or kill. However, she was reluctant to sheath the relic. She felt more secure with it in hand.

Did she have an alternative? Reaching within, she found the gleaming sapphire core. Reaching without, she found moisture in the air. In the dew condensing on the foliage. *Come to me.* She drew moisture in along her kythim like pearls on a string and felt her strength return. The water replenished her wyld reservoir. Could she attack someone with her wyld?

I don't know! But I don't want to die. And I don't want Raeden to die.

The Oathbond sang. Raeden was close. Carefully placing one foot ahead of the other, she crept around the tree and approached a screening bush until her shallow breaths stirred the foliage. Abruptly, the weapons-noise ceased, and she froze. Had they heard her?

A cold, cruel voice spoke. "You weaken, harkhurz. Once I kill you, nothing will hinder me. I will take the wyldling."

Annabelle shuddered as her blood ran cold. The nehmwight leader. Where was the other?

Growls shredded the night, morphing into words. "You can't have her. This one may fall, but he will drag you down with him before you look upon the hairs of her head!" He shouted something in his dialect, and the clanging noises resumed.

Annabelle bit her lower lip and swallowed a whimper. Raeden. His rough voice was almost unrecognizable, a beast's snarl. Despite the fury singing through the Oathbond, her champion grew ragged and worn, no doubt from the battles he'd already fought, while the nehmwight sounded fresh and confident of success. She secured her hold on the dagger and reached for her wyld. It kept slipping through her fingers. Her breathing grew choppy. *I'm no warrior, but I must help Raeden.*

Cautiously, she pushed aside leaves and peered through an opening in the interwoven branches. The other nehmwight lay propped against a standing stone, his throat torn out, weapons abandoned on the ground where he'd dropped them in death. She shuddered.

Looks like Raeden took care of that one.

Annabelle swallowed bile and eyed the two swords. They were both too long and heavy for her, but she needed a weapon. She sheathed Daar-Lûsin and crept from her hiding place, heart fluttering. Oddly, her eyesight didn't dim. Grabbing the smaller sword, she scurried across a narrow gap to the next standing stone; no way was she sharing cover with a dead man.

Had they seen her? Sword in hand and panting, she peered around the menhir. The waystone reared up in the clearing beyond, a faint glimmer stirring in its pearlescent depths. Despite this, the grim beauty of the deadly dance among the standing stones captivated her.

The nehmwight had removed or lost his cloak. Beneath, he wore glistening black full-body armor like insect chiton. Her champion and the nehmwight whirled around one another with consummate grace—moving more swiftly than she could follow—and their weapons moved even faster. Like watching a samurai film on fast forward.

How can they do that? According to what the Oathbond told her, the pace wasn't sustainable. The fierce rage she sensed would soon burn Raeden out.

The nehmwight slashed at her friend with two swords. Raeden blocked with his knife, then parried the other blade with Murder Stick. The nehmwight attacked again. And again. Raeden deftly countered every blow, but his breath came loud and fast and the slightly larger nehmwight was driving him back inside the ring of stones, closer to the waystone. The Oathbond quivered with his growing weariness. If the nehmwight overpowered and killed him ... Her heart gave a lurch. *I can't let that happen.*

Before the central crystal, her champion appeared to stumble with both blades lifted in a cross-block. Annabelle cried out. The kaenhir and the nehmwight both froze. Her champion's head twitched in her direction and his lambent green eyes widened. Recovering quickly, Raeden brought up Murder Stick to block his opponent's short sword, diverting the blade.

Lightning fast, the nehmwight thrust the longer sword. Annabelle watched helplessly as the blade slid into Raeden's abdomen. Shock and pain flared in the Oathbond. Her champion snarled as the nehmwight raised his other sword to deliver the coup de grâce.

From deep inside, a scream rose in a geyser's blast, and she howled a denial. "I won't let you kill him!"

The nehmwight jerked out his blade and turned, wiping blood from the sword and then sheathing them both in a leisurely fashion. He brushed off Raeden's feeble attempts to restrain him as he strode toward Annabelle. Gasping like a fish drowning on land, she clawed for that boiling core of sapphire, but it slipped through her fingers like the water she was supposed to command.

If I don't get control ... No! God has control. I need to be calm. I need to concentrate. God, please, help me.

Peace descended. Time seemed to slow. The nehmwight, so fast before, now moved at a snail's pace. She had to stop him. Trap him in mud? She focused on the ground beneath the nehmwight's boots. Reaching with her kythim, she found water and drew it to the surface. The ground turned to mud, sucking the nehmwight down until it reached his mid-thighs. Quicker than thought, she froze the water.

With a groan, Annabelle clutched her spinning head and fell to her knees. No! She had to get up. Raeden needed her. He was still alive; the bright line of pain humming through the Oathbond told her so. But it was fading into pastels like paint too long in the sun. She crawled toward her fallen champion, past the trapped nehmwight, who snarled at her in a guttural tongue.

Raeden sat hunched over at the base of the waystone, arms wrapped around his middle, trembling. Metal glinted as a faint glow stirred in the depths of the waystone. Had it grown brighter?

"Raeden." She knelt beside him. A crackling noise made her turn. The nehmwight was breaking the ice and pulling his legs out of the quagmire she'd created. And he still had his swords. Why hadn't she tried to take them away while the ice held him?

She looked around wildly. "Help!" Who could she call? The one with the greatest mobility. "Peter! Help!"

"Anna," Raeden whispered. She peered into his face. His eyes were glassy, but lucid. Weakly, he nodded at the weapons lying on the ground. Her sword and his hunting knife. "Take. Go." With a sigh, his chin lowered to his chest. Panic ripped through her, but then she felt the flickering warmth of the Oathbond. Raeden yet lived, but what would happen when his colors faded and his thread snapped?

I can't let him die. Now that Toad is ... is ...

Annabelle swallowed her grief. Where was Peter? As the nehmwight approached, she pawed at the ground, grasping Murder Stick in her right hand and Raeden's knife in her left. Commander Storm had said she must always keep her weapon in hand. Shakily, she rose, straightened, and stood between the nehmwight and her champion.

"Peter!" She shrieked her throat raw.

"Your friend is not coming." The nehmwight's face bore little expression as he stood before her, swords in his hands at his sides. "Come, wyldling. Step aside, and I shall release your scout-hound from his misery." His tone was almost apologetic as he lifted his right-hand blade. "A pity, for he was a worthy opponent—it has been Cycles since I last fought a true berserker—but he would not yield."

No ... Annabelle mouthed the word but lacked the air to make the sound come out. She ought to run. No; she couldn't abandon her champion again. Her mind ached and felt limp as a wrung-out dishrag. She was just so tired. Raeden was willing to die for her. Could she not risk her own life for his sake?

God, please grant me courage!

At last, she found her voice. "No. I won't come with you." She drew a shuddering breath. "I won't stand aside. Because Jesus said, 'Greater love has no one than he who lays down his life for his friends.' You can't kill him." Behind her, the glow intensified, tinged with blue.

"An odd sentiment." Frowning, the nehmwight looked past her. Unease flickered in his gaze. "I give you my word of honor as a Valkyr Golorum, I won't harm you. But the scout-hound must die."

"No. I'll k-kill you first." Galvanized, she squared her shoulders and lifted her right-hand weapon in a ready stance, keeping the knife at her side. Behind her, Raeden wheezed.

He's fading. If only I had some water.

The nehmwight laughed and sheathed his swords. "Wyldling. Your power is spent, and you lack the two-blade skill to repel me." With a sneer, he stepped forward, seizing her right wrist as she thrusted. He twisted, and Murder Stick fell from her grasp even as he reached for her left arm. He did the same thing to her left wrist, caught the knife, and shoved her aside. His tone was clipped, impatient. "I shall do him the honor of dispatching him with his own blade. Do not interfere."

Annabelle fell on her rear. *God, please ...* Sobbing, she drew Daar-Lûsin and threw herself in front of Raeden. Grim as death, the nehmwight loomed, knife raised. The waystone's light waxed, blue swirling inside the pearly glow. Beneath her, moisture hummed in the soil, in plants' roots, aquifers of the rock ...

I can use this.

Reaching down deep, Annabelle *pulled.* Energy from the groundwater filled her reservoir within a heartbeat. She fixed the nehmwight with a glare—his orange eyes widened as he snarled a curse—concentrated on the water flowing inside him, and *pushed.* With a grunt, he skidded backwards a few feet as if punched in the gut, then held steady. Straining, he took a step toward her. His eyes blazed murder.

No, no, no!

Daar-Lûsin raised in guard three, Annabelle held up the other hand in a warding gesture. *"Freeze,"* she told the water inside the nehmwight's body, and she *felt* his blood solidify, cells burst, and organs rupture. As ice coated him from head to toe, he made a terrible groaning sound, then went still. Blood oozed from his mouth. The light in his irises went out.

Did I just …? Gasping for breath, cold satisfaction mingled with a shrinking horror settled in Annabelle's gut. *I saved Raeden from him. That's all that matters.*

An avian screech split the night. Something pink swooped in. Peter caught up the frozen nehmwight in his talons and dragged him into the canopy. The knife fell. Its blade stuck in the soil between Raeden's boots.

A moment later, a headless corpse crashed through the branches and into the bushes beyond the stone circle. She cringed, hugging her fallen champion. Even with the dagger in her hand lit up with a pearlescent glow, a mist obscured the surrounding menhirs.

"Raeden," she choked, touching his face, patting his cheek. "Wake up," she sobbed. "Please, wake up." His eyelids flickered, and he groaned.

From a distance came the sound of battle. Men shouting. Steel clashing. From nearby came the sound of fluttering wings. She clutched at Raeden, then flinched as a feathery warmth curled around her.

"Annie, Annie, Annie-O." Peter's rough tongue rasped on her cheek. A wing cradled her. "Are ya hurt? I settled for the nehmwight afore he got you. Made mince-meat of him. Can you get up? Please tell me you're alright. I hear ya callin' and Dukey's coming. The Shepherd and the Ambassador are too. The battle's coming closer." He leaned over Raeden, eyes round and ears trembling. "Poor Reddy-boy. Is he ...?"

At least the Commander survived. And Dinah and David. But Toad ...

A pain that was all her own sliced through her. Closing her eyes, Annabelle drew in a shaky breath. "Peter. Go get Dinah. Now," she snapped when the syrax hesitated.

He backed away, ears drooping. "Okay, okay, I'm a-goin', Annie. Going, going ... I'm gone." He kicked off from the ground, the draft from his wings stirring loose tendrils of her hair.

Annabelle strained for more water. Dizziness swept over her. Nothing. She turned to Raeden. "Please, God," she prayed through hiccoughing sobs. "He's my friend. I didn't mean for him to get hurt. I'm so sorry for distracting him. Please let him be all right. I swear I won't do anything to put myself—or my champion—in danger ever again."

Once the tears spilled from her brimming eyes and streamed down her cheeks, she could see a little better. She remembered healing Enoch's friend in the glade by the Wall. It seemed so long ago now.

I could heal Raeden. If only I could pull more water in. If only I weren't so tired ...

"Please, God help me," she sobbed, pulling the knife out of the ground. She had an idea to open Raeden's vest to get a better look at his wound, but then realized both hands were full. She put away Daar-Lûsin, then tucked his hunting knife in its sheath.

Can't lose it, she thought, crazily. He'll need it later.

Her tears dripped on Raeden's bloody hands as she leaned over him. The Oathbond flickered; his life hung on by a thread. A fraying thread. When she checked, his hands fell away from the wound easily. She shut her eyes while placing her hands over the slippery rent in his body. Blood. There was blood everywhere, and blood was mostly water. And her tears ... Pulling it all in, she reached for her reservoir. Liquid warmth trickled, then gushed, into her champion.

Annabelle sagged against the glowing waystone beside Raeden. Her left hand still rested over his wound. All her strength had fled into him. Had it made any difference? He murmured, shifting a little. And yet, he faded. There was no more water. She couldn't take any more. She couldn't give any more. She couldn't even move.

Please, please, please. I've lost Toad. I can't lose Raeden, too. God, please, I need water.

Delicate bells chimed. *Sweet Ann, I will aid you.* Reach *through the waystone, then* pull *through Daar-Lûsin.*

There was no time to question. She drew the relic and *reached.* There—far away—a vast amount of water awaited her call. Gritting her teeth, Annabelle *pulled.* Both waystone and dagger flashed blue as a gentle, warm energy infused Annabelle. It flowed into her champion and he tensed, grunting. Beneath her hand, his flesh writhed as the wound closed.

The world grew darker, as if clouds had obscured the moon. Only there was no moon—it had been the light of the dagger fading. She clumsily sheathed Daar-Lûsin, then sagged against her champion, putting her arms around him. Raeden felt chilled under his fur, but she'd healed the damage. His heartbeat throbbed steadily like a distant war drum.

Weakness sank into her bones and she felt thirsty—terribly thirsty. Water. What she wouldn't give for some water right now. Could she reach that place, that vast ocean from which she'd borrowed energy to heal Raeden? A sapphire glow surrounded her, and she remembered the sea where she'd met Hadrien.

From nearby, familiar voices shouted. One of them even sounded like Toad, but how could that be? Weariness sapped away the last of her strength. She closed her eyes.

Just for a minute...

"Kiddo!"

Wait ... was that *Toad?* Eyes snapping open, her head felt lined with lead as she raised it. Raeden twitched and groaned softly. She patted his chest, shushing him, and looked around. The waystone shone brighter and cast a sapphire glow over the environs. Beyond the stone circle, a pale figure hobbled toward them, eyes fixed on her. A shaggy-haired and bearded man who— holy cow! Was he *naked?* She blinked, then furrowed her brow. No, not naked. He was wearing short pants, thank God.

"Annabelle," the man rasped. "I'm coming."

She gasped. "Toad?" That man ... he sounded just like Toad. Could it be? Her heart skipped a beat as hope took root like a willow beside a stream. "Who are you?" It was all she could force past the dry sandpaper of her throat.

Pausing, he grimaced and clutched at his shoulder. It might have been a trick of the bluish light, but dark ridges lined his chest and abdomen, as if someone had been cutting his skin. "Kiddo, it's me. Toad. Sir Thomas."

He's alive? Thank God!

"Toad!" A huge grin spread across her face. He'd been restored to his human form! Joy suffused her, a balm providing strength to raise an arm despite her weariness.

Pale eyes intense, he hobbled closer, lips twitching in an almost-smile. The waystone flared as bright as the suns. Hesitating, the man threw up an arm across his eyes. Then he shouted her name and lunged forward, leaping into the circle.

"Sir Thomas!" She strained, reaching out for him.

The blue light washed out all detail and Sir Thomas faded. The last she saw of him, he held out a hand, and his voice rang in her ears. Everything went white as the waystone activated.

It's too soon! God, please save us!

Raeden shuddered and cried out. One hand gripping Daar-Lûsin, Annabelle clung to her champion as the ground fell out from under them, and they sped down a corridor of shining brightness toward an expanse of endless blue.

Some Time Later ...

Annabelle stood on the promontory as a restless sea crashed into the rocks far beneath her. Normally, the height would make her dizzy, but today the thunder of the waves resonated with her soul and kept her steady. The day was overcast and the waters reflected the dingy gray of the sky. Her hand rested on the pommel of Daar-Lûsin.

"Freylin, away from the edge. Your servant cannot swim."

"Raeden," she said as she turned and walked inland to where he knelt under a spreading oak. "Don't worry. I'll be okay." Patting the dagger, she favored her gaunt and haggard champion with a wan smile. "I've decided. Today, I'm going to reach Enoch. No more failures."

Green eyes haunted, he stared out to sea, but after a moment he nodded. "Your servant will guard your body while you are in the dreamscape."

Annabelle laughed. "I don't think our hosts mean me any harm." She sat down beside Raeden and leaned against the tree. The rough bark dug into her back through the gossamer fabric of the tunic her new friend had given her.

Her champion growled, shifting closer until his warmth seeped into her. "The water sprites cannot be trusted." The Oathbond sang with his ever-present anxiety.

Annabelle sighed. That familiar refrain was growing tiresome. *I wish there was something I could do to make him feel better.* Instead of answering him, she patted his leg, drew Daar-Lûsin, and held the artifact in her lap. She closed her eyes.

This would be her ninth attempt since arriving on the island. With each test, she felt she drew nearer to her goal. She concentrated on her breathing, slowing it, sending herself into a half-asleep trance as Khinjara had taught her. She felt herself become lighter, less substantial, and her mind drifted above a sea of mist. Her sense of Raeden disappeared. When she opened her eyes again, she no longer sat beneath the tree.

She stood in the glade where it had all begun, wearing the dark blue armor, with the Wall a dark gray expanse before her, forest all around, and the sunless, clear blue sky of the dreamscape above. An expectant hush pervaded the area, and her breath caught in her throat at the electric charge in the air.

I'm in the dreamscape, but something's different this time.

She wasn't alone.

Slowly, she turned to her right with Enoch's name on the tip of her tongue. An armor-clad man stood in the gap between clumps of bushes, a thin golden mist swirling around his feet as he also turned to face her. It wasn't Enoch; this man was as pale-skinned as she was and had dark auburn hair. She gasped, and his light blue eyes widened as his hand settled on the pommel of a golden sword. For a moment, they remained frozen, staring at each other in silence.

Her face warmed. *Oh, my gosh ... it's Sir Thomas.*

The man's paralysis broke first. "Kiddo," he said as he strode toward her. Her heart pounded so hard she wondered if he could hear it. He stopped two paces away, his expression grim and his gaze intense. "About friggin' time I found you."

Before she could argue that it was *she* who had found *him,* he continued speaking. "I've been trying to find you in this freak show of a place every night since you and His Excellentness vanished." His mouth twitched into a ghost of a smile. "And before you ask, everyone's fine. Even your stupid deer." She opened her mouth to ask for details, but his next words robbed her of her breath. "Now. Tell me where you are, and I swear by all that's holy, I'll move heaven and earth to get to you."

END OF BOOK TWO
The adventure continues in *Wyldling Armor!*

Glossary

Aethyr - magic of an "elemental" variety, of seven "aspects," limited only by the imagination of the wielder.

Age - (time expression) the same as 1,029 Earth years.

Ahdmerel - title referring to a wyldling attuned to water. High Dwelfnic term translating to "weaver of water" in the trading language.

Alarimet - "mirror twin" in dwelfnic; refers to a psychic bond between two wyldlings.

Aspects - Air (wind), Energy (fire), Flesh (shape), Mind (illusion), Stone (earth/mineral), Water (H2O), Void (space/time.)

Arkhabadh - ceremonial blood magic used by nehmwight sorcerers, heavily reliant on symbolism and objects. Power and ability levels are measured in Circles. Apprentices have between one and six circles. Acolyte sorcerers have between seven and nine. Master sorcerers have ten or more. Thirteen Circles is the highest attainable level, which rarely happens.

Arkhabala - circular tattoos (called Circles) carved into the skin of the back and upper arms made from black ink and blood that store magical energy and aid in casting spells. The tattooed circles have swirling off-shoots that expand on their own as the student advances and can be controlled with one's mind.

Arkhadahn – title used for a master nehmwight sorcerer.

Arkhasuhl – title used for apprentice and acolyte nehmwight sorcerers.

Atropos - The third sun, a red giant star.

Burkheld - robe worn by sorcerers. Apprentices wear brown and masters wear black.

Crane Watch 11am-1pm

Cycle - (time expression) roughly the same as three Earth years; the time it takes for Tehara to complete a revolution around the three suns.

Dwelfn (s) **-im** (pl) - race of humans that resemble Tolkienesque Elves.

Epoch - (time expression) the same as 147 Earth years.

Evainghir - the term used to refer to the son of a Sage.

Evaingynon - the term used to refer to the Sages; High Dwelfnic for "Wise Ones." Each is associated with an Aethyric aspect. It is believed that all perished in the Oblivion Wars. Annabelle refers to them as dragons.

Folken - how the wensallen-kaen refer to themselves as a people/race.

Frog Watch - 5-7am

Golor (s) **Golorum** (pl) - elite nehmwight warrior, one achieves this level for surviving pitched battle and is given a "blooding name."

Generation - (time expression) the same as twenty-one Earth years.

Gwerindawr - refers to what we'd call "merfolk" and can shift to fully human form (land-bound) at will with great pain and effort. Skin and hair can be any color of the rainbow.

-had - female suffix

-hir - male suffix

Harkhurz - what the nehmwights call a wensallen-kaen.

Harrowdwelfnim - the term used by the dwelfnim to refer to nehmwights and their ilk, collectively.

Heron Watch 3-5am

Hisanabyad – a mythical creature resembling a winged unicorn with both fur and scales, among other reptilian features.

Iqorasu (s) **Iqorasulim** (pl) - also called Sky-Dancers and believed extinct; refers to pygmy humans with wings who dwell in the Second Demesne, which can only be reached using a special artifact.

Jay Watch 1-3pm

Kaenhir - term used to refer to a male wensallen-kaen (man).

Kadorei - race of humans; what is considered a human on Earth.

Klotho - The first sun, a white dwarf star.

Kythim - collective noun that refers to a person's "aura;" shows mood and mental state. Used to reach out mind-to-mind. Annabelle uses the word-picture "thought-tendrils."

Lachesis - The second sun, a yellow dwarf like Earth's sun, Sol.

Lark Watch - 7-9am

Loricum - dwelfnic term for an expert in a particular field of science or an art; like a Ph.D.

Nehmwight - race of humans that resemble Tolkienesque Elves (but more like drow), a subset of the Dwelfnim with gray skin and orange eyes. Sensitive to the sun but tolerant of cold.

Nightstalker - a nehmwight/kadorei hybrid that generally favors the nehmwight side. Those few born of a nehmwight mother are sacrificed to one of the various nehmwight godlings. Most often those born of a kadorei mother who survive to adulthood hire themselves out as mercenaries or follow other similarly violent professions.

Oblivion Wars - often mentioned, but little is known about them. Much knowledge of the past civilization was lost during these cataclysmic wars, when the Sages and their magically/genetically engineered constructs fought against the nehmwights and their allies.

Owl Watch 9-11pm

Panther Watch 11pm-1am

Rakt-nasala - nehmwight term for nightstalker.

Raven Watch 5-7pm

Sakkhelt - a multi-pocketed sash worn under the burkheld that holds components for spells.

Serpent Watch 1-3am

Skelsdaran - title referring to a wyldling attuned to air/wind. High Dwelfnic term translates (roughly) to "master of the wind blades" in the trading language.

Skraeling - refers to human shapeshifter who can change into a single type of mammal, called one's totem; mass is conserved.

Sourekghar - magic armor created by the Sages for the wyldlings during the Oblivion Wars.

Sourethol (s) **-im** (pl) - dwelfn who has an affinity for an Aethyric Aspect and can manipulate that Aspect in a limited fashion; confined to what they are in contact with, in many cases.

Sparrow Watch 3-5pm

Syrax (s) **-im** (pl) - race of humans permanently locked in a bestial shape. Refers to what we'd call a griffin, but the avian half can also be corvid and the mammalian half can be something other than a great cat.

Thrush Watch - 7-9pm

Tradespeak - also called "the trading language." The common tongue used by the different races, cultures, etc. for the purposes of diplomacy and/or commerce. Annabelle automatically interprets it as English.

Turning - (time expression) one turning of the seasons, equivalent to an Earth year.

Varazslo - Title reserved for the most powerful Arkhadahn, with thirteen Circles. Translates loosely to "highest" in the trading language.

Vashenta – a talisman, usually a gem, spelled for a specific purpose.

Vashryu - High Dwelfnic term translating (roughly) to "focus gem."

Wensallen-kaen (s) **-im** (pl) - race of humans with canine characteristics; High Dwelfnic for "scout hound."

Wren Watch - 9-11am

Wyld - ability to use magic associated with an Aethyric Aspect.

Wyldling - a kadorei human born of the sel Drayven bloodline who can manipulate and/or utilize Aethyric Aspects.

Ynys Lloches - "Sanctuary Isle," the place where the gwerindawr live.

Acknowledgements

If not for God's blessings and providence—in this case, the wonderful people He put in my life—I probably wouldn't have published any books at all. I feel like I've rewritten and reworked *Wyldling Trials* five times over the past year; it's been a long haul. May God continue to bless my family for putting up with me through these trying times. Ryan, Gabriel, and Michael, fair warning: it's going to continue. Huckleberry, thank you for helping me trim the fat and discover new avenues to explore. Thank you, Wes, for the encouragement, critique, and proofreading. I will be forever grateful to the Sun Prairie Writers group—Gail, Dennis, Jennifer, and Mike—for helping me work through the Gordian knots of this behemoth's storyline. A shout-out to my awesome ARC team: Kelsey, Pamela, Katherine, and Wes. For everyone else I may have forgotten to mention, whether friends from work, church, Facebook, or random passers-by, please know that I appreciate you. And last but certainly not least: thank you, Mom, for continually urging me to "finish writing that story, already!"

About the Author

Born and raised in Wausau, Wisconsin, A.R. Grimes started writing "books" about dinosaurs in the second grade but moved on to writing fantasy after reading J. R. R. Tolkien, Madeleine L'Engle, and C. S. Lewis. She spent over twenty years trying to complete her debut novel, *Wyldling Snare*, and is living proof that any fool can get published nowadays. Several of her poems and short stories won awards in her alma mater Carroll University's literary magazine (1998-2001). Other than reading and writing, she enjoys singing in the church choir, listening to music, making fused glass art, drawing, daydreaming, and going on nature hikes. She is married to a martial arts enthusiast and currently lives in Sun Prairie, Wisconsin. They share the house with two male offspring and two cats who—naturally—are the true overlords.

Find me here: